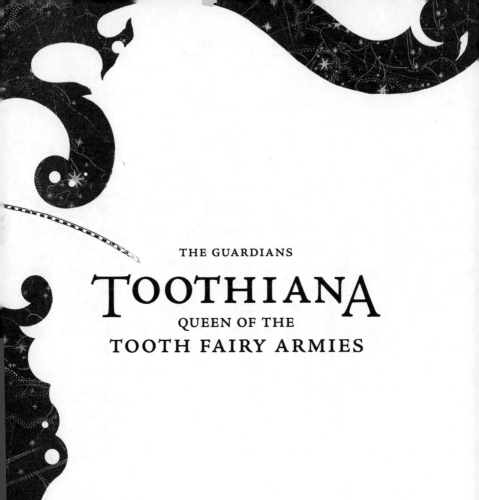

THE GUARDIANS

TOOTHIANA

QUEEN OF THE

TOOTH FAIRY ARMIES

Queen Toothiana

THE GUARDIANS

TOOTHIANA

QUEEN OF THE

TOOTH FAIRY ARMIES

◆———◆———◆

WILLIAM JOYCE

Atheneum Books for Young Readers

NEW YORK ◆ LONDON ◆ TORONTO ◆ SYDNEY ◆ NEW DELHI

Atheneum Books for Young Readers

An imprint of Simon & Schuster Children's Publishing Division

1230 Avenue of the Americas, New York, New York 10020

For information about special discounts for bulk purchases, please contact Simon & Schuster Special Sales at 1-866-506-1949 or business@simonandschuster.com.

The Simon & Schuster Speakers Bureau can bring authors to your live event. For more information or to book an event, contact the Simon & Schuster Speakers Bureau at 1-866-248-3049 or visit our website at www.simonspeakers.com.

Book design by Lauren Rille

The text for this book is set in Adobe Jenson Pro.

The illustrations for this book are rendered in a combination of charcoal, graphite, and digital media.

Manufactured in the United States of America

0812 FFG

First Edition

10 9 8 7 6 5 4 3 2 1

CIP data for this book is available from the Library of Congress.

ISBN 978-1-4424-3052-5

ISBN 978-1-4424-5461-3 (eBook)

───◆───

To Trish,
she IS a Guardian
FOR US ALL.

───◆───

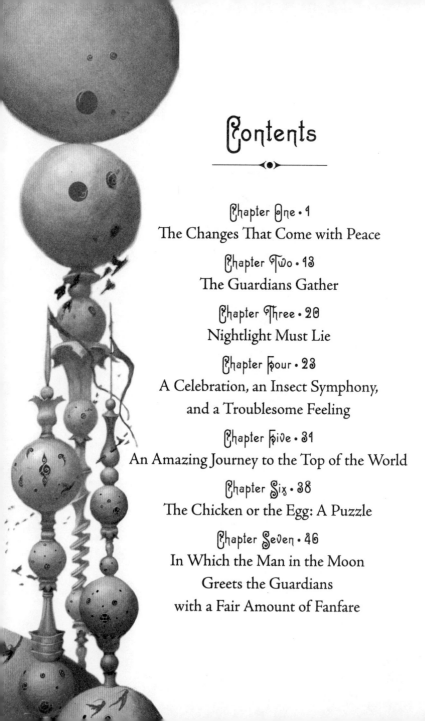

Contents

◆

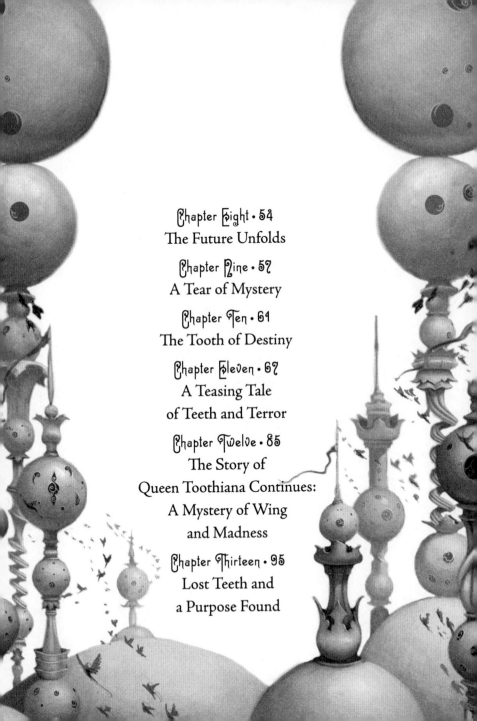

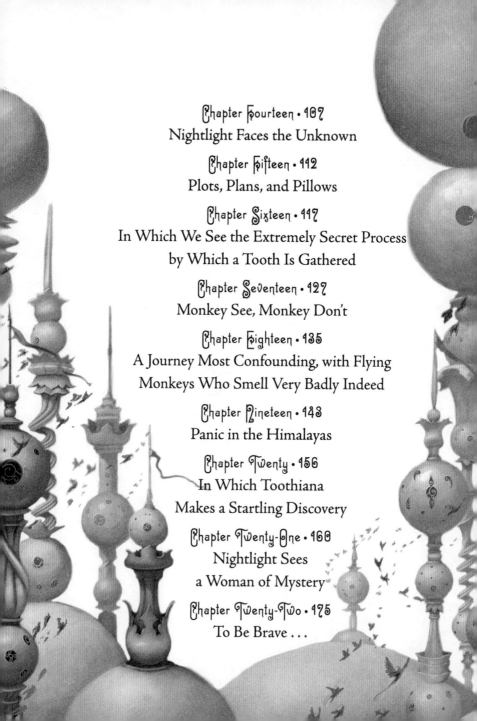

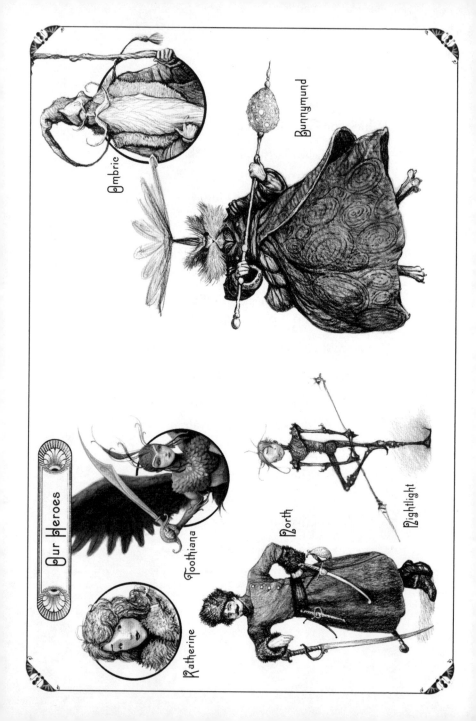

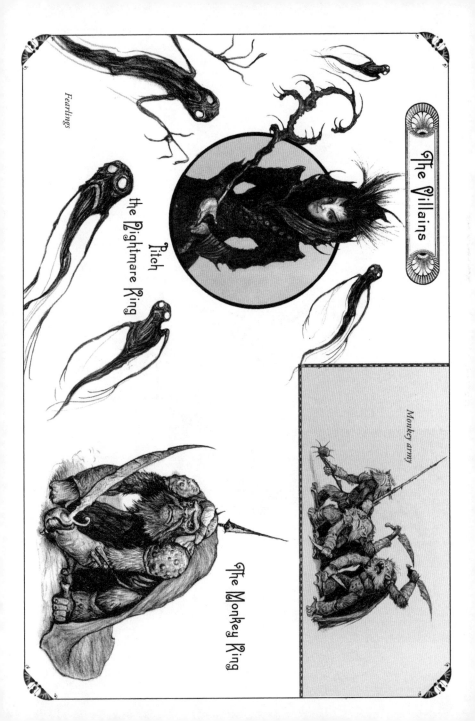

The Villains

Feartlings

Pitch
the Nightmare King

The Monkey King

Monkey army

CHAPTER ONE

The Changes That Come with Peace

WILLIAM THE ABSOLUTE YOUNGEST galloped through the enchanted village of Santoff Claussen on the back of a large Warrior Egg, a gift from E. Aster Bunnymund. "I can't stop or I'll be scrambled!" he shouted over his shoulder to his friend Fog. In this new game of Warrior Egg tag, to be scrambled meant you had been caught by the opposing egg team and therefore, had lost a point.

Sascha and her brother, Petter, were in hot pursuit, riding Warrior Eggs of their own. The matchstick-thin legs of the mechanical eggs moved so fast, they were a blur.

"Comin' in for the scramble shot!" Petter warned. His long tag pole, with the egg-shaped tip, was inches away from Sascha.

"Eat my yolk," Sascha said with a triumphant laugh. She pushed a button, and suddenly, her Warrior Egg sprouted wings. She flew over the others, reaching the finish line first.

William the Absolute Youngest slowed to a trot. "Wings!" he grumbled. "They aren't even in the rules!"

"I invented them yesterday," said Sascha. "There's nothing in the rules that says you can't use 'em."

Soon Sascha was helping the youngest William construct his own set of eggbot wings. She liked the youngest William. He always tried to act older, and she appreciated his determination and spirit. Petter and Fog, feeling wild and industrious, catapulted themselves to the hollow of a tall tree where they had erected a hideout devoted to solving ancient mysteries, such as: why was there such a thing as bedtime, and what could they do to eliminate it forever?

Across the clearing, in a tree house perched high in the branches of Big Root—the tree at the center of the village—their friend Katherine contently watched the children play.

The air shimmered with their happy laughter. Many months had passed since the battle at the Earth's core during which Pitch, the Nightmare King, had been soundly defeated by Katherine and the other Guardians: Ombric, the wizard; his apprentice, Nicholas St. North; their friend Nightlight; and their newest ally, the Pookan rabbit known as E. Aster Bunnymund. Pitch, who had hungered for the dreams of innocent children and longed to replace them with nightmares, had vowed with his Fearlings to make all the children of Earth live in terror. But since the great battle, he had not been seen or heard from, and Katherine was beginning to hope that Pitch had been vanquished forever.

As for Katherine and her battle mates, their lives were forever changed. The Man in the Moon himself had given them the title of "Guardians." They were heroes now, sworn to protect the children of not just Santoff Claussen, but the entire planet. They had defeated Pitch, and their greatest challenge at present was how to manage the peace. The "nightmare" of Pitch's reign seemed to be over.

The other children of the village now filled their days with mischief and magic. Bunnymund, who could burrow through the Earth with astonishing speed, had created a series of tunnels for them, connecting the village with his home on Easter Island and with other amazing outposts around the world, and the children had become intrepid explorers. On any given day they might journey to the African savanna to visit the lions, cheetahs, and hippopotami—Ombric had taught them a number of animal languages, so they had numerous stories to hear and tell. Many of the creatures had already heard of their amazing adventures.

The children also regularly circled through Easter Island for the latest chocolate confection Bunnymund had invented, and could still be back in time for dinner and games with Bunnymund's mechanical egg comrades. The eggs were once Bunnymund's warriors; now they helped the children build all manner of interesting contraptions, from intricate egg-shaped puzzles where every piece was egg-shaped (a nearly impossible and frankly unexplainable feat) to egg-shaped submarines. But no matter where the children roamed or what they did to occupy their days, whenever they returned home to Santoff Claussen, it had never seemed so lovely to them.

As Katherine sat in her tree house, she put her arm around Kailash, her great Himalayan Snow Goose, and looked out on her beloved village. The forest that surrounded and protected Santoff Claussen had bloomed into a kind of eternal spring. The massive oaks and vines that had once formed an impenetrable wall against the outside world were thick with leaves of the deepest green. The huge, spear-size thorns that had once covered the vines grew pliant and blossomed with sweet-scented flowers.

Katherine loved the smell, and drew a deep breath of it. In the distance she could see Nicholas St. North walking with the beautiful, ephemeral Spirit of the Forest. She was more radiant now than ever before. Her gossamer robes were resplendent with blooms that shimmered like jewels. North was deep in conversation with her, so Katherine decided to investigate. She climbed on to Kailash's back and flew down into the clearing, just in time to see William the

Absolute Youngest try out the new wings with which he'd outfitted his Warrior Egg. He landed and trotted over to her.

"Want to race with us, Katherine?" he asked. He gave Kailash a scratch on her neck, and the goose honked a hello.

"I will later!" Katherine said, smiling. She waved to her friends and headed into the forest, realizing that it had been quite some time since any of the children had asked her to play, and an even longer time since she had accepted. In joining the world of the Guardians, she was in a strange new phase of her life—where she was neither child nor adult. As she watched the youngest William fly away with Sascha close behind him, she couldn't help but feel a bit torn.

Then she heard North's hearty laugh and, underneath that, the more musical tones of the Spirit of the Forest. Katherine hurried toward them, thinking that it was hard to believe that when North first came to Santoff Claussen with his band of outlaws, it had been with the intent to steal its treasures. The Spirit of the Forest, the village's last line of defense, had turned North's crew of cutthroats and bandits into stone statues—hideous, hunched elves. But she had spared North, for he alone among them was pure of heart.

When Katherine caught up with the Spirit and North, they were standing in that most strange and eerie part of the forest—the place where North's men stood frozen in time, like stones in a forgotten burial site. With the Spirit's help, North was bringing his bandits back to human form.

As the Spirit touched the head of each statue, North repeated the same spell, "From flesh to stone and back again. To serve with honor, your one true friend." And one by one they emerged from their frozen poses. To North's great amusement, they hadn't regained their size. They were still the same height as their stone selves—about two feet tall, with bulbous noses and high, childlike voices.

"Welcome back," North called out, slapping each of the elfin men on the back.

The men stamped their little feet and waved their little arms to get their blood flowing again, and soon the children, drawn by North's laughter, arrived. They were shocked; they often played among these small stone men, and now that they were moving—were alive, in fact—the children were most intrigued. Tall William, the first son of Old William, towered over them. Even the youngest William was overjoyed—at last he was taller than someone else.

While the children watched, the little men kneeled before North. They took on new names as they pledged to follow their former outlaw leader in a new life of goodness. Gregor of the Mighty Stink became Gregor of the Mighty Smile. Sergei the Terrible was now Sergei the Giggler, and so on.

It was an odd but auspicious moment, especially for North. He remembered his wild, unruly life as a bandit and the many dark deeds that he and these fellows had committed. He'd become a hero, a man of great learning, good humor, and some wisdom. So much had changed since that moment when he faced the temptation of the Spirit of the Forest, when he had rejected her promises of treasure and had chosen to save the children of Santoff Claussen.

North turned and looked at young Katherine. He felt the full weight of all they had been through. They had both changed. It was a change he did not fully understand, but he knew he was glad for it. For though these dwarfish fellows in front of him had once been his comrades in crime, North, in his heart, had been alone. But that was past. This was a different day. And through the friendship he now knew, he could change bad men to good and stone back to flesh.

North gently asked his old confederates to rise. They did so gladly.

Peace had indeed come.

Katherine took North's hand, and together they welcomed these baffled little men to the world of Santoff Claussen.

CHAPTER TWO

The Guardians Gather

ALTHOUGH THE CHILDREN HAD begun to refer to the battle at the Earth's core as "Pitch's Last Battle," the Guardians knew that the Nightmare King was both devious and shrewd. He could still be lurking somewhere, ready to pounce.

Nightlight, the mysterious, otherworldly boy who was Katherine's dearest friend, scoured the night sky for signs of Pitch's army. He even traveled deep into the cave where he'd been imprisoned in Pitch's icy heart for centuries, but all he found were memories of those dark times. Of Pitch and his Fearling soldiers, he could find not even an echo. Bunnymund kept his rabbit ears tuned for ominous signs while burrowing his system of tunnels, and Ombric cast his mind about for bits of dark magic that might be creeping into the world. As for North, he was being rather secretive. He kept to himself (or, rather, to his elfin friends), working quietly and diligently in the great study, deep at the center of Big Root. On what he was working, no one knew for sure, but he seemed most intense.

And every night the children clamored for Mr. Qwerty, the glowworm who had transformed himself

 into a magical book. Because he had eaten every book in Ombric's library, he could tell the children any fact or story they wanted to hear. Mr.

Qwerty's pages were blank, at least until he began to read himself, and then the words and drawings would appear. But most nights the children wanted to hear one of Katherine's stories from Mr. Qwerty, for he allowed only her to write in him. But before any story was read, Katherine asked them about their dreams. Not one had had a single nightmare since the great battle.

There truly was *absolutely* no sign of Pitch. The sun seemed to shine brighter, every day seemed more beautiful, perfect, carefree. It was as if, when Pitch vanished, he took all the evil in the world with him.

Even so, the Guardians knew that wickedness of Pitch's magnitude did not surrender easily. They met together every day, never at an appointed time, but when it somehow seemed right. Their bond of friendship was so strong that it now connected them in heart and mind. Each could often sense what the others felt, and when it felt like the time to gather, they would just somehow *know*. They would drop what they were doing and go to Big Root, where, with cups of tea, they'd discuss any possible signs of Pitch's return.

On this particular day Nightlight hadn't far to travel. The night before, he'd stayed in Big Root's treetop all through the night, having searched every corner of the globe at dusk and found nothing alarming. Though he could fly forever, and never slept, his habit was to watch over Katherine and Kailash. More and more often the girl and her goose slept in their nestlike tree house, and so Nightlight would join them and guard them till morning.

Among the Guardians, his and Katherine's bond was the greatest. It hovered in a lovely realm that went past words and descriptions. The two never tired of the other's company and felt a pang of sadness when apart. But even that ache was somehow exquisite, for they knew that they would never be separated for long. Nightlight would never let that be so. Nor would Katherine. Time and time again they had managed a way to find each other, no matter how desperate the circumstances.

So Nightlight felt most perfectly at peace when watching over Katherine as she slept. Sleep was a mystery to him, and in some ways, so was dreaming. It worried him, in fact. Katherine was there but not entirely. Her mind traveled to Dreamlands where he could not follow.

In his childish way, he longed to go with her. And on this night, he had found a way to trespass into the unknown realm of her sleeping mind.

As he'd sat beside Katherine and her goose as they slept, he'd looked up to the Moon. His friend was full and bright. In these peaceful times the playful moonbeams came to him less often than before. There were no worries or urgent messages from the Man in the Moon, and so Nightlight could now enjoy the silent beauty of his benefactor. But a glint of something on Katherine's cheek had reflected the Moon's glow. Nightlight leaned in closely.

It was a tear. A tear? This confounded him. What was there in her dream that would make Katherine cry? He knew about the power of tears. It was from tears that his diamond dagger was forged. But those tears were from wakeful times. He had never touched a Dream Tear. But before he could think better of it, he reached down and gently plucked it up.

Dream Tears are very powerful, and when

Nightlight first tried to look into it, he was nearly knocked from the tree. He caught his balance and carefully looked at the small drop. Inside was Katherine's dream. And what he saw there seared his soul. For the first time in all his strange and dazzling life, Nightlight felt a deep, unsettling fear.

There, haunting her dreams, he had seen Pitch.

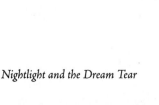

Nightlight and the Dream Tear

CHAPTER THREE

Nightlight Must Lie

Now, as Nightlight shimmered his way into the waiting room of Big Root, he was the last to arrive. He kept his distance, perching high on one of the bookcases. Ombric and Bunnymund were poring over a map of the lost city of Atlantis. Katherine spied Nightlight and could tell immediately that something was troubling him.

North began regaling Ombric with the news about his band of brigands and their new lives as elfin helpers.

Ombric's left eyebrow rose high; he was clearly

amused. "Well done, Nicholas. I see great things in store for your little men," he said.

Though neither man would say out loud how they felt, Katherine could tell Ombric was immensely proud of his apprentice, and North took great pleasure in Ombric's approval. She felt a surge of happiness for the both of them.

Bunnymund's ears twitched. *These humans and their emotions*, he thought. *They are so odd. They are more interested in feelings than chocolate!*

"Any sign of Pitch today?" he asked politely but pointedly.

North shook his head. "The old grump hasn't grumbled."

"None of the children have had bad dreams," reported Katherine.

Nightlight didn't respond. He knew otherwise.

Or, at least, he thought he did.

Bunnymund then answered his own question. "And nothing in my tunnels—nothing evil or unchocolatey or anti-egg anywhere."

Ombric stroked his beard. "Perhaps the children are correct," he mused, "and the battle at the Earth's core truly was Pitch's *last* battle."

North pondered. "Can that really be?"

Katherine turned to Nightlight. She generally knew what he was thinking, but today she couldn't read him. "Nightlight," she prompted, "have you seen anything?"

He shifted on his perch. His brow furrowed, but he shook his head.

It was the first time Nightlight had ever lied.

CHAPTER FOUR

A Celebration, an Insect Symphony, and a Troublesome Feeling

It's now been eight months since we last saw Pitch. I think before we declare victory, it would be best to consult with the Man in the Moon," Ombric said. "And that means a journey to—"

"The Lunar Lamadary!" Bunnymund and North said together. The Lamadary sat on the highest peak of one of the highest Himalayan mountains, and it was there where North had first met both the Lunar Lamas and the Man in the Moon.

North was ready to leave that minute. It was a great chance to meet again with the Yeti warriors who defended the city. They had been quite help-ful when North had been learning the secrets of the magic sword the Man in the Moon had bestowed upon him. The sword was a relic from the Golden Age, and there were five of these relics in total. Bunnymund had one as well—the egg-shaped tip to his staff. The Man in the Moon had said that if all five were gathered together, they would create a force powerful enough to defeat Pitch forever. But peace seemed to be at hand. With any luck, the Guardians would have no need for more relics. But North *had* been wondering how he would keep his warrior skills sharp, or if he even should. With the Yetis, he'd again have able competitors with whom to practice his swordmanship.

Ombric turned to Bunnymund. He didn't even have to ask about making a tunnel, because next to making chocolate eggs, digging tunnels was the Pooka's favorite pastime.

"One tunnel coming up," Bunnymund said. "It'll be ready in twenty-seven half yolks—that's one day in your human time."

"Outstanding," Ombric said with a nod. "We'll take the whole village—everyone is welcome!" he added. "It'll be a grand adventure. We'll plan a celebration tomorrow evening to see us off!"

Katherine clapped her hands together in excitement. *Kailash will be so happy to see the other Great Snow Geese,* she thought. She'd wondered if her goose ever missed the flock of massive birds that nested in the Lunar Lamas' mountain peak.

But her excitement was tempered by her unease about Nightlight. She glanced at him, but he would not return her gaze. Instead, with his amazing speed, he shot out the window and into the clear, blue sky. But he did not seem bright, Katherine noted, and her unease grew.

The next day found Santoff Claussen full of preparations for the trip and for a celebratory dinner. The eggbots whipped up frothy confections, and the ants, centipedes, and beetles tidied Big Root while glowworms set up tables in the clearing—tables that would be heaped with delicious foods. Not to be left out, squirrels made teetering piles of nuts, birds filled their feeders with seed, and mouthwatering smells came from every nook and cranny of the village.

That evening the children led a parade of humans; elvish men; insects, birds; their great bear; the djinni; North's wonder horse, Petrov; and one very tall Pooka to the well-decorated clearing.

The Moon was so luminous that the villagers were sure they could see the Man in the Moon himself smiling down on them. The Lunar Moths glowed, and Ombric's many owls hooted softly. Soon the children were jumping onto the backs of the village reindeer and racing them across the evening sky while Katherine and Kailash flew alongside. Fireflies circled their heads, making halos of green-tinged light.

Down below, North's elves ate plate after plate of jam roly-poly, noodle pudding, and sweet potato schnitzel, topping off the meal with elderberry pie and Bunnymund's newest chocolates—a delectable blend of Aztec cacao and purple plum—all the while asking North to describe the meals prepared by the Yetis (accomplished chefs all) at the Lunar Lamadary. It seemed that being turned to stone and back again was a hungry business.

Even the crickets came out into the moonlight to play a sort of insect symphony to the delight of everyone.

Finally, when all the games had been played, the food eaten, and the songs sung, the village of Santoff Claussen settled down to sleep.

Up in her tree house, however, Katherine lay awake. Nightlight had been the only one who had not joined the party that night. And it bothered her. As did something else: Ever since the last battle, Katherine found that in quiet moments like this, her mind often drifted back to Pitch and his daughter—the little girl he had fathered and loved before he'd been consumed by evil. In the final moments of their battle, Katherine had shown Pitch a locket—a locket that held his daughter's picture. She could not stop thinking about the anguished look on Pitch's face, or her own longing to be loved as deeply as Pitch's daughter had been loved by her father.

Does that feeling only happen between parent and child, a father and a daughter? Katherine wondered. She had lost her own parents when she was just a baby. It was true that here in Santoff Claussen, many people loved her and cared for her. Ombric and North were like a father and a brother to her. But that wasn't the same as a *real* family, was it? She couldn't help wondering whether anyone would feel that same anguish she'd seen in Pitch's eyes if she were lost to them.

And there was Nightlight. She sensed his current melancholy.

He's never had a parent, she thought, *and he had seemed happy enough.* But now something was wrong. She would find out what it was. She would make him happy once more. And then maybe she'd be happy too.

That thought brought comfort to the gray-eyed girl, and soon, like everyone else in the village, she was asleep.

But a strange wind blew through Santoff Claussen. It caused the limbs of Katherine's tree house to gently sway. If Katherine had awakened, she'd have felt uneasy, as though she were being watched by a force nearly as ancient as Pitch. Whose motives and deeds would change everything. If Katherine just opened her eyes, she'd have seen what was in store.

CHAPTER FIVE

An Amazing Journey to the Top of the World

THE NEXT MORNING THE whole village gathered at the entrance of Bunnymund's latest digging extravaganza: a tunnel that would take them to the Lunar Lamadary.

With great fanfare, Bunnymund swung open the tunnel's egg-shaped door and stepped into the first car of the extraordinary locomotive that would speed them on their way. Trains were still not yet invented (Bunnymund would secretly help the credited inventors some decades later), so the machine and its technology were still a source of considerable amazement for the people of Santoff Claussen. Like the tunnel he had created, Bunnymund's railway train was also egg-shaped, as was every knob, door, window, and light fixture. It was easy to tell he was quite proud of his creation.

Ombric, North, Katherine, and Kailash, along with North's elfin comrades, the children, and their parents, scrambled on board. Bunnymund was twisting and turning the myriad of egg-shaped controls.

The Spirit of the Forest waved her shimmering veils at them as Bunnymund started the engine.

"Aren't you coming?" Katherine called out, hanging from a window.

The Spirit of the Forest shook her head, the jewels in her hair casting a glistening, rainbowlike glow around her. "I'm a creature of the forest, and in the forest I will stay. Petrov, Bear, the eggbots, the djinni, and I will watch over the village while you are away." The gardens of flowers around her seemed to be nodding in agreement as the villagers waved good-bye with calls of "See you soon" and "We'll miss you."

As soon as the train began to move, Sascha turned to Katherine excitedly. "Tell us again about the Lunar Lamas!" she said.

"And the Yetis!" her brother Petter added.

But Katherine was distracted. Nightlight hadn't gotten on board. In fact, she hadn't seen him since yesterday afternoon. She looked out the window as the train began to descend into the tunnel. *Where is he?* Then, as the last car heaved downward, she glimpsed him swooping into a window at the back of the train. She felt instantly better.

"Please, will you tell us of the Yetis?" the smallest William begged, pulling on Katherine's shirtsleeve. She turned to him with a smile now that she knew Nightlight was at least on board. She searched through the pages of Mr. Qwerty until she came to the drawing she had made of the Grand High Lama. His round face seemed to beam at them. "The Lamas, remember, are holy men," Katherine told them, "even older than Ombric! They've devoted their whole lives to studying the Man in the Moon. They know all about Nightlight and how he used to protect the little Man in the Moon in the Golden Age before Pitch—"

Katherine cut herself off. She did *not* want to think about Pitch right now.

"The Lamas live in a palace . . . ," Sascha prompted.

"Not a palace, really. But a fantastic place called a Lamadary." Katherine turned the page, revealing the Lamas' home, glowing as if with moonlight. "There's nowhere else on Earth closer to the Moon than the Lunar Lamadary."

"Now tell us about the Yetis," Petter begged.

"The Yetis—oh, they are magnificent creatures . . . ," Katherine said, but her voice began to trail off. "They helped us defeat Pitch. . . ."

"I can't wait to see it all with my own eyes," Sascha said dreamily. "Especially the Man in the Moon."

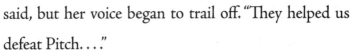

"And mountains so high, we'll be above the clouds," Fog added.

The children began chattering among themselves about the adventures to come, not noticing that Katherine had grown quiet.

She rose from her seat. She felt uneasy again, and the children's company didn't suit her right now. She didn't really know where she wanted to be—with the children or with North and the other grown-ups. Even Kailash didn't comfort her. She was betwixt and between. She started toward the back of the train. The only company she desired right now was Nightlight's.

CHAPTER SIX

The Chicken or the Egg: A Puzzle

WHILE THE CHILDREN WERE anticipating their first trip to the Himalayas, Ombric and Bunnymund were in a deep debate about which came first, the chicken or the egg. Ombric believed it was the chicken. Bunnymund, not surprisingly, believed it was the egg. But the Pooka had to admit that he could not answer the question definitively.

"Eggs are the most perfect shape in the universe," he argued. "It's logical that the egg would come first and the chicken would follow."

"But where did the first egg come from, if the

chicken did not exist?" Ombric asked.

"Where did the chicken come from," Bunnymund pointed out, "if not from the egg?"

Privately, each one believed he had won the argument, but publicly, the wizard deferred to the Pooka. Bunnymund was the only creature alive who was both older and wiser than Ombric. In fact, when Ombric had been a young boy in Atlantis and had first experimented with his magic, it had been Bunnymund who had saved him from a most tragic end.

Ombric had learned so much since he'd become reacquainted with the Pooka. He felt almost like a student again. But perhaps, he thought, he had something to teach E. Aster.

"Have you ever met the Lunar Lamas?" Ombric asked, eager to fill him in on their strange ways.

"Yes and no," Bunnymund replied mysteriously.

"It *was* rather difficult getting that mountain in place before their ship crashed to Earth back, oh, before the beginning of *your* recorded time. So we have what you might call 'a history,' but does anyone *really* know anyone? I mean to say, I've met them, I've talked to them, I've read their minds and they've read mine, but do I know what they'll say or do next at any given moment or what underwear they wear on Tuesdays and why? Do I? Do I *really* know?"

Ombric blinked and tried to take in all that information. It was an answer of sorts. "Indeed," he said at last. "Um . . . yes . . . well . . . all right . . . That must be how they knew to point us in your direction when we sought the relic." He glanced up at the sumptuously bejeweled egg that adorned the top of Bunnymund's staff and raised an eyebrow. "They would tell us only—"

"That I was mysterious and preferred to remain unknown," Bunnymund finished for him, steering the train around a graceful, oval curve. "True. Absolutely true. Etched in stone, so to speak. At least until I made the curiously rewarding acquaintance of you and your fellows. Most unexpected. Utterly surprising. And, as you say, 'a hoot.'" Bunnymund had developed a genuine pleasure in using the new expressions he heard in the company of what he called "Earthlings."

Ombric smiled at the fellow. "I like you too, Bunnymund."

The rabbit's ears twitched. Such obvious statements of Earthling sentiments never failed to baffle him. Yet, while the Pooka would never admit it, Ombric could tell that he was beginning to actually enjoy the company of humans—in small doses, anyway.

+ + +

As they neared the Himalayas, Katherine combed through car after car of chattering villagers and elves, looking for Nightlight. North's elves were busily working on what looked like a drawing or plans for something. They cheerfully covered their pages from her view. She decided not to pry, for she rather liked these funny little men. But more to the point, she was on a mission to find Nightlight.

Then, as it always happened, she suddenly knew that it was time for her to meet with the other Guardians, and she could sense that Nightlight was there with them. She followed this feeling as it led her to the train's front car, or as Bunnymund referred to it, the Eggomotive.

They were all there: North in the back by the door, Ombric and Bunnymund tinkering excitedly with the controls. And out the front window she could see Nightlight, sitting face forward in front of the engine's smokestack. He did not turn around though she knew he could feel her presence. His hair was blowing wildly as the train blasted ahead. The sound of the train was loud, but it was pleasing, like ten thousand whisks scrambling countless eggs. *Perhaps Nightlight misses all the excitement of battle,* Katherine thought, watching him lean forward into the air rushing past.

She wondered if North did as well. He was humming to himself, a faraway look on his face. Something was now different about the young wizard. He was still always ready to leap into action, still loved conjuring up new toys for the children. (Just that morning he'd brought the youngest William a funny sort of toy—a round biscuit-shaped piece of wood with a string attached to its middle. When jerked, it would go up and down almost magically. North called it a "yo-yo-ho.") And he still continued to tease Bunnymund, whom he insisted on calling "Bunny Man" no matter how many times the Pooka corrected him. Nevertheless, Katherine sensed a change, a change she couldn't quite put her finger on. In those moments when he thought no one was looking, North had become quieter, more contemplative.

And yet he didn't seem sad or melancholy or lonely like Nightlight did. His face was alive with excitement. *What is he up to?* she wondered, hoping that, when he was ready, he would tell her about it. If only she could be sure that Nightlight would be so forthcoming. *All this change is so unsettling. Peace is harder than I thought it would be.*

North, sensing her presence, grinned and brushed

a lock of hair from her forehead. "Ready to see the Man in the Moon again?"

Katherine gave him an impish smile, and nodded yes. She could feel the train beginning to climb upward. The engine strained to pull the egg-shaped cars and their festive cargo up toward the Himalayan mountain peak. They were nearly there.

CHAPTER SEVEN

In Which the Man in the Moon Greets the Guardians with a Fair Amount of Fanfare

THE GUARDIANS EXCHANGED LOOKS full of anticipation. Even Bunnymund, who considered anything nonchocolate or egg-related to be of little importance, looked forward to sharing the news that they believed Pitch had been vanquished.

For the last few minutes of the journey the train was traveling completely vertical—Katherine had to hang on to North or she'd slide out the door. Then the first car popped out of the tunnel into the clear, perfect light of the highest place on Earth. A new egg-shaped Eggomotive station was in place, and the train came to rest at the outskirts of the Lunar Lamadary.

The holy men now waited on the platform in their silver slippers and billowing silk-spun robes. They bowed deeply at the sight of Nightlight, who hopped lightly off the engine. Having once been the protector of the Man in the Moon, Nightlight always received their greatest reverence. Their Moon-like faces, normally inscrutable, resonated joy at his arrival. And this seemed to brighten Nightlight's mood as well. But he was still distant with Katherine.

Old William and his sons, along with all the other parents and children, gaped in wonder at the sight of the Lamas' headquarters and the cool, serene, creamy glow of its moonstone and opal mosaics. Sascha nearly tumbled out of the train's window in her effort to see the Lamadary's famous tower, which was also an airship. Even Mr. Qwerty, his pages fluttering, hurried toward the train's doors to get a closer look.

Gongs rang out. Bells—hundreds of them— chimed in the wind. Yaloo, the leader of the Yetis, stood with the Snow Geese at the edge of the platform, and blew a silver horn forged from ancient meteors, as the Snow Geese honked a warm "hello" at the sight of Kailash and Katherine.

As the welcoming reverberations quieted, Ombric stepped onto the platform. "Greetings, my good friends," he addressed the gathering. "We've come to speak to the Man in the Moon . . . and to report what we think is historic news."

The old man was clearly eager to see the Man in the Moon and share their findings, but there were the curiously slow habits of the Lamas to consider. They never did anything quickly and were usually very, very, very talkative. And yet, surprisingly, it seemed that the Lamas were just as eager to proceed. It was highly unusual for them to rush for any reason, but today they whisked everyone off the train and directly toward the Lamadary's courtyard.

The Yetis lined the outer edges of the courtyard as the Lamas led everyone else to the huge gong at its very center.

The children could barely contain their excitement. The Man in the Moon was about to be summoned!

The Grand High Lama glided forward. He smiled serenely, then, with almost shocking suddenness, he struck the great gong with his gilded scepter. The sound was sweet and strong. It grew and echoed throughout the temple, then throughout the mountains around them until it sounded as though the whole Earth was humming a gentle "hello" to the heavens.

The gong itself began to shimmer, shifting from a solid metal to a clear, glasslike substance. And as the children pointed in astonishment, the Moon began to appear in the milky light at the gong's center, swelling in size until a face emerged from the craters—the kindest, gentlest face anyone could imagine.

The Lamas bowed, as did the five Guardians and everyone else in the courtyard. As they stood up, Nightlight and the friendly moonbeam that lived in the diamond tip of his staff blinked a greeting. North raised his sword in salute and noticed that it had begun to glow. So did the egg on the tip of Bunnymund's staff. Katherine held her dagger aloft exactly as she had when she had vowed to battle Pitch so many months ago, and Ombric simply placed the palms of his hands together and lowered his head even farther in greeting.

"Tsar Lunar," he said in a reverent tone, "we've scoured the Earth for Pitch and found no trace of him. Can you tell us, has he truly been defeated?"

The image on the gong flickered and waned like moonlight on a cloudy night. The Man in the Moon's voice was so deep, it almost seemed like a heartbeat. "My valiant friends," he said. "Each night I send thousands of moonbeams down to Earth, and each night they return clear and untarnished by Pitch's dark ways." As he spoke, a wide smile spread across his face.

Cheers rung out throughout the Lamadary.

"It appears

the world is on the cusp of a new Golden Age," he continued, "a Golden Age on Earth. And it is you, my Guardians, who must guide its creation. It is a task of great daring imagination and thoughtful dreaming."

Everyone's eyes turned to Ombric, Katherine, Bunnymund, North, and Nightlight. One old, one young, one from another world, one who overcame a most disreputable beginning, and one a spirit of light. Such a group *could* bring about a Golden Age. But who would lead this historic endeavor?

To everyone's surprise, it was North who stepped forward. "I have a plan," he said.

He sheathed his sword and raised his other hand, opening his palm to reveal a small paper box covered with minute drawings and plans. Katherine recognized it. *It's what the elves were working on!*

"This was a gift, one that I now pass on," North began, stealing a glance at Katherine and then turning back to the Man in the Moon. "A dream for the new Golden Age."

CHAPTER EIGHT

The Future Unfolds

WITH THAT, NORTH CLOSED his eyes for a moment, recalling Ombric's first lesson: The power of magic lies in believing. He began to chant, "I believe, I believe."

Ombric, Katherine, and even Bunnymund joined him, quickly followed by the entire courtyard, and the box in North's hand unfolded into a vast origami wonder.

A magical city seemed to grow out of North's palm. Ombric's eyebrows raised. North was becoming something more powerful than a warrior *or* a wizard. Ombric could sense it.

North tipped his head toward Katherine, whose eyes were shining—this was the dream *she* had given him when all seemed lost during one of the first great battles with Pitch! A dream in which North was a powerful figure of mirth, mystery, and magic, who lived in a city surrounded by snow.

Katherine nodded back encouragingly, and so North started.

"I have a plan for building new centers of magic and learning," North explained. "One village like Santoff Claussen is not enough, and to expand it would be to change it. What we need instead are more places where all those with kind hearts and inquiring minds—inventors, scientists, artists, and visionaries—will be welcomed and encouraged. Where children will always be safe and protected and grow to become their finest selves."

The paper city hovered in the air just above North's palm. There was a great castlelike structure in its center, surrounded by workshops and cottages. A tiny Nicholas St. North could be seen striding through the village center, with his elves and Petrov, his horse, by his side. And a herd of mighty reindeer. The Yetis too were there.

North bowed his head and waited for the Man in the Moon's response. He'd thought he might feel anxious at this moment; instead, he felt peaceful—more peaceful than he could ever remember feeling. He had shared the truest dream of his heart.

The Man in the Moon gazed down at North. He didn't need to say anything. His luminous smile said all that needed saying.

CHAPTER NINE

A Tear of Mystery

WITH ALL THE HURLY-BURLY and hubbub surrounding this new Golden Age and the city North would build, Katherine found herself lost in the shuffle. The adult Guardians were in a frenzy of excitement, talking heatedly among themselves. She didn't mind, really. It made her happy to see North and Ombric in deep discussions again; it was like old times. And watching Bunnymund interject ideas was always amusing. He was enthusiastic as long as the plans involved chocolate or eggs. As the discussions went on, she realized they'd made a slight breakthrough. Bunnymund was now willing to broaden his interest to other types of candies. "Anything that is sweet has great philosophical and curative powers, and as such, could be key to this new Golden Age!" he pronounced with his usual droll pookery.

The villagers of Santoff Claussen were also happily speculating about new innovations and technologies. The children, especially, were caught up in the commotion. Sascha and the youngest William came up to Katherine. "What do you think this all means?" Sascha asked.

Katherine thought a moment, then answered, "It means that there'll be amazing new things to invent and build and see and do." Sascha's and William's eyes grew bright as they tried to imagine what this future would be like.

As if reading their minds, Katherine added, "Everything will be . . . different."

Before they could ask her to explain, she caught a glimpse of Nightlight up on the highest tower of the Lamadary, and she hurried after him. All his dodging about had her increasingly worried. She could not *feel* his friendship. She could feel nothing from him at all.

The steps to the bell tower were steeper than she'd expected and proved hard to climb. North's compass, which she hadn't taken off since he'd given it to her all those long months ago, was swinging back and forth, thunking against her chest in a most annoying way. But she didn't stop to remove it; she just climbed on.

I hope Nightlight hasn't flown off, she thought, trying to see around a corner as she neared the top steps. She began climbing much more quietly. Through an arched window, she could see him on the other side, perched on the ledge. His back was to her, but she could see that his head hung low, almost to his knees. The light from the diamond point of his staff was dim. And for the first time in days, she could sense his feelings; his feelings were sad. Very sad.

She'd never known Nightlight to be sad! She crept closer still, until she could see that he was holding something. Carefully, carefully, without making a sound, she balanced herself out onto the ledge right next to him. In his hand he held something. She leaned forward even closer. It was a tear. A single tear.

Nightlight suddenly realized she was there. He jumped to his feet with an abruptness that startled her. She teetered for a moment, windmilling her arms for balance.

In a terrible instant, she fell from the ledge.

CHAPTER TEN

The Tooth of Destiny

ғALLING TO YOUR DEATH is a strange and unsettling sensation. Your mind becomes very sharp. Time seems to slow down. You are able to think an incredible number of thoughts at astonishing speed. These were Katherine's thoughts for the three and a half seconds before she came in contact with the cobblestone courtyard of the Lunar Lamadary:

Oh oh oh oh! Falling! I'm falling!!! FAAALL-LING!!!!! Not good!! Maybe I'm not falling. Please-pleasepleasepleeeeese say I'm not falling. WRONG!!! FALLING!!! Falling FAST!!!! FastFastFastFast... Slow

DOWN . . . Can't CAN'T . . . Not good . . . Okay . . . think . . . How do I stop? I DON'T KNOW!!!!! Okay, okay, okay . . . I HATE GRAVITY . . . GRAVITY!!! HATE!!! HATE!!! HATE GRAVITY!!!!! Hairs in my mouth . . . My hair . . . Yuck . . . Spit . . . Okay . . . Hairs out of mouth . . . FALLING!!!! STILL FALLING!!!!! A tear? Why was Nightlight holding a tear? . . . Sad . . . real sad . . . SAD!!! SAD THAT I'M FALLING . . . Where is everybody? . . . There are flying people everywhere in this place. . . . FLYING PEOPLE HELP NOW!!!! RIGHT NOW!!! I'M YOUR FALLING FRIEND HERE . . . FALLING FAAAAAST . . . I MEAN IT!!! Where are all my magic flying friends? . . . Hellooo . . . falling Katherine . . . could USE A HAND . . . NOW!!!! Now NOW NOW NOWWWWWW!!! Is that Nightlight? . . . Can't tell . . . OH NO TURNING FALLING FAST DOWN GROUND COMING NOT GOOD

NOT GOOD NOT GOOD . . . GROUND . . .
Happy thoughts . . . kittens . . . chocolate . . . baby mice . . .
family . . . friends . . . family . . . favorite pillow . . . friends . . .
favorite pillow . . . North . . . Ombric . . . MOON . . . Bun-
nymund . . . North . . . Nightlight . . . NIGHTLIGHT!
NIGHTLIGHT! NIGHTLIGHT! SAVE ME!!!

Then, as she screamed and thought her life was
ended, her chin came into contact with the cobblestone courtyard, and she suddenly stopped falling.
Nightlight had caught her left foot.

He was floating.

So now Katherine was as well. Or almost. Her
chin nicked against a cobblestone, but the rest of her
was held aloft. For a moment she was speechless.
And when she did try to talk, she found it difficult.
There was something small and hard in her mouth,
like a pebble. She instinctively spit it onto the ground

beneath her. Out bounced not a pebble but . . . a tooth! Her tooth. Her last baby tooth.

And before she could even say "ouch," chimes rang out as every bell in the Lunar Lamadary began to toll. And suddenly the entire troop of Lamas and the Yetis were surrounding her and Nightlight. They were chanting and bowing and bowing and chanting.

"Most auspicious," said the Grand High Lama.

"A tooth . . . ," said another.

". . . of a child . . . ," said a taller one.

". . . of a Guardian child . . . ," said a roundish one.

"A lost tooth . . . ," said the shortest one.

"The TOOTH . . . ," said the Grand High Lama with a touch of awe, ". . . OF DESTINY!"

Then they started up bowing and chanting again. Nightlight gently lowered Katherine to the ground, then helped her up, and together they stood, baffled.

Katherine, Nightlight,
and the bond of the lost tooth

But even more baffling to Katherine was the strange look on Nightlight's face. He was trying to hide it. But he didn't know how. He was so confused by all that was happening and how close he'd come to losing Katherine. She was growing up. Nightlight's worst fear—his *only* fear—was coming true. He did not understand growing up. He did not know if he could grow up. And he did not want to be left behind if she did. But he had saved her, and as she placed her finger in the empty spot where her tooth had been, he knew that everything would be different. But there was only one thing he could do—smile at the gap in her grin.

CHAPTER ELEVEN

A Teasing Tale of Teeth and Terror

It took North, Ombric, and Bunnymund a few minutes to shift gears from planning a new Golden Age to understanding the importance of Katherine's lost tooth.

They had been gathered in conference in the Lamadary library when the Lunar Lamas filled the chamber, presenting Katherine and her tooth with great pomp and circumstance, proclaiming it "a lost tooth of destiny."

Bunnymund was particularly vexed by the interruption. "If Katherine is unharmed, then what is all this fuss about a tooth?" he asked, one ear twitching. "It isn't actually lost. She holds it in her hand, and now she'll grow another one. It's all very natural and, frankly, rather ordinary. It's not like she lost a chocolate truffled egg or anything."

Then the Grand High Lama described Katherine's fall and hairbreadth rescue.

Bunnymund felt a twinge of shame. He didn't mean to discount Katherine's terrifying accident. But still, a tooth was just a tooth.

The Lamas pressed on.

"We Lamas do not have baby teeth to lose," explained the Grand High Lama.

"At least, not since before recorded time," added the shortest Lama.

"And we've never had a child at the Lamadary ...," said the tallest Lama.

"... who's lost a child's tooth," said the least ancient Lama.

"So we've never been visited by Her Most Royal Highness," stressed the Grand High Lama.

The mention of a "Most Royal Highness" piqued everyone else's collective interest.

"Her Most Royal Highness who?" asked North, certain that if this personage dwelled on this continent, he'd likely stolen something from her in his crime-filled younger years. Ombric leaned forward, also eager to hear the Lamas' answer.

The Grand High Lama actually looked shocked by their ignorance. "Why, Her Most Royal Highness, Queen Toothiana, gatherer and protector of children's lost teeth!"

Well, that raised eyebrows from every one of them. Everyone except Bunnymund.

"Oh, her," he said dismissively. "She dislikes chocolate. She claims it's bad for children's teeth." He sniffed. "For confectionery's sake, they all fall out, anyway."

But Ombric, North, and especially Katherine wanted to know more. "I've read something about her once, I believe—" Ombric was saying, trying to remember, when a quiet cough interrupted him.

They all turned. Mr. Qwerty was standing on one of the library's Moon-shaped tables.

"Mr. Qwerty knows something," Katherine said.

The bookworm bowed and told them, "The story of the Queen of Toothiana lies in volume six of *Curious Unexplainables of the East*."

"Of course! I should have remembered that myself," Ombric said, nodding. "Mr. Qwerty, please enlighten us."

The Guardians sat around the table while Mr. Qwerty began his tale.

A Sister of Flight

"To know the story of Queen Toothiana," he said, "you must first hear the tale of the maharaja, his slave Haroom, and the Sisters of Flight."

"Sisters of Flight?" North interrupted.

"Sisters of Flight," Mr. Qwerty repeated patiently. The image of a beautiful winged woman appeared on one of Mr. Qwerty's pages. She was human-size, with long, willowy arms and legs and a heart-shaped face. But her wings were magnificent, and she held a bow and arrow of extraordinary design.

"Can she really fly?" Katherine asked in awe.

"Please, allow me to tell

the tale," Mr. Qwerty said. "The Sisters of Flight were an immortal race of winged women who ruled the city of Punjam Hy Loo, which sits atop the steepest mountain in the mysterious lands of the Farthest East. An army of noble elephants stood guard at the base of the mountain. No humans were allowed to enter, for the mountain's jungle was a haven for the beasts of the wild—a place where they could be safe from men and their foolishness."

Bunnymund's nose twitched. "Men are certainly full of *that*," he agreed.

North's nostrils flared, ready to argue with the Pooka, but Mr. Qwerty quietly continued.

"Toothiana's father was a human by the name of Haroom. He had been sold at birth into slavery as a companion for a young Indian maharaja. Despite being slave and master, the maharaja and Haroom

became great friends. But the maharaja was a silly, vain boy who had his every wish and whim granted. Yet this did not make him happy, for he always wanted more.

"Haroom, who had nothing, wanted nothing and so was very content. Secretly, the maharaja admired his friend for this. For his part, Haroom admired the maharaja for knowing what he wanted—and getting it."

Katherine scooted closer to Mr. Qwerty, peeking at the images of Haroom and the maharaja that now appeared on his pages. *How had a slave become the father of a queen?*

Mr. Qwerty straightened his pages and continued. "The maharaja loved to hunt and slay all the animals of the wild, and Haroom, who never tired of watching the powerful elegance of wild creatures such as tigers and snow leopards, was an excellent tracker. But he hated to see the animals killed, so when that moment came, he always looked away. As a slave, he could do nothing to stop his master. And so, with Haroom tracking, the maharaja killed one of every beast in his kingdom, lining the palace walls with their heads as trophies. But the one animal the maharaja coveted most continued to elude him.

"In the mountain land ruled by the Sisters of Flight, there dwelled one creature that no slave, man, or ruler had ever seen: the flying elephant of Punjam Hy Loo."

Katherine was impressed. "A flying *elephant?*"

Mr. Qwerty nodded. "Indeed, a flying elephant. The maharaja was determined to do anything to have one for his collection, but every time he tried to force his way up the mountain, the elephant army at its base turned him back. He realized that he must find another way to reach Punjam Hy Loo.

"In those ancient times no man had yet discovered the mystery of flight. But after demanding advice from his wizards and soothsayers, the maharaja learned a secret: Children can fly when they dream, and when the Moon shines brightly, their dreams can become so vivid that some of them come true. Sometimes the children remember, but mostly they do not. That is why children sometimes wake up in their parents' beds without knowing how they got there—they flew!

"The wizards told the maharaja a second secret." At this, Mr. Qwerty lowered his voice, and all the Guardians leaned closer. "The memory of everything that happens to a child is stored in that child's baby teeth.

"And so the maharaja's wizards gave him an idea: fashion a craft of the lost teeth of children and command it to remember how to fly. The maharaja sent out a decree throughout his kingdom, stating that whenever a child lost a tooth, it must be brought to his palace. His subjects happily complied, and it was not long before he had assembled a craft unlike any other the world had ever known."

Once again an image formed on one of Mr. Qwerty's blank pages. It was of a ship of gleaming white, fashioned from thousands of interlocking teeth. It had wings on each side of an oval gondola. The inside was lined with sumptuous carpets and intricately patterned pillows. And a single lamp hung from a mast to light the way.

"Meanwhile, the maharaja ordered Haroom to make an archer's bow of purest gold and one single ruby-tipped arrow. When the weapon was finished, the maharaja ordered Haroom to join him aboard the craft. Then he said these magic words:

"Remember,
remember,
the moonlit flights
of magic nights.'

The maharaja's
Flying Tooth Mobile

"And just as the royal wizards had promised, the craft flew silently through the sky, over the jungle, and past the elephants who guarded Punjam Hy Loo.

"They descended from the clouds and flew into the still-sleeping city. In the misty light of dawn, the maharaja could hardly tell where the jungle ended and the city began. But Haroom, used to seeking out tracks, spotted some he had never seen before—tracks that could only belong to the flying elephant, for although they looked similar to a normal elephant's, his keen eye saw one addition: an extra digit pointing backward, like that of a bird.

"It did not take long to find the flying elephant, sleeping in a nest in the low-lying limbs of an enormous jujube tree. The maharaja raised the golden bow and took careful aim. The tip of the ruby arrow glittered in the first rays of morning sunlight. Haroom looked away.

"Suddenly, there came an intense, cacophonous alarm, as if every creature of Punjam Hy Loo knew of the maharaja's murderous intent. Charging down from the towers above came the Sisters of Flight, wings outstretched, with all manner of weapons at the ready—gleaming

swords, razor-sharp daggers, fantastical flying spears with wings of their own. It was a sight so beautiful, so terrifying that Haroom and the maharaja froze.

"Then the maharaja raised his bow again, this time aiming it at the Sisters of Flight. 'Look, Haroom, an even greater prize,' he exclaimed.

"In that single moment Haroom's whole life changed. He knew, for the very first time, what he wanted. He could not bear to see a Sister of Flight harmed. He ordered the maharaja to stop.

"The maharaja paid his servant no heed. He let loose the arrow. Haroom blocked it. Its ruby tip pierced his chest, and he crumbled to the ground.

"The maharaja stared in shock, then kneeled beside his fallen friend. Weeping, he tried to stop the flow of blood but could not. Haroom was dying.

The Sisters of Flight landed around them. The

most beautiful of the sisters, the one the maharaja had meant to kill, approached them. 'We did not know that any man could be so selfless,' she said. Her sisters nodded.

"With one hand, she grabbed the arrow and plucked it from Haroom's chest, then kissed her fingertips and gently touched his wound.

"Haroom stirred, and his eyes fluttered open. All he could see was the face of the Sister of Flight. And all she could see was the brave and noble Haroom.

"He was a slave no more.

"She took his hand, and in that instant her wings vanished.

"The other sisters lunged toward the maharaja in fury. They raised their swords, and Haroom could see they meant to kill his former master. 'He will no longer harm you,' he said. 'Please, let him go—send him on his way.'

"The sisters looked from one to the other, then agreed. But they declared that the maharaja must leave all he brought with him. The golden bow, the ruby-tipped arrow, the flying craft of teeth, and Haroom, his only friend.

"'And one thing more.

"'You must also leave your vanity and cruelty behind so that we can know and understand them.'

"The maharaja was heartbroken but agreed.

"The flying elephant glided down from his nest, and with his trunk, he touched the maharaja's fore-head, and all the vanity and cruelty went from him.

"But once these things were gone, there was little left—the maharaja was as simple as a baby monkey. In fact, he even sprouted a tail and scampered away speaking gibberish, shrinking to the size of an infant.

"His vanity and cruelty would never be forgotten—the flying elephant had them now, and an elephant never forgets. As for Haroom and the beautiful Sister of Flight, they were married and lived on in Punjam Hy Loo. Within a year, a child was born. A girl. Selfless like her father. Pure of heart like her mother. She was named Toothiana."

Toothiana as a child

CHAPTER TWELVE

The Story of Queen Toothiana Continues:
A Mystery of Wing and Madness

Mr. Qwerty took a sip of tea and continued: "The child of Haroom and Rashmi (for that was Toothiana's mother's name) seemed to be a normal mortal child. As there were no other human children living in Punjam Hy Loo, her parents thought it best to raise her among other mortals, and so they settled on the outskirts of a small village at the edge of the jungle. The young girl was well loved and protected and lived a simple, happy life until she was twelve and lost her last baby tooth. That's when all her troubles began."

"Troubles?" Katherine asked nervously.

"Yes, troubles," Mr. Qwerty said. "For when she lost her last baby tooth, Toothiana sprouted wings. By the end of this first miraculous day, she could fly with the speed of a bird, darting to the top of the tallest trees to choose the ripest mangoes, papayas, and starfruit for the children of the village. She played with the birds and made friends with the wind.

"But while the children delighted in Toothiana's new skill, the adults of the village were bewildered, even frightened, by this half bird, half girl. Some thought she was an evil spirit and should be killed; others saw ways to use her, as either a freak to be caged and paraded about, or to force her to fly to the palace of the new maharaja and steal his jewels.

"Haroom and Rashmi knew that to keep their daughter safe, they would have to pack their few belongings and escape. And so they did, deep into the jungle. The village children, all of whom adored Toothiana, tried to persuade their parents to leave her alone. But it was no use. The grown-ups of the village had gone mad with fear and greed.

"They built a large cage, hired the best hunters in the land, and asked them to capture the young girl. Among these was a hunter most mysterious. He spoke not a word and was shrouded from head to foot in tattered cloth stitched together with jungle vines. The villagers were wary of him, and even the other hunters found him peculiar. 'He knows the jungle better than any of us—it's as if he's more a creature than a man,' they remarked quietly among themselves.

"But Haroom and Rashmi were as wily as any hunter. Haroom, knowing everything there was to know about tracking, could disguise their trail so that no one could follow it. And Rashmi, who could converse with any animal, enlisted their aid in confounding the hunters. Tigers, elephants, even giant pythons would intercept the hunters whenever they neared. But the hunters, eager for the riches and fame they'd receive if they caged Toothiana, would not give up."

Why can grown-ups be so strange and wicked sometimes? Katherine wondered, not asking aloud so as not to stop Mr. Qwerty's story. He cleared his throat and continued.

"The children of the village were also determined to thwart the hunters. They defied their parents, sending word to Toothiana and her mother and father again and again whenever the hunters were stalking the jungle. Toothiana, wiser still, hid in the treetops by day, only visiting her parents in the darkest hours of the night.

"After weeks of the best hunters in the land failing to capture Toothiana, the cunning villagers became more sly. They secretly followed their children and discovered where Toothiana's parents were hiding. They left a trail of coins for the hunters to follow. But only one hunter came—the one they almost feared. It was then that the Mysterious Hunter finally spoke. His voice was strange, high-pitched, almost comical, but his words were cold as death. 'Seize the parents,' he snarled. 'Make it known that I will slit their throats if Toothiana does not surrender. That will bring this child of flight out of hiding.'

"His plan made sense; the villagers did as he suggested. They attacked Haroom and Rashmi's camp.

With so many against them, the two surrendered without a fight. They had told their clever daughter to never try and help them if they were ever captured.

"But the Mysterious Hunter had planned for that. He shouted out to any creature that could hear, 'The parents of the flying girl will die by dawn if she comes not!'

"The creatures of the jungle hurried to warn Toothiana that her parents were doomed if she did not come. Toothiana had never disobeyed her parents, but the thought of them at the dubious mercy of these grown-ups filled her with rage and determination, and she flew straight to her parents' aid. She dove down from the treetops, ready to kill any who would try to harm her parents.

"But Haroom and Rashmi were brave and cunning as well. Haroom, who had never harmed a living creature, was prepared to stop at nothing to prevent his daughter from being enslaved. And Rashmi, like all Sisters of Flight, had been a great warrior. As Toothiana neared, they slashed and fought like beings possessed. Toothiana flickered back and forth, hovering over her mother and father, reaching for them, but she did not have the strength to lift them up over the angry mob. Rashmi thrust a stringed pouch into her daughter's hands. 'Keep these to remember us by. Keep these to protect yourself,' she pleaded to her child.

"'Now go!' commanded her father. 'GO!'

"With a heartrending cry, the winged girl did as her father ordered. She flew away but stopped, unsure of what to do. Her ears filled with the sound of the vengeful mob falling upon her parents.

"'Go!' shouted her mother.

"Toothiana flew wildly and desperately away. And as she went, she screamed from the depths of her soul. It was the scream of two beings: human and animal. It was a scream so pained and fierce that it caused all the villagers who were attacking her parents to go briefly deaf. All except . . . the Mysterious Hunter. He screamed back to Toothiana. His was a scream equally unsettling—a scream of rage and hate that was more animal than human. Toothiana knew in that instant that she had a mortal enemy—one who she must kill or be killed by.

"But for now she would grieve. She flew to the highest treetop and huddled deep inside its foliage. She had no tears, only the blank ache of a now-empty life. She rocked back and forth in a trance of disbelief for a full day and night. Then she remembered the pouch her mother had thrust into her hands. Trembling, she opened it. Inside was a small box carved from a single giant ruby. It was covered in feathery patterns, and Toothiana knew that the box had once been the ruby-tipped arrow that had nearly killed her parents. Inside this beautiful box was a cluster of baby teeth and a note: —

Our Dearest Girl,

These are the teeth of your childhood. If you have them under your pillow as you sleep, or hold it tightly, you will remember that which you need — a memory of happy days, or of deepest hopes, or even of us in better times.

But one tooth is not yours. It is a tooth of amazing power, and from what being it comes from, we do not know.

Use it only in times of the greatest danger or need.

Your Dearest Parents

"Toothiana still did not cry, not even after reading the note. She slept with her baby teeth under her pillow and took solace in the dreams and memories it gave her."

CHAPTER THIRTEEN

Lost Teeth and a Purpose Found

Toothiana stayed in the jungle. She began to hate her wings. Once, she had thought them wondrous things, but now she saw them as the reason for the death of her parents. Her grief and loneliness knew no depths. The creatures of the jungle did what they could to help her, by bringing her food and making her treetop sleeping places as comfortable as possible. The children of the village tried to aid as well, but they now had to be doubly cautious of the village grown-ups.

"As for Toothiana, she became more and more

convinced that she belonged nowhere—not among the creatures of the jungle and certainly not among the humans of the village. She was alone. When she was at her very saddest, she would take one of her baby teeth from the carved box she always carried in her mother's pouch she now wore around her neck, and hold it until it revealed its memories.

"As the lonely years passed, Toothiana saw that the village children lost much of their innocence and some of their goodness as they grew up. She began to collect their teeth, so that, in the future, she could give them back their childhood memories and remind them of their kindness, just as her own parents had done for her.

"Soon the children, not wanting their parents to find out, began to hide their lost teeth under their pillows for Toothiana to find. And she, cheered by this new game of sorts, began in turn to leave behind small bits of treasure she had found in the jungle. A gold nugget here. A sprinkling of sapphire chips there.

"But you can imagine the curiosity that is stirred when a five-year-old sits down to breakfast with an uncut ruby in her palm, or when a ten-year-old boy comes to the table with a pocket full of emeralds. Once again the hearts of the grown-ups filled with greed, and it wasn't long before they forced their children to tell them how they had come upon those treasures. Soon enough they had laid a new trap for Toothiana.

"One dark, cloudy night Toothiana flew to the village to make her nightly rounds. A boy named Akela had lost his two front teeth, and Toothiana had a special treasure saved for him: two beautiful uncut diamonds. But as she entered his open window, it wasn't Akela she found. Instead the Mysterious Hunter leaped toward her. From behind his shroud of rags, she could see the strangest eyes. Close together. Beady. Not entirely human. And cold with hate.

"Toothiana's rage clouded her keen intellect. All she could think was, *I must get rid of this . . . thing!* But before she could act, a steel door slammed down between her and the Hunter. She glanced around with birdlike quickness. The room was not Akela's bedroom, but, in fact, a cleverly disguised steel cage.

"She was trapped! The villagers cheered as the Hunter hauled away the cage. His platoon of slave-like helpers pulled the wheeled prison away from the villagers and into the jungle. The helpers were as strangely shrouded as the Hunter who commanded them was, and seemed excited by the capture. The children wept, begging their parents to let Toothiana go free. But they would not. The Mysterious Hunter had promised them riches beyond their dreams when he sold Toothiana.

"Toothiana flung herself wildly against the cage, like a cornered eagle. But it did no good. The Hunter and his minions traveled swiftly through the night, deeper into the jungle. They knew the creatures of the wild would try to help Toothiana, so they carried the one weapon every animal fears: fire.

"Torches were lashed to the roof of Toothiana's cage. The Mysterious Hunter himself carried the brightest torch of all. The animals kept their distance, but they continued to follow the eerie caravan and keep watch over Toothiana, waiting for a chance to strike.

"After days of travel they arrived at the base of the steep mountain of Toothiana's birthplace—the kingdom of Punjam Hy Loo. The great elephants that guarded the mountain were standing at the ready, shifting back and forth on their massive feet. Toothiana's jungle friends had warned them that the Mysterious Hunter was headed their way.

"The Hunter did not challenge the elephants. He ordered his minions to halt and made no move to attack. Instead, he held his flaming torch aloft. 'I bring a treasure to the Sisters of Flight and the flying elephant king who dwell in Punjam Hy Loo!' he shouted into the night sky. The sky was empty; there was no sign of either the winged women who ruled there, or of the flying elephant.

"The Hunter called out again. 'I bring you the half-breed daughter of Haroom and Rashmi.' At this, an otherworldly sound—like a rustle of trees in the wind—was heard. And indeed wind did begin to blow down from the mountain. It grew stronger and more furious, with gusts that nearly put out the torches.

"Toothiana knew instinctually that this wind was sent by the Sisters of Flight and that they did not trust the Hunter. She also knew that it was time to take out the box her parents had left her.

"As the winds continued to rise, the Hunter grew increasingly nervous, as did his minions. They began to chatter in the oddest way, not in words, but in sounds.

"Then a chorus of voices, all speaking in unison, rang out bright and clear above the howl of the wind: 'Tell us, Hunter, why cage our child? Where be her father and mother? What trick of men do you bring us? What do you seek, you who seem of men and yet are not?'

"The Hunter rocked on his feet, seething with undisguised hate. He held his torch high and stepped forward, leaning into the wind. The elephants raised their trunks but took a step back. Fire was a fearsome thing, even for these mighty beasts.

"The Hunter laughed, then threw down his tattered cloak. He was no man at all, but a massive monkey. 'A maharaja of men I once was,' he screamed, 'and by your doing, I am now a king of the monkeys!' Then his troops dropped their cloaks as well. An array of monkeys revealed themselves, all armed with bows and arrows.

"The Monkey King shrieked above the roaring wind, 'You ask about her parents? Dead! By *my* doing! What do I seek? Revenge! On all who made me thus!' Then he threw his torch into the herd of elephants and grabbed a bow and arrow from one of his men. He had it drawn in an instant, aimed directly at Toothiana's heart.

"Before he could let loose the arrow, the wind tripled in strength. Toothiana knew what to do. She held the ruby box tightly in her hand. 'Mother, Father, help me,' she whispered furiously, clenching her eyes shut. She pictured them clearly in her mind, letting herself feel the bond they had shared so deeply, letting herself remember how much they had sacrificed for her.

"Suddenly, she was no longer in the cage. She was no longer a single entity, but several smaller versions of herself.

"Bow drawn, the Monkey King hesitated, bewildered. *How can this be?* He could not remember the power of love—even though it had been this girl's father who had loved him best—and his own memories were now fueled only by hate.

"So the world turned against him once again.

"The Sisters of Flight circled overhead. It was the flapping of their wings that made the great wind. It grew wilder and stranger, like a tornado. Leaves snapped off trees. Dirt swirled like a storm, and the Monkey King's torch blew out.

"Now the only light came from the Moon, and no jungle creature fears that guiding light. In an instant the elephants stampeded forward. Toothiana's animal friends attacked. Toothiana's mini-selves charged the Monkey King. The monkey army screamed and ran.

"The king tried to grab the Toothianas, but he could not catch them. Then all the fairy-sized selves merged back into a single being.

A mini Tooth

Toothiana was mystified by her new power, but she didn't think on it. With one hand, she grabbed the Monkey King by the throat. It was as if she now had the strength of a dozen. The Monkey King cried out in terror and pain.

"For an instant Toothiana felt the rage within her swell. She would snap his neck and be done with him. But the little box glowed in one hand, and the memory of her parents made her stop. She would not end this monkey man's life. Let the jungle choose his fate.

"So she let him go.

"He fell to the ground, and she did not look back as she flew up to join the Sisters of Flight.

"As they sped away, Toothiana and her kindred could hear the creatures of the jungle do as they saw fit with the fallen Monkey King. And his cries could be heard all the way to the Moon."

Mr. Qwerty then shut his pages. The tale, as it was written, was done.

Toothiana's story made Katherine feel many things, but the strangest was a twinge of envy. *Toothiana* had memories of *her* parents. It was something Katherine wished for more than anything.

CHAPTER FOURTEEN

Nightlight Faces the Unknown

AFTER LISTENING AT THE window to the story of Queen Toothiana, Nightlight flew listlessly around the mountains that surrounded the Lunar Lamadary. He was increasingly troubled. Until now he had viewed the events of his life in very simple terms. To him, the world was divided into good and bad. Katherine and the Guardians were good—absolutely. And Pitch was bad, through and through, without even an ounce of good in him. And yet . . .

Nightlight was confounded by what he had seen in Katherine's Dream Tear. And in this dream, Pitch's hand was human, as it had been since he'd tried to make Nightlight a Darkling Prince.

But there was more.

In the dream, Pitch had held in his human hand the locket with his daughter's picture. But the picture shifted, and Katherine's face took its place. And then *her* face began to change! It became different. Older. A grown-up's face. And then darker. More like Pitch's.

Nightlight was afraid of this dream. It felt true. No Guardian had seen any sign of Pitch of late, yet Nightlight had; Pitch *lived*—in Katherine's dreams. What did this mean?

Would she grow up? Would she become like so many adults, a grim shadow of her youthful self? Or was there a greater danger? Would she somehow be taken over by Pitch? Was her soul in danger? These questions tore at his heart and soul in ways he could not comprehend or put into words. So he turned to his oldest friend.

For hours he waited for the Moon to rise, and when it did, he took Katherine's Dream Tear and held it up. The moonbeam inside his staff began to flash, and moments later, the Man in the Moon responded to his signal. Moonbeams shined down and flickered as they interpreted the Dream Tear. Then Nightlight, waiting anxiously, finally whispered in his rarely used and otherworldly voice, "Will my Katherine go Darkling or stay true?" He stood, still and tense, for a long while until a moonbeam brought back the simple answer, the answer that was the truth of everything:

Believe. Believe. Believe, it said.

And for the first time in his endless childhood life, Nightlight cried. He was not sure why he was crying.

He could not describe the feeling that brought the tears. It was not happiness or sorrow. It was not good or bad. But it was something just as powerful.

Someday he would know what it was, that first mysterious step beyond childhood. It is a strange feeling, to realize that you will grow up, especially for one who has been a child for so long. But he now had the answer he needed to face this uncertainty.

Believe. Believe. Believe. If he could remember that, he would make everything right. And so his tears stopped. He wiped them from his cheeks, then brought them close to his face, so unaccustomed was he to having tears.

Each was bright with light and seemed to take the burden from his anxious heart. He let them spill together with Katherine's Dream Tear.

Then he took the diamond tip of his staff and

touched it to the tears, holding it there until they fused with the diamond. Now the spearlike point of his staff held not just his friend's fear and sorrow, but his own as well.

The moonbeam inside grew furiously bright, for sorrow and fear that are triumphed over make a powerful weapon.

At that instant he heard Katherine calling for him, and he knew that whatever might come, he was ready.

CHAPTER FIFTEEN

Plots, Plans, and Pillows

IT IS NOT EASY to fall asleep when an entire village, an army of Abominable Snowmen, a troupe of ancient Lunar holy men, and all your best friends are coming into your bedroom and wishing you good night. It is also not easy to sleep when you know you are going to be visited by a half-bird, half-human queen with magical powers. And it is really hard to sleep when you have made a secret plan with your dearest friend to do the *one thing* you've been told you absolutely MUST NOT DO when this particular queen arrives. So there Katherine sat, in her huge and feathered bed in her special room in the Lunar Lamadary, as wide awake as any twelve-year-old has ever been.

She'd just checked under her pillow for the eleventh time to make certain that her tooth hadn't somehow rolled onto the floor when North opened the bedroom door again, just enough to stick in his head. "Still awake?" he asked in surprise.

Ombric and Bunnymund crowded in next to him, crammed so tightly in the doorway that Katherine could see only half of Ombric's face and one of Bunnymund's ears, with Ombric's beard tangled around it.

"Perhaps if you chant the ancient Atlantan phrase 'Sleep-o deep-o slumberly doo—'" Ombric began to suggest.

Bunnymund interrupted with, "Counting! That'll do it. Count chocolate eggs jumping counterclockwise over a small wall also made of chocolate—"

Then North interrupted, saying, "A song! We should sing a song!"

Then they all began to talk at once: "It should be about eggs! A sleepy chocolate egg opera would be perfect!" . . . "No, no, no! A good old-fashioned Cossack lullaby. 'Don't cut my throat while I am sleeping, mother, my mother dear.'" . . . "North, that's awful! No, she should chant, 'Dream, dream, dream of chocolate ocean waves . . .'"

And so it went till Nightlight flew down from the rafters and, with a firm but caring swing of his staff, slammed the door shut.

The three Guardians muttered outside the door for a moment or two, then the Lunar Lamas could be heard suggesting that the centuries-old method of simply being left quietly alone tended to bring about sleep quite reliably. And so things finally settled down.

Nightlight leaped to Katherine's bed and sat cross-legged on the footboard. He still seemed . . . different to her; no longer quite so sad or distant. But the cheerful half grin that had always been there was replaced by a look that seemed—well, she couldn't really put a finger on it, but he didn't seem quite so like a little boy now.

And whether it was the Lamas' suggestion or just the result of a very full day, Katherine suddenly felt overcome with sleepiness and ready to close her eyes. But she propped herself up on one elbow for another minute, careful not to shift the pillow that covered her tooth. She wanted to go over the plan she'd concocted earlier with Nightlight one more time. It had come to her when the Lunar Lamas had told her even more details about the workings of Queen Toothiana. It had taken a while, given the Lamas' propensity for vague answers, but Katherine had learned that she had to be asleep for Toothiana to come and take her tooth. And only Toothiana could unlock the countless memories in a tooth, by holding it in her magic grasp. Once the memories were unlocked, Katherine wanted her tooth back.

"You must get my tooth back the instant she does her magic!" she reminded Nightlight.

Nightlight nodded. He could feel how much this meant to Katherine. *She wants to remember her mother and father*, thought Nightlight. *And if she remembers them, then perhaps she'll forget Pitch.*

That's what he believed in his hopeful heart. He had never failed Katherine before, and he would not fail her now.

CHAPTER SIXTEEN

In Which We See the Extremely Secret Process by Which a Tooth Is Gathered

FOR CENTURY UPON CENTURY Queen Toothiana flew majestically on her nightly rounds with her half dozen mini-selves. At the bedside of every child who had left a tooth under his pillow, one of her selves quietly collected the tooth and made a silent wish. The children each were different, but the wish was the same: that the child would grow up to be kind and happy. In the many villages and cities and jungles of Asia, the children knew to place their lost teeth under their pillows. Then a tiny treasure would be left in place of the tooth. And the tooth would be stored in the palace of the flying elephant of Punjam Hy Loo until it was needed again.

Once, Toothiana had loved to spend time at each child's bedside—straightening a blanket that had been kicked off or whispering messages of hope into sleeping ears. She had loved to peek from the windows as the children woke in the morning; their joyful cries when they reached under their pillows and found their gifts—this was *her* treasure.

But she wanted to help all the children in the world, however there simply wasn't enough of her to go around. Since she'd learned long ago that jewels of any kind were likely to bring the wrong kind of interest from adults, she had begun to use coins or other smaller treasures in exchange for teeth. But, oh, the coins! Children loved to receive them; however, as more countries were formed, more currencies were invented, and each child required the coin from his or her realm. It became a complicated business. Even with six of her, there was barely time to outrun the coming dawn.

Yet despite Queen Toothiana's hurried pace, there was something about her presence that calmed every child she visited. And while on any given night she might encounter a bad dream or two, the terrible time of the Nightmare Man seemed to be over. The children in her lands, like children everywhere, called him the Boogeyman, and she'd seen no sign of him for months.

While Queen Toothiana knew less about the Guardians than they knew about her, she'd observed that glimmering boy made of light who had been involved in battling the Boogeyman. She'd seen how brave he'd been saving the girl who wrote stories and drew pictures. She felt a special fondness for the two of them. In a strange way their devotion to each other reminded her of her parents' devotion, and so she was looking very much forward to the last stop of the evening.

For the very first time, she'd received a call to the highest peak in the Himalayas—to the Lunar Lamadary. There, she knew she would find out more about this valiant girl who rode on a giant goose.

Meanwhile, Nightlight waited for Queen Toothiana on the top of the Lamadary's tower with as much patience as he could muster. He remembered the first time he had seen the bird woman: He'd been playing moonbeam tag when she'd flickered by so quickly that he mistook her for an enormous hummingbird. And from time to time they glimpsed each other. She'd never spoken to him, but she always nodded whenever their flying paths briefly crossed. But Nightlight, with his keen intuition, sensed that she distrusted most people and didn't want the other Guardians to know about her, so he had kept his knowledge of her to himself. Besides, there was something about her that made him feel sort of shy.

But Katherine asked for his help. So he kept his eyes trained on the night sky, peering among the bright stars for the first sign of this Toothiana.

Soon, Nightlight spied a glow. It was a shimmer—flickering sparks of iridescent blues and greens. As it came closer, Nightlight made out a feathered head, bright green eyes, and a happy smile. He tried to hide, but Toothiana and her mini-selves saw him before he could leap into the shadows.

Toothiana knew immediately that he was up to

something. Through the centuries, too many children had plotted and planned to wake at the moment she arrived for her to be caught unawares now. She shook her head sternly and held a finger to her lips, warning him not to interfere.

Nightlight wavered. His deepest loyalty rested with Katherine, and yet he found himself acutely aware that he needed to trust this winged being. At least for the moment. With the slightest of nods, he let her know that he would do as she asked. But he followed her closely as she and her selves shot through the window and down to Katherine's bed.

Three of the mini-selves, no bigger than sparrows, each carried a gold coin. They flew silently to Katherine's pillow, then tucked in their wings and crawled gently and silently under it. Another landed by Katherine's ear and plucked at a tiny silver instrument

Katherine and her visitors

while she sang a soft, lulling song. Nightlight was fascinated. *They sing to make her sleep more soundly*, he realized.

Another mini-self stood guard by the pillow while the last one winged about the room and seemed to be keeping watch as Toothiana, an expectant smile upon her face, waited for the tooth to be smuggled from under the pillow.

The pillow puckered here and rumpled there, then, at last, the three small fairies emerged, Katherine's tooth in hand. Toothiana picked it up tenderly. With her other hand, she brought out a beautiful, carved, ruby box from a pouch she wore around her neck, and held it tightly.

She closed her eyes as if in deep thought. A glow began to emanate from both Katherine's tooth and the box. The queen's magical power seemed to be working.

Nightlight had seen all he needed. As willful as the flying woman seemed, he would do as Katherine asked. He readied himself to swoop in to take the tooth, but a quiet, mournful sigh from Toothiana made him pause, puzzled. A sadness came over her lovely face, and then her mini-selves sighed as well, as though they shared her every feelings. She could see all of Katherine's memories.

Toothiana murmured, "Poor child. You're like me—you've lost your mother and father. But . . . you didn't even have a chance to know or remember them." She bowed her head ever so slightly and looked down at Katherine, who slept on.

"I must give you the memory you long for," she whispered. Nightlight leaned forward anxiously as Toothiana lowered the hand that held the tooth to Katherine's forehead.

Nightlight knew he needn't steal the tooth now. Katherine would have the memory. He was glad. He felt a peculiar bond with this bird royal and didn't want to anger her.

But suddenly, a sound most angry stopped Toothiana from granting Katherine her wish.

◆

CHAPTER SEVENTEEN

Monkey See, Monkey Don't

MONKEYS, DOZENS OF THEM, sprang through the windows of Katherine's room and swarmed the chamber. They were huge, hulking, and armed with daggers, spears, and crude weapons.

What is this dark business? Toothiana wondered in shock as a handful of the malicious creatures, screeching loudly, leaped upon her with a swiftness that was unnatural. She crammed the ruby box back into its pouch, then turned, batting her wings at the fiends as she tried to escape their grip, then drew her swords and slashed away. But the monkeys were too quick.

Katherine startled awake and instinctively grabbed for the dagger on her night table as six or eight of her attackers grasped her arms and legs. A monkey with a grotesquely humanlike face pressed his hand against her mouth so that she could not cry out. Nightlight was there in a flash, batting the animals away with his staff, but for each monkey he hit, seven would take its place. The room was overrun with chattering, maniacal monster monkeys.

Queen Toothiana knew she had to protect the girl. As Katherine struggled to free herself, Toothiana lunged for the monkeys. In the tangle of tails and clawing hands, Katherine's tooth was knocked to the floor. Both Toothiana and Katherine cried out at the same time.

Katherine was determined not to lose that tooth. She elbowed one monkey after another, reaching,

reaching, reaching for the tooth. Each time her fingers nearly gripped it, it was kicked away. Katherine darted along the floor on her hands and knees, her eyes never leaving the tooth. Finally, it was within her grasp. One great last stretch, then—got it!

Only then, when her precious tooth was safely tucked in her palm, did Katherine think to scream, to call out for help. She didn't get a chance. Once again a hand covered her mouth. Then another had her leg; another, her arm.

Katherine strained against her captors, trying to squirm away as Toothiana and Nightlight struck at monkey after monkey. The tiny versions of Toothiana dove and charged relentlessly at the primates' eyes. They were making headway when a second wave of monkeys attacked. There were just too many.

The largest monkey, the one who seemed the

leader, snatched the pouch from around Toothiana's neck, raised it over his head, and hurled it to one of his minions, who promptly leaped out the window with the prize, followed by a dark mass of his scuffling cohorts.

Toothiana struggled to follow them, sweeping her wings at the monkeys in her way, but then she stopped short. The monkey who had taken her precious box—she recognized him! *That vile creature . . . That monkey was the one who . . .* Toothiana's rage took hold, and in one swift move, she had him in her grip.

The room became a cyclone of monkeys; they stampeded around the walls and began to bound out the windows in waves. They seemed to be running right across the night sky, as if it had become solid under their feet. And then in a flash of darkness, the monkeys vanished.

All except one.

Toothiana pressed her sword against her old enemy's throat, breathing hard.

The door flew open. North burst into the room, with Ombric, Bunnymund, Yaloo and his Yeti lieutenants, and even a few sleepy-eyed Lamas right behind him.

"Villains, explain yourselves!" North demanded, his cutlass ready.

Toothiana didn't respond. Nor did she remove her blade from the monkey's neck.

North took a step closer, and Toothiana cocked her head, birdlike, from right to left. As North took another step, her feathers flared up, as if to warn him not to come closer. One of her wings hung limp.

The captive monkey, frantic-eyed, whimpered something that sounded vaguely like "Help!"

Everyone froze, wonderstruck at the sight of the flying woman they had heard so much about. They had expected a serene being, but here she was in fighting stance and with a death grip on a decidedly evil-looking ape. Ombric was madly sorting through the various dialects of primate languages to best question the captive monkey. *Odd how humanlike it looks,* he thought. *Very odd indeed.*

In all the confusion, it was Nightlight who was the first to notice that Katherine was not in her bed.

Before he could alert the others, they all felt the surge of his frantic worry.

North whipped his head back and forth, surveying the room. "Katherine?" he called. Then "KATHERINE!" Dread crept through the Guardians when there came no reply.

Ombric and Bunnymund reached out to her with

their minds, but they got only a confusing darkness in response.

North turned his attention back to Toothiana and the strange creatures she held prisoner. He glared menacingly at them, raising his sword.

"Tell me what you've done with Katherine," he demanded, "or you will never take another breath."

CHAPTER EIGHTEEN

A Journey Most Confounding, with Flying Monkeys Who Smell Very Badly Indeed

KATHERINE CLUTCHED HER TOOTH as she tried to push away the putrid cloak that one of the monkeys had thrown over her head. The last thing she had seen had been the monkey with the humanlike face take Toothiana's pouch. Then it dawned on her. *That must be the Monkey King from Toothiana's story!*

The air felt colder, so Katherine knew she had been dragged outside. Her mind raced with so many questions, she hardly had time to be scared. *The Monkey King has come for revenge, but why take me?* she wondered. She felt herself being prodded and shoved and sometimes even thrown from one tight grip to another, speeding along at an impossibly fast pace. The monkeys seemed to be running on solid ground, but sometimes it felt like they were—what? Flying? She pulled at the cloak till she made a small hole. Clouds. Stars. Sky. They *were* flying! And were extremely high.

At that moment the cloak slipped to one side, and Katherine caught a glimpse of solid surface below— a road made of shadows. She gasped. It was like Nightlight's roads of light, but inky and frightening. *There's only one being who could make a sky road of shadows*, she realized with dread.

And then she remembered her dream, her awful dream.

Screeching incessantly, the monkeys sped on. Katherine tried to reach out to her friends with her mind, but something about this dark highway was blocking her thoughts.

Her breath formed tiny icicles around her face and nose as freezing air rushed past. She ripped the hole bigger and was finally able to take a deep, unfettered breath, but it was too cold, and she pulled the cloak shut, now feeling smothered again.

The monkeys had a stink to them that she hadn't expected; they'd looked much sweeter in the pictures from Ombric's ancient book. A fleeting wish that she had taken the time to learn the language of monkeys flashed through her mind. Ombric could speak it, no doubt, but as there were no monkeys in Santoff Claussen, it had seemed much more important to learn languages she could actually use—like squirrel and Lunar Moth. She could likely learn it easily enough. She'd learned Great Snow Goose, hadn't she?

Oh, Kailash! Katherine thought with a groan. *She will be so worried. Nightlight, too.* Then it struck her: What if he were wounded? A wave of fear for her friends swept over her, forcing her attention back to the dilemma at hand. She kicked and pushed against the cloak, but it was futile. The monkeys simply held it tighter around her, until she could barely move her arms.

The temperature was changing again, slowly at first and then more quickly. The icy air warmed. The cloak felt suffocating. Katherine's stomach lurched as the monkeys took a giant leap and then bounced up and down on what felt like a tree branch.

The cloak slipped from her head. This time the monkeys made no effort to cover her face as they swung from tree to tree, dragging Katherine along with them. Sometimes it seemed the branches could never hold them, and then they'd plummet down, down, down, in rapid falls, leaves slapping at Katherine's face and neck. She found herself being thrown from one paw to the next until one of the monkeys would grab a solid branch and begin the ascent again.

Besides the screeching monkeys—were they *ever* quiet?—Katherine saw no other jungle creatures at all, not even birds. It was as if the monkeys were the only animals in this land. *Where are the other animals?* she wondered. *Where are the elephants and the tigers? The snakes and the lizards?*

And then, without warning, the monkeys let go of their grasp and dropped Katherine. She didn't fall far. Just a few feet. When she realized she was unhurt, she began to cautiously look around. She could not see much beneath the jungle canopy, but she was able to pick out what seemed to be the ruins of what once must have been a magnificent city. The jungle had done its best to take it over, but Katherine could see evidence of the city's former glory in the tarnished gold and silver fixtures on the crumbling walls.

Where in the world am I? She looked in every direction and didn't see a soul, just the army of monkeys. But now they kept their distance. It had become eerily quiet. So Katherine decided there was nothing to do but investigate. She headed for the closest buildings, stopping at the first to peer at a dirt-covered mosaic. The design, though half buried under a layer of mud and mold, looked exquisite, so using the side of her fist, she wiped the muck off until she could make out the outline of an elephant—an elephant with wings.

"The flying elephant!" she said with a gasp. *I'm in Punjam Hy Loo!* It seemed almost a dream. Just yesterday Mr. Qwerty had told them all about this city and the Sisters of Flight!

She looked in every direction. *Were the sisters still here somewhere? What has brought this city so low? Were there still elephants guarding the mountain?* She looked for more clues and didn't notice that the shadows around her were growing larger. Blacker. She didn't see that hundreds more monkeys were quietly perching on the derelict walls surrounding her.

It wasn't until an immense shadow loomed directly over her that Katherine looked up and gulped. It was as she feared.

"Pitch," she said, trying to sound calm.

The Nightmare King greeted her with a ghoulish smile. "Greetings, my Darkling Daughter," he whispered in a voice that was anything but welcoming.

CHAPTER NINETEEN

Panic in the Himalayas

"WHERE IS KATHERINE?" NORTH roared again at the winged woman in front of him. He was sure she had some hand in Katherine's disappearance, but his sword was pulling away from this strange being—he'd almost forgotten how the sword, the first relic from the Man in the Moon, could tell friend from foe. The sword knew Toothiana meant no harm to any Guardian. But North resisted it. The woman knew something, and she must tell them.

Nightlight sat on Katherine's bed. Her pillow had been tossed to the floor, but the three coins that had been left for her were still in place.

Toothiana's eyes darted from North to the others, one hand still tight around the struggling monkey's neck, the other still clasping her sword, poised and ready to end this creature's life. With a quick glance, she told her mini-selves to stay back. Her feathers fluffed and quivered. *With rage?* North wondered. *Or panic?*

He had seen that look before. As a boy in the wild, he had known it well. It was the look of a trapped animal, one that had nothing to lose, so would go down fighting. North had learned how to approach them—calmly and carefully.

Then it dawned on North how he and the others must appear to her—this queen who had every reason to mistrust adults. She was facing a sword-wielding warrior, a seven-foot-tall bunny, an ancient wizard, and Abominable Snowmen bearing all manner of weapons. The set of Toothiana's jaw was fierce, but her eyes, almond-shaped and green, betrayed her. *Why, she must feel just like a sparrow caught in a cage,* he thought.

So North held up one hand and sheathed his sword. He approached the queen slowly. Even the monkey stopped his squirming as North took one careful step after another, never blinking, never taking his eyes off her.

"We mean you no harm," North said in his most soothing voice. "But we are most anxious to find our friend—the girl you were here to see tonight. Do you know what happened to her?"

Toothiana cocked her head, held North's gaze in her own for the longest time, then seemed to make a decision: She would trust this hulking man.

"Gone. Taken," she said.

"Taken where? By whom?" North encouraged, forcing his voice to stay steady.

"*This* creature knows," she said, gesturing toward the monkey.

Ombric made one cautious step forward. "Is that creature the Monkey King?" he asked, recalling Toothiana's story.

She nodded, then gave the creature a hard shake. "Tell what you know!"

The monkey spat at her. "Never!" he screeched.

North could scarcely contain himself. "Tell us!" he roared. "Or die!"

The monkey merely sucked on his teeth and smirked.

Toothiana grabbed the simian by his feet and swung him upside down, giving him a good shake with each word. "Where. Is. The. Girl? Where. Is. My. Box?"

"Gone. Taken," the Monkey King mimicked.

North unsheathed his sword and brought its tip to the monkey's chin.

The Monkey King simply continued to suck on his teeth, as if being held upside down with a sword pressed to his chin was a perfectly normal course of events.

Bunnymund's whiskers bristled. He, too, knew the ways of animals, even better than North did. And North—like all poor humans—was beginning to let his emotions get the best of him. It was time for cooler heads. It was time for the Pooka to take charge.

He pressed a paw on North's arm until North lowered his sword. Then he eyed the monkey appraisingly. "You're very clever," the Pooka told him. "Clever enough to fool all of us. To break into the Lamadary. To lead your troops to capture our friend. And steal this lady's precious treasure."

While he was talking, he was pulling a chocolate egg out of his pocket and carefully peeling it, as one would a piece of fruit. The aroma of a perfectly ripe banana, tinged with the scent of milky chocolate, filled the room.

Bunnymund motioned to Toothiana to turn the monkey right side up again. As she did, the monkey's eyes began to gleam. He reached for the chocolate, which Bunnymund dropped into his hand. Popping the confection into his mouth, the Monkey King closed his eyes. "Yum-yum," he said blissfully.

Nightlight watched closely. He had never before wanted to harm a creature of flesh and blood. Pitch was darkness, a phantom, but the monkey man was *alive*—a living being. Nightlight saw the hate in Toothiana's eyes for this creature. And in North's. Even Ombric's. And now he felt it too. And he did not like it.

The Monkey King motioned for another chocolate as Nightlight fought the urge to spear him through with his staff.

"What a wise monkey king. You want more. And more you'll have," Bunnymund said, patting his pockets and backing away. "But first you must answer our questions."

The Monkey King bobbed his head up and down

and answered in the language of monkeys.

Ombric translated. "The King of the Monkeys claims he is much too clever to fall for our tricks."

The monkey's eyes widened. He had never before met a human who could speak monkey.

"You are indeed clever, Maharaja," Ombric said, "but perhaps not as clever as you think you are. Who sent you to kidnap our friend?"

"No one sent me," the monkey said, speaking in the language of men. He raised his head haughtily. "I am a king. I lead my army where I choose. I am not 'sent.' And now I demand to be fed."

"Some army," North scoffed. "They've left you behind."

"They have not!" he howled.

"Then where oh where have they gone?" asked Bunnymund.

No longer a maharajah,
the Monkey King is maha-rose.

The Monkey King stiffened. "They'll be back."

Bunnymund took out another chocolate with a flourish and held it close to the Monkey King's nose.

"You'll get no more answers from me, *Rabbit Man*," the Monkey King spat.

"Then no more yummies for you," said Bunnymund. He handed the chocolate to Ombric, who peeled tantalizingly, then bit it in half. The banana-laced fragrance filled the room.

The monkey eyed the other half of the chocolate and whimpered, "More yum-yum." Bunnymund shook his head.

"I *can't* tell you," the Monkey King whimpered. "I will be killed until dead."

"Who would dare do such a thing to such a clever Monkey King?" Ombric asked, searching for an even tone, though alarm bells were exploding in his head.

The Monkey King saw a chance to bargain. He drew himself up again. "One who can make me human again—make me much, much maharaja. Can *you* do that?"

North was growing tired of this back-and-forth. The longer this went on, the farther away Katherine could be taken. He leaped forward and smashed the monkey onto the floor. "Tell us what we ask!" he demanded.

The monkey giggled and pointed at Toothiana. "In *her* home. They wait at Punjam Hy Loo."

Toothiana trembled with rage. "You lie!"

"No, no, no," cackled the monkey. "'Tis all part of the plan!"

"Coward!" North spat out, pacing in front of him. "You're a pathetic excuse for a king."

"And always have been," Toothiana added.

The Monkey King scowled darkly, his anger building. "Wait until the King of Nightmares makes me the King of Mans again. I will kill you deader than your father!"

Toothiana pulled her sword to his head. How dare he boast of such things in her presence!

But North and the other Guardians barely noticed. The words "King of Nightmares" had stilled them. North ceased pacing; Nightlight glowed brightly. Bunnymund's whiskers twitched, and Ombric's beard began to curl with worry. They all had only one thought.

Pitch was back!

"What does the Nightmare King want with my ruby box?" Toothiana asked now.

"And why take Katherine and leave the rest of us?" North demanded.

The Monkey King's eyes gleamed with triumph. "He seeks to build an army. And turn the girl into his Darkling Princess."

CHAPTER TWENTY

In Which Toothiana Makes a Startling Discovery

INSTANTLY THE GUARDIANS BEGAN to talk in low, tense voices. Queen Toothiana, however, kept her eyes trained on the Monkey King.

The Monkey King looked back at her with a gloat of self-importance.

Toothiana's eyes narrowed; her anger felt venomous. She thought about all of her years on the run. About her parents' deaths. Every sorrow of her life had been caused by this pathetic monkey.

He tried to avert her gaze, but Toothiana grabbed him by the neck again and forced him to look at her.

"How?" she demanded. "How did the jungle law spare you?"

The Monkey King glared at her, his eyes matching her own in the fury they contained. "The tigers tore at me. The serpents bit me. Every creature gave me wounds, but I would not die, for I had to destroy . . . YOU!"

"My father *saved* you," said Toothiana.

The Monkey King glanced away, drawing in a shaky breath.

Toothiana wondered if there was anything about this monkey worth sparing. Her father had saved him once, and he had been repaid with angry mobs and an early death. Did this monkey maharaja have even a shred of his childlike goodness left? There was only one way to know for sure. With an angry cry, Toothiana pried open the Monkey King's mouth.

"No baby teeth!" she shouted. "You die."

The monkey yowled, wrenching his jaw from her hands.

Toothiana swung her sword to strike a deadly blow when North bounded across the room and grabbed her wrist.

"No!" he yelled. "We need the creature. He can help us rescue our friend."

She scoffed at him. This monkey would never help anyone but himself. She lowered her sword.

"I'll leave," she said. "For Punjam Hy Loo. I'll get the ruby box *and* your girl."

"Pitch—he's crueler and more devious than you'd ever imagine," North warned. "You can't go alone."

"We'll come with you," Ombric implored. "Together our power is mighty."

Toothiana scoffed again. "This Pitch scares me not

at all." With that, she leaped onto the windowsill and prepared to spring into the air. But as she spread her wings, she listed to the left. Her right wing, her beautiful, iridescent right wing, hung limp.

CHAPTER TWENTY-ONE

Nightlight Sees a Woman of Mystery

KATHERINE TRAPPED AND ALONE with the Nightmare King was the worst thing Nightlight could possibly imagine.

For a new fear gripped him, one that he could not describe even to himself, for it was a feeling beyond his own understanding. But he knew that Katherine longed for a father's love and that Pitch had lost a daughter. Could this be a dangerous thing for his friend? He thought of what he'd seen in the Dream Tear and shook his head.

As he sat at the tower top, he looked up to the

Moon for reassurance, but it was blocked by dense, fast-moving clouds. There was a strange wind blowing, and Nightlight couldn't shake the feeling that he was being watched; even that his thoughts were somehow overheard. He'd had this feeling before. It was only when he was alone, and it did not seem threatening—but it was strange. He sometimes thought he saw a face—a woman's face, for just an instant—in the shapes of the clouds or in a swirl of leaves that blew past him or even in a mist of falling snowflakes. He never saw it clearly, and he wondered if it was just his daydreaming ways that made him think he even glimpsed this woman, but this time he looked about, trying to see if she was really there. He knew he felt something. He knew it felt tied somehow to Katherine and Pitch. He let his thoughts reach out, as they could with Katherine, but there was no response.

Just a vague feeling that someone, not unfriendly, was watching and waiting.

Nightlight paced about nervously. He needed to calm down, he needed a moment of peace, for his mind was not ready for all these strange feelings and grown-up thoughts. He didn't know what to do. How could he help Katherine? Should he fly pell-mell into the unknown and try to save her on his own? He was brave and clever enough—but this time he felt that it would take more than he could manage. He thought of the Bird Lady, Toothiana, this queen with a mother's heart and a warrior's ways—maybe she would know the trick of saving Katherine. But her wing was hurting and she could not fly.

Then he thought of Kailash. The Snow Goose rarely slept without Katherine by her side, but on this night she had stayed in her old nest, among the Snow Geese she hadn't seen in so very long. Kailash loved Katherine as much as he did. Kailash! Suddenly Nightlight had an idea that was both childish and knowing.

The children of Santoff Claussen huddled with Kailash in the nesting cave. The terrible news of Katherine's abduction had reached every corner of the Lamadary.

When Nightlight arrived at the cave, he found Tall William doing his best to appear brave and strong while Sascha and Petter readied a saddle. The children had decided to try and save Katherine themselves while riding Kailash. Nightlight knew better than to laugh or scold them for attempting this impossible mission.

He reached over to Kailash and gently stroked

her feathers. She gave a low, woeful honk, then rested her head on Nightlight's slender shoulder.

He knew his idea would work. He gathered the geese and the children together.

And so began a strange parade—Nightlight, followed by a dozen or so children and a flock of Giant Snow Geese, made their way through the Lamadary, past Yetis who were sharpening weapons in preparation for a great battle, past Lunar Lamas who were thumbing through their ancient books looking for clues that might help Katherine, and past the villagers from Santoff Claussen, who were standing about in worried clumps, sharing ideas and comforts. They didn't stop, not even to answer Old William's question about where they were going, until they reached Katherine's room.

They found Queen Toothiana there. Her back

was toward them—one of her iridescent wings dangled limply.

North was asking her in a gentle yet urgent voice, "And why in the world would Pitch come after you?"

Toothiana answered; her voice had a low cooing quality. "When I'd left the Monkey King, I flew up to Punjam Hy Loo. I found my mother's sisters, the Sisters of Flight. They had been waiting for me! But as they greeted me, they seemed so very sad. They asked of my mother. When I told them of her death, their leader sighed. 'We felt it, we thought it, now we know it to be true,' she told me." Toothiana's own eyes filled with tears, but she continued.

"The sisters formed a circle around the flying elephant, and one by one—right in front of me!—they turned into wood, like carved statues. Branches began to grow from them, branches that weaved themselves together like a giant basket. And as the last sister began to stiffen and change, she said to me, 'If one of us dies, we all die; you are queen here now. You must tend the elephant. He will protect all the memories of us, the memories of everything.'" Toothiana's one strong wing flapped ever more quickly.

"The elephant never forgets," Toothiana told them again. "It is he who touched the fabled Magic Tooth my parents bequeathed me. It is he who saw the memories that dwelled inside."

"But whose tooth is it?" asked Ombric in a hushed tone.

"The one who lives in the Moon," she answered.

The Lunar Lamas all murmured at once with excitement. "The tooth of the Man in the Moon!"

"Astounding!" said Ombric. "Toothiana has one of the five relics."

North needed to know more. "But what power does it bestow, Your Highness?"

"With it I can see the memories within the teeth. And once, when I was caged by this royal primate," she said, pointing her sword at the Monkey King, who was now bound by heavy shackles and chains, "I asked it to help me. It was then that I became more than I am. That is when there was more of me."

As if to explain better, the six mini-versions of Toothiana fluttered down from their perches in the candelabra that hung from the ceiling. They landed

A mini Toothiana in repose

on Toothiana's shoulders, three on each side, and bowed.

Ombric pulled at his beard, thinking. This he had *never* seen. "Pitch could make much mischief if he were able to use that relic—maybe even harness the power of the flying elephant," he told them uneasily.

Nightlight felt a cold chill. Sascha, standing in the doorway beside him, couldn't help herself. She gasped, and Toothiana and the others spun around. The queen was even grander than the children had imagined. Her wings—they were magnificent—the most beautiful shades of blues and greens. Her eyes were as bright as a bird's, and her headdress was as glorious as any peacock's. And she was covered in a layer of tiny green and blue feathers that caught the light like prisms and filled the room with tiny reflected rainbows.

As the children stood, staring in awe, Kailash and one of the other Snow Geese stepped forward, honking. Kailash went on for quite some time. Toothiana's expression lit up when she learned that they could fix her wing, for she was, of course, fluent in all the bird languages, Snow Goose being a particular favorite.

Ombric placed a hand on North's arm. "Come, it's time to leave the queen to her helpers," he told him. "She's suffered a terrible injury and needs time to recover."

"We must rescue Katherine now!" said North. "Every second counts."

Bunnymund shook his head. He, too, was nearly desperate with worry about Katherine, but he would never let his emotions take over. Why, that would make him practically *human*. "I'll dig a tunnel to wherever we need to go, but first it would be most advantageous to know what to expect when we get there, and whether or not chocolate eggs will be required."

North had been in too many battles in his young life to ignore the sense in Bunnymund's words. He reluctantly agreed, but that didn't mean he was finished questioning the monkey. He grabbed him by the arm and dragged him toward the door, followed by Ombric and Bunnymund. "We'll be back," he called to Toothiana.

The Snow Geese, now cooing, began repairing the queen's damaged wing. Nightlight and the children stayed out of the way, watching the miraculous work of the geese. With unimaginable delicacy, they twined and smoothed each strand of Toothiana's crumpled feathers, layer after layer after layer. And slowly, the wing began to look as good as new.

The queen gave the injured wing a slight flutter. "Still hurts," she said, "but it is much better." Then she cocked her head from side to side, eyeing the children. "You should be asleep."

William the Absolute Youngest shook his head. "We're worried about our friend," he said.

Toothiana nodded, giving her repaired wing another careful flutter. She perched on the edge of Katherine's bed, turning her full attention to the children. Her very presence soothed them, just as it did the sleeping children she visited every night.

The youngest William now ventured a small smile. "We live in Santoff Claussen," he told her.

"It's the best village in the whole world," Sascha added. Then she gave a shiver. "Except for when the Nightmare King comes to visit."

The children began to tell Toothiana all about

their magical village and about the first time that Pitch's Fearlings had attacked them in the forest. "It was Katherine— She was the bravest, and she saved us," Tall William said.

"And that's when we first saw Nightlight!" his youngest brother added.

Petter, Fog, and the others acted out the various battles they'd seen.

Toothiana seemed properly impressed by their derring-do, and so the youngest William ventured to ask for a favor: "Can you—would you—make a wish on my next lost tooth? I don't have any loose ones right now, but you can pull one if you want." He opened his mouth as wide as he could so she could easily choose the best tooth.

"I needn't pull your tooth, but," Toothiana said, trying not to laugh, "name your wish."

"I wish for Katherine to come back to us, safe and sound," said William the Absolute Youngest.

"That's my wish too!" Sascha added.

"And mine," Petter said.

And one by one, the children asked for the same wish: the safe return of Katherine.

Toothiana listened carefully, then told them, "I will try."

Finally, William the Absolute Youngest—who may just have been William the *Wisest*—suggested they recite Ombric's first lesson.

And so, with Toothiana taking Katherine's place in their circle, the children joined hands and recited: "I believe. I believe. I believe."

But Nightlight did not join them. He stood alone. His face was blank and expressionless. Then full of fear.

North burst into the room, pressing through the door just ahead of Ombric and Bunnymund. "The monkey finally talked!" he said.

"We know his plan!" said Ombric.

"To Punjam Hy Loo?" Toothiana asked.

"And right speedily," replied Bunnymund.

Toothiana sprang to her feet, fluttered her wings, and brandished her swords. "Let's fly."

CHAPTER TWENTY-TWO
To Be Brave . . .

AN OMINOUS WIND BEGAN to blow in Punjam Hy Loo. Pitch looked down at Katherine. She was determined not to look surprised to see him.

"Thought I was done for, didn't you?" he asked in a voice icy with scorn. "No, my dear. It's your so-called Guardians who will be destroyed."

Katherine knew that the Nightmare King fed on fear—particularly the fear of children—and so she steeled herself to meet his cold, dark eyes with her own. She reminded herself of when last they'd met, when she'd held up the locket-size picture of his long-lost daughter. One look at it had made Pitch scream in agony. It had defeated him. Caused him and his Fearling army to vanish. And his scream had haunted Katherine ever since. She even felt a vague sort of pity for him. That pity gave her courage. And she was sure that Nightlight, North, and the others would soon fly to her rescue.

"The Guardians battled you in the Himalayas and at the center of the Earth," she said evenly, "and each time, *we* won the day."

Pitch's expression betrayed little. He slid closer to her, his dark cape covering so much of him that it was impossible to tell if he actually walked or if he floated. One thing was apparent: He kept his right hand, the hand that had become flesh, hidden under the cape, and his entire right side seemed stiff, as if underneath the cape he hid a terrible wound.

He stood perfectly still. Katherine looked to where his hand was hidden and wondered about the locket. Did he have it still?

Pitch sensed her thoughts. "You preyed on my weakness, and that was very clever." He brought his face close to hers. "But soon I'll be rid of any weakness. Your new Golden Age," he added, his voice becoming a calm whisper, "will become the Age of Nightmares!"

The monkeys began to screech in unison. They pounded their paws against the ancient blocks of stone they sat upon. One of them swung, paw over paw, down from the top of the ruins and landed in front of Pitch.

"Where is your king?" Pitch asked blankly. The monkey muttered a reply.

"Left behind?" said Pitch with a hint of

bemusement. "Betrayed by his own. All the better! Do you have the relic?"

The animal held up a pouch. From within this small sack there came a bright red glow, emanating from the ruby box snatched from Queen Toothiana!

Katherine recognized that glow—it was the same glow she'd seen coming from the orb of North's sword and on Bunnymund's egg-tipped staff . . . It was the glow of an ancient Lunar relic! She immediately averted her gaze, not wanting to arouse Pitch's suspicions as to the box's importance. But, she realized, this must be what gave Queen Toothiana whatever powers she possessed. Was this what Pitch was after?

Hoping to distract him, she blurted out, "You'll fail. You always do."

Pitch drew himself up, growing ever taller until he towered above her, and then he leaned over, his icy breath in her face. The air suddenly felt as cold as Siberia in winter.

Too late, Katherine realized her mistake. She had insulted Pitch's intelligence. Drat! She should have let him keep talking, let him talk all night, give her friends the time they needed to get to her.

"But what do I know," Katherine stammered, trying to placate him. "You're the Nightmare King and I'm just a girl."

Pitch permitted himself a small smile. "That's exactly right. The Man in the Moon's *toys* are of some use to me. But the prize I seek is of greater value—*much* greater. With it I can make an undefeatable army."

"What prize is that?" Katherine asked, using her sweetest, most innocent voice.

Pitch stared at her but said no more.

Katherine had to keep him talking, she had to! She had to trick him into revealing his plan—it was vital. She racked her brain for a compliment that he might believe, a compliment that would make him want to tell all—just so that he could boast.

"You've been brilliant at coming up with ways to thwart us—like sneaking into North's djinni or creating armor from the Earth's core," she said. "Why, I can't begin to imagine how astounding and dreadful this new prize will be."

Then she held her breath, waiting, while Pitch considered her words.

His eyes lit up. Katherine's heart pounded. *Pitch's need to boast would win out over his need for caution!*

She did not realize was that her lost tooth, which she held tightly in her hand, had begun to glow almost as brightly as the ruby-carved box.

Before she knew what had happened, the tooth was harshly snatched from her hand. A monkey soldier shuffled away from her, clutching the tooth. He tossed it to Pitch, who caught it easily with his left hand. He wrapped his fist around the tooth and pressed it against his forehead. His eyes closed, and he began to chuckle with diabolical glee. He was reading her tooth's memories!

"Stop, stop!" Katherine cried. "Those are *my* memories!" But a pair of monkeys sprang upon her, holding her tight, keeping her from attacking Pitch. His eyes stayed shut as if sleeping, and he saw every memory of hers he needed.

When at last he opened his hand again, the tooth was black and rotted.

It turned to dust and blew away in the wind.

Desperate, Katherine reached for the dust, but it

was gone. She sank to the ground. She felt so lost and alone. She began to clutch the compass around her neck. It was the first gift that North had ever given to her—a compass with an arrow that pointed to a single letter *N*, to North himself. Katherine had once used it to find North and Ombric in the Himalayas, and now—she was absolutely sure—it would show her that North was on his way to rescue her. Together they would put an end to this Nightmare Man.

But before she could look, Pitch crooked one of his long, black fingers, and the compass flew to him. His eyes still closed, he held the compass for a moment, then lobbed it at her feet.

"Your North isn't coming," he said, an edge of triumph in his voice. "The arrow isn't moving."

Pitch had learned enough of Ombric's magic to damage the compass. And now he also knew Katherine's most precious memories as well as many things about her and the Guardians. And he was quite sure he now knew how best to defeat them all.

Katherine grabbed the compass back. She stared at it in disbelief. The arrow spun uselessly, pointing nowhere. Why weren't North and the others on their way?

"They've abandoned you, their precious Katherine. To me." His voice turned smooth and cunning as he pretended to comfort her. "Your rightful place is at my side. Everyone's known that from the very moment you reminded me that I once had a daughter. I lost her, just like you lost your parents."

Katherine winced. "Don't," she cried. "Please, please don't!" Fighting back tears, she pressed North's compass to her heart. She closed her eyes and tried to recite Ombric's first spell: *I believe, I believe.* But doubts flooded her mind. She'd never recover her memories of her parents. She'd never know if they had loved her with the same fierce love that Pitch harbored for his daughter. An empty feeling filled her soul.

"You long for that, don't you?" he asked. "For the love of a parent—a father. I can give that to you...." His voice was low, coaxing. "The locket—you know the one—it has your face in it now. You've seen it in your dreams, haven't you?"

Katherine shook as doubt and fear coursed through her. She *had* seen it. She'd *had* that nightmare—of being Pitch's daughter.

"You couldn't count on your parents," Pitch continued, his eyes once again glittering. "They left you.

When you were just a baby. What kind of parents do THAT? And your friends—your *Guardians*—why, you can see for yourself that they aren't coming." Pitch pointed to the compass again. The arrow still hadn't budged. "Without me, you'd be alone. Abandoned. Again."

Suddenly, Pitch swirled around. The monkeys, whose chant had been drumming quietly in the background, now began to screech.

With a ghoulish laugh, Pitch flew off, a trail of black smoke, into the night, leaving Katherine alone— more alone that she had ever been in her young life.

CHAPTER TWENTY-THREE

In Which the Guardians Fly to Punjam Hy Loo

BACK IN THE LUNAR Lamadary, North was filling Toothiana in on the best ways to battle Pitch. "If we surprise him, we will have an advantage," he told her.

Toothiana and her six mini-selves understood. They took to the sky. Nightlight started after her, then stopped, looking over his shoulder at the other Guardians. Toothiana made a trill-like noise and the mini-selves hovered in midflight, too.

"Go!" Bunnymund urged. "I'll tunnel the rest of us there."

"Pitch will be watching the skies," Ombric mused. "If we come from both air *and* underground, we may surprise him."

Queen Toothiana nodded sharply and set off toward Punjam Hy Loo, Nightlight on her heels and her six mini-selves flying just ahead.

The train was ready, filled with Yetis and Lunar Lamas and the villagers. If the Guardians were surprised to see the villagers already on the train, they didn't take the time to say so. Tall William, Fog, Petter, and all the children were aboard, as were North's elves. Bunnymund walked toward the front, North dragging the Monkey King after him. He shackled him to a door in the engine car.

"You might make a useful bargaining chip, Your Royal *Monkeyness*," North growled. "Just don't cause any trouble."

North and Ombric stood at the controls in the front car as Bunnymund readied himself near the tip of the digging device. "Let's get going, Bunnymund!" North urged. "We've got to *move!*"

Bunnymund turned to his friends. He held a particularly large chocolate egg in one paw. "It's time again to unleash the inner Pooka," he said with a flourish. Then he swallowed the chocolate whole.

North grimaced. "Oh, boy. I'm never sure what's going to happen when he goes nutty with the chocolate."

"He told me that once he grew an extra head," Ombric offered cheerfully.

And indeed, Bunnymund began to twist and grow and change with alarming suddenness, and before they could tell if he'd grown anything extra, he became a giant blur of digging. Even for a Pooka, he was moving astonishingly fast. All they could see in front of them was a blizzard of dirt and rocks.

At the same time, Ombric's beard and eyebrows began to twirl. He was finally sensing bits of thoughts from Katherine, and he was most concerned. The thoughts that made it through to him were full of despair. North sensed this too, but he had more immediate concerns.

"We've never had a crazier plan," he confided to Ombric.

"Nicholas, we have what we need. Brave hearts. And sharp minds," Ombric reminded him. "And as you might recall, we always abandon our plans and end up doing things we never imagined."

North smiled. The old man still had a thing or two to teach him.

CHAPTER TWENTY-FOUR

Anger, Despair, and a Wisp of Hope

KATHERINE HUGGED HER KNEES to her chest and tried to quell the feeling of hopelessness that was starting to overwhelm her. Sweat formed on her temples and on her upper lip. She felt as if disaster was closing in, and indeed it was. The monkeys dropped down from the ruined walls and formed a circle around her.

She tried to block out their howling, but it grew louder and more insistent as the animals came closer. Her heart seemed to be beating to the rhythm of their chant.

Where are my friends? They have to know where I am by now! She gazed at the compass and its motionless arrow: North was not on his way to rescue her. And her tooth—its memories were lost forever.

She'd never felt such rage.

Katherine got to her feet and glared at the monkeys. They were spinning faster and faster in a circle around her, chanting louder and louder. She covered her ears and screamed, "Stop it! Stop it!"

But the monkeys' grins only widened. And then they resumed their shrieking chant.

Katherine sank to her knees, gripping the compass in her hands. She didn't know what to do. *Where is North? Where is Nightlight? How can they not have come to get me?* And the despair overtook the anger, overtook the outrage, overtook reason.

Why did my parents die when I was too young to remember them?!

Maybe it would be easier to give up, she thought. *To go along with Pitch and become his Darkling Daughter.* At least this terrible pain would go away. She looked up at the sky and tried to make out the Man in the Moon's face. But swirling clouds blocked him out. It was as if even the Man in the Moon had turned his back on her.

Ignoring the monkeys, Katherine began to scratch at the ground with her fingers; the dirt was soft, and soon she'd made a small hole. She paused for a moment, then dropped the compass in. She pressed dirt over it. Then she curled up and lay upon the small mound.

I'm tired of fighting, she thought. *I don't want to grow up.*

A breeze stirred the air, and Katherine was glad for at least that, at least a moment of coolness. And that's when she saw, in the distance, what appeared to be a hummingbird making its way toward her.

CHAPTER TWENTY-FIVE

A Brief Exchange as the Watchful Are Watched

As NIGHTLIGHT AND TOOTHIANA flew toward Punjam Hy Loo, the wind and clouds seemed to be moving with them. For the second time in as many days, Nightlight had the feeling he was being watched. Toothiana, he noticed, was glancing about from side to side, as if she felt the same. Nightlight tried to see if Toothiana could hear his thoughts. *Are you having this "watching" feeling?* he asked her in thought.

For a moment she did not respond, but just when he'd decided she didn't share the same gift he and the Guardians did, she turned her head in her sudden, birdlike way and looked him in the eye, her glorious wings never missing a beat. "I do, Quiet Boy," she said above the wind. "I've felt 'the watching' many times. She is a mystery. But she is always there. In the wind. The rain. The snow. The thunder and the lightning. I do not know if she is bad or good. But what interest she has in the battle to come? I cannot say."

CHAPTER TWENTY-SIX

The Reckoning

THERE WAS A STRANGE moment as they approached Punjam Hy Loo. Every Guardian felt it, including Toothiana. They no longer wanted to merely defeat Pitch or imprison him or send him into exile. They wanted him to die.

Because of rage or sorrow or hate or revenge or even cold, calculated logic, they wanted to kill him. It was a dark reckoning. Each of them looked for the Moon, hoping that their friend and leader would tell them what to do. But a storm had blackened the skies.

And they were on their own.

CHAPTER TWENTY-SEVEN

—◆—

Can a Pooka Grow Six Arms?

THE JOURNEY WAS EXTREMELY swift; the first car of the egg-shaped train popped quietly above the earth near the peak of Punjam Hy Loo. North unshackled the Monkey King, grasped him by the neck, and dragged him out. The Cossack's sword was aglow. Ombric climbed out right behind him.

Bunnymund motioned for them to be quiet. And quiet they were. Dumbfounded, actually. For Bunnymund was a hulking mess, covered with layers of mud and pulverized rock dust that made him look more like a statue than a giant rabbit. His cloak was gone, torn to nothingness. But what was most surprising—the chocolate he'd eaten had turned him into a massive, muscular warrior version of himself, and as an extra little surprise, he now had six arms, three on each side.

North frowned. "This is too odd, even for me."

"Oh, don't worry," replied Bunnymund cheerfully. "I'll go back to being bi-armed when we're done." Then he shushed North with all three right hands. North thought the gesture pointless—how could they be heard above the strange chanting that echoed through the dense jungle?

They looked around. The darkness was nearly total. Not a star shined through what seemed to him ominous-looking clouds, and the wind seemed to be blowing in gusts from every direction. Toothiana and Nightlight flew down from the topmost

Bunnymund ate the six-armed chocolate again!

branches of a huge banyan tree to join them.

"Just ahead. In a clearing," Toothiana said quietly. "Katherine."

"Any Fearlings?" asked North.

Toothiana shook her head. "Monkeys. An army of monkeys."

"Our relics won't have the same effect on creatures of flesh and blood," said Ombric, worried.

"Pitch is most cunning," said Toothiana.

"Indeed," replied North. "But we can handle them."

"The monkeys are a dangerous mix," she cautioned. "Part man. Part animal. The worst parts of each. And they obey no law, not even the jungle's. They are an army to be feared."

"My army!" the Monkey King screeched.

"Silence!" North hissed. He threw him to his elves. "Guard him," he ordered. Then, tossing aside his overcoat and using the glowing orb on his sword to light the way, he stormed through the thick, steamy jungle toward the chanting primates.

The wind picked up and swirled around them. Toothiana knew the way so she sped ahead of North to lead them through the vines. They pushed past immense tropical plants and webs of vines for what seemed an eternity, until the chanting suddenly stopped.

The Guardians could tell they were edging into the clearing now; the jungle seemed less dense, and they could just make out the shapes of structures and buildings ahead. North's saber grew brighter, as did the egg at the tip of Bunnymund's staff. But Nightlight kept dim. To do what he had planned, he needed to be stealthy.

The relics provided enough light for them to see

the monkey army that had gathered along every stone, pile, and tower that filled the city of Punjam Hy Loo. Toothiana flared her wings and hissed at them. "We are just outside the Temple of the Flying Elephant," she whispered.

The Guardians pressed forward until they came to a wall of monkeys. The Guardians drew their weapons, expecting to be set upon, but to their surprise, the creatures shuffled aside to let them pass. They were armed with all sorts of weapons: daggers, swords, spears, and each was crudely armored.

Bunnymund's whiskers twitched. "Pitch is quite resourceful in his choice of henchmen. Or should I say henchmonkeys?"

North was unimpressed. His sword would make quick work of these monkey boys.

With a nod from Toothiana, Nightlight darted

past the others and disappeared into the dark. As the others moved past the last layer of monkeys, they could see a single torch shining in the dark just ahead, its flame being battered by the winds. Then they spied Katherine, bound by thick vines and lashed to a post in front of the giant doors of the flying elephant's temple. Behind her stood Pitch. Around his neck hung Toothiana's ruby box.

"One step more," warned Pitch, bringing one of his long, black fingers to within a hairbreadth of Katherine's cheek, "and I make her *mine.*"

They stopped. The wind picked up. A spider's web of lightning lit the sky.

Pitch smiled a sly smile and then roared a command.

The monkey army launched its attack.

CHAPTER TWENTY-EIGHT
◆
A Monkey Battle Royale

THE MONKEYS ATTACKED WITH a fury that surprised even North. The hilt of his sword wrapped itself tightly around his hand, and he slashed at the screaming creatures they descended upon them.

"Do your magic, old man!" North shouted to Ombric, hoping the wizard had a spell or two that would help combat this onslaught. North swung left and right, but he missed his mark more often than he wished. *With humans,* he thought, *you can anticipate what they'll do, but these monkeys are insane.*

Toothiana flew above the fray, expertly wielding

Ready to attack!

her swords, bucking and spinning whenever a monkey landed on her back, trying to rip at her wings.

Bunnymund was able to do considerable damage to any simian within reach of his six massive arms.

All the while, Nightlight was creeping quietly along the top of the temple, staying in the shadows. And with him? Toothiana's six tiny selves. They were waiting for their moment.

The timbre of the monkeys' screeches was deafening. And for every monkey the Guardians felled, three more seemed to arrive to take its place. They swooped down from the treetops like giant locusts. Their swarms made it nearly impossible to get closer to Katherine. And the heat, the dastardly heat! Sweat poured from his brow; North could hardly see.

And so he was unaware of the villagers and the Yetis and his elf men, dragging the pitiful Monkey

King with them, joining in the fight. Even the boys—Petter, Fog, and Tall William—grabbed on to thick vines and swung into the middle of the action, sporting Yeti-crafted daggers. "Free me!" the bedraggled king cried out, but his army paid him no mind; they followed Pitch now.

Ombric, for his part, was doing his best to calm the unnerving wind. At one moment it seemed to favor Pitch and the monkeys, pushing North back as he neared Katherine, but in the next, a blast of air sent a monkey's arrow into the trunk of a banyan tree instead of into North's forehead. Even the huge Yetis fought to make headway against the hurricane-force gales. But despite trying all his meteorological enchantments, Ombric failed to still the eerie gusts that coiled and twisted about the combatants.

And even with all their manpower, even with all

of their weapons, and even with all of Ombric's wizarding capabilities, the Guardians could not keep up with the monkey horde. It was as if Pitch had called every monkey in the world into his service.

Pitch stood back and surveyed the scene with satisfaction. He taunted Guardians and monkeys alike, enjoying the chaos he caused.

"Bravo!" he cheered as a monkey catapulted itself toward Toothiana's back. Then he laughed out loud when Toothiana dodged the flying creature and it plummeted to the ground in a broken heap.

He smiled with gruesome delight as a trio of monkeys waged a game of catch with Gregor of the Mighty Smile and Sergei the Giggler. They tossed the pair about like toys while the other elves tried to rescue their hapless friends.

The Guardians themselves were beginning to

stagger with exhaustion. North found he was missing more than he was hitting—never had he found himself in such a situation. Even Bunnymund could barely lift any of his six arms to fight off the endless, screeching horde. At last Ombric raised up his staff and called out frantically, "Enough! Enough! We are beaten, Pitch!"

"Never!" North immediately contested. But he, too, was incapable of continuing—if his relic sword had not been attached to his hand, he would surely have dropped it.

The monkeys encircled them and readied for the kill.

Pitch was delighted. This was exactly what he wanted: for the Guardians and all who followed them to feel defeated.

He raised his dark hand, and the monkeys froze.

They did, however, keep their weapons poised.

The Guardians and Toothiana stumbled forward, panting. Bunnymund had to hold up North with one set of arms and Ombric with the other.

"What is it you seek, Pitch?" Ombric asked, gasping.

"The flying elephant," he said simply.

Toothiana's eyes narrowed. "He will do only as I command," she told Pitch.

"Oh, I know that, *Your Highness*. Please remind me—what is it you are queen of? Ah yes, a bunch of ruins. A handful of little fairies and a flying elephant. An elephant that no one *ever* sees. Not much of a kingdom."

Queen Toothiana spread her wings and hissed at Pitch.

"Most articulate, Your Highness. Now, BRING

OUT THE ELEPHANT, or I'll take this child"—
Pitch placed his hand dangerously close to Katherine's
brow—"and blacken her soul forever."

Toothiana took a step toward Pitch, her swords
still ready. Her face was set; she seemed determined
to attack.

He gave her a shriveling look. "Oh, my dear girl.
Your dinner knives can't harm me."

At that moment the Monkey King wrenched himself away from his elf captors and hobbled quickly to
Pitch. "Master!" he blubbered. "You'll make the elephant give me back my humanity?"

Pitch looked down at the pitiful creature and
laughed. "No, you fool. I'll ask him to remove *all* of
mine."

The monkey looked almost comically confused.

"It's my only imperfection," Pitch went on. "I can

feel things. *Human* things. It's my only weakness." He glared at Toothiana. "You should understand that, Your Highness, being half human yourself. Think of what you might accomplish if *you* didn't have that burden."

Toothiana just stared at him.

"If the elephant can take away all of this miserable creature's weaknesses," he said, pointing to the monkey, "then it can surely take away mine."

"If that is what you wish," Toothiana said evenly.

"It's the only way you'll get her back," said Pitch, motioning to Katherine.

North, his face a storm of fury, called out, "He'll become invulnerable!"

Toothiana refused to look at North. "I cannot let harm come to any child."

Then she lowered her weapons and closed her

eyes. "Sisters of Flight, forgive me," she whispered. The Guardians gazed up at the wooden statues that ringed the base of the temple. They were magnificent effigies. Beautiful winged women standing straight and tall, but frozen forever.

"If only they could help," moaned Ombric. The wind calmed somewhat as the massive doors of the temple creaked slowly open.

At first they could see only darkness in the temple. Then the shuffle of heavy footsteps shook the ground.

CHAPTER TWENTY-NINE

The Dark Surprise
Or
All Is Given for the Sake of Pity

IT WAS TIME. THE trap was sprung. Everyone knew their part. The flying elephant exploded from its temple. Wings outstretched, trunk and tusks raised, it knocked Pitch away from Katherine and pinned him to the ground. At that exact moment Toothiana leaped to Katherine and, with one slash of her blade, cut the vines that bound her to the post. Her six mini-selves flew like darts from their hiding places atop the temple and yanked Toothiana's ruby-carved box from Pitch's neck. The monkey army, momentarily stunned by the surprise attack, quickly recovered and fell upon the Guardians, certain that they would kill them on the spot.

They were in for another surprise.

"No more playacting!" North shouted out, brandishing his swords with characteristic fury. Bunnymund and Ombric dropped their exhausted posing and became dervishes of action, knocking out monkeys by the score. The Yetis, elves, and citizens of Santoff Claussen followed suit. It had all been an act! They weren't beaten at all! The battle became feverish within seconds.

But there were more surprises yet.

Toothiana grabbed her ruby relic from her mini-selves, held it to her chest, and repeated the call she'd made only once before: "Mother, Father, help me." No sooner had she spoken these words than hundreds—no, thousands—of mini-versions of herself

*Nicholas St. North will do his best
against the worst.*

began to stream from her like waves of light.

They swarmed the monkeys like an endless army of hornets, their tiny swords and arrows slicing the monkeys to ribbons.

Pitch struggled against the elephant's weight, and from the roof of the temple, Nightlight took careful aim. The final blow would come from his staff.

Katherine knew what was coming. One of Toothiana's mini-selves who had flown to her outside the temple had told her every detail of the Guardians' bold plan. Now that Katherine was free from Pitch's clutches, he would die. In a moment Nightlight's diamond-tipped staff, sharper than any spear—and the only weapon that had ever pierced the villain's heart—would do so once more.

All around was the crazy havoc of battle. Monkeys, Yetis, wizard, villains, and heroes were locked in a battle to the death. Everyone but Katherine. She stood still, looking down at Pitch. In that moment he knew her thoughts. He knew that his doom was an instant away. And Katherine saw fear in his eyes.

There was one thing she must know before the end. So she did something that was not in the plan.

CHAPTER THIRTY

The Winds of Change

NIGHTLIGHT BLINKED. HE COULDN'T throw his staff. Katherine was in the way!

Move! he thought as hard as he could. But Katherine did not answer.

He knew that something was terribly wrong. As fast as his considerable powers would propel him, he flew. But the disaster unfolded faster than could be reckoned with.

Katherine stared at Pitch's hand. Its flesh color had spread up his arm, all the way to the shoulder. But that's not what held her mesmerized. It was the locket. In his hand, Pitch still gripped the locket. In fact, the locket seemed to have fused to his fingers, become a part of him. The same locket that she had shown him at the battle of the Earth's core. The locket that had carried a picture of Pitch's lost daughter. But whose picture would be in it? Would Katherine's face be there? Would her nightmare be true?

It took all her courage to look. And then she saw. The picture was almost gone; only scraps of it remained—Pitch had clearly tried to tear it away. But Katherine could see just enough to know that it was the old image of Pitch's daughter. She felt a sort of relief, but then she looked in Pitch's eyes again. They were so anguished, afraid, lost in pain. *He doesn't deserve to die,* she thought. *Even the worst villain needs pity. He was a father and a hero once. He did not chart his past or the present.*

Pitch is fallen.

What Katherine felt, that strange mix of revulsion and sorrow that overwhelmed her, was instantly felt by all the Guardians.

Then Pitch's other hand reached out and grabbed hers. Her eyes widened. Pitch's touch was unexpectedly gentle.

Nightlight tried to break Pitch's hold on Katherine, but before he could do so, the wind picked up again, gusts of it whipping through the clearing, bending trees in half, ripping leaves from their branches.

The sky darkened faster than any of them ever experienced before. A swirling mass of clouds broke through the treetops and descended into the clearing. In the midst of it all was a tall, cloaked woman who held herself with a regal air. Her face was long yet lovely, and years older than they remembered from the picture they had seen. Icy nuggets of hail

Mother Nature makes
a dramatic and unexpected appearance.

and bolts of lightning churned around her as the cloud mass moved toward Pitch and Katherine, then engulfed them.

Then, as suddenly as the cloud had arrived, it was gone.

And with it, Katherine and Pitch.

The monkey army had scrambled back to the jungle. All who remained stood there speechless. Katherine was gone! They'd failed.

North was the first gather his wits. "That woman in the clouds. Pitch's daughter?"

Ombric looked at Nightlight. He did not have to ask the question out loud for Nightlight to understand.

Nightlight shimmered a response.

But his answer was one that Ombric never expected. He turned to Toothiana. She nodded. The old wizard blinked rapidly, processing what he'd just learned. North cleared his throat impatiently. "Spit it out, old man."

Ombric tugged at his beard once, then a second time, then at last he said, "She has another name, apparently. By some she's known as Mother Nature."

Bunnymund's left ear twitched, then his right one did same. "I've encountered this being before," said the Pooka. "She's not always a benevolent soul, and she is very unpredictable."

The villagers, the children, the Yeti—all of them gathered. The Guardians looked to the coming dawn, bound by one emotion. Not fear or hate or vengeance. It was that feeling of pity Katherine had for Pitch.

Toothiana spoke what everyone was feeling. "We didn't fail, but we did lose our way. We wanted to kill," she said softly.

"We were no better than Pitch. Perhaps worse," said Ombric.

"But Katherine remembered," said North quietly.

So they stood on the peak of Punjam Hy Loo, weary but alive and certain of one thing: Katherine's strength had been greater than theirs. And they hoped and believed that this strength would keep her safe past the dawn of this new day.

TO BE CONTINUED . . .

THE NEXT CHAPTER
IN OUR ONGOING SAGA

THE
SANDMAN

AND THE WAR OF DREAMS

*Featuring the desperate mission to save Katherine
and the appearance of a wayward lad of considerable
interest named Jackson Overland Frost.*

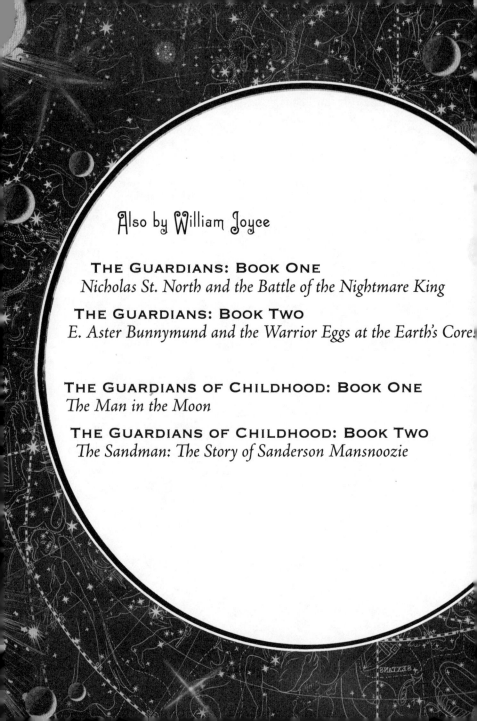

Also by William Joyce

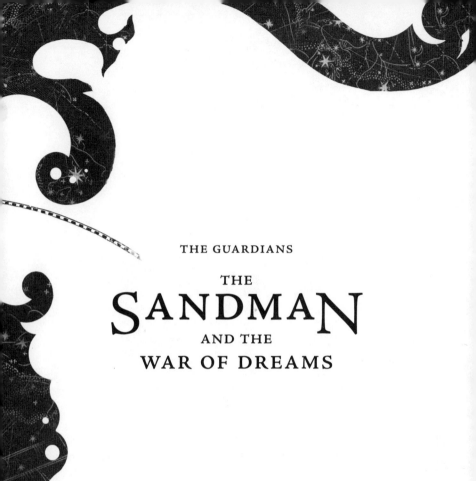

THE GUARDIANS

THE
SANDMAN
AND THE
WAR OF DREAMS

Sanderson Mansnoozie

EXTANS

THE GUARDIANS

THE
SANDMAN
AND THE
WAR OF DREAMS

———◦———

WILLIAM JOYCE

A
atheneum
Atheneum Books for Young Readers
NEW YORK • LONDON • TORONTO • SYDNEY • NEW DELHI

Atheneum Books for Young Readers

An imprint of Simon & Schuster Children's Publishing Division

1230 Avenue of the Americas, New York, New York 10020

For information about special discounts for bulk purchases, please contact Simon & Schuster Special Sales at 1-866-506-1949 or business@simonandschuster.com.

The Simon & Schuster Speakers Bureau can bring authors to your live event.

For more information or to book an event, contact the Simon & Schuster Speakers Bureau at 1-866-248-3049 or visit our website at www.simonspeakers.com.

Book design by Lauren Rille

The text for this book is set in Adobe Jenson Pro.

The illustrations for this book are rendered in a combination of charcoal, graphite, and digital media.

Manufactured in the United States of America

0913 FFG

First Edition

10 9 8 7 6 5 4 3 2 1

CIP data for this book is available from the Library of Congress.

ISBN 978-1-4424-3054-9

ISBN 978-1-4424-8146-6 (eBook)

———◆———

To my Dream Captains:
George Melies, Jean Cocteau,
and
George Auric

———◆———

Contents

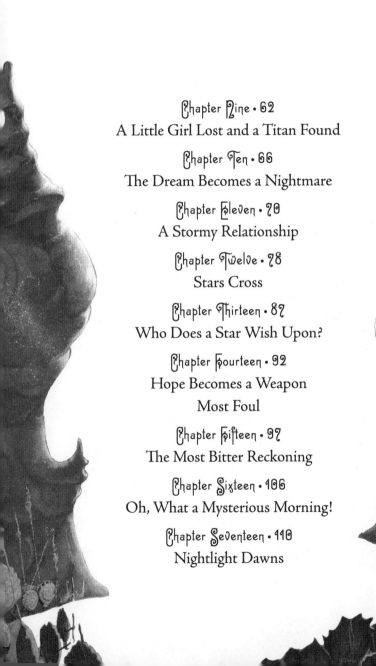

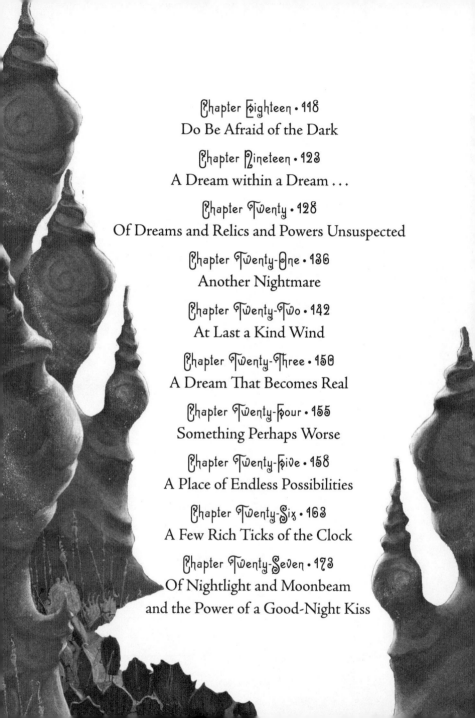

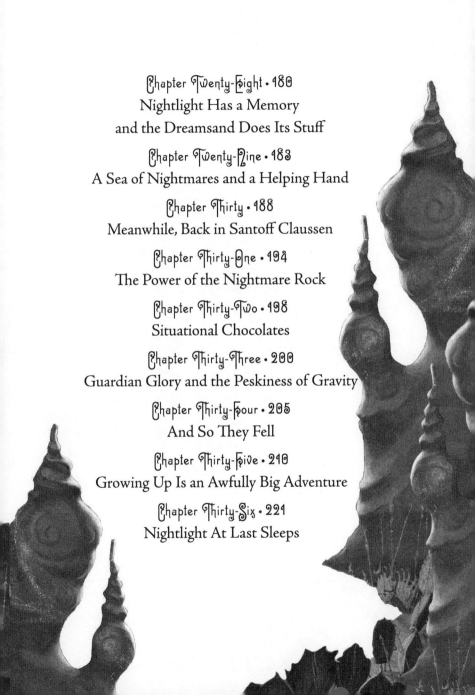

Mother Nature

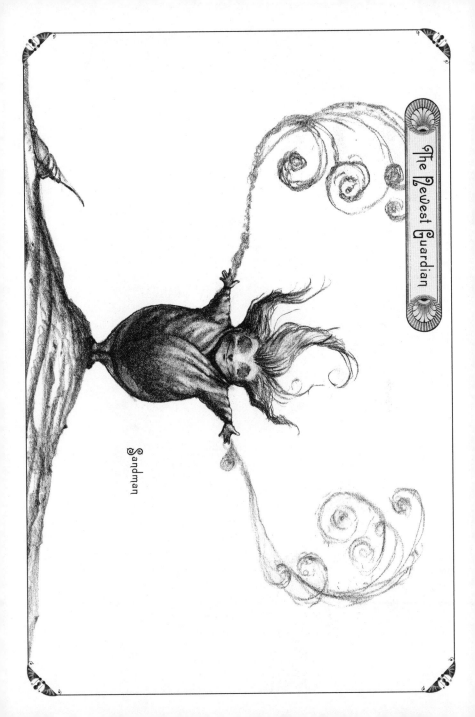

The Newest Guardian

Sandman

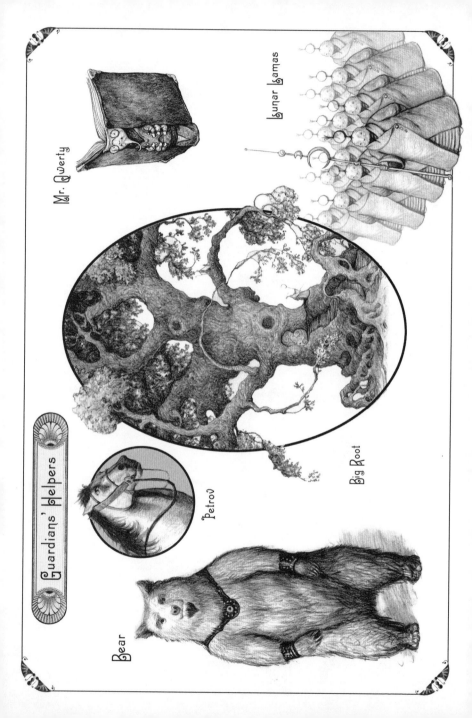

Guardians' Helpers

Mr. Qwerty

Lunar Lamas

Big Root

Petrov

Bear

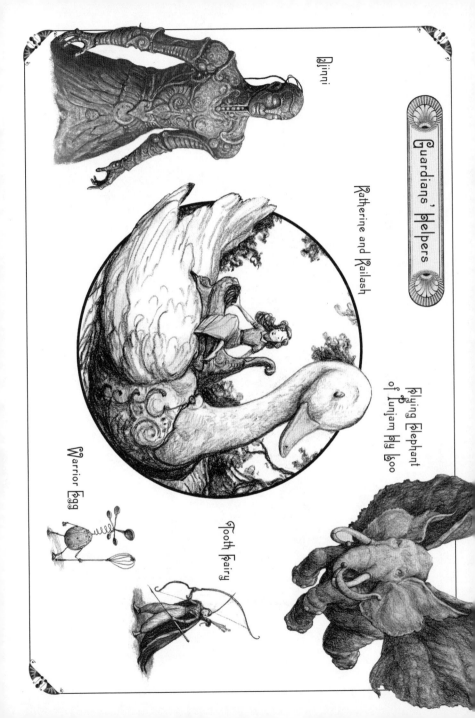

Guardians' Helpers

Djinni

Katherine and Kailash

Flying Elephant
of Punjam Hy Loo

Warrior Egg

Tooth Fairy

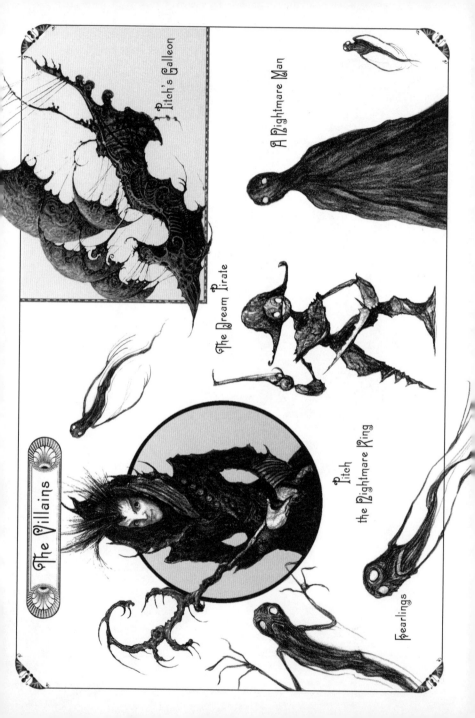

The Villains

Pitch's Galleon

A Nightmare Man

The Dream Pirate

Pitch
the Nightmare King

Fearlings

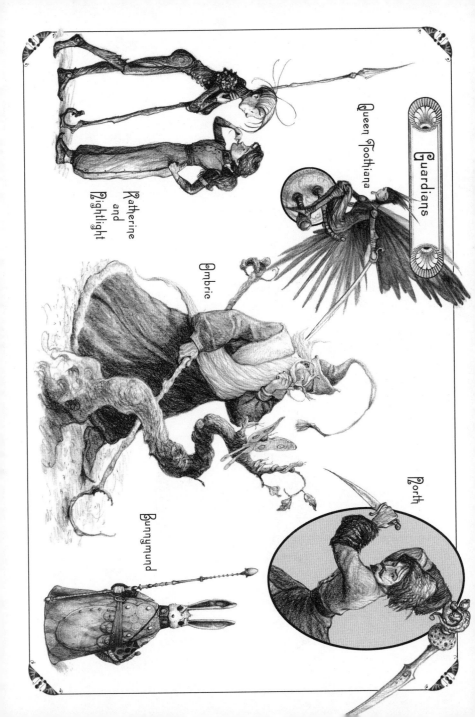

Guardians

Queen Toothiana

Katherine and Nightlight

Ombric

North

Bunnymund

CHAPTER ONE

The Dreams That Stuff Is Made Of

TIME PASSES STRANGELY WHEN you are sleeping. You can close your eyes when it is night, then open them again and see morning. Yet the hours that went by seemed no longer than the drifting journey of a leaf in a soft breeze.

Strange, wondrous, and terrible adventures are the norm in dreams. Uncharted lands come and go. Dream epics play out. Wars are fought and won. Loved ones are lost or found. Entirely different lives are lived as we sleep. And then we awake, with disappointment or relief, as if nothing at all had happened.

But sometimes things do happen.

In the waking world, the Guardians had lost one of their own to a powerful entity known as Mother Nature.

But an odd little man had been sleeping for more days and nights than any calendar could count. The snoozing fellow was the color of golden sand—indeed, he seemed to be made of the stuff. And his unruly hair twirled and twisted as he slept. He rested in the dune-covered center of a tiny star-shaped island that was nearly impossible for humans to find, for it was not originally from the Earth. The island was not connected to anything; no landmass beneath the ocean anchored it in place. As such, it was the only island on our planet that truly floated atop the water. Because of this, it drifted. In June it might be in the Pacific Ocean, and by July it might be off the coast of Madagascar, its whereabouts known only to the Moon and the stars.

Which was fitting, for this island had once *been* a star. It had been saved by the leader of the Guardians, Tsar Lunar, or as we call him, the "Man in the Moon." But that was ages ago.

The island, from above

On *this* most auspicious night, Tsar Lunar called upon the small and harmless-looking fellow who softly snored among the island's magic sands.

But how should one awaken a man from the past? A man who had traveled oceans of time and space. A steadfast fellow who had piloted the fastest shooting star in the heavens. A hero of ten thousand battles against Pitch, the Nightmare King. This smallish warrior had once been the most valiant granter of wishes the cosmos had ever known. How does one wake a man who has not opened his eyes since the great ancient days of the Golden Age?

As with most things, the answer was simple.

The Man in the Moon sent a moonbeam messenger with a single whispered request: "I wish that you would help. Your powers are needed."

In an instant the little man's eyes opened. The

centuries of sleep fell away. There he stood, tall as he could: Sanderson Mansnoozie. The Man in the Moon then proceeded to relay his full message. Sanderson Mansnoozie listened intently.

So very much had happened while he had slept.

Pitch had returned and was threatening the galaxies again. But Sanderson Mansnoozie's long sleep had been most productive. He was now more powerful than he had ever been: He had power over the world of dreams. In fact, every grain of sand on his island now contained a dream—one dream from each night of his nearly endless sleep, and all of them good dreams, strong enough to fight any nightmare.

When the Man in the Moon finished, Sanderson Mansnoozie, with a wave of his hands, brought his island to life. Its sands swirled around him, and the island transformed into a cloud that swept him up from the sea and into the sky.

With moonbeams to guide him, he sailed the golden cloud toward his mission: to aide the Guardians. To save and rescue a girl named Katherine. And to stop Pitch forever.

This "Sandman" was ready to seek out his ancient enemy and oldest friends. He was ready to face whatever dangers lay ahead.

And there were many.

CHAPTER TWO

A Return to Where Things Started

FOR THE GUARDIANS AND their allies, it had been a hectic and miserable trip from Queen Toothiana's mountain palace in Punjam Hy Loo. After the horror of seeing their Katherine, and Pitch, abducted by Mother Nature's cyclone, the Guardians had decided they should return to the village of Santoff Claussen. Santoff Claussen was the place where magic, goodness, and bravery were tended and protected. It was where they had been linked and where their new lives as Guardians had been born. It was a place that felt like home.

But the Guardians felt lost and broken. They could not sense Katherine. Where she might be. If she was in peril or safe.

Home. They needed that feeling of "home"; the safety and warmth, the dreamlike comforts that are "home."

E. Aster Bunnymund was the last of the giant rabbits of the Pookan Brotherhood, and while he had been to Santoff Claussen only a few times, he had found his first friends in the enchanted village.

Nicholas St. North had been the greatest thief in all of Russia and had once tried to rob Santoff Claussen of its treasures. But the kindness he had found there had changed his brigand's heart, and now he was a hero of unparalleled skill and valor.

For Toothiana, Queen of the Tooth Fairy Armies, this would be her first real visit. She had heard from her many animal friends that the village was a haven of kindness and respect for all living creatures. She already felt a great kinship with any who came from Santoff Claussen.

Ombric Shalazar ached to return to the village he had founded. This most ancient and wise of wizards hoped that by going back to Santoff Claussen, the Guardians would heal from their battles with Pitch. Such a cunning and relentless villain was this Nightmare King! Three times now the Guardians had defeated him. And three times he had returned, with deeply devious plans that had tested them beyond what they thought they could ever do. They were weary and heartsick. But Ombric . . . Ombric was close to collapse. His weariness was now equal to his wisdom, and he feared that perhaps he was losing the delicate balance that kept him ready for any fight.

Going home must mend me, he thought. He hoped it would steady them all, give them a chance to regroup, gather their strength, and re-sharpen their wits. They would need to if they stood any chance of finding Katherine.

This lost girl may have been the youngest of their troop, but in many ways she was its oldest soul. She was orphaned, as all the Guardians had been, and like them, she had found a path out of that sorrow. Unlike them, however, her path was not through daring deeds or the study of magic or the use of miraculous powers. She had been gifted with something almost as rare: an open and eager mind. She had the gift of watching and listening, the gift of taking all the hurts and happenings of others' lives and understanding their purpose.

Katherine's heart and mind would take their

adventures and reimagine them, sometimes exactly as they had occurred or—most miraculously of all—as new stories. She had become the historian of what had happened and what should have happened. No one could tell a story better than Katherine. No one understood what needed to be as well as she. This was a singular and important power in the ranks of the Guardians.

But Nightlight was the most eager of them to be back in Santoff Claussen. He was well named, this quicksilver boy of brightness and unending youth. His pureness of heart could cast away the darkest shadows. Katherine was his best, closest, dearest friend. He had first met her in the village, and their friendship had changed him, made him more of what was best inside his joyful, restless soul. With Katherine at his side, he felt he could light up the world. And he quite likely could. But now she was gone.

And so the remaining Guardians would return, along with all the villagers and children and animals who had joined them on what was intended as a celebratory journey.

It had been a time so full of hope and promise. Peace was coming. A new Golden Age was at hand.

But war and disaster had come instead.

They now boarded Bunnymund's Eggomotive and made the long trek home. As the wondrous locomotive rose from its tunnel and into the village, they immediately sensed an unfamiliar air of worry.

All who had stayed behind in the village came rushing out to greet them.

In front were Petrov, North's uncannily smart stallion, and Bear, the most magnificent of his species to ever walk the forests of Europe. Bear was as gentle as he was powerful. The robot, Djinni, was beside him. This extraordinary metal being, built by North, was capable of untold amazements. Flanking the three were Bunnymund's Warrior Eggs of all sizes, standing at attention. Hovering above them was the Spirit of the Forest, her robes shimmering in unseen winds. Behind them were all the creatures of the forest and the villagers, each smartly dressed in the customary Santoff Claussen attire. Even the beetles and worms wore dapper vests and hats.

And of course Ombric's owls were there as well. These mysterious birds had the ability to absorb knowledge from out of the air, so they knew everything that had happened during this fateful trip of the Guardians. Within Big Root, the massive hollow tree that was the center of the village, the owls had been able to activate the magical screens that hung in Ombric's laboratory.

From the minds of the owls, the screens had projected to everyone in Santoff Claussen the story of what had happened in Punjam Hy Loo. So everyone in the village had seen the meeting of Queen Toothiana and the twisted Monkey King who had allied with Pitch. They had learned of the battle against the monkey army, in which Pitch's long-lost daughter had returned and taken Pitch and Katherine. They knew everything except the one detail the owls did not know. It was the one detail that would put all their minds at ease: Where was Katherine?

As the engine of Bunnymund's Eggomotive stopped and its egg-shaped puffs of smoke cleared, the village and all its citizens came together again.

Cautious hellos and welcomes were exchanged. Parents hugged their children. Old William embraced all his younger Williams. But the joy in this reunion was shadowed. The children who had just returned from the journey broke from their parents' clutches and clustered around Kailash, the Great Himalayan Snow Goose who had been raised by Katherine. The huge bird's graceful neck hung low. The villagers had hoped beyond hope that the Guardians might have an answer as to Katherine's whereabouts, but because they did not, the band of heroes was lowest of all. And when the smallest William raced up to Mr. Qwerty, the former glowworm who'd transformed himself into a magic book in a moment of dire need and whose pages were filled with Katherine's every story—his pages were Katherine's pages; her stories, his stories—Mr.

Qwerty opened himself and showed one blank page after another. His life, without her, was on pause. There were no new stories beyond her first ones— no clue as to where Katherine was or if she was all right.

CHAPTER THREE

In Which We See Many Terrors in the Shadows

KATHERINE WAS WORRIED AS well. She was straining to hear the volatile discussion between her captors, but it was difficult. She had no idea where she was, but she was certain it was unlike any place she'd ever been. And she'd seen many amazing places: the enchanted forest that surrounded Santoff Claussen. The eerie majesty of Pitch's lair at the Earth's core. The gilded splendor of Bunnymund's underground city, where everything—right down to the doorknobs— was egg-shaped. Queen Toothiana's haunting palace at the highest peak of Punjam Hy Loo.

She assumed this densely wooded place where she was being held must be part of Mother Nature's empire. The ground seemed to be made of an ever-changing mix of earth and water. Oddly, it never became muddy; the elements stayed separate. Spirals of water encircled the trees' roots like minia-ture moats, and widened and narrowed whenever Katherine moved. Mist and fog spun through the air in delicate patterns. They looked like layer after layer of glistening lace that heaved and rippled in the con-stant breeze.

The trees were of every size and sat close together. The high canopy of leaves was so thick that almost no direct sunlight filtered through. The few low-hanging branches curled and swayed with the haunting grace of a dancer's arms.

It was these armlike branches that held Katherine

tightly at the base of one particularly massive tree. Every time she pulled against them, their grip intensified. If she tried to take even a single step, the moats around the tree would widen and deepen. The water was black and menacing.

So, for the present, she resigned herself to the fact that she could not break loose, and she instead concentrated on eavesdropping. The mist muffled almost all sound, but she could manage to make out the voices of Pitch and Mother Nature. What she heard fascinated and terrified her.

"You saved me," Pitch was saying, his voice a curious mix of pride and vulnerability.

"No," Mother Nature replied dismissively. "It was the girl who saved you. The one who *you* would make your Darkling Princess."

Katherine knew they were talking about her. She

had taken pity on Pitch and stopped the Guardians from killing him. But there was a hardness in Mother Nature's voice that made Katherine uneasy.

"Had you forgotten me?" Mother Nature demanded. "Your own daughter!"

Katherine was amazed that this magnificent woman of the elements was Pitch's long-lost child.

The breeze began to strengthen. The air grew considerably colder. Katherine could now see her breath.

"No!" Katherine heard Pitch cry out. "I never for a moment forgot you."

"Then why did you not come for me?" Mother Nature asked with a chilling calm.

"I tried! I tried. . . . For so long, I tried—" Pitch's voice broke off in anguish.

Mother Nature's silence after this pleading admission was telling.

The air became wintery. The lacy mist froze into sheets of stiffened frost. Katherine realized what was happening. As Mother Nature's voice grew colder, so did the air around her.

"You failed me, Father," she said, her voice low and dangerous. "I was lost. I had nothing but my rage at you to feed me. I came to your aid only out of . . . curiosity. To see how a once-great man could become so fallen and low."

It began to snow furiously. Katherine was freezing. She could now faintly see Pitch crawling toward her, as if in agony. Mother Nature walked behind him, calmly and regally.

"You will receive only indifference from me, Father. I will neither hinder nor help you," she was saying. "I demand only one thing for my neutrality: You cannot make this girl yours. Not ever. Leave her be, or I will destroy you. *I* am your only daughter, for good or ill."

By now Pitch was less than a dozen feet from Katherine. The snow was blinding. He looked up at her. The look on his face changed from deepest mourning to calculating evil. He seemed on the verge of laughing.

"Yes, my daughter," he said with a sneer. "I will not touch her."

Those were the last words Katherine was to hear for a long, long time.

CHAPTER FOUR

Djinnis and Jests

It had been a long day for everyone in Santoff Claussen. Unpacking is always wearying, even when using magic.

Without the robot djinni, however, it would have been exhausting. The djinni had been particularly useful when North had summoned it to unload the train. The djinni's strength was almost unlimited, so it had been able to carry many dozens of large bundles and to give every child in the village a piggyback ride at the same time.

"Thanks, Djinni," called out the youngest William as the metal robot dropped all the Williams and their belongings at their house.

"It was my pleasure," said the djinni in its usual way—crisp and exact and with a chimelike quality, as though it were a talking music box.

North, Ombric, Toothiana, and Bunnymund were busy settling into the comforting hollow of Big Root. The interior of the gigantic tree was tidier than they had left it. While they had been gone, the owls had organized the insects and squirrels into a very efficient cleaning brigade.

North, Ombric, and Bunnymund were scouring the library's newly constituted volumes for any hints that could lead them to Mother Nature's whereabouts, while Toothiana, who also spoke fluent owl, quizzed the wise birds on many points of mutual interest. They were desperate to begin their attempt to rescue Katherine.

From the very beginning, the Guardians had the ability to feel the thoughts and emotions of one another when needed. If one Guardian was in the next room or on the other side of the globe from the others, a call for help could be sensed. But that made it all the more strange that they had heard nothing from Katherine. And they were deeply alarmed that the woman who had taken both Katherine and Pitch was, in fact, Pitch's daughter. Though this Mother Nature clearly possessed enormous power, the Guardians had no clue as to how she had acquired it. They weren't even certain of the extent of her powers. Or whether she was good, evil, or both.

North was particularly frustrated and echoed

all their thoughts. "We know more about making chocolate milk than we do about Pitch's daughter and how she came to be this so-called . . . Nature Mother or Mother Nature. We're supposed to be the wisest men on the—"

Bunnymund felt obliged to interrupt his friend. "The two of you are indeed *men*, and you possess an impressive amount of knowledge for humans of your generations. But, my dear North, must I remind you that I am a Pooka and not a man?"

Sometimes Bunnymund's precise and exact nature could be inadvertently funny . . . or inadvertently irritating. Often at the same time. North looked at the enormous rabbit, who stood even taller than himself. He poked a single finger at one of Bunnymund's impressively large ears. "Holy smoke, you're right! I've never noticed your ears."

Bunnymund blinked twice. One ear twitched slightly. As did his nose. "Really? You never noticed my ears? Oh. I understand," he responded. "That was an example of the peculiar human method of communication known as 'sarcasm.'"

"Or a joke." North smirked. "Someday I'll make you laugh, Bunnymund."

"Me, laugh?" The rabbit looked particularly baffled. "That would be historic. Pookas don't laugh."

North grinned. "No kidding."

"Actually, no. I mean, yes. Well, either way, I'm not, as you say, 'kidding.' Pookas never laugh, as far as I know, and have difficulty in kidding."

"I *know!*" said North.

"Then why did you say it? Oh! You were restating

an obvious fact, to underscore your perception that I needn't have stated the fact in the first place. In other words, you were again being sarcastic and or making a joke."

"Nope," North said. "I was just kidding."

The rabbit's ears, nose, and whiskers were now twitching like mad. "I . . . you . . . that . . . doesn't entirely make sense."

"Really?" asked North. "Are you kidding?"

"No. I mean, yes. Wait. Yes to the first question and no to the second one. But are you kidding or joking with me?"

"Neither," said North. He was deeply pleased. He had finally discovered a way to confound the brilliant rabbit. "I was just being silly."

"Look," said Bunnymund, twitching all over, "I have tried to embrace this thing you call 'humor,' but I do not see the difference between 'kidding' and 'joking' and 'being silly.'"

"Or jesting?" North said.

"That . . . Well . . . it's . . ."

"Or making a quip?"

"No . . . I mean . . ."

"How about a wisecrack?"

"A crack? In something solid? How can that have wisdom?!" asked the rabbit.

"It can't. It just needs to tickle your funny bone," North said, smiling.

The rabbit, however, was panting with frustration. "What are you talking about?! There is no such bone in any known creature. Humor is a mental activity, and it has nothing to do with the skeletal system. To claim so is complete nonsense!"

"EXACTLY!!!" bellowed North.

Ombric had been deliberately ignoring his two comrades. He was buried deep in one of Bunnymund's egg-shaped books.

Ombric was astounded: The rabbit had vast records of all the natural occurrences of the Earth. This wasn't unexpected. He was a creature attuned to nature, more so than any human. But it was how his books were written that was so surprising— in the highly technical phrasing that was typical to Pookan literature. The Earth was usually described as "the planetoidal orb." Earthquakes were referred to as "high-volume terra firma displacement events," and so on.

Midway through the chapter titled "Peculiar Interstellar Phenomena from the Dawn of Time till Last Tuesday," Ombric found something described as an "extraterrestrial solid matter of some interest hurtled through the atmosphere and into a large body of oceanic fluids in the southern Pan-Pacific region in the two millionth equinox cycle." In other words, a meteor or a shooting star had crashed somewhere in the Pacific Ocean, sometime near the end of the Golden Age. Ombric was startled to discover that soon after this event, the weather on Earth changed profoundly. Before, there had been almost no storms of any kind, but since this meteor had arrived, nature had become far more dramatic. Unpredictable. *Is this the beginning of Mother Nature? Has Pitch's daughter come to be here on a shooting star?* wondered Ombric.

At that instant Nightlight flew through one of Big Root's knothole windows. As the Guardian who was most deeply connected to Katherine, Nightlight always knew before any of them if she was in trouble or not. Now the poor boy looked stricken.

A sudden, terrible dread came to them all. They felt certain that Katherine was in grave peril. The owls began to hoot. Toothiana's feathers stood on end.

CHAPTER FIVE

Grab a Tear, Save a Story

THE NIGHT WAS OPPRESSIVELY dark. The stars themselves seemed to shrink. Nestled into the upper branches of Big Root was Katherine's tree house. Though it was empty of Katherine, it was not exactly empty. Kailash, now fully grown, sat dejectedly in an impressively large nest, which also served as the tree house's roof. Being full grown meant Kailash was considerably larger than other species of geese. She was quite large even for her own breed. Her wingspan was roughly forty-five feet, and even while sitting in her nest, she was taller than any man.

But her nature was gentle and her emotions still childlike. She was heartbroken over Katherine's disappearance and could barely raise her long neck to respond to the kind attention of the village children who had snuck away from their own beds to comfort her. Petter and his sister, Sascha; the brothers William; and even Fog, who was usually too sleepy for such late-night adventures, were there. They petted Kailash, smoothed her feathers, and tried to convince her to eat. But the giant goose would only make a sad peeping sound.

Petter, who had a fine sense of how to cheer everyone up, suggested that Mr. Qwerty tell one of Katherine's stories.

He opened himself to read one of Katherine's earlier tales, but his voice cracked and faltered. Tears filled his eyes and spread slowly down the handsome leather binding of his book spine.

None of the children had ever seen a book actually cry, which was not surprising, as there had never before been a book that was able to. But the tears that fell from the page to the soft leaves around Kailash's nest surprised them further. Each tear had inside it a letter or a question mark or some other form of punctuation.

It was Sascha who understood the ramifications of this.

"That's Katherine's handwriting!" She gasped. "Please don't cry, Mr. Qwerty. You're crying out Katherine's stories!"

But this caused the poor book to sob even harder. Tears and letters began to spill out at an alarming rate. If this continued, all of Katherine's stories would be drained away.

The children became desperate, and Kailash also began to weep. They reached out to comfort the goose, then turned at the sound of something landing on the far side of the nest. Nightlight was back! He had been with them earlier and had not seemed like himself at all. He was moody, dark, and almost afraid. Then he had left hurriedly. But now he was like the Nightlight of old. He flashed and flickered and grabbed at every fallen tear. Nightlight had amazing abilities with tears. The children had seen this before. He'd once taken their tears and used them to repair his broken diamond dagger that could cut through any armor. But these tears were different. He cradled them in his hands with extraordinary tenderness, as though he held a most delicate treasure. These were Katherine's words and thoughts. This was a treasure that must never be lost. He tucked the wordy tears into his pocket.

Then he looked from the children to Kailash to poor Mr. Qwerty, who thankfully had stopped his sobs. What hope could he offer them? He knew Katherine was in terrifying peril, and he had no idea how to help her. How could he possibly comfort his friends—Katherine's friends?

He felt himself dimming again. Now they'd see for themselves his own desperation.

But Nightlight was a creature of light, and he could shine or feel more in a shadow than any other being. So of course he was the first to see, in the evening shade of Big Root, a light in the sky coming toward them. A sort of lustrous, radiant cloud.

He could feel his hope returning, and he

brightened, leaning toward the light. The others turned to see what he was looking at. One by one, they cried out as they began to see the cloud, a cloud unlike any they'd ever seen—one that left them feeling that hope can sometimes travel in the darkest night.

CHAPTER SIX

The Sandman Cometh

Moments earlier North had been in midsentence when Nightlight had flown suddenly out the window. The boy was frantic to help Katherine, and North had been trying to calm him. For all his bravery and powers, Nightlight was not used to controlling his feelings. Especially feelings like hurt and worry. He wanted to do something. He wanted to help Katherine right then!

North was the closest to understanding what Nightlight was going through, for he had been almost as wild and carefree when he was a lad. Why, he'd lived as a wild child of the Russian forest, raised by Cossack bandits, which is almost the same as being raised by bears. But his attempts to ease Nightlight's anxiousness had lasted about six words before the boy vanished.

Bunnymund sensed North's concern. "In my observations, beings between childhood and adulthood are even more prone to confusing behavior than during any other of the confusing times that inflict most species," the Pooka said.

"He wants to think he can figure everything out for himself," said North, eyeing the rabbit. "A characteristic common in many species, no matter their age." He poked one of Bunnymund's ears.

"I don't know what you're trying to infer, North," said Bunnymund. "I do not *like* to figure everything out. I simply always do!"

Before North could make a snappy response, they became keenly aware of an intense sensation of lightness around them. Not only was there an other-worldly glow to the air inside the tree, but gravity itself seemed to have less pull. They literally felt light on their feet.

"Is someone casting spells?" asked Ombric, glancing around at the others.

A soothing sound enveloped them. Ombric hazarded a guess as to its origin. "It's like the falling sand from a thousand hourglasses."

Under normal circumstances, the orb at the tip of North's sword would have sent out some sort of alarm, but evidently, it found nothing to be alarmed about. Even when the three Guardians began to float from the floor—first a few inches, then higher and higher—the orb stayed silent. Graceful twists of golden glowing sand ebbed up through the floor-boards, pushing them gently but firmly out the giant knothole window and up toward Big Root's upper branches.

As they floated ever higher, none of them, oddly, sensed they were in any danger. Rather, they felt incredibly calm, as though this unprecedented occurrence was simply the way things were somehow supposed to be, which was equally odd. Were they all being drugged? Was this some new magic? If so, they sensed it wasn't a dark sort.

As they approached the treetop, the whorls of sand seemed to be settling more at their feet. To their amazement, they could see that every other creature of Santoff Claussen, human or otherwise, was also floating through the evening sky. Bear, Petrov the horse, even the Spirit of the Forest and Queen Toothiana—they were all rising up and rotating around Big Root.

When they all reached the top and were level with Katherine's tree house, they saw Kailash surrounded by the children. Those in the nest were transfixed by something else. Just above them floated a rotund little man. He had wild swirling golden hair, and he seemed to be glowing from within.

Nightlight stood just below the little man, and as the villagers watched, he began to kneel, as though the man were a king of some kind. The man seemed very friendly; his smile was radiant. It was a smile of total reassurance and gave all who saw it a feeling of intense well-being. Not joy, but something akin to a sleepy peace. A sort of not-a-worry-in-the-world sensation. None of them, not even the Guardians, were able to do anything more than gaze at this gentle fellow. And though he did not speak, they felt as though they heard him say a single whispered phrase: *Time now for a dream.* Then, with a wave of his little hands, the sand began to spin around them. It did not sting, nor did it get in their eyes. It felt rather like the tickling of a soft bed sheet. Then everyone, right down to Bear, fell into a deep, restful sleep.

But this was no ordinary sleep: They began to share an experience that seemed like a dream, for it was dreamlike, but every moment of it was amazing, and somehow, they knew it was absolutely true. They felt they were being given a history in the very best way this friendly little man knew how. And they were certain to remember every detail, for Mr. Qwerty, who was the only one not asleep, was recording the story of this dream experience on his pages. He knew Katherine would not mind. She loved a good story.

This one might also help save her life. And here was how it began. . . .

CHAPTER SEVEN

A Dream Pause

My name is Sanderson Mansnoozie, and I have no age.

My story is the story of many dreams. Dreams do not exist within the realm of hours or minutes or any measure of the day. They live in the space between the tick and the tock. Before the tolling of the bell, past the dawn, and beyond the velvet night. I am from a place that was a dream, a place called the Golden Age. And though it may be a place of the past, it is not gone. The dream of it lives still.

My telling it to you will make that so.

I was once a Star Captain in the Golden Age, born to guide the stars that would not stay still. Stars are an amazing phenomenon—all but the rarest stay in place. You see them in the night sky, and you always will. But a few—a precious few—are restless, driven on and on by too much energy or curiosity or even anger. . . . These are the ones we call "shooting stars."

As a star pilot, I belonged to the League of Star Captains, a cheerful brotherhood devoted to the granting of wishes. We each had a wandering star that we commanded. In the tip of our star was our cabin, a bright compact place, much like an opulent bunk bed. We journeyed wherever we pleased, passing planets at random and listening to the wishes that were made to us as we passed. If a wish was worthy, we were honor-bound to answer it. We would send a dream to whomever had made

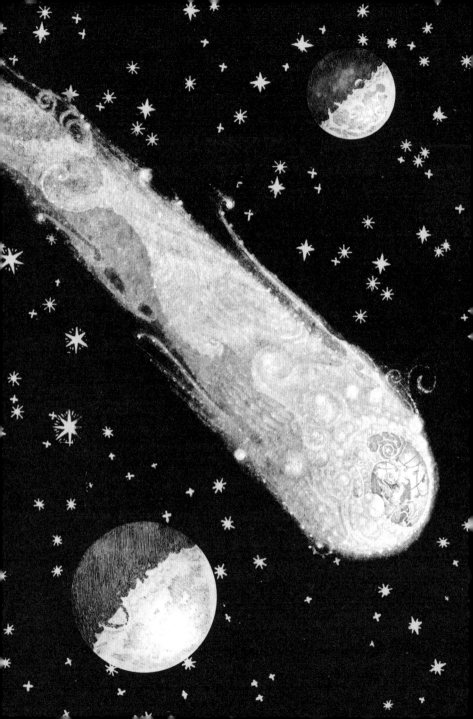

the wish. The dream would go to that person as they slept, and within this dream, there would be a story.

If the story was powerful enough, the person would remember it forever, and it would help guide them in their quest to make the wish come true. These dreams were considered one of the greatest treasures of the Golden Age. But to create the dream in the first place, we had to be asleep. So we were often asleep and dreaming, even as we flew, and our stars would awaken us if trouble lurked.

And trouble wasn't difficult to find. Dream Pirates prowled every galaxy. They were nasty, stunted creatures who lived by stealing dreams. At first they ruthlessly plundered these dream treasures of the Golden Age for the bounty they could raise for their return. But then they discovered an even more wicked motive for this crime. If they consumed a dream, it made them stronger, tougher, and more powerful in every evil way.

So we Star Captains fought hundreds of battles with the Dream Pirates, at least until the great war that ended them. We weren't without help—the other planets and Constellations of the Golden Age banded together and formed the greatest fleet in the known universe, led by the most brilliant and fearless captain in history, Kozmotis Pitchiner, Lord High General of the Galaxies. It was Lord Pitch (as he was called by his sailors) who sailed unceasingly to every corner of the heavens and hunted down legion after legion of Dream Pirates. Though he was victorious and had become the greatest hero of the Golden Age, he paid a most terrible price. And that is where this story of my life takes an unexpected turn.

The tragedy of Pitch and what brought him low

became the center of my journey. It is the story of Pitch and his lost daughter.

Of how she became lost.

Of how Pitch was broken past healing.

And of how his daughter became the one you call "Mother Nature."

CHAPTER EIGHT

The Heart Becomes the Hunted

The War of the Dream Pirates was vicious and bloody. The pirates knew that if they lost, they would never again be as powerful as they were at that very moment. So they became more clever, devious, and cruel with their tactics: They would destroy whole planets. Extinguish stars. Eliminate entire Constellations.

For eons the pirates had been seen as dangerous criminals. Now the people of the Golden Age viewed them as an evil that had to be eradicated. Soon hate became the center of how this war was waged, and hate is a powerful force.

It can make bad men worse and good men nearly mad.

Lord Pitch had been noble and fair at the start of his campaign. He'd fought honorably against the pirates. When he bested their ships, he took the survivors prisoner. He fed them well and urged them to renounce their wretched ways.

But the pirates saw this thread of humanity as a weakness, a weakness that could be used against Lord Pitch. They'd thus far failed in their attempts to assassinate him, and their attempts had been many. Now, however, they realized with cold calculation, if they failed to kill him in body, they would simply destroy his spirit.

They began to hunt for that which mattered most to the valiant sailor: his family. Lord Pitch kept his wife and child housed safely on the small moon of a planet deep in the heart of the

Constellation Orion. It was a lovely moon and was well protected by the many asteroids that encircled it. Each asteroid was a small fortress, armed with a platoon of the elite of the Golden Age Armies.

Lord and Lady Pitchiner were doting parents, their palace a thrilling place to raise their young daughter, Emily Jane. She was a wild and joyful child, with raven-black hair as thick and flowing as a horse's mane, which was fitting, as she was always on the run. Like her father, she loved to sail. She was constantly in her own small schooner, venturing around her moon and its asteroids.

Lady Pitchiner, ever vigilant in her care of their only child, often ordered Emily Jane to stay close, to take a guard with her, or simply to stay home. But Emily Jane disobeyed her mother frequently. She couldn't stop herself from slipping out alone and doing as she pleased. Her father loved his girl's wild heart, so he turned a blind eye to her disobedient sailing ways.

Fate can be as peculiar as any dream or story, for it was one of these little secret adventures that saved Emily Jane's life.

Dream Pirates had been reported off the tip of Orion's sword. Lord Pitch hurriedly said his farewells to his wife and daughter before preparing to hunt down the scoundrels. The family never liked saying good-bye; they tried not to think of the dangers that would be faced. But this time Emily Jane had made for her father a silver locket containing her picture. He was very pleased by it and put it around his neck as he kissed her.

"I'll be back soon," he told her.

"Promise?" she said.

"On my soul," he replied.

Lord Pitch was a man of his word. And he reassured himself that his family was safe. Their moon home had many defenses against a large attack.

But the Dream Pirates had not planned a large attack. They had something more intimately sinister in mind.

Several dozen pirates, shadowy and expert, slipped past every guard, every outpost, every defense and made their way to Lord Pitch's villa.

The villa was spacious, columned, almost castlelike. It was carved from moonstone, so the rooms had a soothing, cool glow of reflected light, even in the darkest night. But this night seemed particularly dark.

All in the villa were asleep except one— Emily Jane. After bedtime she had slipped out her bedroom window and into her schooner docked close by. She hadn't yet traveled far when she spied a school of Star Fish, swimming low in the moon's atmosphere. She loved Star Fish—a favorite game was to tie her schooner to the leader and ride along with them as they swooped and dove through the canyons near her home.

The Dream Pirates, so intent on infiltrating the villa, had not seen the girl sneaking out. Emily Jane had already cast off when the pirates were surrounding the villa and readying to strike. They could feel the sleeping dreams of Lady Pitchiner and of the entire household. To the Dream Pirates, dreams were like blood to a vampire. Dreams made them hungry and sometimes stupid. Could they feel the dreams of Lord Pitch's daughter? They were too impatient and crazed to make sure. "She must be in there somewhere," they reasoned.

And so they charged.

A Dream Pirate attack is swift and ragged. Like awkward phantoms, the pirates often fly in lurches and jerks, and they usually destroy everything that gets in their way.

Lady Pitchiner startled awake as the pirates smashed their way through the house, coming closer and closer to where she lay. She could hear the alarms sounding, but would help come in time? She doubted it. She ran into Emily Jane's bedroom and locked the door. But the bed was empty. The covers hadn't even been pulled down.

Good! Lady Pitchiner thought. *She's out on her ship!* For once, she was thankful rather than angry that her daughter was so rebellious.

The pirates were smashing down the door.

Lady Pitchiner had only an instant to act. *They'll be looking for us both,* she thought. So she grabbed a large doll and held it in her arms, as if it were Emily Jane, and sat very still. The door splintered into pieces, and the pirates poured in. Lady Pitchiner knew the awful fate of those taken by Dream Pirates—their souls sucked dry of dreams, leaving them to become mindless slaves . . . or worse.

They must be made to think that we have died, she thought desperately as the pirates clamored closer. Keeping just enough of the doll exposed under her cape so the pirates would see it, she ran for the window. Straight into and through it. The glass shattered. Lady Pitchiner was gone.

The pirates pressed at the window, staring down. The fall was more than a mile.

Emily Jane had heard the alarms and the explosions echoing through the canyons she was coasting. She knew the ruckus could only be coming from her home. She knew the sound of a Dream Pirate attack. They had attacked her father's ship when she and her mother had first come this moon. And though she was wild, she was not foolish. She stayed with the Star Fish. Perhaps if she rode among them, she would not be seen. The Star Fish swam swiftly through the canyons, in a near panic from the sounds of battle.

Between gaps in the canyons peaks, Emily Jane watched in horror as her palace was riddled with explosions. She could make out the window of her own room, then the awful sound of shattering glass, and there was the unmistakable figure of her mother falling.

Emily Jane turned away. She closed her eyes tightly and would not open them; she let the Star Fish take her where they would. The Star Fish darted on and on, away from the embattled moon, through the rings of meteors, and out into the ocean of space. Soon Emily Jane could no longer hear anything but the lulling sound of the wind as she was pulled farther and farther from her doomed home and into the eternity of space.

CHAPTER NINE

A Little Girl Lost
and a Titan Found

And so Emily Jane traveled far from her home
and far from her sorrow, until she came to an
unexpectedly safe place—the Constellation called
Typhan. Before the War of the Dream Pirates,
Typhan had been a maker of storms and was a
powerful ally of the Golden Age. He could conjure
up solar winds so vast and terrible, they would scatter
whole fleets of Dream Pirate galleons when required.

But the wily Dream Pirates had managed to
ravage him and render him harmless: They had
extinguished the stars that had been his eyes. Once
blinded, he could no longer see the pirates as they

attacked. And they had been merciless, killing so many of his stars that his once-vivid outline was nearly gone. He was now a forgotten ghost of his former self, and he had lost the will to make storms or to fight. He was a mournful, pitiful Titan. Only the harmless Star Fish ever swam among Typhan's few remaining stars and moons.

Now, as the Star Fish weaved their way past Typhan's head, Emily Jane was as blind to the damaged giant as he was to her. Her thoughts were only of her poor mother, her vanished home, and the feeling of being as lost as any child could be. "Father," she cried at last. "Come find me! Please! Please!! I am so alone!"

Typhan heard these cries. He had only heard the taunts and laughter of the Dream Pirates since his sight was destroyed. He thought he would never again hear a voice that was not forged by cruelty.

"Child?" he whispered. "How come you here?"
Even in a whisper, his voice could fill a galaxy,
but his was a strong, unthreatening voice, like a
summer storm that has recently passed.

Startled, Emily Jane looked up and saw what
remained of the starlight giant. Like all Golden Age
children, she had been schooled in the names and
shapes of the Constellations, so she immediately
recognized his dimmed face.

Through tears, she told Typhan who she was
and all the awfulness of her journey. This stirred
Typhan, and for the first time since his blinding,
he felt an echo of his former might. They had both
been victims of the Dream Pirates and had been
left to lonely fates. He summoned up a breeze
that took Emily Jane and her Star Fish to a moon
near the stars of his right ear. The travellers were
exhausted, and resting was very welcome. As they

landed among the powdery craters, Typhan spoke
once more.

"Child," he said. "You are not alone."

Those words were like a shield of comfort for
Emily Jane. She felt safer, and even hopeful. And as
she fell into a long, weary sleep, she thought over
and over: *Somehow, my father will find me.*

CHAPTER TEN

The Dream Becomes a Nightmare

When word reached Lord Pitch that his home and family were under attack, he knew he had been duped. There were no pirates waiting where he had been told. So he pushed his fleet to return with a speed none thought possible. The palace, and most of his moon, was now nothing but scorched ruins. The pirates were reboarding their sleek escape vessels when Lord Pitch's warships surrounded them. They never expected him to return so swiftly.

Lord Pitch wanted these pirates alive. "My wife and child may be among them," he told his lieutenants.

The pirates were impossibly outgunned. They knew it was hopeless to fight, and they also knew they could count on Lord Pitch's compassion. They surrendered without the firing of a single shot.

But as they were hauled aboard Lord Pitch's flagship, they did not face the same noble warrior they had come to begrudgingly respect. They faced a man on the brink of madness.

"My wife and daughter? Where are they?" Lord Pitch demanded.

The captain of the Dream Pirates said with a sneer, "We were denied the pleasure of draining them of their dreams."

"Because you were caught?"

"No, my lord."

"Have you harmed them?"

"No, my lord," replied the captain. Its lips curled into a small, satisfied smile. "They are dead."

Lord Pitch stood stoically. He was a gentleman of the Golden Age, a commander of its armies. Even now, he felt he must maintain his judgment and composure. But the pirate captain was too keen to bring forth his hurts.

"Your lady so feared our company that she threw herself to her doom, and the child with her," the captain gloated.

Lord Pitch could barely speak. He looked from one pirate to another. "Is this true?"

The captain grinned. "'Tis true, my lord. I saw it myself. As did we all."

Lord Pitch, bringing his face within inches of the captain's, said with a measured calm, "Then feast your eyes on mine. They are the last things you will ever see." And with startling suddenness, he drew his sword and cut the captain's head from its body.

He stepped quickly to the next pirate, and before another word could be said, he sliced again. Another head tumbled to the deck. The pirates gasped and pulled against their chains, but Lord Pitch continued on.

His own crew shuffled and murmured uneasily. Was this their general? The most gallant of the Golden Age? Lord Pitch was methodical and never paused. All the pirates, and Lord Pitch's mercy, were dead in less time than it takes to sing a song.

CHAPTER ELEVEN
◆
A Stormy Relationship

Emily Jane's life with Typhan suited her nature. He had been a god of storms, and now he delighted in conjuring up tempests for her to ride. At first she rode her Star Fish over the waves of solar wind that Typhan blew, but in time he taught her the trick of making storms herself. He anointed her as his daughter, and from then on, she could wield the power of the heavens. Wind, starlight, gravity were hers to command. She now was a sister of the heavens and was honor-bound to use her power only for good.

Emily Jane never tired of summoning playful

squalls; she rode them until she was exhausted. It was the only peace she knew from the heartaches that ate away at her. Where was her father? Why did he not come to find her? Typhan was kind; he even loved her. In time she regarded him with awe, but awe is not affection or love. It didn't heal her pain. She stayed with Typhan because she hoped against hope that if she remained in one place, there was a chance her father could still find her. But while the Star Fish swam as far as they dared to try to send word of Emily Jane, they could never make it far enough. Days turned into weeks, weeks into months, months into years.

Occasionally, passing wrecks of abandoned ships drifted by the Constellation. Emily Jane became an expert forager. She discovered that the contents inside these ghostly vessels could supply her with all her needs. She positioned dozens of scavenged telescopes all over her small moon so she could be the eyes of Typhan. Food, supplies, clothes, furniture, books—everything she might need—all were found in the abandoned wrecks that strayed close enough to her moon that she or the Star Fish could retrieve them. The hull of a crashed galleon served as her home. So she lived in a sort of ramshackle magnificence. There was even treasure. Great heaping chests of it, which she stored in the moon's small, hollow core. But the more treasure she amassed, the less the treasure came to mean to her. She even began to hate it. It reminded her of the past. Of her home. Of the Golden Age.

In those early weeks and months with Typhan, she had scanned the heavens in every direction, each hour on the hour, ever hopeful, looking for her father's flagship. But the years bore on without a single sighting. *He has forgotten me,* she decided one fateful day. It was the morning of her sixteenth birthday.

She had tried to forget the date. Year after year, her only wish had been a simple one: that her father would come. But ten birthdays had passed, and each one left her harder and more bitter.

On this day a ship finally appeared in the distance! Her hope came back. She could tell in an instant that it wasn't a Dream Pirate vessel. Their ships were always twisted, spiked, and foul to look at. This was a Golden Age craft to be sure. Elegant of line and sail. It was beautiful . . . too beautiful. It was no warship. But it did not fly the flag of her father. It was a peaceful liner and nothing more.

Why has Father never come? she wondered bitterly. And she felt an anger that clouded her good sense. She hated her father now. She hated the world that she had so ached to return to. She'd rather stay lost. And in that dreadful moment, something changed in her. Her heart became consumed with rage.

Typhan could feel that something was terribly wrong.

"Daughter?" he whispered. "What do you see? Friend or foe?"

Her answer surprised even herself. "I see only foes!" And without warning, she raised up a murderous storm.

Typhan knew the sound of pain and rage. He feared that she had lost her reason.

"Daughter!" he cried out. "What ship approaches?"

"Not the ship I hope for!" she shouted back. Her violent winds sped toward the helpless vessel.

"Stop this tempest!" Typhan ordered her. "We never harm without cause!"

"From now on, my cause is harm!" she screamed.

Typhan knew then that she had gone mad, and gathering all his strength, he sent forth winds to counter hers.

But her rage was equal to Typhan's goodness, and she fought him, hurling a galaxy of hate-filled torrents at the ancient colossus.

"Daughter! Stop!" he pleaded, summoning every last ounce of strength he possessed.

"You are not my father!" Emily Jane shrieked.

Meteors! Comets! Hunks of broken planets came smashing into Typhan's stars and shattered the Golden Age galleon that neared.

The old Constellation's heart was cleaved by her words. He was stunned and heartsick. Her deeds were a betrayal that could not be forgiven.

"From forever on, you are cursed!" he bellowed,
stunned and heartsick. "You have broken your
vow!"

It scorched his soul to punish her so harshly,
to cast her out of his life. But an oath had been
broken. So with one mighty blast of his lungs, he
sent Emily Jane's moon shooting away from him.
It flew at such a speed that it began to brighten,
brighten till a hot white light burned, until the moon
itself became a shooting star streaking through space
like a spear.

Emily Jane fled to the moon's hollow core just
as the old galleon where she had slept was burned to
ash. Her telescopes disintegrated. In nanoseconds
everything on her moon's surface was gone. Because
she had fled to the moon's core, she became
entombed by the melting chest of treasure for which
she cared nothing. Emily Jane was indeed doomed.

She would have to live within this new star's center and never leave it until it crashed.

If only she had known her father thought her dead.

If only she and her father had known the truth.

Two hearts that had once been united at the center of the Golden Age would not have become hardened, embittered, and so very cruel. These wounded hearts would not have brought an end to the Age of Wonders.

*T*his dream continued for all in Santoff Claussen,
but the Guardians were taking particular note.
They knew, even in this dream state, that they were
learning a great deal about Pitch, which could be
useful in fighting him. But they also began to feel the
pity Katherine had felt. Pitch had not always been evil.
His heart was once as strong and good as theirs. But
for Nightlight, this was a feeling that confused him.
He thought only in simple terms. He didn't want to
feel pity. He wanted only to save Katherine, and he
could not see how pity could help him.

Then Sanderson Mansnoozie appeared and

became part of the story he had been telling. The dream had been so intense and dramatic that even in their deep sleep, the villagers and Guardians were glad to at last see him. Sandy had a manner both soothing and blissful. He smiled, sending a blanket of calm to one and all, and then continued the tale. . . .

We in the League of Star Captains quickly became aware of this "new" star. I was born into a family of Star Captains. For generations we had steered stars to every corner of the universe, our primary duty to bestow the wishes made to our stars. But the stars we harnessed needed greater and greater speed, for the Dream Pirates were especially intent on capturing Wishing Stars. You see, in all the galaxies, there are few things with more dreams in them than a Wishing Star. These stars are concentrated dream matter, and their pilots are the key to unlocking those dreams. When someone made a wish that was judged worthy, then a Star Captain would send back one of those dreams to help that person fulfill their wish.

But within each star was stored tens of thousands of undreamed dreams that were made by our brethren since time began.

And so when I heard of this wild new shooting star, I pursued it. I didn't know its origins. I didn't know Emily Jane was at its cursed core. But I saw that this star could outpace any Dream Pirate vessel. If I was to saddle it, I would need to be clever.

Many other Star Captains were also after this star, but it had outrun them all. Shooting stars are generally very solitary. They live for speed and wildness. But I had noticed that this particular star would sometimes slow down for schools of Star

Fish. The Star Fish seemed to have a kinship with the star, which was most intriguing.

My brother Star Captains tried to sneak up on the slowing star when it neared a school of Star Fish, but they failed. The star was no fool. It could sense a trap and would blast away, leaving any who chased it choking on its stardust.

I don't like to boast, but I was well liked among the creatures of the cosmos. Star horses and Star Fish have always been my friends. I have a soft spot for them and liked to feed them a star spice they find most delicious, much as you humans do with sugar for your horses. So one day I rode near a school of Star Fish. They were glad to see me and let me swim along. I'd brought supplies of that special spice, and soon they had completely surrounded me, each hovering beside me to have a taste, hiding me completely.

In time the wild star came near.

I waited till it was gliding right by me, keeping pace with us. Then I charged through the Star Fish and lassoed the star with my line. The stun of surprise lasted only a second. The star shot away with more speed than any I'd ever seen, but I held on.

This is not uncommon in trying to catch a wild star. There is an ancient method for bringing them to heel, and I followed it to the letter. I skied along in its fiery wake for ten thousand leagues, pulling myself closer and closer to its burning apex. But it dove and snaked with such fury! It even tried to scrape against a planet or two to knock me off! It seemed . . . enraged, something I'd never witnessed before in a star. It needed to serve my more gentle purposes if only to calm itself—otherwise, it would burn out.

It was the toughest fight I've ever had with a star. Days are difficult to measure in deep space, but it took me the equal of fourteen Earth days to finally tame this wild one. And in the end it was tame in only one regard: It would let me steer it.

Not a lot is known about shooting stars. Mortals, of course, never have a chance to do more than watch and wish when they see one. But something happens when you master a star. You come to understand it. Each has an individual personality that you can sense and feel. All are vivid, but this star had an energy that far exceeded any I'd known. It had a voice. It spoke to me. At first it would not tell me its name or anything about its past, but in time it came to trust me. It could tell I meant it no harm, that I wanted to be its friend and ally. And a friend is like a savior to one so angry and lost. But still the star did not tell me its name.

We sailed from one end of the cosmos to
the other. I would answer dreams whispered up to
us. When the Dream Pirates would attack us, my
star would not pause, as most stars did, but would
charge them head-on, fearlessly.

Together we won every battle.

Then for a year we traveled in peace. Not
once did we happen upon a single pirate. We were
curious about our good fortune. In the vast reaches
of space, news is slow to arrive. Then word came
that the war with the pirates was over. It was said
Lord Pitch had been victorious and all the Dream
Pirates imprisoned. The Golden Age was safe
again! And I thought this would be a cause for
great celebration for my star and me. But upon
hearing this news, my star broke free of my will.
It flew at breakneck speed, trying to crash into any
heavenly body in its path—planets, stars, fields of

asteroids. I could barely keep it from destroying us both.

Then, when it began to career directly toward a small green planet, a thousand wishes rose up from the children of that doomed world. These weren't the common hopeful wishes sent to a shooting star. These were terror-filled wishes. "Please, bright star, don't kill us."

I urged my star to stop. *Think! Think of the children who fear your coming! You are no better than a Dream Pirate!*

And at that moment my star stopped.

If shooting stars ever stop, they quickly become a sun. It takes only a few minutes for this process to become irreversible. In all my eons as a Star Master, I had never ridden a star that had just . . . stopped. I sat at my controls and wondered what my wild star would do next. Then

I heard what sounded like crying from the star's core, and the words, "My name . . . is Emily Jane. Please, I do not want to be feared."

CHAPTER THIRTEEN

Who Does a Star Wish Upon?

I listened to the long, sad tale of Emily Jane. Now I understood her mysteries. She was driven by a child's rage that had never been soothed, never been healed, and now this rage had the power to destroy worlds. She was moments away from becoming a stationary star. If she continued to refuse to move, she would never fly again. Her anger or strength wouldn't ever again threaten any living being. This would be the safest outcome, surely, but what would it do to Emily Jane? To be imprisoned forever in her star with nothing but her anger did not seem . . . fair. Terrible events had

twisted her better instincts. But if she could tame
her fury . . .

So I offered her a choice.

*Emily Jane! You can stay here with your rage
until you burn yourself out. Or . . . fly again. Let me
guide you, and together we will do wonders.*

There was only silence from her. I added
hopefully, *Perhaps we can find your father and with
him . . . peace.*

The minutes went by and still Emily Jane said
nothing. There were mere seconds left before she'd
become fixed forever in this spot. In that moment
she suddenly flamed brightly and jerked forward just
a little.

"I will ride," she whispered with a new calm.
And before I could communicate how pleased
I was, she shot away with a speed that took my
breath.

From the start, she had been difficult to steer, always pulling against me, so now I feared the worst. But after that initial burst of speed, she followed my lead contentedly. We inquired about the whereabouts of her father from any ship or planet we neared, but in these faraway regions of the galaxies, very little was known. So we worked our way toward the great center of the Golden Age, to the Constellation of Zeus. It was a peaceful journey. And when wishes came, Emily Jane listened.

She heard every kind of wish there was. Wishes for ponies and pets. Wishes for riches. Wishes for revenge on enemies. Wishes for love. Emily Jane came to understand all the things that people yearn for. In time she could see the difference between wishes that were worthy of being granted and those that were not.

"People are often . . . confused," she said to

me one quiet night as we streaked through the sky. "They want what they don't need, or can't use, or won't ever make them whole."

True. I was proud that she was learning.

"I think all wishes are the same, really," she continued. "Whether they ask for this, that, or the other, what they are really asking for is happiness."

And what do you wish? I wondered. *What would make you happy?*

She did not answer for a while.

The silence of a peaceful night in the deep oceans of space can feel almost holy. The vast darkness is dotted with stars that go on and on—farther than any light or thought can seem to travel. But they do. In that quiet solitude that wrapped around us, Emily Jane answered my question.

"I wish to be washed clean of my old life. To

let go of my tide of sorrows and find my way to a new shore."

This was a good and worthy wish. It was a wish I wanted to grant.

But fate had other plans.

CHAPTER FOURTEEN
—◆—

Hope Becomes a Weapon Most Foul

We were leagues away from any planet, and no other wishes could reach us. And I began to think about Emily Jane's wish. To answer her wish would take all my thought and wisdom. I must go into a sleepier trance to fashion an Answer Dream.

It is during this trance that a Star Captain must let the star steer itself and be on the lookout for any trouble. Our travels had been peaceful for so long that I had no worries, and Emily Jane had always been up to the task of dealing with any attack.

But there was a danger neither of us had foreseen.

In all the time that Emily Jane had been trapped in her star, she had been dreaming one dream over and over: that her father would rescue her.

Lord Pitch had decided that imprisoning the pirates was a worse fate than death, so the Dream Pirates were confined to a planet-size prison on the other side of the cosmos. But they could still detect a dream no matter how far away and faint it might be.

They had heard Emily Jane's dream.

At first it had puzzled them. How could this be? *The child of Pitch died in a raid years before,* they thought. But every night they heard the dream again and again, and after a time they realized the dream was indeed coming from Lord Pitch's daughter. So they hatched an awful plan.

The Dream Pirates knew how badly the loss of his family had wounded Lord Pitch. And he was their one and only jailer. He guarded the single door into the prison that held them; it was such a grim and dark place. Made from giant plates of dark matter, it was a place where no being from outside could ever hear or feel any pirate who coiled inside. Only Lord Pitch could hear them faintly. He had volunteered to be their single guard. He felt he had nothing left since the loss of his family.

The Dream Pirates, with the help of the other dark creatures imprisoned with them, listened each night to Emily Jane's faint dream until they knew the sound of her voice and could imitate it. Then, one awful night, they huddled next to the single door and whispered to Lord Pitch, in his daughter's voice, the one thing they hoped would set them free. "Please, Daddy. Please, please, please open the door."

Emily Jane? he thought to her. He pulled the silver locket from his tunic pocket and stared at the photograph inside. He did not stop to wonder how she could possibly be inside the prison.

"Daddy, I'm trapped in here with these shadows, and I'm scared. Please open the door. Help me, Daddy, please."

What father could ignore such a plea? Lord Pitch opened the door, his aching heart suddenly hopeful that Emily Jane was somehow alive and near enough to be saved.

He opened the door and sealed his doom.

The Dream Pirates poured out and enveloped him. The cold, calculated betrayal was more than any being could withstand. The locket fell from Lord Pitch's neck. With his hope shattered, his heart withered and he died inside. At first he resisted valiantly, but there was no fight left in him. Numb and utterly empty, he let the dark creatures take his soul. And they did—they possessed him completely.

He became their leader, their king, their warlord.

With Lord Pitch as their general, the Golden Age had lost its greatest strength, its greatest ally. And so began the awful second War of the Dream Pirates, and Pitch was proving unstoppable.

But now he could hear Emily Jane's dream. He had ten times the wicked thirst and need for dreams as his pirates. And her dream haunted him and fed his new hunger.

All this had happened without our knowing. Emily Jane's newfound hope was like a beacon, drawing evil and awfulness toward us.

CHAPTER FIFTEEN

The Most Bitter Reckoning

The first harpoon that hit us came as a surprise, but by the second and third, I was fully awake and Emily Jane was already charging the Dream Pirate galleon that had fired upon us. It was a massive vessel—tarnished, ragged, and beastly to behold.

Its decks were swarming with Dream Pirates, who fired harpoon after harpoon with withering swiftness. But Emily Jane displayed amazing agility at dodging their rusted dagger points and using her blazing tail to burn us free of the first harpoons that hit.

She was heading straight for the ship's bow,

her star fires flaming with determination. I braced for our impact, but the pirate galleon swerved to port at the last instant. We shaved so close to the ship, we could see the shadowy faces of the grisly crew who leered and taunted us as we passed. At the ship's helm stood its captain, tall, gaunt, and unmistakable. It was Lord Pitch himself. Or at least what he had become.

His skin was now a spectral white, his eyes dark and soulless; he was a creature to be feared.

For Emily Jane, this was a shock beyond all reckoning. Her father had arrived at last, but now he was a nightmare come to life.

Then Pitch shouted out to me. "Ahoy, Dream Master!"

I tried to slow Emily Jane, so I could better hear Pitch's hail, and though she pulled against me, she yielded to my maneuver.

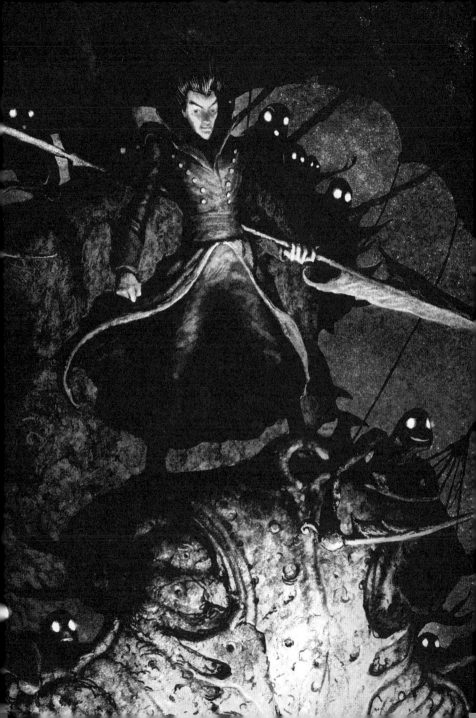

"Why do you send this dream of my dead daughter to plague me?" Pitch shouted again.

Before I could send him an answer, Emily Jane implored, her voice trembling with terror, "Please, be careful what you say, Captain Sandy. He is so changed. We can't know what to expect."

I sent this thought, taking care with my words: *The dream this vessel sends you, it is no plague! It is a dream of hope!!*

"I have no hopes!" he bellowed. His voice was edged with rage. "This dream you sent is what killed my soul and made me what I now am! DEATH, I say, to who made me thus!"

Emily Jane had never backed down from a fight. But she understood the madness of rage. Her rage at this man had driven her to the brink of despair. But she had pulled back. Could he? He had not seen her since she was a little girl. If she were free from her star, would he recognize her? Would his hate die as hers had? In an instant her instincts told her a grim truth.

"We must run, Captain Sandy," she said. "I can feel it. If he finds me, we both shall die."

Go then, I agreed. *As fast as you ever have.*

Away we flew. But Pitch's harpoon men were too skilled and quick. Before we could get out of range, a dozen of their weapons slammed into us, their chains linking us to Pitch's galleon. Emily Jane frantically tried to burn them away, but as one disintegrated, three more ensnared us. Our speed no longer mattered, for now we pulled the galleon with us. The pirates winched the chains and inched their malevolent ship closer and closer.

I had fought the Dream Pirates time and again and had never been defeated, but never before had they been led by Pitch. I'd never encountered such fury. But Emily Jane swerved and breached with a power that even Pitch's galleon could not contain. With one great last buck, she snapped free of the chains and we tumbled away.

We spun and spiraled at speeds beyond

endurance. I remember seeing a small green and blue planet just ahead of us. I could barely stay conscious. I knew we would crash. I could hear the wishes of children coming from the planet, so I pulled at my controls. We must crash over water so as not to harm any child. I could no longer feel or sense Emily Jane. As we plummeted toward a vast ocean, I did hear one thing: a single wish above all the others. It was bright and clear.

"I wish you well" was all

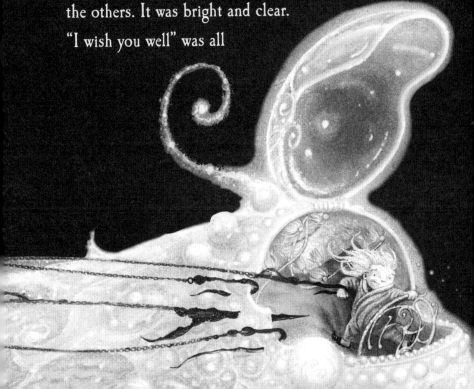

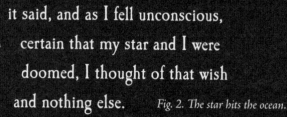

Fig. 1. The star falls.

it said, and as I fell unconscious,
certain that my star and I were
doomed, I thought of that wish
and nothing else.

Fig. 2. The star hits the ocean.

We skipped across the ocean's
surface like a giant stone, then
came to a spray of water, and
all went black for me.

I did not wake for many,
many years. When I did, I
found that my star was shattered,
pulverized into a sandy island. I was awakened by
that same voice that had comforted me all those
years ago, the voice that had wished me well. It
turned out to be your Man in the Moon.

And so it is I come to
you, with the Moon's
instructions. I will help

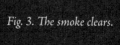

Fig. 3. The smoke clears.

you save your friend, Katherine, and fight Pitch. But to do so, I must finally see the girl who lived in my star, Emily Jane, daughter of Lord Pitch and the one you call Mother Nature.

Fig. 4. The star is now the Island of the Sleepy Sands.

CHAPTER SIXTEEN

Oh, What a Mysterious Morning!

AND AS SANDY REACHED the end of his story, everyone awoke from the dream. They blinked their eyes and roused, surprised to find that it was morning. Those who had fallen asleep while floating in the air around Big Root awoke in their usual beds and under the covers. North was in his customary Cossack bed shirt and sleeping cap. His trusty elfin men were on the floor in a row at the foot of his bed. They snorted awake like a litter of young piglets. Bunnymund was all comfy in his egg-shaped bed, which he always traveled with, his head propped up by half a dozen egg-shaped pillows. He was wearing satin pajamas with matching ear warmers that had small egg-shaped pompoms dangling from the tips. Bunnymund lifted the egg-shaped patches that covered his eyes and gave his ears a wake-up shake.

Ombric was, of course, roosting in his huge globe, surrounded by his owls. They woke in unison, as always, though Ombric did not hoot as he usually did. Toothiana found herself perched in a marvelous twig structure that hung like a bell from one of the limbs that formed the top of Big Root's canopy. It was the perch she had back in Punjam Hy Loo. *How has it arrived in Santoff Claussen?* she wondered.

The children were in the same place they had started the evening, at the top of Big Root, nestled next to Kailash in her gigantic nest. They looked around, utterly perplexed. The Dream had seemed so real. Yet here they were, feeling rested and ready, but for what, exactly? The host of their dream was nowhere to be seen. Nightlight stood up and looked at the spot where Sandman had hovered. There was nothing. Not even a grain of sand.

Mr. Qwerty peered at his pages. They were filled—the entire dream had been written down, and at the very end was a tiny drawing of Sandman.

Nightlight gazed at the illustrated page. He was unsure what to think about what he saw. But he reached out and touched the sparkling sketch. The drawing was made from a sort of sticky sand. It had been left by Sandman himself!

Golden grains clung to Nightlight's fingertips. He looked at them closely. He could feel the magic in them. Then he had a sort of flash of memory, of a song from so long ago: *Nightlight, bright light, sweet dreams I bestow. . . .*

"Is there a message there, Nightlight?" Petter asked.

Nightlight closed his eyes and held his sand-covered fingertips to his forehead. The sand told him many, many things.

Nightlight rarely, if ever, spoke—only the direst of circumstances could compel him to use his mesmerizing, otherworldly voice. So it was all the more alarming when he quietly replied: "Only that he's gone to help Katherine. And that none of us should follow."

CHAPTER SEVENTEEN

Nightlight Dawns

THE FIVE GUARDIANS WERE in a full frenzy for the rest of the day. Or more accurately, Ombric, North, Bunnymund, and Toothiana debated all morning while Nightlight remained still and quiet. He watched his friends study grain after grain of Mansnoozie's sand under a never-ending array of magnifying glasses, microscopes, spyglasses, cosmic ray detectors, and even a crystal-clear egg that Bunnymund assured them could pinpoint the precise origin of the sand and its exact age. It did neither.

After hours of testing and studying, the only

conclusion they came to was that this sand was . . . well . . . sand. It obviously had magical properties, but what exactly were those properties, and how were they triggered?

No one knew. And so they argued on, about everything. Whether to try to follow Sandman. How to follow him if they ever could agree to follow him. Where he might have gone and what to do if they found him. Should they split up and try to find Katherine? Should they call the Lunar Lamas? Should they try to contact the Man in the Moon?

And, most irritatingly, why hadn't Sandman asked them to join him? They studied charts, they consulted clouds, they looked into the past, they tried to see the future, they grumbled and worried and fussed.

Though Nightlight remained silent, it was not

without purpose. He had not yet told his friends that he could "read" the sand. Which was not unusual. He spoke only if he thought it necessary. He was always curious about the ways of the "Tall Ones," as he called adults. He did not think of them as smart or intelligent. He thought of them in terms of other qualities, those things that made a Tall One "good": kindness, bravery, trust, fun. But if they were cruel, lied maliciously, or were mean? Then Nightlight viewed them as "bad."

North, Ombric, Bunnymund, and Toothiana were Nightlight's favorite Tall Ones. He understood that they were the "most good." And he understood that they had "knowing," which was his way of calling them wise. Then he thought about Sandman's dream story and the new Tall One—Mother Nature. Was Mother Nature good or bad?

Now that he knew her story, he was not sure. As a child, she had been kind and wild and brave, like Katherine. And like himself. But so much hurt had come to her. So much loss.

It had changed her. And it had changed Pitch.

Nightlight stared at his friends. They seemed changed too. Like they'd lost their knowing and bravery and tallness. Now all they did was "talk the loud," as he referred to arguments, and "do the nothing." This scared Nightlight.

He put his sandy fingertips to his forehead again.

The sand.

Just having it touch his brow made him feel calm and clear. Suddenly, he felt himself understand his friends' behavior. The sand had given him a bit of the "knowing." His friends—they were hurting too. Katherine being gone was hurting them so much that they were scared. Just like he was. And he hated feeling scared. And hated all this hurt. He hated it so much, he couldn't stand it any longer. He thought of the words of Katherine; stories that had washed away when Mr. Qwerty had cried. He could almost hear them from his pocket. It was as if Katherine herself was calling out to him. He had to do something.

He leaped up and slammed his staff on the floor as hard as he could, over and over till the room began to shake. The other Guardians stopped in midargument and looked at him with bewildered awe.

Now that he had their attention, he began to dart about the room in his faster-than-light way, herding them toward the center of the room.

"Hey, squirt," North harrumphed. "Who do you think you are? You can't shove—" Nightlight kicked the Cossack firmly in the rear, moving him along.

"He's gone mad!" said Bunnymund just before Nightlight grabbed him by both ears and yanked him into place.

"Or he's playing some sort of game," mused Ombric as Nightlight jerked his beard firmly and pulled the old wizard along with it.

Toothiana began to see what the boy was up to. She moved to the room's center without any coaxing.

There they stood as Nightlight had insisted, in a sort of circle looking at one another, perplexed and curious about what the boy was up to.

Nightlight now sat cross-legged on the floor in the center of them. He held up Mr. Qwerty and turned the magical book's pages slowly. Then, when he found the right spot, he stood and thrust the book close to each of their faces.

Those four—those magnificent four, the bravest

and most wise of all the Tall Ones who had ever lived, these guardians of the worlds of children—stood sheepishly as a boy (admittedly a magical boy, but still, a mere boy) showed them what Sandman's sand was capable of doing and how to unlock its magic.

Nightlight held his sandy fingertips to his lips and blew. The sand drifted toward them, and as it sprinkled around their eyes and faces, for the second time in twenty-four hours, the four instantly fell asleep. In perfect unison, they teetered, teetered some more, then fell backward onto the floor. They were snoring before they'd landed.

Nightlight again pointed to Mr. Qwerty and said to his napping friends, "Katherine's story! Her life! Her hurts! HER! That's what we save. Remember your knowing. Be stronger than the scared and the hurt, and *dream* a way to save our Katherine!"

Then Nightlight spoke to Mr. Qwerty: "Be writing what just happened on your pages, Mr. Q. That today Nightlight, the boy Guardian, had the knowing of a Tall One."

That's the most Mr. Qwerty, or anyone, had ever heard Nightlight say.

And though Ombric, North, Bunnymund, and Toothiana were away in the land of dreams, they could still hear him. And in their sleepy minds they each were in agreement that what Nightlight had told them was exactly what they needed to hear.

CHAPTER EIGHTEEN

Do Be Afraid of the Dark

KATHERINE WAS SURROUNDED BY total darkness. She could see nothing. She couldn't tell if her eyes were open or shut. She tried to blink but wasn't even sure if she'd succeeded—in such darkness, it was impossible to tell. She then attempted to flash her hands back and forth in front of her eyes, but she realized she couldn't move. Her brain was telling them to move, but they didn't budge. And then she realized that nothing would move—not her legs, not her toes, not her smile. She tried to cry out, but nothing happened.

Strangely enough, she didn't feel afraid . . . yet.

Then she began to hear voices . . . low murmurs of speech . . . a little louder than whispers . . . She couldn't make out any of the words. . . . It was just an unnerving babble . . . of wordlike sounds. The voices were deep and menacing . . . mocking . . . as if amused by her being trapped—

It hit her. She was *trapped*. But where? By what?

The voices came closer. She still couldn't grasp what they were saying. But then she recognized a different sound. Crying. It was a girl crying. The other voices were becoming quieter, and she could hear the crying more clearly. . . .

Then Katherine became afraid.

That was her voice crying. But it was the strangest sensation—the crying was somehow separate from herself, as if behind a wall. Then she heard an actual door opening. Light, white with brightness, began to shine in front of her. It was coming from the opening doorway, and she could see the room inside. It was so bright. Almost blinding. Then she began to make out a shape sitting on the floor. It was a girl.

It was her!

But she looked older. *How can this be?* This older Katherine's crying continued. It sounded like a young woman's.

Her clothes were faded and nearly rags. *Why?!*

And in her hands was . . . *Mr. Qwerty! Good!!*

She saw herself start to turn the pages, one by one by one, from the beginning. This Katherine was reading the book very intently, but as she finished a page, a dark hand reached out and tore the pages from the book. She glimpsed her entire history as it was taken away. There was one set of drawings that she could clearly make out. The images she had made for North for his city of the future. She watched her older self close the book and close her eyes. She was going to sleep. She looked unspeakably sad. Tears escaped from her closed eyes.

Then the sounds of the murmuring voices grew louder. . . . They came closer to Katherine, and closer, till it seemed as if they were inches from her . . . just next to her ears . . . They mumbled on and on . . . then began to laugh . . . She could feel breath against her ears and cheeks . . . but she couldn't see . . . Who was it?! What was this awful language? The door—the door allowing the light in—began to slowly close. The bright glow of that other room, the only light, began to vanish. But then she realized it wasn't a door closing, but Pitch himself blocking out the light. He held the pages of her book in his one good hand. He looked at them gleefully and began to laugh.

This is like a nightmare, Katherine thought. And her fear deepened. *This* is *a nightmare,* she realized. Her fear swelled then because she knew—she could *feel* it: She was caught in a nightmare from which she could not awaken.

CHAPTER NINETEEN

A Dream within a Dream . . .

NICHOLAS ST. NORTH DIDN'T realize he was asleep on the floor of Ombric's library in Big Root. The Dreamsand had felled him in midthought, and it was such an odd thought. He was thinking of Nightlight and what in the world the boy was doing. But at the same time he had been briefly distracted by Bunnymund's ears. One of them was definitely longer than the other—by about three-quarters of an inch—then BAM! He was asleep, and while he could still hear Nightlight talking, it was as if the boy were a thousand miles away . . . Something about Katherine . . . about saving her.

And so that's where his mind began to wander as he dreamed—to Katherine. He saw bits and pieces of his time with her. How she had tended his wounds when he was so near death after his fight with Pitch and Bear. How she had brought him out of his bitter, lonely shell. How the two of them had saved each other time and again. Then he dreamed of Nightlight. Of the enchanted friendship between Katherine and the spectral boy.

He was worried, though. Katherine was growing up, but could the same be said of Nightlight? He was an otherworldly creature who never changed; he never grew taller or thinner or fatter—even his hair didn't grow. He'd been a young boy for who knows how long. This was troubling, and then more so as

North's dream began to darken. He saw Katherine becoming older, and growing. Then Nightlight seemed to vanish, to fade away into nothing, and as he did, Katherine's eyes closed. Darkness folded around her like a shroud, a shroud that became Pitch's cape. Then Pitch's face appeared atop the cloak and began to spin faster and faster, making a dreadful sound, a most awful sound, a squealing, screeching, laughing sound. North felt terrified. He felt far away. He felt helpless.

Then, like a bright bolt, everything changed.

Now Katherine was standing over him. Her face was huge. This seemed familiar. . . . It was! It was when North had been turned into a toy by Pitch during the battle at the Himalayas: Katherine had picked him up, held and protected his tiny paralyzed body, and dreamed a dream that had saved him: the dream of his future. The dream had been so glorious. So beautiful. He would build a great city of snow and ice, and it would be filled with magic and good works. It would be like Santoff Claussen, but on a grand, magnificent scale. In bright, brief flashes, he saw Katherine's dreams for him more clearly than he ever had before; he saw it as a reality, of what *could* be: There was a great tower—a polelike spire that rose up from the center of this city—and from this pole, lights would shine out into the world....

And now—now he could clearly hear Katherine's voice urging him to "build this place.... It will destroy Pitch. . . . It will save me." Then she said the words they all used, the most powerful words in all of magic: "I believe. I believe I believe."

Believe, indeed! North thought in the wakeful part of his sleeping mind. Katherine was sending him a message from wherever she was being held—he just knew it! It was as strong as any feeling he had ever had. Nightlight had told him to find a way to save Katherine. But he hadn't had to find it. It was being sent to him. By the bond of their friendship, Katherine was telling him how to save her!

He fought now to awaken. But that dratted Dreamsand was so very powerful.

CHAPTER TWENTY

Of Dreams and Relics and Powers Unsuspected

DREAMSAND WAS INDEED POWERFUL, but when the Guardians share an identical dream, the power of their struggle to wake up was even stronger. They had all felt as if Katherine was reaching out to them by sending this dream. So they roused themselves, shaking the sleep from their minds and rising with a cry—a unanimous call to action.

"This dream must be made real! For Katherine's sake and for the good of all," proclaimed Ombric. He felt reenergized. He felt like the Ombric of old. He quickly thought through all the possibilities and circumstances. He nodded to himself as he pondered.

First, this Sandman fellow had gone to help Katherine and insisted they not follow. Now they had their first message from her since she'd been abducted. Ombric nodded once more. Sandman must be making progress. And so the choice was obvious: The city of North's future must be built. Ombric wasn't yet sure why or how, but he knew it would somehow be Katherine's salvation.

He looked up to see his fellow Guardians all nodding along with him, agreeing with the very same thoughts they themselves were having. They all knew what had to be done. It was bold. It was ambitious. It was unlike anything they had ever attempted. A new city had to be built. And an old one changed.

Toothiana flew to the knothole window of Big

Root. "No time can be lost," she called down to the whole village, then she sent out her bright, musical call, singing all the way to Punjam Hy Loo. "The magic elephant must come and help," she added. She called out once more, cocked her head as if listening to the wind, and then, with one flap of her wings, she filled the air around the village with legions of her tiny flying warrior helpers.

Bunnymund tilted one ear appraisingly, then tapped his foot four times on the floor. Within seconds, hundreds of Warrior Eggs popped forth from fresh tunnels surrounding the outer edge of the thick forest around Big Root. They scurried toward Ombric's home on sticklike legs. "The creatures of the air will need help from those of the earth," the Rabbit Man explained wryly.

Ombric took this all in approvingly. He held his

staff aloft. "Guardians!" he boomed out. "Place your relics together, my friends. This mission will require all of our powers!" His owls began to hoot madly, as if they could sense that something unprecedented was about to occur. Bunnymund held his staff against Ombric's, and the jeweled egg on its tip began to glow. Toothiana took out her ruby box and joined it to the staffs. The glow shifted from pale to red, growing ever brighter, glistening. Then they all looked to Nightlight and North. Nightlight motioned for North to go next.

The valiant buccaneer kept his head down; he seemed almost . . . bashful. His voice was barely a whisper when he said, "You are indeed the truest of friends." He paused for a moment, overcome. At last he added, "That you would help make true this dream given to me—"

"My dear North," Bunnymund interrupted. "It is, I believe, a dream we share."

The Pooka's words were true. It was by now a dream that belonged to them all.

North grabbed his sword and swept its crescent-moon tip up to the other relics. The light of North's blade was almost too bright to look into. There was a moment's hesitation.

Ombric said what each of them had suddenly realized. "Will this work without the final relics?" There were five relics from the Golden Age that Tsar Lunar had told them were necessary to defeat Pitch, and they had only three.

Bunnymund's ears suddenly began twitching wildly in opposite directions. Then, just as suddenly, they stopped. "Nightlight!" he yelled. "Your staff! Its powers, combined with the power of Ombric's staff, might be enough . . . if my calculations are correct!"

The others agreed and urged Nightlight closer. But Nightlight resisted—he knew they were wrong. Yet they needed convincing, so he walked up to them and raised his staff up to the other relics. Its diamond tip did indeed begin to glow. The moonbeam that lived inside—his moonbeam, sent by the Man in the Moon himself—flickered and shined brighter than ever. But it was not what was needed. Nightlight could feel the worry and disappointment of his friends as their collective light failed to grow brighter, despite the addition of Nightlight's staff.

"It's still not powerful enough!" Ombric said in a strained voice.

Nightlight felt frustrated. His fellow Guardians were all so knowing, but sometimes they failed to see the most obvious things. Or forgot to look.

Again only Nightlight's childish mind could understand the truth, but if Sandman had been brought to them by Tsar Lunar, then surely he had brought with him something invaluable to the Guardians. *If Sandman was from the Golden Age, then so was his sand.* Nightlight took up a few grains of Sandman's sand and blew it into the light of the relics.

A flash as bright as a dozen suns filled the room instantaneously. At that moment Katherine's dream for North began its journey from the dimension of dreams to the realm of the real.

In the same moment, every other tree in the forest began to uproot itself. Every other creature from Santoff Claussen began to be affected by the magic that was washing through the village. They began to feel that something amazing was about to happen to them.

Half of this wondrous place would make the journey; the other half would stay and hold.

Friends old and new would be separated. But for the good of all.

CHAPTER TWENTY-ONE
◆
Another Nightmare

KATHERINE WAS RUNNING. SHE was in a forest. It was night. There was a bright moon, which made seeing easier, but it also made the shadows even denser and darker in contrast. There was no wind at all; the air lay thick and heavy all around her. There were no insects singing or the usual low commotion of a forest at night. Just an unnerving quiet. The only sound was her footsteps on the grass.

And the sound of the Thing that was pursuing her.

It seemed as though she'd been running for days. Even though she was going as fast as she could, her feet were as heavy as lead. She could barely raise them. She heard the Thing coming behind her. Its movements were smooth and agile. It was coming closer, and quickly.

She had to hurry! Why were her feet so leaden? She seemed to be slower with each step.

She'd glimpsed the Thing, but only for a few fractured instants as it moved from leafy shadows into the moonlight, then back into shadow. Light. Shadow. Light. Shadow. A horrible flickering. Never long enough to see the Thing clearly. It was a squirming, lumpy mass, as big as Bear, but not like a bear at all. Not like anything she could name. It was coiled and knotted, like a tangle of giant snakes, but there was an arm too; a man's arm, Pitch's arm, coming from the Thing's center, clawing at the ground and pulling it forward. Large snaky tails, each as thick as a small tree trunk, twisted out from the main mass, helping the arm move its bulk over rocks and roots with a disturbing ease.

Katherine was desperate to get away from the Thing. She had to go faster. But her feet grew heavier still. Stepping over tree roots grew harder, then almost impossible. The Thing was getting closer.

Ahead was a small clearing where the ground was level. Katherine willed herself to reach it—maybe she could run faster from there. She staggered toward it. The sound of clawing behind her—a lean whisper of slithering—was getting closer. Now she didn't dare look back.

She reached the clearing. Her first dozen steps were a victory; swift and strong, she was gaining speed!

Her feet were light now; she was running! She

could feel the strength surging through her legs as they quickened their pace. She felt revitalized, as if she could run like this forever. Fists tight, she pumped her arms up and down in perfect rhythm with her stride.

Up ahead there was a huge tree. It looked familiar. It was Big Root! Faster! FASTER! If she could just make it to the door, she knew she'd be safe. She tried to call out—someone would hear her, help her.

"Nightlight!" she gasped, but she was too winded. She didn't dare slow down. The Thing was right behind her. It would catch up. She tried again, "Nightlight, help!" But her voice was barely a gasp. Faster. Faster. Faster.

Then her foot came down onto ground that was like mud—softer even. Her leg sank past her knee; her next desperate step went even deeper. She tried to push herself forward, but it was no use. She was sinking.

She could hear the Thing hurrying behind her. She was too afraid to look. She was sinking quickly. She struggled to free herself from the sucking mud, looking yearningly at Big Root all the while. The tree began to pull away from her. How could that be? The distance between them—the ground itself—began to pull up into the air. Were her friends leaving her?

The Thing. She didn't dare turn around, but she knew it was only steps away. As it covered the last bit of distance between them, she heard it reach the mud. It couldn't be more than ten feet away. Five. She closed her eyes. It did no good. She could still see the Thing in her mind. Then she felt the hand of it on her collar.

She tried to scream. But nothing came out. Not even a whimper. If her friends could only hear her, they would come. They always had. Why couldn't they hear her?

CHAPTER TWENTY-TWO
◀•▶
At Last a Kind Wind

Sanderson Mansnoozie had been extremely busy. He had scoured the entire planet searching for Katherine with no success.

He had not searched in any conventional manner. He did not prowl about actually looking with his eyes to find her. Nor did he ask people or creatures if they had seen her or noticed anything unusual that might lead him to her. He could have asked any passing cloud about her—he had the ability to communicate to clouds and to other natural phenomena, such as wind and rainbows, but he knew they would not tell him a thing. He'd come to realize they were under the influence of Emily Jane. Of course, they did not know her by that name. They only knew her as Mother Nature. In fact, he was sure they were watching him and reporting to her his every move.

He was not entirely surprised by this. The many tragedies of Mother Nature's previous life had turned her into a solitary and mistrustful being. It wasn't unexpected that she had watchers everywhere. Still, he hoped that if she were being informed of his whereabouts, their old friendship would perhaps spur her to contact him—and hopefully help— but so far no such gesture had come. This did not surprise him either, for even as a girl, she didn't often reach out to others. There were some crea- tures that were willing to tell him what they knew of how Emily Jane became this nature matriarch.

Sea creatures were more sympathetic to his mission. Especially seashells and mermaids. They had become familiar with Mansnoozie and his island during his long sleep and had watched over him. They saw what had happened when his island had first formed. They'd seen the explosion of his star, and the girl who had been freed by its destruction. They too did not know her as Emily Jane. To them she had no name at all. But they saw the power she had over wind and clouds and natural phenomena. They saw her use the magic she had learned from Typhan. But she remained a mysterious force to them. Always moving. Never resting. Calm one day. Stormy the next.

So Sandy searched for Katherine the best way he knew how: by listening for her dreams.

Nearly every living thing has dreams. Dogs, frogs, gazelles, centipedes, guppies, and certain plants, such as dandelions and weeping willows. Sandman could hear the dreams of every creature—and every person—on Earth. He was certain he had not heard Katherine's. The dreams of the Guardians were distinct from any other dreams he had ever encountered. Not only were their dreams extraordinarily vivid (they had a lifelike clarity unlike any others), but he could also tell that the Guardians had the ability "to dream-share"—their minds could bond while dreaming. But in Katherine's case, that bond had been damaged, and now, perhaps, destroyed. Even creatures as powerful and mysterious as Pitch or Mother Nature had dreams, though Sandy had no clue what those were like; they both had successfully blocked his efforts to read them. But he could still feel the distant presence of their dreams, so he knew they were somewhere.

He also knew North and the others had received a dream from Katherine while he had been searching for her. He had felt their dreams while they experienced this message from Katherine. But he had not *felt* this dream. How could that have been? He was suspicious of Katherine's dream, even though it seemed to be of good intent. How had she sent it? Or *had* she sent it?

For with Katherine, he could feel nothing. Only one thing could stop a person from dreaming, and this was what worried Sanderson Mansnoozie as he sat drifting over the Earth on his cloud of Dreamsand. He was trying to avoid asking the question he most dreaded, but the time had come: Was Katherine no longer alive?

The thought was so dark and sad. Though he had not met this girl, he had heard her dreams many times during his great sleep. So he knew how extraordinary she was.

Could Pitch have been so evil as to end her?

Sandy felt sadness well up inside him, and his cloud of Dreamsand began to drizzle. It was a light rain made of drops of pure sorrow. *That poor girl,* he thought. *As alone and lost as Emily Jane . . . and now perhaps lost forever.*

Dense, dark clouds began to form spontaneously and billow toward him. They were gigantic and storm-like, but they held no wind or thunder. Once Sandman was fully encircled by the storm, he heard a familiar voice bloom around him. It came from the clouds.

"I can stand anyone's tears but yours." It was Emily Jane Pitchiner, now the Queen Mother of Nature! "Besides, I control the rain here. Hold on, I'll send you to the girl."

She will take me to the girl, Mansnoozie thought as relief flooded to even the tiniest grain of sand in his being. *Katherine must be alive!*

He looked up into the cloud nearest to him as it began swirling ever more tightly, narrowing into a sort of tunnel. For the briefest moment, he saw Emily Jane standing at the opening. Her majestic robes whirled around her, and it seemed as though they were what powered the clouds. He felt a deep satisfaction at seeing her at last. She had grown up without his realizing it. Even more gratifying was knowing that his time with her had left some echo of kindness in her soul.

He nodded gravely to her, and she returned the nod. Old friends sometimes need no words to understand each other. Then her winds guided him swiftly up and away, toward Katherine.

CHAPTER TWENTY-THREE

A Dream That Becomes Real

THE COMBINED POWER OF the three relics with the Dreamsand was extraordinary. Their collective energy was nearly nuclear, but smooth and efficient rather than destructive. A quadrillion molecules had been released, all with the intent of instantaneously transporting many of the vast resources of Santoff Claussen to a spot nearly halfway around the planet without damage or upset. Trees from the enchanted forest; books from Ombric's library; the bear; North's elves; dozens of forest creatures of every species, including a small herd of the mighty reindeer; Mr. Qwerty; the robot djinni; Guardians and their helpers—all found themselves in a wondrous frozen landscape.

But there was even more!

From the Lunar Lamadary came dozens of Yetis, the clock that could enable time travel, the magnificent flying tower—accompanied by a note from the Lamas:

May come in handy. Or perhaps useful. Or perhaps necessary. Or even essential. Or not. But perhaps.

Everything arrived and landed at its final destination according to a precise design that had been formulated in North's imagination. North was thunderstruck. He had been working on plans for this "New City to the North," as he called it, ever since Katherine first sent him his dream of the future. But he'd done so alone, during moments of quiet. He'd shown his fellow Guardians a paper model of the city, but that had been a simplistic thing, barely more than a childlike sketch. This . . . this was as if he'd witnessed part of his imagination unfold into reality.

Another reality was that where they had landed was cold. Very cold. They huddled together in a large group, looking around at the icy landscape that surrounded them. They were on a snow-covered peak— miles and miles of snow and glaciers spread before them in every direction. The towering cedar and pine trees from the enchanted forest that had uprooted themselves only a short time ago in Santoff Claussen had been magically replanted around the base of the peak, forming a wall around the city-to-be.

Ombric stroked his beard, cleared his throat, and looked at North inquisitively. His former apprentice had become a wizard of rather astounding accomplishments. And though the old wizard might never admit it aloud, in some ways, North was now more than Ombric's equal.

"Nicely done, my boy," he said. *Now, where exactly are we?*

North could tell that his old teacher was much impressed. In the past he'd have gloated and said something to vex the old man, but he knew this wasn't the time for that. They had the most important mission of their lives ahead of them, and time was short.

North swept his arms wide, as though to include everyone in his response. "We are at the magnetic pole of the northern hemisphere," he called out, loud enough for all to hear. "The first city of the new Golden Age will be here."

"The North Pole," Bunnymund murmured thoughtfully. "I remember when I first magnetized it. Good choice."

Toothiana, her troops, the Warrior Eggs, the Yetis, reindeer, and everyone seemed to agree.

Nightlight just smiled. He was glad to have helped, but he had plans of his own.

CHAPTER TWENTY-FOUR

Something Perhaps Worse

EMILY JANE AND SANDMAN arrived on their clouds at the entrance of a small cave outside the town of Tanglewood in the northeast part of a country called America. The surrounding forests were thick with craggy pine and hemlock, and a great many bats flittered through the trees and in and out of the mouth of the cave. An old, well-worn Indian trail led to the cave, and if Nightlight had been with them, he'd have remembered this dark and mournful place as the spot where Pitch had been frozen for centuries, pinned by Nightlight's diamond dagger embedded in his heart.

Emily Jane enshrouded both herself and Sandman within dense cloud cover so as not to be seen, then said to her old friend, "This is as far as I will go. He is, after all, my father—for good or ill."

Sandy nodded again. He never spoke except through dreams or thoughts. But he understood her reasoning. So he was surprised when she said more, giving voice to her fears.

"He promised me he would not make the girl his princess," she told him, "but he did something perhaps worse."

Sandy frowned.

"You'll see for yourself," she said, knowing Sandy so well, she knew his question without the asking. She took his hand just for an instant. "Be careful. Father is past saving and is now . . . savage, through and through."

Then she turned away hurriedly, her robes swirling around her. Within seconds, her cloud had billowed away into the night sky, taking her with it.

Sanderson Mansnoozie had faced countless dangers in his long and varied life, but this time he felt a fear that was darker than the depths of space.

CHAPTER TWENTY-FIVE

A Place of Endless Possibilities

THOUSANDS OF MILES AWAY at the North Pole, things were progressing with astounding speed and ease. A small but fantastic city was taking shape.

The varied talents of the Guardians and their allies were on full display. The strength of the Yetis, Bear, and the robot djinni had been put to great use in cutting and forming the ice and wood that would make up many of the city's fanciful structures. Toothiana and her tooth fairies zipped in and out of the towers and outer buildings, carving intricately ornate windows and doors through the solid ice walls.

Bunnymund was busy everywhere. From digging out massive blocks of ice to burrowing a network of elaborate tunnels that would connect every building in the city to the rest of the world, he was a blur of city-creating activity.

Ombric and North focused most specifically on the great central tower that would officially mark North's city. The centerpiece for this was the original flying tower of the Lunar Lamadary, and once they had it in place— a tricky maneuver that at

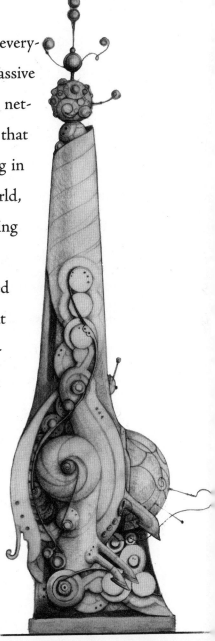

The North Pole

first seemed to defy the laws of gravity—they started in on building an extension to that older structure. They made it taller, bigger, and even more grand.

North had it all planned out: This tower would become a beacon to the world. It would generate a multicolored shimmering of light that could reach almost to the heavens and that he had already named the "northern lights." These lights would be capable of sending forth all sorts of messages to the Guardians and their allies, no matter where on Earth they might be.

Additionally, the tower's precise placement would enable North to see any part of the planet beyond. Best of all, it could also fly. Its transportive power was unlike any that had ever been since the old Golden Age. It could break past the Earth's atmosphere and fly out into the cosmos.

"Think of it, old man," North said to Ombric excitedly. "We will be able to visit the Moon. Meet Tsar Lunar himself! In person!"

Ombric was putting the finishing touches on the new library. All his knowledge, all his wisdom, he was now passing on to this most amazing young man, one whose start had seemed most dubious. The thought made Ombric feel both satisfied and perhaps a little sad. His pupil was now the master. But that's how it should be. He put his hand on North's shoulder.

"The Moon," he said quietly. "After we save Katherine, we'll go meet the Man in the Moon together."

They looked up into the sky. The Moon was just over the horizon. From where they stood, the possibilities were endless.

CHAPTER TWENTY-SIX

A Few Rich Ticks of the Clock

SANDERSON MANSNOOZIE WAS A luminous being. He was infused with shards of starlight, which made him glow rather brightly. This would be a problem if he was to sneak into the dark of Pitch's cave. The bats that clung to the bony tree limbs around the cave's opening noticed him the moment Mother Nature's clouds had left. He was dangerously exposed, and he knew it. The bats fluttered their wings and were about to sing out in alarm, but Sandy was quick. With the flick of one wrist, he sent a fog of Dreamsand that put every bat into a deep and instantaneous sleep. The creatures dropped from the trees by the hundreds, thumping lightly on the ground. There was a quiet hum of snoring bats as Sandy crept into the cave. The strange curling rocks at the mouth of the cave gave way to a long tunnel-like chute.

Sandy spotted something in the shadows, something wispy and dark. He whipped his right hand at it. A bullet of Dreamsand shot toward the thing. There was a light *pff* as the sand hit its mark. Sandy flew down to inspect the target. It looked like a Dream Pirate, only a bit smaller and somehow more vaporous. *One of Pitch's Nightmare Men*, thought Sandy. It was fully asleep and exactly what Sandy needed. He cloaked himself with the nasty, dark creature, completely covering his glow. Now he could proceed unseen.

The inky dark of the cave was nearly total, but

Sanderson Mansnoozie could make out the faintest light emanating from the floor below. He slipped past dozens of Nightmare Men without notice, leaving just enough Dreamsand in his wake to make sure they were put to sleep. This rescue would be difficult, and he needed every advantage in order to succeed.

As he came to the cave's bottom, the light grew only slightly brighter. Mansnoozie was very comfortable with darkness. He'd spent eons in the black of space, and he dwelled most of his time in the land of dreams with his eyes shut. In fact, the only real weakness he had was in staying awake. He could fall asleep with such ease and quickness that on occasion it was a problem. As he peered around the edge of the cave's tunnel and into its main cavern, he felt the telltale twinges of sleepiness starting to lull him. He shook himself awake, not realizing that in just a few more steps he would see something that would jar him awake completely.

He found the source of the cave's only light. It came from a girl, a brown-haired girl who lay sleeping on a coal-colored slab of marble that had been carved into a coffinlike shape. *Katherine! It had to be!* And he could see that she was breathing—she was alive! But what was that around her? He crept closer. She was surrounded by an unearthly glow.

This glow fascinated him. It twisted and spiraled around Katherine like a living thing, and within it, he could see the shifting shapes of tiny Nightmare Men, dozens and dozens of them.

It must be some sort of shield, Sandy thought, feeling a deep unease. Was it to keep her dreams from getting out or to keep nightmares in? Perhaps it was both. Or perhaps it tripped some sort of alarm? He stepped back. He'd thought he knew everything there was to know about dreams, good or bad, but this "shield" had him stumped. He scanned the room. There was no sign of any other Nightmare Men or of Pitch. He was certain the room was empty except for Katherine. So he cautiously lowered his Dream Pirate cloak.

If it's an alarm or a trap, so be it, he decided. *If I act quickly, I can get out of this cave before anyone can nab me.*

And so he crept forward once more.

Looking down at the sleeping girl, he saw that she had a lovely face, but her brow was furrowed, her expression almost tortured.

She's having a nightmare!

Then he looked closer. Small, glowing Nightmare Men were being sucked into her nose and mouth with each breath. His heart began to pound. *She has no*

way of waking! Pitch has doomed her to an eternity of nightmares! Sandy fumed. *The fiend!*

Heedless of potential dangers, he tried to reach through the glowing dome of nightmare light that surrounded Katherine, but his hand was deflected by a painful burst of energy. He snatched his arm back and cradled his blistered hand. He forced himself to keep his mind clear, to not lose his temper. To him, dreams were precious, noble things. Seeing them twisted into something evil was an abomination.

If Sanderson had grown more powerful during his centuries-long sleep, then evidently, so had Pitch. Sandy knew he'd have to be clever and quick to get Katherine from this place. He was certain he'd be discovered at any moment. But how to remove her? Any effort to break through this formidable shield of nightmares would take time and draw attention. Ideas bombarded him, but none were correct, and he was stymied.

He noticed a slight brightening of light behind him. *Pitch has caught me,* he thought, his heart sinking. Still, he spun around and shot streams of Dreamsand from each hand at whatever was sneaking up on him.

The darts of sand were deflected easily. And in the scattered dust Sandy saw not Pitch but Nightlight! Nightlight with his diamond-tipped staff in one hand and a fistful of just-caught Dreamsand in the other. The boy smiled at Sanderson Mansnoozie. Sandy was torn between feeling relief at not being caught and being a little perturbed. He felt he had been quite specific when he'd told the Guardians not to follow him. Still, he couldn't deny he was glad to see this strange, glowing boy. He also was very curious as to why the boy had not been affected by the

Dreamsand. Why had it not put him to sleep?

Nightlight had had an intuition that Mansnoozie might lead him to his Katherine and also that the little fellow might need a bit of help. He'd slipped away from the other Guardians at the North Pole and had been tracking the Dream Captain from a discreet distance, but he knew it was time to take action. Without saying a word, Nightlight leaped forward with his staff and slashed at the base of the coffin-shaped rock upon which Katherine lay. With a single stroke, the diamond-tipped staff cut through the stone completely.

Amazing, Sandy thought, looking on with surprise.

Nightlight enjoyed the little man's astonishment. As did the moonbeam in his staff. But the moonbeam suddenly sense danger. It flashed a warning to

Nightlight. The moonbeam remembered this place well; didn't his boy? The moonbeam had found Pitch here, pinned through his black heart to the very same rock upon which Katherine was now entombed. Pinned by the diamond dagger in which the moonbeam now lived. Nightlight's dagger.

Sanderson turned to the moonbeam, hearing its thoughts. He could see all the details of the memories that flooded through this brave little flash of lunar light.

And as Sanderson Mansnoozie listened, he became sleepy, then sleepier. And in one more blink he was dreaming the moonbeam's memories, about how the moonbeam came to be the light of Nightlight's staff and the amazing story of Nightlight himself.

It all happened in an instant, as thoughts and dreams often do, but what a rich few ticks of the clock this proved to be.

CHAPTER TWENTY-SEVEN

Of Nightlight and Moonbeam and the Power of a Good-Night Kiss

SANDY HEARD THE MEMORIES of the moonbeam exactly as the young light remembered them:

"I was tumbling down like," the moonbeam began. "Into this dark place. I sees things that first time, in the Cave Dark, all Shadowy and nightmare-like. The Cave Dark looks like now, 'cept the Pitch was there. On this same rock. The Nightmare Rock where he was trapped for all that time. That rock must have dust and darkness of the Pitch's hate living ins it still. Trapping Nightlight's Katherine. Making Nightlight's

Katherine dream the nightmares terrible over and over, on and on.

"The thinking of it is a cold horror. I'm remembering the last time. I felt that same cold. When I wents into the diamond dagger. The one that speared through the Pitch, through the Pitch's cold heart and into the stone and held the Pitch prisoner. Kept him so he wasn't alive or dead, just . . . There. All the while, inside the dagger was my boy Nightlight. Surrounded by the coldness awful. For almost longer than ever. It froze my boy. It made him still. And made his memories separate from him. But my light warmed him and wakened him and made my Nightlight boy free. He broke out of the diamond 'cause of me. He needed a bit of the Moon's light to make him strong again.

"But the diamond traps me as it does any

magical light that comes into it. But I'm not minding. 'Cause I know I helps the Nightlight be free. And he should be free. He's the hero of us all. But none really knows the all of his story. Only me. 'Cause his memories stayed here in the diamond. And I can feels them.

"Some knows he was a friend of the Man in the Moon. Some knows about his battling with the Pitch. But only I knows what came before: that Nightlight was the guard of the baby Prince of the Moon. The Nightlight was a special being. The only one there ever was. A boy of light who would live forever and never grow old. And he would always protect the royal young of the Golden Age, especially from nightmares. He would never sleep. And be always watchful.

"But he was doomed to a heartbreak. For though

he cherished and cared for the prince, there would be a sadness time when the prince would become grown and need him no more. And so sorrow would be his life until another child was born to rule, and then the joy and heartbreak would begin again.

"But Nightlight knows this and takes the burden, and every night he stayed and protected the sleep of the prince baby. Every night the Nightlight waited for the Mother Queen and the Father King to come give the kiss good night to their prince. The Magic Kiss of the Good Night. So powerful is this kiss. Takes away all the hurts. Makes the scare and sad go to nothing. My Nightlight has that power too. But he don't know of it. He can't ever give it and stay a nightlight. But his magic is like the parents'. And when they leaves after the kiss, my Nightlight boy says his song:

"'Nightlight, bright light,
Sweet dreams I bestow.
Sleep tight, all night.
Forever I will glow.'

"Then he sprinkles Dreamsand over the prince and watches all the night. Every night. Never to sleep, my Nightlight boy. And he kills any nightmare from the Pitch that could do the princeling harm.

"But then the Pitch so terrible comes, and the Father King and Mother Queen, they know the Pitch will take their boy. To end the Golden Time, the Pitch must do away with the baby prince. So they give Nightlight an oath:

"'Watch over our child,
Guide him safely from the ways of harm. . . .

For he is all that we have, all that we are,
And all that we will ever be.'

"And all around the Pitch is battling terrible, and he captures the Mother Queen and the Father King. And Nightlight hides the prince, but the baby is fearful. The prince baby cries, and this hurts my Nightlight's soul. My Nightlight, he takes the prince baby's tears—he holds 'em tight like treasure next to his heart thumping, and he says the oath, and that makes a magic thing. My Nightlight's hand—the tears burn it, they burn till my boy can't stand it, but he does.

"And then the tears they change; the tears they become strong, the tears they become the diamond dagger. And my Nightlight knows that only he can use this dagger to end the Pitch. My Nightlight knows he will likely die and never see his prince again, so he whispers nice, so nice, to the prince baby, 'Remember me in dreams.' And he flies off to face the terrible, the Pitch.

"And stop him he finally does. And crash here they finally did. And Nightlight felt cold for longer than any should inside that cold heart of the Pitch. He still will never grow up or old, and all the ones he loves will grow past him and leave him, but he must always stay the same. But he 'members almost none of this. Which is my doing. I held on to his memories. So he wouldn't know all his hurts. So he won't be made sorrowful. So me and now you knows of how grand he is in the history of the brave and the good."

Nightlight Has a Memory and the Dreamsand Does Its Stuff

KNOWING THEY NEEDED TO make their escape, Nightlight leaned down to the fresh cut in the stone and opened his fist full of Dreamsand. He held it palm up and blew the sand with one gentle breath. The sand settled quickly into the slice, and once the last little grain had slipped in, the entire block of stone magically lifted a foot or so into the air.

But of course, thought Mansnoozie, having snapped awake as soon as the moonbeam's story had ended, making an instant connection. *Nightlight remembers the powers of Dreamsand, if nothing else.*

Sandy instantly added his own stream of Dreamsand, and soon a sparkling cloud formed under Katherine's stone bed, lifting it even higher. It was time to leave. They were certain to be seen now. Nightlight peered in at Katherine and felt an awful ache. She looked so sad. His beautiful friend was imprisoned in almost the exact same place where he had been. He hated the feelings this brought into his heart.

Sandy let the sand continue to stream forth, its glow brightening the room like sunlight. As Sandy had anticipated, alarms began to sound. The rumble of approaching armies of Nightmare Men and Fearlings rang out from every part of the cave.

Mansnoozie himself wasn't alarmed. He knew that the magic of the Dreamsand cloud was potent. And sure enough, in an instant the three of them flew up and out of the cave and into the evening sky.

They could already see traces of the northern lights of North's faraway tower, showing them the way to safety.

The Nightmare Men tried to follow, but a trail of Dreamsand put all of them to sleep.

Our heroes had made their escape. It had been fairly easy, really.

Pitch was nowhere in sight.

CHAPTER TWENTY-NINE

A Sea of Nightmares and a Helping Hand

KATHERINE WAS ASLEEP AND silent within the energy of the nightmare stone that was now being sped toward the North Pole. She could nonetheless tell that something was happening outside the nightmare world she'd inhabited for . . . days? Weeks? She had no way of knowing. Night, day, twilight—she was oblivious to the real world, for from where she now dwelt, it was always half past terrifying.

At least now she believed she'd been dreaming—that the terrors that hunted her were only nightmares. But they seemed so real. As sharp and true as life. And their fearfulness was just as strong. But something had changed.

In the dream she was now dreaming, she was on an endless and stormy sea. The water was as black as tar and the sky heavy and dim with clouds. She was floating in North's sleigh, but it was rotting in the water and slowly falling to pieces. The waves, huge and coming to mountaintop-like peaks, weren't cresting, but rather each one rose and fell at a continuous roll that was dizzying.

Floating past her were all the people and things she knew and loved: North's horse, Petrov; the giant bear of Santoff Claussen; all her young friends—Petter, Fog, Sascha, and all the Williams—but they were as stiff and lifeless as driftwood. They could not help her, nor she them.

More friends bobbed by: the Spirit of the Forest,

the Warrior Eggs, the owls, the reindeer, then Ombric, North, Bunnymund, Toothiana, and even her beloved Kailash. But not Nightlight. That was her only relief. At least Nightlight had been spared.

Then the dark, murky sky above her flashed and brightened, like an exploding star. She glimpsed a hand, a huge hand. It was visible for only a moment, but she was able to see it distinctly.

Golden colored, it glistened like sand. It was the first bright and hopeful thing she'd seen in all her nightmare journeys. She reached up toward it. It was so close. She lunged and just grazed the tip of one gigantic finger.

Then the hand vanished.

The sky darkened again, and the waves grew even more violent. But now there were dozens of small figures in the water around her. They were quite active, not frozen like the earlier wooden totems of her friends. These were unfamiliar, and they amused her. There were three mice wearing dark-lensed glasses, a dish and a spoon, a leaping cow. All of them happy whimsies, compliments of a friend and ally who knew just what might be needed in this dark place.

So Katherine wasn't fearful as a huge whirlpool began to form, drawing her crumbling sleigh into its swirling vortex. She would be sucked down, surely! The inky spray of the tumultuous sea soaked her and made her cold. So cold. It was Pitch! He was under this awful sea, waiting for her.

But through the dread that now flooded her, something gave her courage. Her hand tingled. The tips of her fingers seemed to glow, as if covered in something barely there. She looked closely. *Is it sand?* she wondered. There were just a few grains—three, four at the most. Then, in a blink, she thought she saw a funny little man who glittered like gold, and she could feel something else . . . Nightlight! Nightlight was near.

As the sea closed around, spiraling her down into its wake, she felt less alone. She knew that somehow, her friends were trying to rescue her. But, oh, the coldness! She could feel that Pitch was so close. She knew that murderous things were afoot.

CHAPTER THIRTY

Meanwhile, Back in Santoff Claussen

EVERYONE IN SANTOFF CLAUSSEN had been a little homesick. Oddly enough they were already home, but half the village was now at the North Pole. So the home half missed the gone half. Petrov, for example, missed his best friend, Bear. They had patrolled the edges of the village together for a very long time. Thankfully, there were others to keep the gallant horse company. Many of the children now rode him on his daily rounds. They had formed their own militia to guard the village. Sascha and Petter were the generals of this young troop. They had enlisted the other children and many of the remaining forest creatures as their captains and lieutenants. No one had a rank below captain, which was one of the fun parts of inventing your own army. The squirrels, chipmunks, beetles, ants, and butterflies all had new military-like uniforms with SC (for "Santoff Claussen") embroidered on their jackets. They had been sent by North himself and had arrived by the train tunnel that now linked Santoff Claussen to his city.

Every few days an Eggomotive train would arrive from the pole, sometimes to bring gifts, news, or returning visitors. The three Williams had just come back and told everyone tantalizing stories of how North's city was growing into the most beautiful place they had ever seen. An enchanted forest now surrounded the city, like the one around Santoff Claussen, but the trees were evergreens—they'd never lose their leaves and all were pointed, like giant cones.

"They are covered with tiny egg-shaped lights, crafted by Bunnymund," explained the youngest William to the others. The city itself sat atop a mountain of ice and snow and was sculpted from the same materials, at least on the outside. Inside, the palatial towers and pavilions, the floors and walls, were grown from sampled hunks of Big Root itself.

On the night of what was now named "the Great Migration," half of Big Root had been transported to the North Pole. But in Santoff Claussen this halving was barely noticeable, for the fantastic tree did not split in half; rather, it divided itself into two trees. Every other limb and root had formed over a new trunk. When the new tree flew away, the original Big Root simply shifted its remaining limbs and roots in a way that made it difficult to imagine that any part of it was gone.

The new Big Root at the pole had then grown itself to take the shapes of all the rooms, stairs, and furniture in North's plans. It was now the only city in history in which every wall, chair, ceiling, and door was alive and able to change upon command.

"If North or Ombric needs a chair, one will come running into place," explained Tall William.

"And North needs a much bigger chair now," added William the Almost Youngest. "He's gotten kinda fat!" They all laughed at the idea.

"The Yetis are great cooks," said Tall William.

"North loves their chocolate and vanilla Moon cookies," blurted William the Absolute Youngest. "White on one side, dark on the other."

"Just like the Moon?" asked Sascha.

"Yep," replied the youngest William. "And *all* good."

"And what of Katherine?" asked Petter.

The Williams glanced at each other. Tall William spoke first. "Ombric received a message just before we left. Sandman found her."

"Is she all right?" asked Sascha.

"We don't know for sure," said Not-as-Old William.

"They are bringing her to the pole," said Tall William.

"What's that?" asked Fog, scratching his head under his SC cap.

"The most magicalist place in the city of North," said William the Absolute Youngest with awe. "Its giant tower in the center of the city—it can do anything. It can even go to the Moon, they say."

That pronouncement drew a collective "wow" from all who listened, even the bugs and squirrels.

Above them, they then saw what looked like a slowly moving shooting star arc across the twilight sky. They looked at it curiously. It was bigger than a star, they realized. It was more like a small cloud. A familiar, slightly sleepy feeling came over them all. Then they knew.

"It's not a star, it's the Sandyman," said the youngest William.

"Yeah. And Nightlight," said Sascha. "They must be traveling with our Katherine!" There was a sudden feeling of hope and excitement among the group.

"Then we must wish them well," said Fog.

So they repeated the words that make all magic possible. The first magic words they had ever learned. The words they hoped would help Katherine.

"I believe, I believe, I believe."

CHAPTER THIRTY-ONE

The Power of the Nightmare Rock

SANDY AND NIGHTLIGHT WERE anxious to get Katherine to safety. Mansnoozie was worried that she had perhaps been trapped inside a nightmare for too long. That she might never recover from such a stream of horror. The black slab of Pitch's Nightmare Rock seemed to be devouring the Dreamsand cloud beneath it; Sandy was using an alarming amount of sand just to keep them flying.

At last they were nearing North's new city. The luminous northern lights ebbed and flowed around them in giant graceful waves. Sandy's fingertips still hurt from his brief attempt to break through the layer of nightmare energy that surrounded Katherine. He paused from spreading Dreamsand to look closely at his aching fingers. The Dreamsand at each tip was scorched with small black bruises that were starting to spread.

He'd never before encountered any nightmare that had had such an effect on his Dreamsand. An odd, sudden urge now compelled him to bring his fingertips to his ear—to listen. And what he heard astounded him. Tiny screaming voices! His Dreamsand was being turned into nightmare sand—each grain of blackening sand now held a nightmare!

As Sandy brought his hand from his ear, staring at the spreading black, thinking of what to do, Nightlight was still watching Katherine. For much of the journey, her sleeping face had been growing ever more peaceful, but now she looked terrified.

The dream cloud beneath them began to lurch and rock unsteadily. Nightlight glanced down. The bright golden sand was churning. Streaks of black began to appear throughout its billowing shape.

Nightlight turned to Sandy, but the little man was already grabbing at him. He jerked the diamond tip of Nightlight's staff to his blackening fingers and began to furiously scrape them. Each scrape peeled the nightmare sand from his fingers; within seconds, his hand was free of the spreading darkness.

But the scraped-away sand began to form into an entity—a small Nightmare Man. And all the sand beneath Nightlight and Sandy was darkening as the dream cloud grew more volatile. They could barely stand as it twisted and jerked, as if fighting for its soul. From both hands, Sandy shot streams of fresh sand into the cloud, but it blackened faster than he could send forth his sand.

They were directly above North's amazing city now, its dazzling lights shining up around them, but they were in desperate trouble.

CHAPTER THIRTY-TWO

Situational Chocolates

DOWN BELOW, THE OTHER Guardians and all the citizens of the new city watched in awe and alarm.

"Just when things seemed to be going so well," said Ombric, rolling up his sleeves and thinking through his list of fighting spells. He wondered if he was still up to the task. *This is for Katherine's sake*, he thought, and strength came roaring back.

"Time to do a little multiplication," said Queen Toothiana, fluttering her wings and clutching her ruby relic.

"Get my sleigh," North said to his elves.

"I believe this situation calls for a particularly potent chocolate," said Bunnymund. Chocolate had quite an effect on the Pooka. It could transform him in a variety of ways, all of them extraordinary. His ears were already twitching with anticipation.

CHAPTER THIRTY-THREE
Guardian Glory and the Peskiness of Gravity

THE CLOUD ITSELF BEGAN twining around Nightlight's legs and feet, trying to pull him into its blackness. Sandy made long whips of Dreamsand and began to snap them at every coiling tendril, shattering the dark attackers. Nightlight was equally effective with his staff. He stabbed and slashed at the black sand, hacking deep rips and troughs into any shape that threatened.

But the cloud was possessed now. It could change faster than Nightlight and Sandy could manage. It reached out and wrapped itself around that

magnificent pole North was building, sending the rock that Katherine lay upon pitching forward.

Sandy and Nightlight grabbed at the marble slab, trying to steady it, but each touch blasted them backward. The blackened sand beneath them began to change before their eyes; creatures by the hundreds began to form from the dark grains—a cloud of Nightmare Men. They clawed and stabbed at Sandy and Nightlight in numbers impossible to vanquish. The two fought on fiercely, cutting away at the tendrils that were twisting around the pole. But they were simply outmatched by the enemy.

Then, as they were beginning to lose hope, the sky around them filled with able helpers. Queen Toothiana and her warrior fairies. Ten thousand fairies! More! Arrows and swords hitting every mark!

At that point Ombric astrally projected himself

into twenty places at once and obliterated the clouds of Nightmare Men in each place!

And Bunnymund, his mighty ears twirling with the speed of a splitting atom, shot through the air like a bolt of lightning. He'd grown a dozen arms, and each held a sword made of meteor metal.

Then came North on his newly crafted sleigh of his own design, flying at the speed of light and pulled by a team of the Giant Reindeer from the forest of Santoff Claussen.

Together they smashed and blasted through the barrage of Nightmare Men with withering force. The power of the Guardians was awesome to behold.

But the moment of triumph vanished quickly.

The rock that held Katherine slipped through the faltering mass of Nightmare Men and fell with sickening speed toward the ground below.

CHAPTER THIRTY-FOUR

And So They Fell

THERE WAS NO DOUBT that Nightlight was the fastest boy who'd ever lived, but he was not the strongest. As Katherine, on her stone tomb, plunged, Nightlight speared the dense rock with his diamond dagger. Gripping his staff, he used every ounce of his flying strength to try to slow the fall. But not even a hundred Nightlights could have slowed a stone of its mass.

And so they fell.

Precious seconds passed as Nightlight tried desperately to smash his fist through the murky shield of nightmare energy that encased Katherine. At the same time his mind was racing, finding that place where time seems to slow and fate can sometimes lend a hand.

The shield. How to break through?! Can't use the diamond dagger. Could hurt Katherine. How to break? How?!

Bits of Sandy's dream cloud, the grains that had not yet been corrupted, still clung to the Nightmare Rock, stinging Nightlight in the face as they plunged. Several bits peppered his eyes and made him blink. There wasn't time to brush the grains away. They could not make the spectral boy sleep—Nightlight had never slept—instead they made him *remember*, just as the Sandman had predicted.

He remembered so much, so fast, all from his long-ago life with the Man on the Moon. Treasured moments flickered by like leaves in the wind. The oath he had taken, the song he sang every night to the young prince, and the Dreamsand. *Before the Dreamsand! What? What happened before the Dreamsand?* He knew it was important. It could show him how to save Katherine.

It was the most powerful thing of all.

It was stronger than dreams and nightmares, or diamond daggers made of tears, or actions bold and relics ancient.

It was the kiss.

The kiss of the good night. He remembered the Man in the Moon's parents. Every night they'd say good night and kiss the baby. Then he, Nightlight, would bring the Dreamsand to keep the nightmares away. *The kiss! It's magic. It takes away all the hurt of the day!* At least that's what they'd told him.

Would a kiss from me have any power? he wondered. There was just enough time to try.

Then valiant Nightlight, hero of so many battles, faced the most bewildering moment of his endless boyhood: a kiss.

How is it done?! What do I do? What if I do it wrong?! Something with the lips?! How?!

Just Go! GO!

He closed his eyes and lunged face-first toward Katherine. The nightmare shield gave way like vapor. Its powers only worked against force and fear. And a kiss is neither. It is a hopeful thing. For one eternal instant, Nightlight's lips touched Katherine's, and all of Pitch's dark spells were gone. Her eyes opened. Her tortured sleep was done. The Kiss made everything all right. Katherine was fine. There was no time for even a smile. Nightlight grabbed her hand and flew her away from the plummeting rock. And as it crashed to the ground, he glimpsed a gash in the stone. It was beneath where Katherine had lain. Just under where her heart had been. It was the hole his diamond dagger had left when, so long ago, it had pierced through Pitch and kept them both imprisoned and asleep for ages.

Nightlight felt Katherine's hand in his. He had saved her. And he had saved a part of himself, too—a part that had been forgotten. He had never felt more awake or alive.

CHAPTER THIRTY-FIVE

Growing Up Is an Awfully Big Adventure

WHEN IT LANDED, THE Nightmare Rock had blasted a crater of impressive size at the base of North's city, sending the Nightmare Men retreating. Then Mother Nature swirled up a tempest so strong, it sent them spiraling away and past the horizon. She gave a nod to them all from where she hovered and then flew away before anyone could say a word.

"Mysterious creature," remarked North. Sandy just smiled. He knew that better than anyone.

"One can seldom predict the weather," said Bunnymund. Then they turned their attention to

the fallen stone.
Though the cra-
ter was twenty
feet deep and
twice as big around,
the damaged ground
beneath it was made of
Big Root wood, so it instantly
began to restore itself. As the other Guardians gath-
ered around the disappearing crater's edge, the floor
began to level, the slab of black stone rising with it.
Since the Nightmare Men had retreated the moment
the rock hit the ground, the battle was, for now, over.

"And no sign of Pitch," said North, stroking his
beard.

"Not like him at all," Bunnymund added, sheath-
ing his dozen swords.

Toothiana flared her wings. "My human side says 'beware.' My other side says the same, but louder."

"We'll meet whatever comes," said Ombric philosophically. As he gazed up at Katherine and Nightlight, the weariness that had plagued him seemed to pass. Having Katherine back was a tonic to him. To all of them. "For now, let's bask in the victory of friends reunited!"

Hand in hand, Katherine and Nightlight floated down and landed gently beside the rock. The entire city rushed to the site, and there were cheers and instant jubilation. Katherine was safe! North immediately picked her up and hugged her tightly, his laugh now as deep as his waistline was thick.

"You've grown!" bellowed the Cossack.

"So have you." Katherine giggled as she poked her old friend in his now-ample belly.

"The hazards of Yeti cooking," explained Ombric, who joined in the hugging.

The Yetis were clustered nearby. Strangely enough, they were weeping like babies.

"They always do that when they're happy," chirped Mr. Qwerty, who paused from frantically writing everything down in himself so Katherine could read all about it later.

"That is *exceedingly* odd," muttered Bunnymund. "I mean, it's peculiar enough when humans cry, but Abominable Snowmen? That's a bit much."

"Oh, and twelve arms isn't?" countered North.

"I'd have grown one hundred and twenty arms to save Katherine," the rabbit replied curtly, then gave her a dozen simultaneous salutes.

"Is that all, Bunnymund?" asked Toothiana, smiling. "I made thousands of fairies."

The rabbit sniffed and wiggled his whiskers. "Hmm. I hate to say it, but you have a point, Your Highness." His ears twitched like mad. "I'll have to start working on a stronger chocolate. Now, if the ratio of cacao beans to each arm is four to one, then I'd need—"

Bunnymund's calculations were interrupted by Kailash, who waddled up between North and Katherine, honking like mad. Katherine was ecstatic to see her beloved Snow Goose. She hugged the massive bird's neck till Kailash pecked her.

The bustle of conversation was joyous and loud and went on till dusk. Katherine was in awe of North's city glittering around her. She gazed up at the turrets, admiring the exacting carvings and sculptural work, delighting over the colors—red and white stripes—North had chosen. And though Katherine was very happy to see it all—and them all—there was one to whom she very much wanted to speak. She looked through the crowd. Where was he?

But Nightlight knew.

As he brought Sandy through the excited group, Katherine motioned for the little man to come closer. He bowed as he neared her. She smiled at him, and he smiled back. His magnificent, peaceful smile. Though they had never actually met, they knew each other well. They were comrades from the land of sleep and dreams.

The other Guardians began to all talk at once.

"Ah!" said North. "Mansnoozie! At last we actually meet."

"Such remarkable sand," commented Ombric. "I am ashamed I didn't recognize it at once."

"I don't often dream, you know," Bunnymund

told him. "Pookas dream only one night in every thousand years. I do hope you haven't damaged my sleep cycle."

Toothiana smacked one of her wings across Bunnymund's left ear. "You don't have to say *everything* that comes into your head!" she whispered.

"Oh no, not you too," the rabbit said, groaning. "I have to have human lessons from you *and* North?"

But one by one, they all grew quiet. They once again knew what Katherine was thinking. The great link of their friendship had finally been restored. In the silence that surrounded them, Katherine looked at Sandy. He didn't say a word. *He's like Nightlight and me,* she thought. *He doesn't need to say much to be heard. His greatness was in his* doing. *He risked his life to save mine! Is there any greater gift?* She'd not heard his story, but from the other Guardians, she knew: He was one of them. And she knew exactly what was required.

"Kneel," said Katherine to the little man, her voice carrying out over the crowd. "And take this oath." Sandy kneeled before them.

Then they all said the Guardians oath together:

"We will watch over the children of Earth,
Guide them safely from the ways of harm,
Keep happy their hearts, brave their souls,
and rosy their cheeks.
We will guard with our lives their hopes
and dreams,
For they are all that we have, all that we are,
And all that we will ever be."

"From now on," said Katherine, "you will be known as His Nocturnal Magnificence, Sanderson Mansnoozie, Sandman the First, Lord High Protector of Sleep and Dreams, and Guardian to the Children of Earth. Rise, Sandy!"

Sandy rose. *I've traveled to every corner of the universe*, he thought. *But this is where I belong now.* The full Moon shined down upon them. Deafening cheers filled the crystal clear air. Katherine had returned. A great new city had been built. The Guardians were reunited and stronger by one.

The northern lights shimmered out from the North Pole and could be seen all the way to Santoff Claussen.

Nightlight looked out at North's beautiful new city, and for the first time in his ancient life, he felt he was no longer separate from these people he'd called

The city of North's dream

the "Tall Ones" and "Short Ones." He was no longer Nightlight, the boy without a past. Nor was he Nightlight, the boy of endless tomorrows. Tonight he was different. Villains had been vanquished. Spells had been broken. And new spells had been made.

Katherine and Nightlight stood together amid the cheering crowds. Their happiness was linked with everyone else's, but distinct. It was a private happiness that only the closest friendships know when they have weathered a great change. Nightlight took a small pouch from his pocket and

gave her the words of the stories that Mr. Qwerty had cried out of her book. He had saved her past and her present. And she his. But his future? That was now like all who grow up: a tantalizing mystery. As the moonbeam had told Sandy, he couldn't use the power of the kiss and stay a Nightlight. Change was coming. Nightlight could feel that. But he was not alone. Katherine once again took his hand.

CHAPTER THIRTY-SIX

Nightlight At Last Sleeps

THE CELEBRATION LASTED TILL very late, long past everyone's bedtime.

Good dreams were had by all. Even Nightlight. For the first time, the boy who never slept finally did. Such dreams! Mansnoozie was amazed by their power.

If only Nightlight hadn't slept.

He'd have been on watch, as he always was before.

He'd have seen Pitch crawl from his Nightmare Rock as it sat in the empty center of the city that was meant to bring about his end.

Pitch's plan was almost complete. He'd read all of Katherine's memories when she was under his nightmare spell. It was he who sent the dream of North's city to them. They had built everything as he had hoped. Unknowingly, the Guardians themselves had smuggled him into the one place he most needed to be. Now he could win this war once and for all. . . .

Also by William Joyce

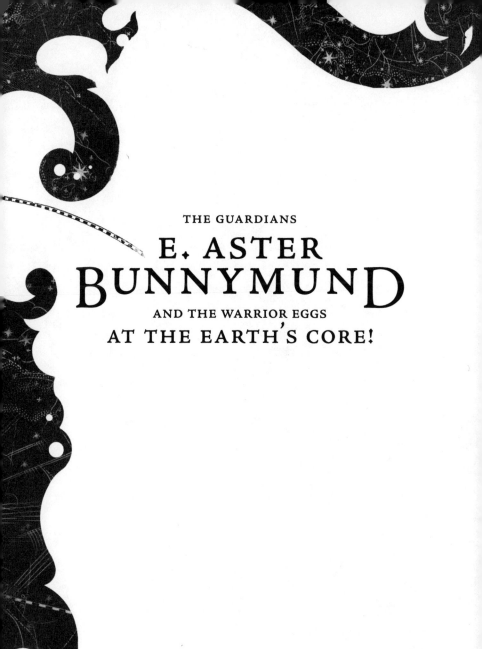

THE GUARDIANS

E. ASTER
BUNNYMUND

AND THE WARRIOR EGGS
AT THE EARTH'S CORE!

E. Aster Bunnymund, last of the Pookas

THE GUARDIANS

E. ASTER
BUNNYMUND
AND THE WARRIOR EGGS
AT THE EARTH'S CORE!

◆

WILLIAM JOYCE

Atheneum Books for Young Readers
NEW YORK · LONDON · TORONTO · SYDNEY · NEW DELHI

Atheneum Books for Young Readers
An imprint of Simon & Schuster Children's Publishing Division
1230 Avenue of the Americas, New York, New York 10020
This book is a work of fiction. Any references to historical events, real people,
or real locales are used fictitiously. Other names, characters, places, and incidents are products
of the author's imagination, and any resemblance to actual events or locales or persons, living
or dead, is entirely coincidental.
ATHENEUM BOOKS FOR YOUNG READERS is a registered trademark of Simon & Schuster, Inc.
For information about special discounts for bulk purchases, please contact Simon & Schuster
Special Sales at 1-866-506-1949 or business@simonandschuster.com.
The Simon & Schuster Speakers Bureau can bring authors to your live event. For more
information or to book an event, contact the Simon & Schuster Speakers Bureau at
1-866-248-3049 or visit our website at www.simonspeakers.com.
Book design by Lauren Rille
The text for this book is set in Adobe Jenson Pro.
The illustrations for this book are rendered in a combination of charcoal,
graphite, and digital media.
Manufactured in the United States of America
0812 FFG
First Edition
10 9 8 7 6 5 4 3 2
CIP data for this book is available from the Library of Congress.
ISBN 978-1-4424-3050-1
ISBN 978-1-4424-4991-6 (eBook)

———◄●►———

To my lovely wife,
Elizabeth,
the grandest lady in all the cosmos

———◄●►———

Contents

————— ◁•▷ —————

A Recap, a Prelude, and a Premonition of Terror

SINCE THE BATTLE OF the Nightmare King had been won, the planet seemed to be relatively quiet.

Katherine, North, and Ombric had stayed in the Himalayas with the Lunar Lamas. They knew Pitch and his Nightmare Armies would strike again. Pitch had escaped wearing the robot djinni's suit of armor and had vowed revenge against them all.

But the Man in the Moon had given North the magic sword that had belonged to his father. He had told them of four other relics from the Golden Age that could be helpful, perhaps essential, in defeating the Nightmare King, once and for all. But where Pitch was hiding or what they should do next was a puzzlement.

Similar questions were being pondered on a faraway island, in a secluded section of the Pacific Ocean. On this island there resided the most ancient, mysterious, and peculiar creature the world had ever known. Or not known, actually. Though he possessed extraordinary wisdom and power, he had given up on the comings and goings of history and humans. He had not allowed himself to be seen in living memory. This being, however, knew something was in the air. He knew about the battle of the Nightmare King, and he knew of Ombric and Pitch. He'd had dealings with them in the distant past. He could see and sense signs most unwelcome. Deep beneath the Earth (which was his realm), he heard ominous sounds. He kept to himself and liked it that way, but his animal instincts told him that, like it or not, he would once again be asked to help save the world he had so carefully cut himself off from.

His nose twitched. His massive ears flinched.

He wondered about the terrible battles to come and what, if any, part he would decide to play.

Our Heroes

North

Petrov

Nightlight

Ombric

Bear

Katherine

CHAPTER ONE

We Begin Our Story with a Story

IN THE HINTERLANDS OF eastern Siberia was the village where Katherine, North, and Ombric called home. The village of Santoff Claussen felt somewhat lonely without them, but a dozen or so adventurous children played in the enchanted forest that protected their homes from the outside world. The surrounding oak trees were among the largest in the world. Their massive trunks and limbs were a paradise for climbing.

Petter, a strong boy of twelve who imagined himself a daring hero, catapulted onto the porch of his favorite tree house. He landed just ahead of his little sister, Sascha. She was testing her latest invention: gloves and shoes that allowed her to scamper up a tree, like a squirrel. But Petter's catapult was faster.

"I'll beat you next time," Sascha said, hoping that a small engine on the heel of each shoe would do the trick.

She peered down at the clearing hundreds of feet below. The village's bear, a massive creature, loped around the perimeter of the clearing along with Petrov, the horse of Nicholas St. North. Sascha was wondering if she'd ever be allowed to ride Petrov when she spied Tall William, the first son of Old William, squatting on his heels, talking to a group of centipedes. The children of Santoff Claussen had begun to learn the easier insect languages (ant, worm, snail), but Tall William was the first to tackle the more difficult speech of centipede.

Sascha pressed a trumpet-shaped sound amplifier to her ear.

Tall William reported what the centipedes said, that all was well—Pitch, the Nightmare King, was nowhere to be seen. It was a warm summer day, but the memory of that terrible time when Pitch appeared in Santoff Claussen made Sascha shiver as if it were the darkest night in deepest winter.

Pitch had once been a hero of the Golden Age, an ancient time when Constellations ruled the universe. His name in those days long ago was General Kozmotis Pitchiner, and he had led the Golden Age Armies in capturing the Fearlings and Dream Pirates who plagued that era. These villains were wily creatures of darkness. When they escaped, they devoured the general's soul, and from that moment on, he hungered for the dreams of innocent children and was known simply as "Pitch." He was determined to drain the good from dreams until they became nightmares—every last one of them—so that the children of Earth and then other worlds would live in terror. And the dreams of the children of Santoff Claussen—who had never before known fear or wickedness—were the prizes he coveted most.

Sascha, like the other children of Santoff Claussen, had survived that terrifying night when Pitch's Fearlings had nearly captured them in the enchanted forest, thanks to a glimmering boy with a moonlit staff who drove back the inky marauders.

Now she climbed out onto a branch and hung by her knees, still holding the ear trumpet. *The world looks different upside down, but it sounds the same,* she thought.

Sascha listened once more, then lowered the

sound amplifier. The insects had said all was well. *Even so, what if Pitch and his Fearlings come back again?* She frowned, but before that thought could darken her mood, Petter called out for a new contest. "Race you to the clearing!" he shouted, leaping for the nearest branch.

Scrambling down the tree, Sascha's shoes and gloves now gave her the advantage. She landed proudly in front of Tall William and his brother William the Almost Youngest. Her own brother was still half a tree behind.

She was about to brag about her victory when she spotted the stone elves hunkered amidst the vines and trees. There were at least ten statues in total, and they made for an eerie and unsettling sight, some with arms raised, swords at the ready; others frozen in midscream.

They were Nicholas St. North's band of outlaws, turned to stone by the Spirit of the Forest. The Spirit had spared North for he alone was true of heart. Rejecting her offer of riches, he had gone to the village's rescue when Pitch attacked again. He then decided to stay in Santoff Claussen, and became their wizard Ombric Shalazar's apprentice.

The Spirit of the Forest was just one of the magical barriers their wizard had devised to protect the village when he first created it. He'd also conjured up a hundred-foot-tall hedge, the great black bear the size of a house, and the majestic oaks that blocked the advance of anyone who tried to enter Santoff Claussen with ill intent. But none of these had been able to protect the children from the shadows and Fearlings at Pitch's command.

Petter and his friend Fog began crossing stick

swords with each other, acting out the battle that took place when Nicholas St. North had come face-to-face with Pitch.

Everything they knew and loved had seemed lost until North had galloped up to the rescue on Petrov. Though badly wounded, North had been able to drive Pitch away, but the children all worried that the Nightmare King would return. At this very moment Ombric, North, and their friend Katherine were far from Santoff Claussen, searching for the weapon—some sort of relic!—that would conquer Pitch forever.

The youngest William was near tears. "I'm afraid. Pitch told us he would come back."

"North, Ombric, and Katherine will find a way to stop him," Petter told him reassuringly.

William the Absolute Youngest wasn't entirely

convinced. "But Pitch's magic is strong. What if it's stronger than Ombric's?"

"What does Ombric always say?" Petter asked.

The youngest William thought for a moment, then his eyes grew bright. "Magic's real power is in believing," he proclaimed, clearly pleased to remember Ombric's very first lesson.

And he began to chant. "I believe! I believe! I believe!"

Sascha joined in. "I believe! I believe! I believe Katherine and North and Ombric will come home!"

CHAPTER TWO
—◄•►—

In Which Old Friends Are Reunited

WHILE WILLIAM THE ABSOLUTE Youngest and Sascha chanted, the light around the children began to glisten and shine. The Spirit of the Forest was coming! In a whirl of shimmering veils laced with tiny gemstones, she appeared before them.

"Time for lessons," she whispered, her soothing voice cheering the children as always. And her luminous, otherworldly beauty banished all worries. "Today you have a special surprise."

Lessons in Santoff Claussen were always a surprise. On any given day the children might learn how to build a bridge to the clouds or how to make rain come from a river rock. So if the Spirit of the Forest said the surprise was special, it must be amazing indeed.

The children broke into a run toward the village, with Petrov and the bear galloping beside them. The Spirit of the Forest glided above them, enveloping the children with trails of light that tickled and swirled around them. They paused only to stomp on the rift in the ground where Pitch had disappeared when he'd retreated. William the Absolute Youngest stomped the hardest of all.

Lessons took place inside Ombric's home in Big Root, the oldest tree in the village and the center of its magic. The huge branches swayed and waved as the children dashed up its massive roots and into its hollow. Ever since Ombric had set off on his mission with North and Katherine, the children's parents had been helping them with their lessons. But on this day, there was a surprise indeed. A towering stack of packages—all identical—cluttered Ombric's library. There were so many that the bees, spiders, and ants who kept Ombric's workroom tidy couldn't keep up with them.

In charge of the library was Mr. Qwerty, a glowworm who loved books above all other things. He could generally be found meandering up the spine of one book or down another, cleaning the covers or repairing torn pages. Roughly six inches long, he was a bright, springlike shade of green; had quite a number of legs; and wore small, round glasses perched on his nose. He was also the ultimate authority when Ombric was away.

He had wriggled down from the book stacks to oversee the package deliveries.

"Careful, now," he told them in a surprisingly humanlike voice. He was the only insect in the known world who spoke human languages.

Of course the children examined the presents with keen interest. "They look like North's work," said Fog.

The comment caused a wave of excited chatter. Then they noticed a small army of ants hauling a package larger than the others through Big Root's entrance.

"I wonder who *that* one is for," said William the Absolute Youngest, a hint of hopefulness in his voice.

"Are there any labels?" Sascha asked.

Just then the giant globe in the center of the room—the one that Ombric slept in—swung open. The inside was hollow except for a single wooden rod near the bottom, which Ombric stood on to sleep. The children always wondered how he managed to not

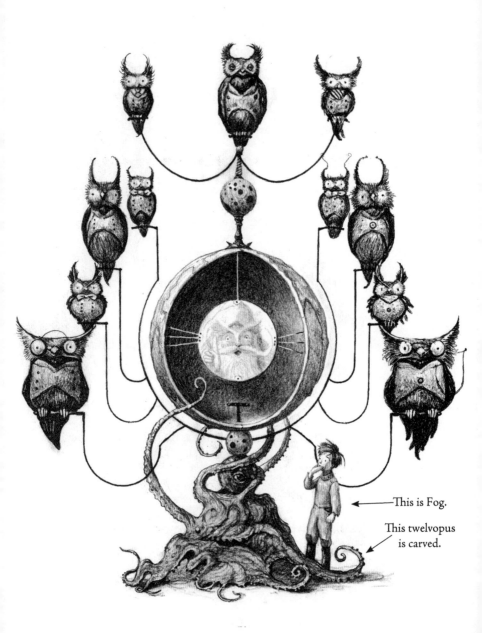

This is Fog.

This twelvopus
is carved.

fall off, but apparently for wizards, this was normal. As always, the dozen or so owls sat on their perches around the globe. They had the singular ability to communicate with the wizard with their minds.

The owls spent a good portion of their day preening, but now they began to hoot, slowly and deeply. At the center of the globe, a flat, circular glass plate appeared and started to glow. An illuminated image shimmered across it, and a familiar face came into focus. The children cried out happily. Ombric! It was Ombric! It had been weeks and weeks since he'd left, and questions tumbled out in shouts. "Where are you?" and "How is Katherine?" and especially, "Whose presents are these?"

The old wizard held up his hands. "First things first," he said with a laugh. "Tell me, has anyone had a nightmare?"

The children looked from one to the other, shaking their heads.

"No," said Fog.

"Old William had his birthday," Petter added.

"So did William the Absolute Youngest," Sascha reported.

"We're still the youngest and the oldest in the village," the youngest William piped up. "Even when I have a birthday, I'm still the littlest," he concluded with a frown.

"Then everything is as it was and as it should be," Ombric said with a satisfied nod. "I knew everything would be in order in the capable hands of Mr. Qwerty."

Upon hearing Ombric mention his name, Mr. Qwerty momentarily stopped resewing the binding of *Interesting Unexplainables of Atlantis, Volume 8,* and gave them all a little wave.

"Tall William," Ombric said, nodding at the boy. "I do believe you've gotten seven-eighths of an inch taller."

Tall William sat up a little straighter, a pleased smile on his face.

"Sascha, I hear you've figured out how to climb trees faster than a squirrel."

Sascha raised her feet and hands so that Ombric could see her invention.

"Ingenious," he said, stroking his beard. For every child, he had a cheering observation or a bit of praise or encouragement. Finally, he reached William the Absolute Youngest, who only wanted to know about the mysterious boxes.

Ombric could tell it was taking every ounce of the boy's self-control to not snatch one up. "To answer *your* question, young William, these boxes are presents from North. There is one for each of you. Each is exactly the same . . . until you pick it up," he said mysteriously.

"Since I'm the smallest, may I have the largest box?" asked the youngest William in his sweetest voice.

"*That* gift is special," said Ombric. "It's for all of you and should be opened last."

So each child chose one of the other boxes. Petter hefted one in his hand. It was surprisingly light.

Ombric smiled. "Now, think of a thing you would like, and it will be yours."

Petter closed his eyes and thought his very hardest. When he opened them, instead of a box in his hands, there was a pair of special shoes that would allow him to glide over water.

William the Absolute Youngest found a small mechanical soldier that could move about on its own.

It carried two swords, which it waved wildly. "It's just as I daydreamed," the youngest William cried. "Tell North thanks!"

There were even presents for Petrov (a carrot that would last a week) and the bear (an elegant ring for the paw that had been hurt in the battle with Pitch).

When all the wishes had been granted, the children turned to the larger box.

"That one is from Katherine," Ombric told them.

The ants carried the oversized package to Ombric's cluttered desk. As they set it down, the package began to unfold on its own, and out came a book.

"Katherine has written a story about our adventures since we left you. She misses you all and wishes she could tell you in person, but until then, her book will tell you the story. Now, before we start, we must begin with the first spell I ever taught you. Do you remember?" Ombric asked.

The children glanced at one another, grinning. Did they remember? Why, Sascha and the youngest William had just said that spell in the forest. Pleased to be a step ahead of their teacher for once, they began to murmur.

And as the words "I believe, I believe, I believe" filled the air, the green leather cover of Katherine's book opened with the contented sigh of a brand-new story entering the world. The pages turned, stopping to reveal a delicate drawing of Katherine. A gold ribbon marked the page. At the top, in Katherine's crisp handwriting, were the words "The Beginning."

CHAPTER THREE

Katherine's Story of Their Recent Amazements

To the children's surprise, the drawing of Katherine began to move and talk, and then her voice filled the room. The insects stopped their tidying, and the owls quieted their hooting. Mr. Qwerty paused in his work on the other books. The only other movement in Big Root came from the turning of the pages and the fluttering wings of the moths and butterflies that cooled the children against the summer heat. Standing watch outside, Petrov and the bear leaned forward to listen too, for even a horse and a bear love a good story.

"Did *you* also get a present?" William the Absolute Youngest asked the Katherine drawing. "If you didn't, I'll share mine with you when you get home."

"I got a wonderful present," Katherine assured him. "It's all a part of the story." And so she began, the pages of the book turning as she talked.

"Do you remember how Pitch disappeared into the ground to escape the sunlight?"

The children all nodded. Light was the one thing that Pitch could not stand.

"And remember how North made the mechanical djinni?"

The children nodded again.

"Good. Now I will tell you what became of the djinni."

The children leaned in closer, unable to take their eyes from the drawings as Katherine filled them in on what had happened over the last several weeks. "Pitch had possessed the djinni, disguised as a spider, and he had learned Ombric's spells of enslavement. He'd turned Ombric and North into porcelain toys and was going to destroy them. But the spectral boy named Nightlight saved us all."

The children gasped at this news. Petrov whinnied. Even the butterflies stopped fluttering.

"Nightlight is a great hero," Katherine said, her face beaming. "He was once the protector of the Man in the Moon, and he kept Pitch trapped for centuries! He is fearless and powerful, and now he's *our* friend and protector."

The children looked at one another, eyes wide.

"Nightlight and I found Ombric and North in the high Himalayas—the tallest mountains in the world. But since Pitch had gotten inside the djinni's metal shell, no light could get through to him, and he was practically invincible. He'd gathered a huge army of Fearlings, there was a terrible battle, and all hope seemed lost. Then—then!—Nightlight brought his own army to help us."

"What kind of army?" Petter had to ask.

Katherine grinned. "Moonbeams! And the Lunar Lamas sent Abominable Snowmen. You know, the ones Ombric has always talked about? They're real, as big as our bear, and there are hundreds of them. They're actually called Yetis."

The children cheered as Katherine's drawings showed scene after scene of the battle.

Then the pages paused at a sketch of Katherine, Ombric, and North as they stood within a sort of castle.

"Where is that?" Sascha asked.

"Ah! That is the Lunar Lamadary! It was built by the Lunar Lamas. They're holy men older than even Ombric."

The next drawing showed Ombric, North, and Katherine surrounded by Yetis and Lunar Lamas, then the page turned, and there was a drawing of the kindest-looking face they had ever seen.

"Who's *that?*" asked Fog.

"*He* is the Man in the Moon," Katherine told him. The children murmured amongst themselves. The Man in the Moon!

"The Man in the Moon told us Pitch had crashed to Earth, and it was Nightlight who'd trapped him, deep underground, for all of those centuries when he'd disappeared!" Katherine recounted. "The Man in the Moon told us that now that Pitch has returned, he will never stop, and he asked us if we would join the war to destroy Pitch forever."

"So there will be more battles?" William the Almost Youngest gulped.

"Does that mean we won't see you for a long time?" asked Fog.

"When are you coming home? We miss you," Sascha added.

The children's questions, and Katherine's answers, were drowned out by a loud honking noise.

Katherine began to laugh. "I'll tell you more later—I have my baby goose to take care of!"

A drawing of a very large gosling appeared on the page.

William the Absolute Youngest jumped closer for a better look. "Is that your present?"

"Yes! Her name is Kailash. She's a Himalayan Snow Goose, and she's going to grow as big as a horse. She thinks I'm her mother. But tonight at bedtime, my book will tell you all about her, I promise."

Then the book closed itself slowly, and the children were left with the impossible task of having to wait till bedtime to hear the rest of the story. Yet they were the children of Santoff Claussen! Mischief and magic would speed their day.

But, for a glowworm named Mr. Qwerty, there could not be enough time. Of all the books in Ombric's library, Katherine's was the most amazing. He would spend the rest of the day polishing it till it shined like a jewel.

CHAPTER FOUR

A Short Frolic Across the Planet

MEANWHILE, FAR AWAY IN the highest Himalayas, Katherine sat at one of the Moon-shaped tables in the library of the Lunar Lamadary. It was there that the Grand High Lama had taught her how to make her magic sketchbooks. How, if she thought hard enough, the drawings and the words she wrote could come to life on the page. The ink and paper she used were ordinary, but her mind, her imagination, was what gave the words and pictures their great power: the power to connect her to anyone who read her stories.

This was the first time she had tried to contact her

friends through one of these charmed books, and she was thrilled by how well it had worked. It was as if she were right there in Ombric's library, sitting next to the youngest William and the others. But it also made her miss her friends even more.

Nightlight sat perched on one of the library chairs, also listening to Katherine's story. He especially enjoyed the parts about himself. Katherine was never happier than when Nightlight was nearby. Though he never uttered a word, they had become very close. He was a miraculous friend. He could fly and speak to moonbeams with his mind. He made her laugh and always kept her safe. But it was in the nearly silent times that the real strength of their bond was evident. A friend who understands everything without being told is the rarest and best kind of friend. So this evening, without Katherine having to say a word,

Nightlight could tell that she missed the children back in Santoff Claussen and worried for their safety.

While Katherine fed her gosling—a process that involved several Yetis and an astonishing amount of oatmeal—Nightlight set off for Santoff Claussen to make sure that the children were safe. Katherine didn't see him leave, but she knew that he had left. This was the time of day when he would fly across the world to check for signs of Pitch.

Nightlight's life was divided into three parts: First was the time when he was guardian and protector of the little Man in the Moon, a time he could barely remember. He did not like to think about the second part—the long, dark years trapped in a cave with the Nightmare King, locked inside Pitch's cold heart. The third part of Nightlight's life was the present— the time of freedom and friendship. This part of his life was happier than any time he could remember. Whenever he leaped onto a breeze or a cloud or helped guard the children, he felt brave and strong and bright.

What made him happier still was Katherine. She was clever and kind and always ready to help her friends. And because Santoff Claussen was Katherine's home and was special to her, Nightlight checked the village extra carefully on his nightly patrols. If Pitch returned to hurt these people— Katherine's people—Nightlight would do everything in his power to stop him. Even at the risk of being imprisoned again inside Pitch's heart or, even worse, destroyed.

It was night when he arrived in Santoff Claussen. He scoured the forest, looking for danger. Was that the silhouette of a leaf in the moonlight—or the grasping fingers of a Fearling? Was it Pitch who momentarily blocked out the Moon—or a cloud drifting across the night sky?

After Nightlight had examined every out-of-the-way crook and corner of the forest and was assured that all was well, he moved on to the village. He peered into each cottage and yard. He even checked the layers of ground around Big Root. Finally, he held his moonlit staff over the dank, smoky scar in the dirt where Pitch had retreated. The moonbeam in his staff's diamond tip glowed brightly, and Nightlight was able to see that the scar looked just as it had the night before and the night before that. He checked a second time, just to be sure. But he saw no dastardly Fearlings disguised as shadows. No trace of Pitch anywhere.

On most nights this was enough to satisfy the

spectral boy. He would laugh his perfect laugh and hop onto the nearest cloud for a game of moonbeam tag. But tonight something felt wrong. Perhaps it was nothing, but all those years near Pitch had given him an instinct for evil. So he stayed back in the shadows, searching the sky as the children of Santoff Claussen made their way to Big Root for their bedtime story.

By now he knew their names: Sascha, Petter, Fog, all the Williams, and the others. He watched them secretly while they talked about the story Katherine would continue telling them tonight. As they hurried to prepare for bed, the Nightmare King was far from their minds. But as much as Nightlight loved Katherine's stories, he would be watchful. While the children gathered, his attention was in the shadows.

The Villains

Pitch,
the Nightmare King

Fearlings

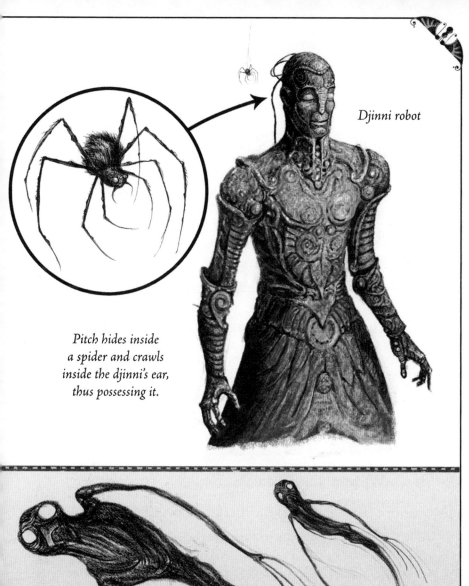

Djinni robot

Pitch hides inside
a spider and crawls
inside the djinni's ear,
thus possessing it.

CHAPTER FIVE

A Bedtime Story with a Girl, a Goose, and Snowmen Who Are Not so Abominable

As THE CHILDREN OF Santoff Claussen tumbled into Big Root that evening, bunk beds materialized from the tree's hollow center. Each row, fanning out like the spokes of a giant wheel, was stacked five beds high. Twisting up and down the center was a spiral staircase.

William the Absolute Youngest scrambled up the stairs and was the first to reach his bed. He propped up his metal soldier against a pillow so he could see Katherine's book, which was suspended from the ceiling by a strand of Mr. Qwerty's silk. In another moment the rest of the children had found their bunks. Warm cocoa hovered in the air by each bed. Cookies also appeared. The children sipped and snacked and waited for Katherine's story to start again.

"She's going to tell us about the giant baby goose," Sascha said.

"And Nightlight," William the Absolute Youngest added. "He's my favorite!"

Nightlight, hovering outside, moved closer to the window at the sound of his name. Though worry still nagged at him, Petrov and the bear stood watch by the door, so Nightlight allowed himself to relax. He pressed his face against the glass, just in time to see Katherine's book reopen.

As it had that afternoon, Katherine's voice filled Big Root; the pages turned and the story started again. "Tonight I'm going to tell you about my gosling," Katherine's voice began. "The tale of the baby Snow Goose is sad—"

Sascha protested immediately. "I don't like sad stories."

"It only begins sadly," Katherine assured her.

Satisfied, Sascha leaned back against her pillow. A moth settled beside her, and together they watched the pages stop at a drawing of a giant pile of snow and ice.

"After the battle, Pitch had retreated inside the djinni's body," Katherine's drawing told them, "but as he left, he caused an avalanche that buried the nests of the Great Snow Geese."

The children oohed as the pages turned to a sketch of one of the enormous birds. Katherine explained how she helped them dig out a most beautiful silvery egg that had been buried in the snow. "The parents could not be found," Katherine said sadly, then she paused.

The children of Santoff Claussen all knew the story of Katherine's parents. They too had perished, in a blizzard when Katherine was just a baby, so it was no surprise to the children that Katherine's heart went out to the little orphaned gosling.

"We looked closer at the egg," Katherine told them. "It shuddered, and we heard a tiny tapping sound. A small hole appeared, then a little orange beak pecked through the eggshell, and then a white, feathered head pushed its way out!"

A picture of the baby goose half in and half out of the shell appeared before them.

"I wish you could feel how soft her feathers are. Maybe I'll be able to bring her home. I named her

Kailash—that's the name of the smallest mountain in the Himalayas."

"Kailash," repeated Sascha. "I like that name."

"Nightlight and I helped the geese rebuild their nests. They're enormous, nearly as big as a room. And the geese stand taller than North—and they are big enough for a person to ride upon!

"Ombric laughs every time he sees Kailash waddling behind me," Katherine continued. "I think he feels like a grandfather! We filled the nests with white goose down to make warm beds. Sometimes I even sleep with Kailash, so she won't feel lonely. But I'm very glad the Yetis know how to cook baby Snow Goose food."

Pictures of the giant hairy Yetis cooking for the gosling and of Kailash waddling behind Katherine made everyone laugh. Then more images followed as the book's pages turned: Katherine and Nightlight flapping their arms to try to teach the gosling to fly, and Kailash's first hops into the sky.

"Now she can fly for two or three hours at a time," Katherine announced proudly. "She's growing so fast, we have to keep making her nest bigger. She grows two or three inches a day."

A growth chart appeared, measuring Kailash against a wall.

"And I'm learning to speak Snow Goose. It's almost as hard as owl, but easier than eagle."

Now Fog sat forward. "Can Nightlight speak Snow Goose?" he asked.

Katherine answered, "He never says a word, but he seems to understand everything. With many creatures, I think he can talk just by thinking. But he likes to talk to me with pictures. Look!"

The children all leaned forward to see Nightlight's drawings, which were different from Katherine's—simpler and more childlike, but quite beautiful in their own way. There were sketches showing his old life in the Golden Age; pictures of the giant Lunar Moths, huge glowworms that lived on the Moon; the Man in the Moon when he was a baby; and the last battle of the Golden Age. There was also a darker picture of all those years Nightlight was trapped in a cave with Pitch. Finally, there was a picture of him being freed by his moonbeam friend, and then another of him saving the children of Santoff Claussen from the Fearlings that night in the forest.

Nightlight pressed his fingers against the glass. He loved seeing the children's reactions to his drawings.

"Yesterday morning Nightlight had a surprise

for me," Katherine said when the children settled back against their pillows. "I'd been waiting and waiting for Kailash to be big enough to ride, and secretly, Nightlight and Kailash had decided that it was the day! Kailash nudged my arm with her beak and lowered herself, so that I could climb onto her back.

"So I did. She unfolded her beautiful wings, and we took to the air. It felt as if we could fly forever. We flew all over the Himalayas, even the tallest mountain in the world, and of course we flew over the mountain Kailash was named for. We flew until it was dark. And then I tucked Kailash into her nest and told her a bedtime story about all of you till she fell asleep, and now it's time for all of us to do the same." The book began to close. "Good night, everyone. Dream of Kailash and me, and we will come home to see you soon."

The story had ended happily, as Katherine had promised.

William the Absolute Youngest yawned and rolled over with a quiet snore. Sascha kicked off her covers, and a troop of beetles pulled them back up over her shoulders. Petter was soon dreaming about giant geese and Abominable Snowmen.

Katherine hadn't told her friends that North and Ombric were trying to discover where the other relics from the Moon were hidden; she hadn't told them that the Nightmare King had vowed to turn her into a Fearling princess and to make nightmares real. Those things scared her and she knew they'd scare her friends too. Besides, she was sure Nightlight would be watching over them. Nightlight, who never slept and never dreamed, would keep nightmares, both imagined and real, away.

Petrov and the bear stood watch at Big Root's entrance while Nightlight sat just outside the window. His guard was up.

The night was too still. Something was wrong.

Something was coming.

CHAPTER SIX

Amazing Discoveries and Ancient Magic

WHILE KATHERINE WAS TELLING her bedtime story, North was studying the sword the Man in the Moon had bestowed upon him. He knew he was in a race against time. Pitch would return, and when he did, Nicholas St. North wanted to be ready. He prided himself on being the best swordsman in the world. Indeed, in his bandit days, he had once defeated an entire cavalry regiment with nothing more than a bent steak knife. But this sword was—blast it!—confounding.

Etched on its handle in a clear, handsome script

was the name TSAR LUNAR XI. The Man in the Moon's father had been the last tsar, or ruler, of the Golden Age, and his sword had been crafted with more care than even North himself was capable of. North had hammered out many a fine weapon, even some forged from bits of ancient meteor, but nothing like this amazing blade. It never seemed heavy, no matter how long North practiced with it. Its hilt closed tightly around his hand whenever he began to wield it, then loosened when he was ready to put it away. It could slice whole boulders in half with one slash. It wasn't a sword for slaying your average enemy, that was certain. But he wanted—needed—to understand all of its hidden powers. How else would he make the best use of it, especially against Pitch?

The Yetis did what they could to help. The crafty warriors possessed an amazing arsenal of arrow guns, pikes, bludgeons, spears, dirks, knucklers, and daggers, and they used all of them against this amazing sword. North was victorious every time, but it wasn't always his skill that won the day. It was the blade itself.

The sword had a mind of its own. It would leap from its sheath and into North's hand whenever there was danger—even during the friendly pretend attacks of the Yetis. It seemed to guide him to block an opponent's every thrust.

This piqued North's pride. The sounds of him yelling, "Quit that! I'm the best swordsman who ever breathed air!" and "Do what I say, you ancient pile of stardust!" could often be heard echoing through the Lamadary during sword practice.

That morning, in a practice battle with Yaloo, the fierce and friendly leader of the Yetis, North vanquished the hairy giant easily. And Yaloo carried the most feared of all Yeti weapons, an Abominable Mood Swing! Yaloo didn't seem to mind, but North was starting to feel sorry for him.

"You'll get me next time," North said with a good-natured chuckle. As he reached up to shake hands with Yaloo, the sword flew from his grasp. It appeared determined to fall from the tower.

North grabbed wildly for it, but it was too quick. He and Yaloo looked down in horror. Tashi, one of Yaloo's lieutenants, was just below, with the Grand High Lama. They were both standing on their heads meditating. The sword was heading straight for them.

What does one shout to a meditating Yeti and an ancient warrior Moon monk when a magic sword is about to impale them? North wondered fleetingly.

"Get off your heads before you lose 'em!" he bellowed.

Then a remarkable thing happened: As the weapon neared them, it stopped its fall. It hovered in the air for a moment, then began to rise. North reached out, his hand beginning to tingle. And even though the sword was a hundred feet below, it instantly flew back up to him and slapped into his palm with a satisfying *thwack*. Down below, Tashi and the Grand High Lama remained in their headstands, completely unaware of their near demise.

North turned the weapon over and over in wonder. The sword had fallen on purpose, to show him one of its secrets—that it could change direction to avoid causing harm. So he tried to test its sharpness with his thumb, but the sword's tip pulled away. "Can the sword wound only my enemies?" he asked out loud.

Yaloo motioned for him to try to slice him.

North paused, but Yaloo was adamant. So North took a breath and then slashed the blade directly toward Yaloo.

The Yeti didn't flinch, and once again the sword veered off, refusing to cause harm.

"The blasted thing. I expect a sword to do what I want. Why give me a weapon that fights *against* me?" North fumed.

The Yeti eyed North with an amused expression. "Perhaps the weapon is fighting *for* you," he suggested.

That pleased North. He was nodding in agreement when he heard a quiet "Ahem" behind him. North turned. Ombric stood there. He seemed eager to talk.

"I've been working on something that might help

us," the wizard said, as if picking up from a prior conversation—one that had nothing to do with North's sword.

North saw great excitement in the wizard's eyes. Ombric had already discovered that the Lamas had a magnificent clock that recorded every second of time. It was one of the few possessions the Lamas had been able to bring to Earth before Pitch had destroyed their home planet. They told Ombric the clock was as old as time itself, and it could send its user back a day, a year, or even an eon.

The wizard had been relentlessly studying the great, round clock. He couldn't believe that he—the prince of invention—had never tried to create such a marvel himself. The clock, more than thirty feet high, looked like nothing he had ever seen before. It was made up of dozens of interlocking rings that spun and rotated inside of one another. The rings were formed from a pale metal known only on the Lamas' home planet, and in the center stood a column of round clock faces of various sizes. These were used to set the clock to the exact time and place in history to which one wanted to journey.

With some trial and error, Ombric had learned how to go on short visits into the past.

No matter how much time he actually spent in the past, he returned to the present within minutes of when he left. Everyone in the Lamadary got used to seeing him pop up out of nowhere, with fantastic tales of his adventures.

One day he told Katherine he went to see the Great Pyramid of Giza being built. "Good thing they'd learned to levitate solid rock back then or they would never have finished the thing," the wizard declared. "Odd, though, that it was once topped with egg-shaped stone."

After another journey, he landed in the middle of the courtyard at the Lamadary, red-faced and panting, a large tear in his robe.

North had never seen the wizard so out of sorts. "What's wrong, old man?" he asked.

"Most dinosaurs are really very friendly creatures," Ombric answered once he caught his breath. "But those rex fellows, Tyrannosaurus? A bit snappy when hungry."

All of these journeys back and forth through time made for interesting stories, but North didn't see how they could help them defeat Pitch.

But this time Ombric planned to do more than merely go back in time. "I'm going to travel back to the moment when Pitch attacked the Moon," he told North. "I'll be able to see exactly where the relics fell. Finding them is our best hope of defeating him." And off he went.

But on this trip, something unusual—baffling, even—occurred. Ombric was very disturbed as he told them his latest adventure. They were eating supper in the busy dining hall of the Lamadary. Yetis, Lamas, and Snow Geese ate noisily as he related what had happened.

"I was back in time, just before the last battle of the Golden Age," he told them. "I could see Pitch's ship hiding on the dark side of Earth, lying in wait to attack the Moon. Suddenly, it occurred to me to warn the Man in the Moon and his family. I hoped to stop this whole history *before it could even begin*. But I sensed someone standing next to me.

"I turned to look, and there, to my utter amazement, floating beside me, was a most curious fellow. He was at least seven feet tall, wearing robes of a most peculiar design, and holding a long staff with an egg-shaped jewel at one end."

"Who was he? Did he say anything?" asked Katherine.

"He did indeed," confirmed the wizard. "One word, which he repeated: 'Naughty. Naughty.'"

"Is that it?" North demanded, lowering his soup spoon.

"Not quite," explained Ombric. "He touched my shoulder with the jeweled egg, and I suddenly found myself back here!"

"You've told me of many strange things, Ombric, but this takes the soup," said North, sipping again at his dinner.

"I left out perhaps the strangest part," added the wizard ominously. "The fellow's ears . . ."

"Yes?" said North.

Ombric leaned forward. "Mr. North," he said with dramatic relish. "They were the ears of a gigantic rabbit."

CHAPTER SEVEN

A Tall Tale for a Rabbit

KATHERINE AND NORTH SIMPLY did not know what to say about a seven-foot-tall talking rabbit. They'd seen so many amazements with the great wizard, but this struck them as, well . . . outstandingly odd.

North was the first to voice his doubts. "An interstellar talking Rabbit Man?" he questioned. "Are you sure all this time travel isn't scrambling your brains?"

Ombric raised an eyebrow at his former pupil.

"It does sound, hmmm . . . very *unusual*," added Katherine.

Ombric's eyebrow rose even higher. He was stunned that they doubted him. His temper began to rise. Then his mustache began to twist into tight curls.

But then Ombric remembered that he, too, had doubted the existence of this rabbit when he'd first read about him in an ancient text from Atlantis. In fact, he'd discounted the creature as merely a myth until he saw it floating next to him.

"If I am not mistaken," began the wizard in his most patient teacher voice, "this Rabbit Man, as you call him, is a Pooka—the rarest and most mysterious creature in the universe."

North and Katherine were intrigued; it was their eyebrows that now rose.

"They are among the oldest creatures in creation," continued Ombric, "so little is known about them and even less understood. It is said that they oversee the health and well-being of planets."

"This Pooka is mysterious indeed," interrupted the Grand High Lama. He and the Lamas stood serenely in their usual V formation. They'd entered the room, as always, in complete silence and had startled our heroes with their arrival.

"You *know* him? It?" asked Ombric, visibly surprised.

"We know he is a him, not an it," replied a tallish Lama.

"We know he has a vast knowledge," said another.

"We know he is difficult to know," said the shortest.

"We know he prefers to be unknown," said one of the others.

"We've heard he likes eggs," said another.

". . . and chocolate," added the shortest one.

"We *think*," concluded the Grand High Lama.

Katherine, North, and Ombric mulled over that uncommonly informative aria of information from the Lamas.

"A robe-wearing Rabbit Man who time travels and likes eggs," summarized North, trying not to laugh.

"And chocolate!" said Katherine mischievously.

"A substance he apparently invented," interjected the Grand High Lama.

"I thought *I* invented chocolate!" said Ombric indignantly.

"That, my dear Ombric, is what the Pooka *wants* you to think," replied a Lama.

"We *think*," added another.

Ombric shook his head in confusion. "I'm going time traveling. At least the past is certain. That much I do know."

"But do not tamper with events in the past," warned the High Lama.

"It is forbidden," said the tallest Lama.

"And the Pooka will not like it," said another.

As the wizard entered the time machine and made his settings, he replied, "Good!" And vanished into the certainties of the past.

North and Katherine stared at the clock for a few moments, then shared a concerned glance.

"I always worry about him when he goes back there. Wherever 'there' is," North admitted.

Katherine gave a small nod. "Me too."

"But he's a tough old bird," North reasoned just as Kailash came waddling up and began nuzzling her head against them. "This tough young bird needs feeding," he chuckled.

He picked Katherine up and set her on Kailash's

back. "Your goose is as big as Petrov—and still growing!"

"Want to help me feed her?" asked Katherine.

"Maybe tonight. I've got to keep working," North told her, reaching up to brush her hair out of her face. Her hair was always falling over one eye, and North would often brush it back.

Katherine looked down at her dashing friend. She was a little worried about him too. He'd been working so hard, trying to figure out how to use the new magic sword.

"That's all right. Nightlight will help me," she assured him.

She thought back to the day she, North, and Ombric had bowed before the Man in the Moon, had pledged their oath to continue in the fight against Pitch. North had sworn to use his sword wisely and well. So study he must. She was grateful for Nightlight's help, for being a Guardian was harder than any of them had realized. And it was about to get harder than they'd ever imagined.

CHAPTER EIGHT

A Hop, Skip, and a Jump Through Time

DEEP INSIDE THE CLOCK, Ombric was somersaulting through time at a furious pace. The world around him flickered from day to night faster than the blink of an eye. He saw seasons pass in seconds. Centuries flew by as he drifted up and away from the Lamadary. He looked skyward as the sun and stars spiraled past him at rocket speed. Day. Night. Day. Night. Faster than could be said and in reverse. The Moon was there too, and in a flash he saw the explosion of Pitch's galleon and the last great battle of the Golden Age. But it all happened too fast. The relics fell from the Moon too quickly for him to track them.

Ombric wasn't worried. He would slow down his trajectory on the return trip and take note of their whereabouts. And if his plan worked, he wouldn't need to.

He began to drift away from Earth, going deeper and deeper into the vast dazzlements of space. He was traveling so swiftly through time that comets, planets, and galaxies pivoted and sparkled around him like fireworks, but their size was beyond description.

Then Ombric realized that the flashes he was seeing were the deaths of the Golden Age worlds. What he was watching was Pitch's galleon destroying one Constellation after another. Then, as Ombric continued to pinwheel backward through time, the universe around him brightened.

Golden Age ships coursed through the sky around

him. This was it! The age he had studied for so long but never dreamed he would see. He could barely take it all in. The cities he saw were colossal, magnificent, more magical than anything he had ever imagined. It broke his heart to think of the vanished wonder and glory of this perfect era, and he became more determined than ever to implement his plan.

He soon found himself at the infamous prison planet, the huge rusted dungeon where the Fearlings had been locked after the Golden Age Armies had captured them. As time slowed down, he stopped his journey just moments before Pitch was overtaken and the Fearlings had escaped. Ombric hid behind a large pillar an arm's length away from Pitch, who was standing in a guard's station in front of the prison's only door.

It was remarkable to see his nemesis as he had been before his change to evil. He looked every inch a great hero. Stalwart. Valiant. Even noble in his Golden Age military uniform. But his determined expression was weary and tinged with sorrow.

From behind the massive door, Ombric could hear a drone of whispers and mutterings from the prisoners. The noise would rise to a crescendo, then sink low, pulsing eerily from within.

What an awful sound, thought Ombric. *It's like evil itself. To hear that day after day would drive any man insane.* And indeed, the ghostly noise seemed to weigh on Pitch. His face was drawn, his fists clenched in anxiety.

But then he pulled a silver locket from his tunic pocket; the chain hung around his neck. He tapped the clasp and it swung open, revealing a small photograph. Ombric could just make out the face of a little girl. Pitch stared at the image, seeming to take great solace in the picture. His face softened and his

sadness eased. Ombric knew that expression. He'd seen it countless times. It was the look of a father gazing at his child. *Pitch had a daughter!* The wizard could feel Pitch's longing to see his child in person.

The Fearlings sensed his longing too. Their strange mutterings shifted in tone, their pleadings took on the voice of a small girl. "Please, Daddy," they whispered. "Please, please, please open the door."

A momentary spark of hope crossed Pitch's face. His eyes lit up, and then they dimmed as he recognized the sound for what it was: a Fearling trick. He visibly steeled himself against the evil, bracing his shoulders, clenching his jaw, but the Fearlings started to beg again.

"Daddy," they cried. "I'm trapped in here with these shadows, and I'm scared. Please open the door. Help me, Daddy, please."

Pitch looked again at the photograph. The

pleading grew more desperate. More hypnotic. Pitch seemed to be slipping into a trance.

Suddenly, his face grew wild with panic. He reached for the door. The locket fell from his neck. Ombric caught it in midair and was about to block Pitch from opening the prison door when the mysterious Pooka reappeared. Ombric found he could neither move nor utter a sound.

The Pooka held up his hand and shook his head. "That's a no-no," he scolded.

The Lamas had told Ombric he could not change events in his journeys through time, he could only observe them. The Pooka, it seemed, was there to stop his trying.

Ombric looked from the Pooka back to Pitch in time to witness agony and shock in the jailer's eyes— the desperation of a loving father trying to save his daughter from the Fearlings. As the door swung open, all that was visible was a roiling mass of dark, serpent-like creatures. Of course Pitch's daughter was not there. Before Pitch could even scream her name, he was surrounded by malevolent shadows. In less than an instant, they poured over, around, *into* him! It was a horrifying sight. One that Ombric would never forget.

Pitch struggled valiantly, but he soon succumbed to the evil flooding him, twisting him into a madman. He swelled to ten times his normal size; his face became monstrous and cruel.

As Ombric stared, transfixed, he felt the familiar touch of the Pooka's egg-tipped staff on his shoulder. He was being sent back to the present again. But as he began to dim and vanish, he saw Pitch throw his head back and roar with the menacing laughter of ten thousand Fearlings.

CHAPTER NINE

The Secret of the Sword

WHILE OMBRIC WAS WATCHING history unfold, North was in the Lamadary library studying the new sword. He'd examined it for weeks with all the methods at his disposal: magnifying glasses of every shape, size, and purpose. Microscopes, maxiscopes, telescopes. He'd come to so many mystifying discoveries, it boggled his agile mind. The metal of the sword could change itself. Sometimes it was mostly iron, then it shifted to steel, then to metals that North couldn't even classify. It could become highly magnetic or immeasurably strong, and at times it could emit various kinds of light. Sunlight. Moonlight. Comet light. Lights that had no name. North began to realize that the weapon was indeed a living thing.

In battle it would transform into a conventional sword—a long blade with a protective covering over the handle. But depending on the circumstances, it would sprout various mechanical additions. In darkness, for instance, a curious light-emitting orb would appear. When danger was imminent, the jewels on the hand guard would glow red. And at other times the hand guard itself would change, sometimes revealing maps of the stars or the Moon or the Earth itself.

But the how, why, and what of these gadgets were still a mystery to him.

North thought about what Ombric always said about magic—that its real power was in belief. North knew for certain that this sword had powers beyond explanation. The sword, he hoped, could tell him what he most needed to know. So he closed his eyes and concentrated on that belief with all his mind and heart. "I believe. I believe. I believe," he said very quietly. As he chanted the phrase over and over, his thoughts began to grow uncluttered, pure, sharp, until he had only one question. Where were the other relics? It was as if the sword now guided his mind.

And then, with the subtlest of clicks, North felt the sword change.

He opened his eyes to see that a metal orb had appeared. It opened, unwrapping like an intricate puzzle. Inside was a map of the Earth, and on the map were four glittering jewels. *Four jewels*—North's mind raced—*four jewels. . . . Were they the four relics?* That had to be it! Each jewel marked their position. They simply had to follow this map!

Eager to share the news with the wizard, North raced through the Lamadary, finding Ombric in the tower just as he was reappearing from his latest time travel.

"I have the answer, old man!" North cried, slapping him on the back.

"And I have new questions," said Ombric wearily.

At that moment Katherine ran into the room.

"Nightlight is missing!" she shouted.

CHAPTER TEN

Revelations, Terror, and Daring Deeds

KATHERINE TRIED TO REIN in her panic, but her quivering voice betrayed her. "He hasn't returned since last night. No one has seen him," she explained in a rush.

Both Ombric and North tensed. They knew that Nightlight's visits were as regular as clockwork. They also knew that Santoff Claussen was always his last stop before he returned to the Lamadary.

"Only one thing could delay the lad," said North, his voice low.

"Pitch," whispered Katherine.

Even as they spoke, Ombric was already trying to contact his owls. They were constantly on watch in his library and forever at the ready to report to him telepathically. He concentrated with all his might, but the line of mental communication was severed. How could that be? He could not sense even an echo of emotion from the owls. If they could not speak to him, he should at least be able to *feel* them. Especially if they were in danger or afraid. But there was nothing.

It was this nothingness that frightened him most. He spun around and caught North's eye. He didn't need to say a word—North understood immediately.

"To Santoff Claussen?" North asked.

"And right speedily" came Ombric's answer.

The question was, which method would get them there "right speedily"? Ombric knew he didn't have the stamina for astral projection[1]—time travel always

---

[1] *Astral projection: When you mentally project yourself from one place to another. It is also an ancient method of mystical travel. Only the most brilliant and daring are able to astrally project themselves.*

left him exhausted. Besides, North and Katherine couldn't join him in that mode. The reindeer? They needed the spectral boy to create the highways of light upon which they flew. The djinni, of course, was gone. Ombric's mind was anxiously calculating all the possibilities when he was interrupted by the sudden appearance of the Lamas.

"We have adequate conveyance," said the Grand High Lama.

"It is swift," said another Lama.

"And comfortable," added a third.

"And easy to pilot," agreed a shortish one.

Ombric dreaded the series of answers his next question would cause; the Lamas answered questions only in fragments.

"Where is the craft?" Ombric tried to sound patient and urgent at the same time.

The Lamas looked at one another, deciding who would answer first.

Ombric, North, and Katherine shifted impatiently. Time was wasting.

Finally, the Grand High Lama spoke. "The craft? Why, you stand within it," he said with stunning simplicity. "You need merely to say where you'd like to go, and this tower will rocket you there with both speed and accuracy." Then the Lamas began to shuffle silently toward the courtyard.

"We are certain you can handle the situation," said the Grand High Lama as they reached the arching doorway.

"But we suggest you sit down for the trip," said the tallest.

"The trajectory is most speedy," said the shortest.

"At least when last we used it," said another.

"Thirty thousand years ago," added the Grand Lama as he exited last.

North, Ombric, and Katherine looked quizzically at one another. They each took to a chair and then glanced up at the glass-topped ceiling of the tower. It was perfect for observing a journey.

"We have all we need, I think," said North, gripping his sword.

Katherine suppressed a smile. She knew Kailash,

asleep under a nearby table, was aboard for the trip.
But she thought it best to keep that to herself.

Ombric turned to her. "My dear, give the order."

She grasped the arms of her chair tightly. "To
Santoff Claussen as fast as—"

But before she could
finish the sentence,
they were already
blasting off.

The Lamadary Tower is a swell way to travel.

CHAPTER ELEVEN
As the Tower Flies

THE LAMAS WERE TRUE to their word. The tower was a marvelous airship. No sooner had they taken off than the entire interior began to mechanically transform. As the tower shifted horizontally in its trajectory, their chairs glided toward the glass ceiling. The floor began to pivot and lean, as did the walls, until they formed a sort of ship's cabin with large Moon-shaped windows.

The woodwork, the mosaic floor tiles, the wallpaper, the instrument panels—every aspect of the cabin took on different shapes of the Moon: full or half or crescent. It was enchanting and, as promised, comfortable.

North examined all the charts and instruments carefully. "This screen shows our present position," he determined, then pointed to another and another. "This one our speed. This one our route. This one our time of arrival."

He seemed pleased by the instruments' reading. "We should be there within the hour," he told them.

Katherine was relieved to hear North's prediction. To travel from the Himalayas to the farthest corner of eastern Siberia in a matter of minutes was an astounding thing. Even the reindeer had not been able to achieve that kind of speed.

But Ombric was quiet. Katherine could tell from his expression that even this was not fast enough. Then she saw the locket he clutched in his hand.

"What's that?" she asked. Ombric was lost in thought and didn't seem to hear her. She gently took the locket from him and opened it to see the picture of the young girl, who was close to her own age. Katherine looked intently at the lovely girl with raven-black hair and haunting eyes.

"She's Pitch's daughter," said Ombric, his own eyes closing as he tried in vain to reach the owls. "I saw him holding it, back in time, before he became evil."

Katherine was amazed. She had no memory of her own father. And though she tried to imagine what he looked like, the image in her mind was never very clear—she'd been too young when she had lost him. It was equally difficult to imagine Pitch ever being a father. Or that he had ever been good. She remembered with a shudder that Pitch had vowed to turn her into a Fearling princess. But mixed with that feeling of dread was now a sadness that twined with her own sense of loss and longing.

Pitch had a daughter. What had happened to her?

And what had happened to Nightlight?

Kailash had found her way from the back of the tower. She honked and struggled to squeeze through the door of the main cabin, and with one great shove, she made it. She snuggled next to Katherine, her long neck twisting around her protectively, her feathered body a warm brace to lean against.

North looked at Katherine's sorrow-filled face. He was glad that Kailash was there to comfort her. He knew from Ombric's concentrated silence that things in Santoff Claussen would be perilous.

So he steadied himself for the darkness that lay ahead.

CHAPTER TWELVE

Delicate Darkness

BEFORE THE TRAVELERS KNEW it, their craft started dropping in elevation, flying lower and lower, until it was practically skimming the tree-tops of Santoff Claussen's enchanted forest. They had to squint to see the village. Clouds blocked the Moon and the stars. More unsettling was that not a single light shined from any window. The village was a shadow.

The airship landed with surprising silence at the edge of the forest. North carefully opened the Moon-shaped door, and they all gazed out on their village. It had never been this quiet. North looked to Ombric with a tense, questioning expression, then unsheathed the magic sword and climbed out first. "Stay behind me. Run if I say so," he told Katherine. The sword was transforming itself as he spoke, its light emerging magically from the blade. The glow lit their way. North sensed a vibration—was the sword signaling danger? He was not sure.

They walked toward Big Root slowly, scanning the mournful landscape for any signs of life.

Katherine had never seen a night so black or heard a silence so quiet—not even on the night when Pitch had first found her and her friends in the forest. It was as if all the life of the place had gone away. There was no movement. No breeze. Not one firefly or night bird flew to greet them. Even the raccoons and the badgers were nowhere to be seen.

Katherine reached for North's hand and kept the other on Kailash's neck. "Where is everyone?" she whispered.

Instead of answering her, Ombric stopped short. Something was glinting in the light from North's sword. Ombric stooped to pick up what appeared to be a small piece of glass. He held it up to the light: It was a tiny porcelain squirrel. It was like a toy. Turning it this way and that, he said, "It appears that Pitch has further mastered the spells of enslavement." He looked troubled and began to walk forward again, his eyes continuing to search the ground.

Though the eerie quiet persisted, the thick cloud cover began to dissipate as the threesome made their way into the village, so at least some moonlight began to penetrate the gloom. But this simply allowed them to better see the horror all around them.

In every direction, Katherine saw small porcelain versions of living things. Whole platoons of squirrels, raccoons, and foxes all looked to be frozen in mid-battle.

Try as she might, Katherine couldn't keep the tears back. Had Pitch frozen everything? She nearly stumbled over the Spirit of the Forest. The Spirit's normally flowing veils hung still and stiff, her gemstones were dulled with the lifeless shine of ceramics. Her frozen expression was one of fierce determination. In her hands she clasped a jeweled sword. She had clearly been petrified at a moment of intense struggle, just as she had once done to all who had fallen under her spell.

Katherine peered into the Spirit's glassy eyes and noticed something she had never expected to see there: fear. Then Katherine wiped her tears and willed herself to shed no more; she needed to keep alert. She jogged to catch up with North and Ombric.

North was barreling ahead. Katherine desperately hoped to find that at least one living thing had escaped Pitch's enslavement spell, but when they neared the village and Big Root, she realized that that was not to be. Every breathing creature in Santoff Claussen had been turned into a china doll. Even the bear. Again Katherine had to fight back tears. The bear looked so small and helpless now.

North's horse, Petrov, was lying on his side in front of Big Root's shattered door. He looked as if he had been on his hind legs in the midst of kicking the shadows away when he'd been overwhelmed by Pitch's spell. North ran to him, speechless.

Ombric walked among the parents of the children. They lay surrounding the tree, frozen, terrified expressions marring their faces. His fears turned to outrage as he swept into Big Root itself. The owls sat immobile on their perches around Ombric's globe. The dozens of honeybees and ants that resided in Big Root lay scattered on the floor like tiny china game pieces tossed aside by an unruly child.

Ombric and North surveyed the damage in stunned silence. The library was stripped bare. Not a single book remained. The beakers and test tubes Ombric used for his magical experiments had been dashed to the ground.

"No books and no children," Ombric said quietly. "And where is Mr. Qwerty?"

Katherine came up behind him. Where was Petter? Sascha? All the Williams? She sank to her knees, carefully brushing her insect friends to one side so they wouldn't be stepped on. Then one glittering piece of crystal caught her eye. She reached for it. Only then did she notice a sliver of a blade nearby. Then another. And another.

Her hand shook as she examined the pieces. Glistening drops, like beads of light, surrounded them. "It's the tip of Nightlight's staff," she gasped.

Ombric and North crouched beside Katherine. A small tarnished moonbeam—Nightlight's moonbeam!—was hidden beneath the largest piece of the shattered blade. With great care, Katherine cupped the beam into her hands.

"What happened, moonbeam?" she asked gently. "Where is everyone?"

Only Ombric spoke moonbeam, so he waved his staff and suddenly the little fellow's memories were displayed on the round glass of the globe bed.

The moonbeam shimmered with all the strength it could muster, and though it wavered and flickered, Ombric, North, and Katherine could see and hear the terrible story of Pitch's return.

CHAPTER THIRTEEN

The Moonbeam Tells His Tale of Woe

WE ARE IN THE Big Root tree, began the moonbeam, on the limbs outside a window. We watch the children in their beds. The Katherine book is telling stories of the Kailash. All warm and happy the children are! And so are we, my Nightlight boy and I. But we feel something that is a bother to us. A Pitch kind of scariness. It comes like a wind. We cannot see it. But we are feeling it. The clouds come dark and quick, and the moonlight and the stars are gone all suddenly. So my Nightlight boy looks out to the forest. All around is a badly sound. The forest creatures from every side are a-chatter and screamly.

So fiercely fast the shadows come. Out of the forest. Toward the village. Toward the Big Root. Toward *us*! The Forest Spirit lady, she is fighting most ferocious, but the Pitch cannot be stopped. He wears the metal djinni suit and has a sword so dark. It takes all light that comes near. The Pitch says words—spells, I thinks—and all who are close go changed. They're made small and still, and they move no more.

My Nightlight boy, his face is wild. He has the look of a knowing plan. This look I seen whenever he is about to do a deed most smart and daring.

So I listens as he tells me with his thinking talk: *The game I try will be most tricky. Don't be fooled by what you see.*

Then he looks close at me and says fiercely strong, *Fly straight and true and never fear.*

Then he takes the staff on which I am tied and points me at the Pitch. He throws me with all his mights. So fast I go. Fast as light. And into the metal I hits. The diamond dagger in which I live goes quick through the metal of the djinni armor and into the darkness of the Pitch himself. I hear the Pitch make a moan of deepest hurt, and I feel him fall. But I can see the cold black heart of him. I have not pierced it. All around me is the darkness. The cold heart still beats.

The Pitch, he is moving, I can tell. But what is happening outside I cannot see. I hear many shouts and screams most loud. I hear the bear a-roaring and the horse make his battle sounds, but one by one, they all go quietlike.

I hear the Pitch.

He breathes hard and heavy, but he is a-shouting

now. "WHERE IS IT! TELL ME!" he's asking most meanly.

Then he makes a groan sound, and I feel the pulling. Then I am out of the Pitch, but he is pointing *me*. Pointing me at my Nightlight boy. We are in the Ombric library, but there be no books. All are gone. The little wormly is gone. Just my Nightlight boy and the childrens. He is a-front the childrens, as if to protect them, but he is much hurt. On his knees from the hurt. But his face is not fearish. Neither are the children's. And this makes the Pitch anger get bad. Very bad.

So he's a-shouting, "I WANT THE BOOKS! THE BOOKS OF SPELLS!" Not any of the Williams or the Petter boy or the Sascha girl tells a word. Fearlings, they are all around the room now. Coming closer, closer to my Nightlight boy and the childrens.

But my Nightlight boy says loud and clear, "We fear you none!" I've never heard him speak with his voice. It is a magic voice he has. Like faraway memories and echoes of long ago. Then he laughs at the Pitch and leaps to attack. But the Pitch throws me and the staff at my Nightlight boy, and then all around is strangeness. The diamond tip hits my boy! And there's lights and shatterings. The diamond, it did not pierce my boy, but it is brokened into many pieces. And my boy lays still. On the ground! He shines not bright, but dim and flickering.

My broken dagger has let me loose. I am free. So I goes to my boy, but the Pitch hits me with his dark sword and it hurts me. Takes some of my light. So I am weak-feeling and cannot help my boy. The childrens look a little feared, but they muster strong and stare angry at the Pitch and his Fearlings.

"I need those books!" says the Pitch, all quiet and scary. "Ombric must give them to me. So you little ones will be my bait!" Then he opens his dark cape. It seems to eat the light as it wraps around the room. In a blink all is gone. The Fearlings gone. The childrens gone. My Nightlight boy gone too. And the Pitch.

Just me left. And the toy-turned owls.

Then the moonbeam turned to Ombric and the others. The childrens need us! My Nightlight boy said his game was most tricky and to never fear. I am trying. I hates the feeling I am having. A scaredy feeling. But I am stronger by the telling of the tale!

CHAPTER FOURTEEN

A Moonbeam, a Mystery, and a Muddle

MOONBEAM WAS EXHAUSTED AND dimmed again as he lay in Katherine's palm.

Ombric, North, and Katherine were each trying to make sense of everything the moonbeam had told them. They knew the situation was dire, but they kept surprisingly calm. They had been growing increasingly confident since taking the Man in the Moon's oath. And now the three began to work almost as one, as one mind. Ombric had read that friendship could produce a sort of magic. North was new to the concept, but he was keenly aware of its possibilities, and Katherine, the youngest, was, in this case, the wisest. She knew in her bones that friendship was a magic with powers beyond words or possibilities. And so the magic grew stronger. They could feel one another's thoughts coming together, sorting through the various threads of what the moonbeam had reported. Discovering questions. Searching together for answers. This curious union caught them completely off guard, especially Ombric. Never in his centuries of conjuring had he felt this sort of shared purpose. A mental mind melding of sorts, he mused. It was strange. Thrilling.

Katherine wondered the first question aloud. "Where has Pitch taken Nightlight and the children?"

"What is this new sword he wields that can devour light?" North asked next. "And why the devil did Pitch want the library?"

"The diamond dagger was shattered!" Ombric declared. "All is strangeness."

The wizard's mind became totally focused as he tried to fathom the muddles and mysteries the moonbeam had presented to them. His mustache and beard began to twirl on their own at a lively pace. He felt Katherine and North connecting to his thoughts.

Ombric suddenly strode over to his empty bookshelves and began examining each intently. Only a few tiny scraps of paper remained, a bit from *Spells of the Ancient Egyptians,* another from *Interesting Unexplainables of Atlantis,* some tattered corners of random maps and charts. Even Katherine's storybook was missing. There was no denying it. The library Ombric had carefully amassed over hundreds of years had utterly disappeared.

Ombric closed his eyes and concentrated, casting about for remnants of leftover magic. "I find no evidence of a vanishing spell," he said, his voice edged with small relief. "No magic was used. The books still exist—somewhere." Then his eyes grew wide. The tips of his shoes stood on end. Katherine and North stared at him warily.

"He's taken them to the Earth's core!" Ombric proclaimed triumphantly. "That's where Pitch obtained the lead. His saber and cloak are made with it!"

North cocked his head. "Lead? What's so special about this lead?"

"Lead found at the core of Earth has been there since the planet was first formed," Ombric explained. "It has never known light—of any kind—so no light can penetrate it. It absorbs it. That's how Pitch was able to attack Nightlight and the moonbeam. He stole some of their light."

"The madman is growing more wily by the day!" North exclaimed. "And the library? Why was he after that?"

Ombric spoke more carefully, as if figuring it out as he went. "Pitch needs all the spells and enchantments in my volumes to become more powerful. To become, perhaps, invincible," he added with some measure of awe. "But, somehow, the library disappeared before he could get it." Ombric frowned. "And that's the part I can't make heads or tails of."

"Without magic, how can all those books just disappear?" North asked.

"Exactly!" said Ombric. "That's the puzzlement."

Katherine took in all of this new information. Her mind worked with lightning speed as she pieced together all the clues herself. What the moonbeam had told them, what they had found here, and what she thought it might all mean. Then suddenly she knew. "It's Nightlight!" she shouted. "He told the moonbeam not to believe everything it sees. He found a way!"

North and Ombric considered the idea, both becoming lost in thought. Then North's mustache began to twirl on its own, as Ombric's had moments before.

"If Pitch is at the planet's core, it's a trap!" North said, restraining his rage. "He knows we'll come to rescue the children." He drew his sword. "But he has not faced this blade since the Golden Age. And never with me at its command." He turned to Ombric. "How do we get to the Earth's core, old man?"

Ombric felt so proud of them. They were becoming a very potent and powerful team. But this elation gave way quickly to disappointment. He had no answer to the question. "*That* is a journey no man has ever made," he said with a furrowed brow.

Then North's sword began to glow and clatter. The cover of the blade's grip began to twist and unfold as it had before. One of its stones started to shine brightly.

All three of them peered at it. North's heart surged. "This is what I'd started to tell you about earlier, old man!" he cried. In a flurry of words he laid out what he'd discovered thus far of the sword's powers. "The sword is telling us where we must go. Where the next relic lies."

Ombric nodded sagely. His brows unfurrowed. He almost smiled. He *almost* began to laugh.

"What is it, old man?" asked North impatiently.

"Why, it's a map of Earth!" replied the wizard. "We must go to Easter Island!"

"Easter Island?" asked North.

"Yes! The legend says that's where the Pooka lives."

The trio began to think very hard.

Mustaches, beards, and eyebrows were twirling wildly on the men as they concentrated. As for Katherine, though she did not notice it, a single curl right in the middle of her forehead was twirling too.

CHAPTER FIFTEEN

Wherein the Friends Must Separate

KATHERINE SPOTTED PETROV AND the bear lying just outside Big Root's door and winced. They didn't look as though they were in pain, but still, it must be terrible to be unable to move or talk or even blink. "Can we unfreeze them now?" she asked Ombric. "Maybe they can tell us where the books are."

"I say we fly to the center of the Earth and rescue the children!" North blustered. Every muscle in his body strained to do something—anything—to help the children.

"How do you plan to do that?" Ombric asked,

folding his arms across his chest.

"I'll figure it out on the way," North said.

"Let's take things one at a time, shall we?" Ombric told him, looking around. "Perhaps Katherine is right, and the animals can tell us what became of my books. But an enslavement spell this powerful can't be reversed quickly. It needs to be done carefully and well." He shook his head. "It's the work of many, many hours."

"Then they'll have to stay like this until we return," North said to Ombric. "You can release them after we've crushed the Nightmare King. We'll help you."

Ombric tugged at his beard, frowning. "Some of these spells are trickier than others. If I wait too long, I fear this spell could be irreversible." He looked at the porcelain creatures scattered across his floor. "There are no two ways about it. I'll have to stay behind in

Santoff Claussen, and you'll have to continue on to Easter Island."

"Easter Island! We have to get to Pitch!" North bellowed.

Katherine added, "Nightlight is hurt!"

"The Pooka, if he can be found, will be able to lead you to the Earth's core," Ombric explained. "Pooka lore indicates that he has a series of tunnels that span the interior of the globe."

North began to object, but Ombric insisted. "By the time you reach Pitch, I expect to have restored our friends here and discovered the whereabouts of my library."

Looking up at him with her steady gaze, Katherine said, "You can do whatever you set your mind to."

Ombric raised an eyebrow. "The student reinterprets the teacher's lesson," he said. "Well done."

"Just do me a favor, old man," North conceded. "Release Petrov first. I can't stand to see him like this."

Ombric agreed. Then, with no time to lose, Katherine, Kailash, and North left Big Root.

On their way to the forest, Katherine looked into Old William's frozen eyes. "We'll be back," she promised him. "And so will all of your Williams."

She climbed into the air shuttle, strapped Kailash into a seat, and then did the same for herself.

"To Easter Island! Let's hope this Bunnymund creature actually exists," North said, scanning the sky for signs of trouble. "There's no setting for the Earth's core."

As he watched them rocket away, Ombric knew he could trust the brave girl he had raised and the young man who had been his apprentice. They would do what needed to be done.

CHAPTER SIXTEEN

The Curl Twirls

KATHERINE'S CURL BEGAN TO twirl again as she and North streaked toward Easter Island.

She did not like that they could not all stay together. But she was certain that Ombric was correct. Only he could manage the delicate and lengthy task of undoing all the enslavement spells that Pitch had conjured against Santoff Claussen. The parents, the owls, the insects, the Spirit of the Forest, the bear, Petrov—everything that breathed would have to be individually "un-toyed," as Katherine had termed it.

Still, she had been brave for so long, and truth be told, she was a little weary of having to be such a grown-up. She wanted Ombric near. He was like a father to her. And in times of danger, it feels good to have one's own father near, not thousands of miles away. But she bore this anxious feeling silently.

She knew they would need to be at their best, perhaps even more than their best, to save their friends and once again undo the dark plans of Pitch.

They were far above the ocean of the Pacific now. The Moon was clear and bright, and so close that they thought they could see the Man in the Moon and his Moonbots smiling down at them.

They rocketed forward—faster even than they had flown on their way to Santoff Claussen. And the stone on the magic sword that marked Easter Island blinked steadily.

Katherine looked at it with alarm. "Is that a bad sign?"

North shook his head. "Quite the opposite! It means we're getting closer."

Kailash honked. "She's glad," Katherine said.

"Of course she is; we're on the wildest goose chase in history!" North joked.

Katherine was glad for the joke, and even more glad to know that North sensed her worries and was trying to cheer her.

The dials of the airship let out an alarm. Up ahead was Easter Island! The sun was just beginning to rise when the ship settled gently on a sandy beach. It cast a soft glow over the island, and Katherine could hardly wait to get out. North opened the shuttle's door and climbed down the ladder.

Katherine patted her pocket to make sure she had

her dagger. Satisfied, she turned to Kailash. "Stay here until I know it's safe," she told the gosling, then she jumped onto the sand after North.

Together they began to explore the island.

Hundreds of giant stone heads sat ominously across the barren beach. Katherine had seen drawings of these colossal sculptures in Ombric's library. But they were much stranger than she'd expected and larger than she'd imagined.

North ran his hand across a mouth—a narrow slit below an enormous stone nose. "These were carved," he said. "But by who?"

There were no signs of life. No humans running over to see what had landed on their beach. No birds cawing in alarm. Katherine and North walked among the stone heads and wondered if there were any living creatures on the island at all. The only sound was that

of the waves coming in and going out again. Oddly, Katherine thought she smelled a hint of hot cocoa in the salty sea air. And she had the strangest sensation that they were being watched.

And they were! One of the stone heads had turned in their direction. Then another. And another. With the screech of stone scraping against stone, all the heads, as far as they could see, were slowly rotating toward them.

The orb on the magic sword was glowing even brighter. North took a chance. "Where can we find the Pooka?" he shouted out. "We need to get to the Earth's core—on the double!"

The heads didn't answer.

But as the echo of his shouts died away, something began to emerge from the top of each of the stone sculptures. Two stone shafts, almost like ears, slowly rose, stretching to sharp points at the tips. The heads had grown stone rabbit ears! Every one of them! Katherine and North exchanged uneasy glances.

Then something, or someone, twisted up out of the ground a dozen feet away, sending sand and grass flying in all directions.

Katherine and North found themselves looking at an extremely tall rabbit. He stood completely upright, not crouched like a bunny. He was at least seven feet tall (with ears) and wore green egg-shaped glasses and a thick green robe with golden egg-shaped buttons. Around his waist was a purple sash and waistcoat with egg-shaped pockets. He held a tall staff with an egg at its tip.

Katherine gave the Rabbit Man an uneasy smile.

The rabbit did not respond. He didn't even blink. In fact, he was so still that Katherine thought he might be a statue too. She took a step closer, but to her utter surprise, a group of armor-covered eggs with tiny arms and legs emerged from under the hem of the rabbit's robe. The eggs raised their bows. Their arrows, she noticed, had tiny egg-shaped points.

Katherine pulled back again, but North was less cautious. He had seen the rabbit's nose twitch and had an inkling.

"You are the Pooka, I presume?" he asked.

The rabbit became a sudden blur of motion. In less than a blink he was standing directly in front of them.

"I am E. Aster Bunnymund," he said in a deep, melodious voice. "I've been expecting you."

E. Aster Bunnymund,
last of the Pookas

In Which Pitch Appreciates North's Ingenuity but Proves to Be a Dark Customer Indeed

NORTH'S MECHANICAL DJINNI WAS a truly inspired invention. Pitch took delight not only in the theft of his enemy's creation, but also in the wonderful things it could do. When he was inside the djinni, Pitch could not only venture out into the sunlight, he could turn it into any number of machines, most notably, one that could fly—the perfect way to quickly transport the children across a vast distance.

With the children and Nightlight trapped within his lead cloak, Pitch had transformed the djinni into just such a machine.

He cared nothing for beauty, but he appreciated the elaborate design of the flying sleigh machine that swelled out from the djinni's shoulders, back, and arms—every floorboard, deck, and bolt was a mechanical marvel. A surge of envy roiled through him, for it was clearly a combination of ancient magic and human invention that had created this masterpiece. The Nightmare King had never imagined anything that even approached North's genius. But he would. Oh, once he had all the books in the wizard's library, he would.

He narrowed his eyes and issued a curt command to the djinni. "Take me to the core!"

Propellers began to spin, and within seconds, the sleigh was piloting across the sky, crossing continents, then oceans, finally landing upon one of the most desolate places on Earth: a volcano at the very top of the Andes Mountains.

Inside the cloak, the children of Santoff Claussen whispered to one another about where they might be and whether or not Ombric and North had already started their rescue mission.

William the Absolute Youngest fumed in the darkness. "I wish I had a sword," he muttered.

"I do too!" said his oldest brother. "If I had North's new sword, why, I'd—"

"Silence!" roared Pitch. The volcano was a shortcut to his new lair. As they entered the open fissure of the volcano, the flying machine's propellers folded tight. They were speeding down faster and faster, straight for the center of the Earth.

The children, trapped in the inky darkness of Pitch's cloak, could see almost nothing, though their ears began to pop. Their only light was Nightlight's considerably diminished glow.

Tall William and Petter, aided by Fog, tried to push their way out of the cloak prison—to no avail. The black cloth wasn't woven, but made of a metal mesh that was flexible but impenetrable, no matter how hard the boys pushed and clawed at it. Sascha did her best to comfort William the Absolute Youngest and some of the other children, but she was most concerned about Nightlight. He lay slumped against the cloak, his eyes closed. His light grew more and more faint—it started to flicker.

William the Absolute Youngest cried out, "Is he dying?" Tears slipped down the children's cheeks. They held their breaths, watching and hoping that the youngest William was wrong.

Sascha grasped Nightlight's hand. It felt strange in hers, like it was made of air and light and crystals, but in a moment he began to glow—faintly—again, and she breathed a sigh of relief.

To her surprise, Nightlight reached out, collected her tears in his hand, and then did the same with those of the other children. He closed his fist tight around them, before pulling his fist to his chest. The children could see where the bookworm was hiding under Nightlight's jacket. "I hope Mr. Qwerty is all right," said Sascha.

"Remember," whispered Petter, "we mustn't tell Pitch about Mr. Qwerty." Just as they were all nodding in agreement, they slammed down on a rocky surface. The children tumbled onto a hard floor, scraping their knees and elbows. Then Pitch flung open his coat, sending them spinning and rolling in all directions. Sascha banged into a wall. Petter rolled away from Pitch's raised foot only seconds before he brought it down, hard. Tall William did his best to gather the youngest children in a tight group.

They were in a giant room with walls of grayish melted-looking metal. The air reeked of sulfur— shallow pools of milky lava flowed around one end of the room. The children could feel Fearlings weaving in and out of their legs like shadowy black cats. Fog flinched and batted furiously at one that seemed to be whispering in his ear. Sascha pressed her lips together and swallowed a scream as another slithered around her face and head.

Nightlight had helped them see inside the cloak, but here the walls seemed to absorb his dim glow, leaving them in a darkness so thick that they began to wonder if Pitch had swallowed up all the light in the world.

Then there was a sound like fingers snapping, and blue flames appeared from the lava pools, casting everything in an eerie glow. The Fearlings pulled back from the light, but couldn't resist continuing to reach for the children, their long, tentacle-like fingers creeping within inches of their faces.

The older boys drew the younger children behind them, and they all instinctively formed a protective circle around Nightlight.

Pitch smirked at their efforts. He commanded the djinni suit to transform itself back into a mechanical man. Then an inky vapor rose out of the djinni's ear, oozing outward and sharpening into the shape Pitch most preferred for himself. He kicked the mechanical suit aside and loomed over his hostages.

Sascha felt the hands of the smaller children reaching for hers, pulling at her sleeves. She forced herself to stay calm. Ombric, North, and Katherine would move Heaven and Earth to come to their rescue; she knew that as surely as she knew that the sky was blue, the grass was green, and fireflies cheated at games of tag. Still, she couldn't keep herself from averting her eyes as Pitch's gaze lingered on each of them. When he reached Tall William, however, the boy stared back.

"You said you had no plans to hurt us," Tall William said as Pitch loomed over him.

"I remember what I said, boy," Pitch answered. "If your precious wizard hands over his library, perhaps I'll keep my promise. Or perhaps not." Then he pointed his long skeleton arms toward Nightlight.

"But you," he added with a malevolent smile aimed directly at the spectral boy, "you are another story."

Nightlight stared back at Pitch with a weak but mischievous grin. The children's strength was feeding his own, and his light was steadily brightening.

He thought of Katherine, of how much he wanted to see her again, and became stronger still. He had spent thousands of years trapped inside this monster. He could survive whatever it wanted to do to him now.

Enraged by Nightlight's smirk, Pitch raised his hand as if to crush him. Sascha shrieked, but Nightlight's grin only grew wider.

"I'll turn you into my Fearling prince," Pitch threatened. "And your friend, Katherine—when she arrives—will be my princess."

Nightlight knew exactly what Pitch was doing: trying to frighten him by threatening Katherine. He deliberately smiled wider.

Pitch reached out his long, gnarly hand and, with agonizing slowness, let his fingers hover just an inch from Nightlight's head. "Now *you* will be *mine*. You kept me imprisoned for centuries. Day after day, year after year, I dreamed of revenge. . . ." He lowered his hand, but the instant he gripped Nightlight, there was a brilliant explosion of light, sending Pitch staggering backward.

He grasped his hand in pain, and for a moment his palm and fingers seemed to glow, then became flesh-colored. The look on Pitch's face was an unsettling mix of fury and something else. Something the children had never expected to see. Something that looked like . . . sorrow.

Pitch screamed. He covered his injured hand with his cloak, pulled out his sword with his other, then pointed toward a small, cramped cell that hung suspended from the ceiling. A swarm of Fearlings picked up Nightlight and threw him inside the small lead cage. "Please be my guest," Pitch said, his voice suddenly taking on a cheerful tone, "in this solid lead prison, created especially for *you*."

Pitch slammed the door with the tip of his sword. The sword's point then transformed and sharpened into the shape of a key. He locked the door, and the key transformed back into his sword.

"The only way to open that door now will be to kill me," he said with a gleeful smile. "And who amongst you is up to that?!"

Then he laughed in a way that left the children feeling helpless.

CHAPTER EIGHTEEN

A Surprising Twist with a Chocolate Center

THE RABBIT AND NORTH eyed each other, sizing one another up.

North had been dubious about this fabled Rabbit Man since Ombric had first described him. North liked to think that he and Ombric were the world's greatest hero and wizard. The idea of this *rabbit* as their equal—perhaps their superior—did not sit well with the prideful Nicholas St. North. But he would give the Pooka a chance.

"You've been expecting us?" North asked wryly.

"Yes and no. I have and I haven't. Maybe. Maybe

not. I did, however, have an inkling," the rabbit answered. He opened one of his egg-shaped pockets and withdrew some egg-shaped candies. Their outer shells were pebbled with an astonishing variety of delicately iced decorations. "Please, have a chocolate. I make the best in the universe," the rabbit said.

That was the sweet scent Katherine had noticed earlier—chocolate—but this was so alluring that she could barely think of anything else. This wasn't just a whiff of some common candy; it was a hypnotizing mist of taste possibility.

"This one has a caramel center made with the milk of an intergalactic bovine creature that on occasion jumps over the Moon," the Pooka told her, waving it under her nose. "And this one—marshmallow made from the whipped eggs of Asian peacocks!" Bunnymund's eyes glistened. His nose twitched and he leaned forward, holding out a pair of chocolates.

Katherine wavered—she was so hungry. In all their dashing about, she and North hadn't remembered to pack anything to eat. So she reached for one of the chocolates.

Before North could object, the Pooka turned to him. "You, sir, would likely enjoy something darker . . . wilder." He pulled forth a candy of impressive size. "This egg is made with cacao leaves that grow in the dark center of the great caves of Calcutta; it contains a pinch of mint from the ice caps of Mars. It also has three molecules of Hawaiian lava sprouts for a little extra kick."

Never had North smelled something so tantalizing. It was almost as tempting as the jewels the Spirit of the Forest had used to lure his band of outlaws in the enchanted forest. She had turned his men into stone elves, so he couldn't help but be a little suspicious of this offering. Besides, the Pooka's egg warriors were still pointing their bows at them.

"You have a piece first," North countered.

"I should," the rabbit agreed. Then he sighed. "But I shouldn't. Couldn't. Shan't. Won't. It's a long story, full of woe."

That made not a lick of sense to North. But he could not resist the chocolate egg—he was even hungrier than Katherine was. "All right, but call off your warriors," he demanded.

"Yes, of course." Bunnymund waved a paw, and the eggs lowered their weapons and stepped away in perfect unison. *Impressive*, North noted, *and deeply peculiar*. He decided that the Pooka was probably harmless enough, but still, one could never be entirely sure.

The air was rich with an overwhelming scent of chocolate, and Katherine could resist its spell no longer. She had been waiting politely for North to take a chocolate before eating her own, but now she popped the caramel egg into her mouth. A look of bliss crossed her face. Her eyes closed.

Both North and Bunnymund watched her carefully—North out of concern, and Bunnymund with an eagerness to hear her reaction. Katherine began to sway slowly back and forth as if in a dream. She was bewitched by the chocolatey goodness.

The Pooka could wait no longer. "You liked it?" he asked, a single twitching whisker betraying his intense interest.

Katherine smiled, her mouth still flooded with the flavor even after she'd swallowed the candy. "The best chocolate I ever had or thought I would ever have!" she answered dreamily.

"Perfect!" said the rabbit, the rest of his whiskers

now twitching along with his nose.

Then he slammed his staff against the ground, and the Earth opened up beneath them. Katherine and North tumbled forward, spinning down a hole that seemed to be digging itself as they fell. Clumps of rock and dirt whirled past them.

When they stopped, the hole above them closed, and they saw that their chamber led to another egg-shaped chamber, and another and another. There was an endless row of them, stretching as far as they could see. Hundreds of living eggs of various sizes, designs, and uniforms strode about on their toothpick-thin legs, engaged in a wide array of duties. Mixing chocolate. Making candy eggs. Decorating eggs. Painting eggs. Polishing eggs. Packaging eggs. It was all very, very egg-centric.

Katherine gazed about in wonder, then spied

A warrior chocolatier egg

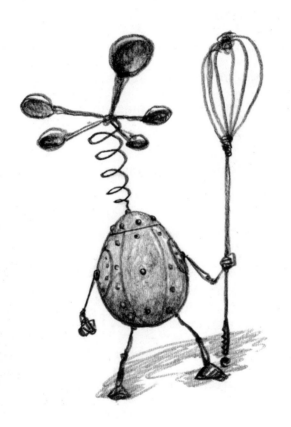

something familiar in a chamber up ahead. It was their ship! Bunnymund had somehow brought it underground too. She sighed with relief: Now she wouldn't have to worry about Kailash being left behind. Still, she wanted Kailash to stay put until she was completely sure this strange underground world was safe.

"Come," Bunnymund invited them, gesturing grandly. "I have much to show you." They passed a vast display of every conceivable type of egg. "I have eggs from every species that ever laid them," Bunnymund said expansively. "Dodo birds, pterodactyls, dinosaurs, the Egg Men of Quacklandia . . ."

On one wall North and Katherine saw a picture of a familiar green and blue planet, only it was egg-shaped, not round. "Is that supposed to be Earth?" Katherine asked.

Bunnymund traced the image reverently. "Yes, many zillions of years ago," he answered. "At that time it was egg-shaped. Unfortunately, ovals have an unstable orbit. If left unchecked, the planet would have swirled closer and closer to the sun and eventually been cooked like a hard-boiled egg."

Katherine stared again at the picture. "But . . . how did it become round?"

"Oh, I fixed it—a nip here, a tuck there," the Pooka said matter-of-factly. "It's rather sad, really. Ovals are such an interesting shape. And circles? Well, so ordinary, common, *dull*." Then he sighed deeply as if saving the planet had been a particularly distressing household chore. "I used the excess dirt to make a few more continents. Australia is my best work, I think," he said. "I'm quite good at digging."

Katherine blinked. "You made *Australia?*"

"Right after I finished the Himalayas," he replied. His whiskers gave a twitch. "But enough geography; I have many, many more eggs to show you."

He spun on a back paw and leaned in toward Katherine. "The egg is the most perfect shape in the universe, don't you agree?"

"We do," Katherine said, nodding enthusiastically, sensing that this would please the rabbit and that pleasing him would make things go faster. "But, well, we're in a hurry. Our friends are in trouble, and our teacher, Ombric Shalazar, believes you can help us." Katherine looked hopefully at him.

"The wizard from Atlantis," Bunnymund said, his ears now twitching. "I had high hopes for that city, but then it vanished." He shook his head. "I did what I could, but . . . humans."

Katherine wasn't sure how to respond to this, but

she had to keep him on subject. She tried to make her face express chagrin at being a mere human, then she pressed on. "Can you help us get to the Earth's core from here?"

Impatience was bubbling up inside North. The light on his sword was blinking more and more frequently, which could only mean that they must be very close to the relic. "Blast it, Man Rabbit! We need your help! We need the Moon relic and we need to get going. Will you help us or not?" he demanded.

Bunnymund sniffed. "I am neither a rabbit nor a man. I am a Pooka. The name is Bunny*mund*. E. Aster Bunnymund, to be precise."

He leaned forward and asked Katherine, "What other chocolates would you care to try, human girl?"

North had never liked being dismissed, and his temper was about to turn blistering, so Katherine jumped in before he could say anything more, trying to remain polite. "It's not easy to choose," she said, trying to sound confounded.

The Pooka stared at her. She had to do something to make him like them. So she began to lick the last dustings of chocolate from her fingers.

Bunnymund watched her closely. "You do love my chocolate," he said. But then he looked rather glum. "If only chocolate didn't . . . ," and he stopped.

"Didn't what?" Katherine encouraged.

Bunnymund closed his eyes and breathed in. "Alas," he sighed, "chocolate is bad for Pookas."

Well, this is interesting, North thought. *The Pooka surrounds himself with what tempts him the most.* He gave Bunnymund an appraising stare. "Bad how?" he asked.

Bunnymund shot him a look. "It makes me more like you. Illogical. Racing about. Always trying to save the day." He shook his head, as if disgusted with himself.

North began to object to the rabbit's tone, but Bunnymund had turned his back to them and was now throwing open the door of a cabinet filled top to bottom with shelves of chocolate eggs. The display was dazzling.

Katherine stopped him. "You've been very generous," she said. "But we'd be most grateful if you would let us borrow the relic—and help us get to the Earth's core. Please."

"Oh, no, no, no," the Pooka said, pulling out a tray of confections. "My expertise is in chocolate. I don't get involved in human affairs. Not anymore."

"Untrue!" said North. "You stopped Ombric from changing history when *he* went back in time. Twice!"

"Indeed. But tampering with the past is not allowed for any living creature—Man, Beast, Plant, or Egg. I've been watching that Ombric of yours since he was a boy. He doesn't believe in rules very much."

"Yes," agreed North. "Especially stupid ones."

The rabbit didn't seem to like North's manner.

Katherine shrewdly changed the subject. "You know what Pitch did to the Golden Age. Don't you want to stop him from doing any more damage?"

Bunnymund shrugged. "Humans come. Humans go. They leave many relics. I've been on the planet much longer than humans have, and I will be here long after there are no more."

"Balderdash!" said North. "So you won't help us?"

"My dear fellow, I didn't say I wouldn't help you," Bunnymund replied. "I am just not *interested* in helping you."

North and Katherine did not know how to respond.

CHAPTER NINETEEN

Nightlight Is Dimmed

DEEPER BELOW GROUND THAN any human had
ever ventured, the children of Santoff Clausen hung
in metal cages in the center of the Earth. The cages,
which hovered a few feet above the floor, were freshly
made just for them. The strange swirling shapes of
hastily poured molten lead surrounding them was full
of airholes and gaps so the children, at least, could see
out. There was much activity around them. Countless
Fearlings were building and shaping innumerable
lead weapons, armor plates, and shields. The children
could hear Pitch's frenzied shouting of orders and

they looked repeatedly toward Nightlight's prison for reassurance. Just knowing he was nearby helped, which was the only comfort they had.

Unlike their cages, Nightlight's prison was made of solid lead. There wasn't a window, there wasn't a crack, there wasn't a pinhole. And the door was sealed so tight, no light could make its way inside.

Nightlight lay on the floor of the cage. He did not move. His eyes were closed. His light grew dimmer with every passing minute. The lead seemed to be leaching all his brightness from him. But Nightlight was not alone.

Something stirred under his jacket. And for a moment Nightlight glowed brighter.

CHAPTER TWENTY

In Which We Find Munch Marks of Mystery

Back in Santoff Claussen, Ombric was slowly and carefully releasing prisoners of another sort: the residents of the village who were caught in Pitch's enslavement spell. It haunted him to see his beloved village, the focus of his long and brilliant life, frozen in a moment of struggle and terror. He began with Petrov, the bear, and the Spirit of the Forest, for they would need to keep watch in case the Fearlings were planning to attack again.

As they stamped and roared and spun themselves awake, Ombric told them the terrible news of the children's capture. Despair hung over them like a shroud—they had failed to protect the children from Pitch. Ombric urged them not to blame themselves.

"Even I once was caught by Pitch in such a spell," he explained. Urgently, he told them that Pitch was holding the children hostage and that the library was the ransom he demanded. None of them knew where his books had gone, so Ombric moved on to release the owls and the other creatures in Big Root. They seemed the most likely to be able to help him solve the mystery.

To each creature raised from Pitch's spell, Ombric asked the same questions: "What happened to the books in my library? Where are they?"

And each time he got the same answer. No one knew. But from the moonbeam, Ombric *had* learned one important detail: His shelves were already empty when Pitch smashed into the library.

Before she had left, Katherine had carefully gathered the pieces of Nightlight's shattered diamond dagger and placed them in a box. It was in this box where the moonbeam now rested. The poor little fellow seemed comforted to be with the diamond shards that had become his home, and Ombric found himself wondering if the dagger could ever be repaired. It was the physical manifestation of the Man in the Moon's spirit and of Nightlight's courage, forged during that last great battle of the Golden Age. But now Ombric knew that the dagger could not be used to hurt anyone or anything good. That was why it had shattered when Pitch tried to kill Nightlight with it.

Once all the creatures in Big Root were up and

stretching, Ombric headed outside. He had saved the parents for last. They had likely been unconscious while under Pitch's spell, so he would have to tell them that their children had been taken.

The parents seemed to have just reached Big Root when Pitch had bewitched them, for that's where they lay, most of them on their sides or on their backs, where they had fallen when the Nightmare King turned them into toys. Their china faces expressed dread and alarm, the only exception being Old William's.

Ombric released him first. Old William contorted his lips again and again to get them moving. Then, as soon as he was able to speak, the father of all the Williams told Ombric his story: "I'm no swordsman, but I fought with all my might. We used stardust bombs against him! But they did nothing. His cloak and sword sucked up all the light! He stormed

Big Root, boasting that he was going to be a more powerful wizard than you."

Old William's voice cracked with desperation. "Will I see my Williams again?" he asked.

"Yes," Ombric promised him.

Old William walked with Ombric as he moved from parent to parent, transforming them from tiny, porcelain versions of themselves back into living, breathing human beings. And Ombric told them to be brave, that their children had been taken hostage.

He met the gaze of each and every parent, taking in their worried frowns and wishing he could ease their burdens. "Nicholas St. North and Katherine are on their way to the Earth's core even now," he told them. "I will do my utmost to find the books Pitch covets, and when I do, they'll make the exchange. But I must know where the books are."

But all the parents assured Ombric that the children had been working on lessons in his library up until the moment Pitch's Fearlings began to seep into the enchanted forest.

"And yet all the books disappeared *before* Pitch could get to them," Ombric mused, stroking his beard.

The Spirit of the Forest hovered above him. "He took pleasure in what he had done to us," she told him. "He swaggered about, enjoying his handiwork." She began to weep tears of angry frustration. They hardened to emeralds and pearls that spilled uselessly to the ground, reminding her once again that her treasures were not what Pitch was after.

Ombric grew increasingly puzzled, and as soon as every living being in Santoff Claussen had been restored, he returned to his shattered library to investigate more diligently. The owls could remember nearly nothing. They'd seen a flash of light just as Nightlight rushed in. He made what looked like a protective shield around the children with it. Then Pitch's spell began to take hold of the owls, and everything had gone dark. Ombric saw that bit of information as a clue. He plucked up one of the tiny scraps of paper that littered the floor, turning it over and over. He held it up to the light and noticed funny little markings on one edge. He picked up another scrap, then another. They all had the same choppy shapes along one edge.

Ombric sat back in his chair, closed his eyes, and tried to remember where he had seen similar markings. Suddenly, it hit him.

"Teeth marks!" he exclaimed. "Those are teeth marks!"

CHAPTER TWENTY-ONE

The Egg-cellent Exchange

BUNNYMUND'S "JUST NOT INTERESTED" still hung in the air.

The Pooka's nose twitched, and with a sharp twist of his staff, he disappeared.

Katherine and North were alone.

"I think you made him mad," said Katherine.

"Who needs his help?" North declared. "Let's find that relic ourselves. Perhaps it can get us out of here and to the Earth's core." He let his sword lead them. Its blade pulled them through one egg-shaped chamber after another.

The first few chambers were similar to the one they had already been in—equipped for candy making. One smelled curiously of cinnamon and another of a sweetness that was so powerful and tempting, they had to fight the urge to stop and inhale its trancelike perfection forever.

But the next chamber they found themselves in was a curious kind of egg museum. There were shelves upon shelves of intricately crafted, jewel-encrusted eggs.

North whistled. "I know a Russian tsar who would pay a fortune for some of these," he said appraisingly as the sword pulled him on to yet another chamber.

The next room, too, was a kind of museum, but the eggs here were natural. A bumpy yellow and orange shell labeled SEA MONSTER sat beside the green speckled egg of a MESOPOTAMIAN DRAGON.

Rows and rows of eggshells lined the walls, ranging from the giant egg of a mega-octopus (pure white and bigger than North's head) to the miniature ones of a hummingbird (smaller than Katherine's thumbnail). There were chicken eggs and goose eggs, duck eggs and swan eggs, and even the tiny illuminated yellow eggs of a glowworm, barely the size of pinpricks. There were so many sizes and colors and patterns and speckles that these eggs seemed to Katherine to be even more beautiful than the eggs carved of gold and jewels. Then North let out a long, slow whistle.

Katherine ran to the next room.

Inside was just a single egg. It sat on a podium of gleaming silver. The egg looked as if it were made of the same mysterious metal as North's sword and was covered in gorgeously wrought carvings of suns and moons and stars. At its center was a crescent Moon that glowed with the same intensity as the orb on the magic sword. In fact, the egg and the sword seemed to be reaching for each other.

"That's it!" North cried out triumphantly. "That's the relic!"

He raced forward, reaching out to snatch up the egg. But before he could get his hand on it, he found himself being hurtled across the room. He landed against the wall, his head pounding.

When he could focus again, Bunnymund was standing over him. "Naughty. Naughty," he said.

North jumped to his feet, rubbing the back of his head. "Did you do that?" he shouted.

Bunnymund again went so still that he didn't appear to be breathing. Then his nose twitched.

Katherine sensed a fight coming on. So, it seemed, did the Warrior Eggs. A mass of them trotted into the chamber on their tiny legs, bows again at the ready. Katherine ran over to stand between North and the Pooka.

"That egg does not belong to you," the rabbit told North firmly.

North clenched his teeth to keep from yelling. "Don't get your whiskers in a twist, Man Bunny," he said. "I doubt you even know the power and significance of that precious egg of yours! That it was fashioned by *people*, not by rabbits or Pookas, but humans from an age more grand than you can imagine. And that it was intended for purposes of good and honor and bravery, not to be used as some useless bauble that satisfies the puny whims of your precious collection!"

It was clear that North's argument had a powerful effect on Bunnymund. The rabbit stepped closer.

He then stood ramrod straight while his nose and whiskers twitched and stilled. Twitched and stilled. The twitches were soon as fast and blurred as the wings of a hummingbird in flight. Then the Pooka spoke very calmly and firmly.

"I know the egg's powers and its origins quite well, Mr. North. I helped, in fact, to make it." He paused for a moment, letting North absorb that information. He drew himself taller, adding, "Inside its curved shell is the purest light in all creation. Light from the exact beginning of time. It is the light that all Pookas were sworn to wield and protect. But men, *people*, cannot be trusted with it. We tried once, during the Golden Age."

"Fine! Then *you* must help us stop Pitch," North pressed. "*He* killed the Golden Age! He is a creature! A monster—"

"But," Bunnymund interrupted, "he was first a *man.*"

North was not ready with a fast retort, but the Pooka raised his hand as if he were and continued: "Pookas were the gatherers of this light. We brought it to worlds that we felt were ready for its power. We thought that the people of the Golden Age showed the most promise of all, and they used it well. But then Pitch came. He destroyed everything. He is why I am the last of my kind. I came here with the hope of a new Golden Age." He fixed North with a stare. "That is why Tsar Lunar, the Man in the Moon's father, sent this 'relic,' as you call it, to me.

"And since it has been in my possession, I've tried over and over to help the world of humans. I've invented most of your trees, flowers, grass. Spring. Jokes. Summer vacations. Recess. Chocolate. But none of it seems to have changed anything. Humans still behave badly and never seem to cherish the light." A look that could only be described as forlorn crossed the Pooka's face, and his voice grew solemn. "Man cannot be trusted."

"All that you invented—all of it—will be lost if Pitch has his way," argued North. "He'll drain *all* the light out of the world. Can you let that happen?"

Bunnymund seemed to think about that for a moment.

"Pitch and his Fearlings don't even like chocolate *or eggs!*" Katherine added. She wasn't sure if that was true, but it sounded good.

Bunnymund was deeply disturbed by that remark. He puzzled. And puzzled. The egg warriors seemed unsure. They lowered their weapons a few inches. Finally, the rabbit spoke.

"The fiends! Not like chocolate? Not like"—he gasped—"eggs? Now, won't you please stop talking—you humans use so many, many words. And so few of them are about eggs. It's exhausting."

Bunnymund eased the relic from its shimmering stand and held it aloft. "I will return in approximately one hour and seven minutes, human time—with your friends."

"I'm ready," North said. "Let's go."

"Oh, no, no, no," Bunnymund said. "I work alone."

CHAPTER TWENTY-TWO

One Mystery Begets Another

"TEETH MARKS!" OMBRIC SAID again. "But *whose* teeth marks?" His beard twirled as he pondered.

His exclamation echoed throughout the village. The creatures of the forest, bristling with pent-up energy after having been trapped as toys for so long, joined forces to help Ombric search for clues. Dragonflies and moths flew through every inch of the forest. Spiders and ants crawled into every hidden nook in Big Root. Birds and squirrels checked the treetops.

The parents, too, joined the search, combing

through every home and every yard, upending mattresses and vegetable gardens.

Ombric examined the gnawed pieces of paper with his microscope. "Who would eat my books? Nightlight had some hand in it, I'm sure, but what . . . ," he wondered. He pressed his fingers against his temples, not wanting to admit it, but his last journey through time had taken a great toll on him. The long, slow process of releasing the entire village from Pitch's spell had added to his weariness. For the first time in his very long life, Ombric felt not old but ancient. But he couldn't wallow in this unfamiliar feeling—the children needed him, old or not. So he shook away his fatigue and examined the paper scraps again.

Mr. Qwerty would never allow—

Ombric stopped in midsentence. His eyebrows,

beard, mustache, hair, shoes, and even eyelashes began to twirl.

"MR. QWERTY!" Ombric shouted, leaping up. "MR. QWERTY!! MR. QWEEEEERTY!!!" He hadn't seen the glowworm since he returned to the village! And now he knew the reason. "Mr. Qwerty has eaten my books! To keep them out of Pitch's hands!"

First things first. He remembered what the owls had said: They saw a flash of light before everything had gone dark. Ombric opened the box where the moonbeam rested and asked, "Was Nightlight holding anything when Pitch took him away?"

The moonbeam, sensing Ombric's excitement, grew stronger himself and glowed: *Yes.*

"Was it white? Rather oblong? About the size of my hand?"

The moonbeam pulsed twice.

"That's it!" Ombric said, sitting back down with a knowing nod. "Mr. Qwerty ate the books! Then he wrapped himself in a cocoon! Nightlight's flash of light protected the children and gave Mr. Qwerty time to eat the books. The little fellow was always hungry for knowledge, but this is *epic!*" Ombric was almost laughing now. "Nightlight took Mr. Qwerty! He has him still. The library is in Mr. Qwerty's stomach."

The old wizard stroked his still-twirling beard. "Right under Pitch's nose. . . ."

CHAPTER TWENTY-THREE
The Honk of Destiny

WE WILL NEVER KNOW what furious argument might have followed Bunnymund's insistence that he go to the Earth's core without North and Katherine, for in the incredibly tense seconds after the Pooka had made his declaration, Kailash came waddling into the chamber and honked loudly.

They all three turned and looked at the goose—North with slight irritation, Katherine with concern, and Bunnymund with complete and total awe.

"Is this one of the Great Snow Geese of the Himalayas?" Bunnymund asked, his nose not twitching but sort of rotating slowly in amazement.

"Yes. Her name is Kailash," Katherine told him hesitantly, a little rattled by the rabbit's shift in interest. "She thinks I'm her mother. I was there when she hatched."

The Pooka inhaled deeply. "Tell me everything," he insisted. "Was the egg very beautiful?"

North fought his every impulse not to shake some sense into this strange, long-eared creature. Time was tumbling by, and the rabbit wanted to talk about eggs! But North's calmer self sensed an opportunity.

"Tell him about the blasted egg," he said, motioning to Katherine to hurry.

Katherine put an arm around Kailash's slender neck. "Well, her egg was large and silvery, with swirls of pebble-size bumps that glistened like diamonds and opals," she said.

"As I've always imagined it! Come," Bunnymund said, pointing to his egg museum. One of the shelves had an empty space labeled HIMALAYAN GREAT SNOW GOOSE. "It's the one egg I don't have. My collection is not complete." He stared at Katherine. "It's silvery, you say?"

"Silvery and blue," Katherine elaborated.

The Pooka could scarcely contain himself.

"Kailash would be grateful to anyone who did as we asked," Katherine said.

The Pooka was almost quivering. After a long moment his former reserve seemed to return. His nose twitched. Then he spoke: "My army is already assembled. I am at the ready. As I hope you are. Any friends of the Great Snow Geese are friends of mine. Come this way. We'll take tunnel number seventeen twenty-eight." He paused dramatically, then added with a flourish, "Straight to the Earth's core!"

"Finally," North grumbled, placing his hand on the hilt of the magic sword. The weapon began to glow. Bunnymund's egg relic did the same.

CHAPTER TWENTY-FOUR

In Which There Is a Fearful Discovery and a Whisper of Hope

To THE CHILDREN'S GREAT relief, Pitch and his Fearlings had disappeared into another chamber.

The chamber where they were kept was as wide and as tall as Big Root. But it was nothing like Big Root. This was a dark and fretful place. If Big Root was a treasure chest of wonders, Pitch's lair at the Earth's core was like the fabled box of Pandora: filled with doom and darkness. The children had managed to ever so quietly wiggle through the openings in their cages and climb down. Half a dozen tunnels led out from the chamber, but Tall William and Petter had explored and reported that every one was being guarded by Fearlings. Not that it mattered. The children wouldn't try to escape without Nightlight.

Fog, Petter, and Sascha stood watch while Tall William ran his hands over the door of Nightlight's cage, seeking a knob, a keyhole, anything that would help them free their friend. But there was nothing, not even a crack. Whatever dark magic Pitch had used when he removed his sword from the lock had left the door smoother than fresh ice on the skating pond in Santoff Claussen.

Tall William knocked hard to let Nightlight know that he was there, then placed his ear against the cage.

"Did he hear you?" Sascha asked, putting her own ear against the metal. "Did he knock back?"

Tall William shook his head. "I don't think so,

but it's hard to hear anything with all that banging going on."

That banging was the incessant clamor— clanking, hammering, striking—coming from the next chamber. Every now and again it was peppered by the Nightmare King's booming laugh.

"What do you think Pitch is up to?" Petter whispered.

"Let's find out," Tall William whispered back.

They crept stealthily to the entrance of the next chamber and peered around the wall, just out of sight of the Fearling guards.

What they saw made their eyes go wide. Hundreds of Fearlings were working furiously under Pitch's direction. Some were chipping away at the lead walls, making the room larger, dropping the lead chips into a bucket. Other Fearlings melted buckets of lead over an eerie blue lava. When the lead melted into a sticky liquid, they poured the mixture into molds.

Tall William watched uneasily—something was different about these Fearlings. They seemed more solid, less shadowy, than the others. One of them tested the lead in a mold with a thin rod. It was solid now, and the Fearling popped what looked like a heavy vest out of the mold and then handed it to the creature next to him. They passed it from one to the next, down the line, until it reached a Fearling that looked normal. Or at least what Tall William and the others had come to think of as normal. The creature slipped the object over his shadowy body. Then he, too, took on the more solid look of the others and skulked into the light.

"They're making armor," Tall William breathed out.

Petter stared hard. "It covers them completely."

"Now they'll be able to go out in the sunlight!" whispered Tall William, struggling to keep the dread out of his voice.

Then they saw rows of swords and spears being fashioned from the same thick liquid.

"Like Pitch's sword!" Petter hissed.

They crept back to the others and reported what they had seen.

The smaller children just stared after hearing this alarming news. The smallest William hid his head under Fog's arm.

Sascha drew a deep breath to keep her voice steady, then said, "I wish Ombric and the others would hurry."

Tall William tried hard not to seem scared, but he was. "The Fearlings will be too strong for them now with that armor and those weapons," he said quietly.

Petter grew very serious. "And if they bring Ombric's library, Pitch will know all the magic there is!" he said. "He'll be unstoppable.

"But we mustn't be afraid," he added, trying to convince himself as well as the others. "It only makes Pitch stronger."

The children knew he was right. But it was getting very hard to stay brave.

If they'd only been able to hear the conversation that was taking place inside Nightlight's tiny, cramped cage. Nightlight was listening to the muffled voice of Mr. Qwerty. The cocoon shifted and wiggled under his jacket. "Change is coming," said the valiant little worm. "And it cannot be stopped."

And Nightlight brightened.

CHAPTER TWENTY-FIVE

The Egg Armada

IF THERE ARE SEVEN Wonders of the Known
World, Bunnymund's tunnel to the Earth's core
would be the first of the *unknown* world. It was
shaped like an egg standing on end and seemed to go
on forever. North was intrigued by how quietly the
Pooka's train was traveling. Despite their remarkable
speed, the train barely made a sound, just a quiet sort
of clucking noise. He'd have to ask the Pooka how
he managed that . . . even the mechanical djinni had
emitted squeaks and hums.

And though Katherine was increasingly worried

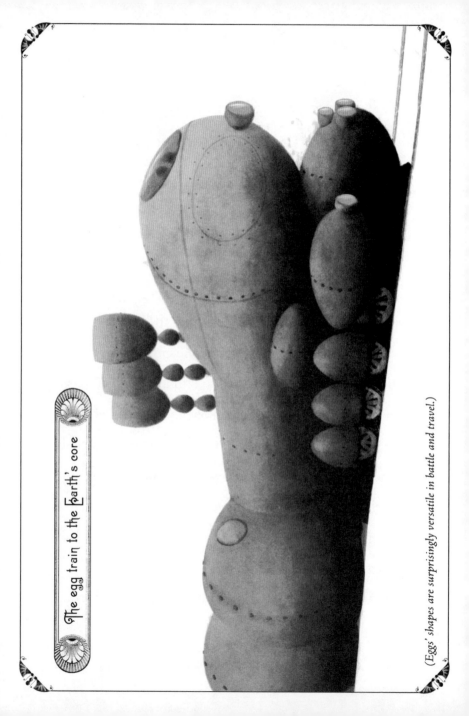

The egg train to the Earth's core

(Eggs' shapes are surprisingly versatile in battle and travel.)

about Nightlight and her friends, she couldn't help noticing how enticingly strange everything about Bunnymund's conveyance was. The railroad cars that were whisking them deeper and deeper underground were of course egg-shaped, as was virtually every knob, hinge, door, window, light fixture, and mechanical component. It was even more opulent than the Lamas' flying tower.

Plus, the cars immediately behind her held an imposing army of well-armored Warrior Eggs wielding an impressive array of weaponry. The smallest eggs were the size of a common chicken's egg, while platoons of other eggs were nearly as big as a good-sized suitcase, and a surprising number of eggs were huge—more than ten feet tall. Katherine was very interested about where *those* eggs could have come from!

North, on the other hand, was having a difficult time taking these Warrior Eggs seriously. *They're eggs!* he thought to himself. *EGGS!* But he tried not to betray his doubts and instead asked his host in a tone that at least hinted at politeness, "Very pretty eggs, Bunnymund, but can they fight?"

The Pooka regarded him evenly, his nose not even twitching. "The Greeks thought so at Troy," he replied, sounding a bit bored. "Though why they built that clumsy horse instead of an egg, as I suggested, I'll never understand."

Katherine, sensing another potential argument brewing, thought it best to interrupt. "Are we getting close?" she asked.

"At our current rate of speed, we'll be there in exactly thirty-seven clucks," Bunnymund replied.

Clucks? North and Katherine both wondered,

then decided not to ask any more questions for a while. Bunnymund's answers always left them feeling, well, they just weren't sure. Bewildered? Uncertain? Odd? Doomed?

Meanwhile, Bunnymund regarded the two humans. He found himself concerned for them. *But why?* Here was this headstrong young man, so determined to be daring. And the little girl, worrying about her friends. Even that lovely goose was all a-twitter about the danger the girl faced. So much disorder and upheaval!

Still, he had to admit that there was a certain satisfaction in working with others, even humans. Never would he acknowledge that out loud, of course, but the Pooka had been alone for so many, many years. Having these other creatures about presented a change of pace. The girl did have excellent taste in chocolates. And there was something to be said for adventure. And what was this if not an adventure?

Bunnymund's musings were interrupted by an insistent clanging sound—far off at the moment, but growing louder and closer as his train barreled forward.

"We're very nearly there," he told the others.

Katherine could tell, for she could smell the dank, sulfury odor of Fearlings. She held her dagger tighter.

At the same time North's sword and Bunnymund's staff both began to glow. Danger was apparently just ahead.

An egg-straordinary way to travel.

CHAPTER TWENTY-SIX

The Now-Rotten Core

Bunnymund ordered the train to stop, and it did so as smoothly as a duck landing on a pond. He, North, and Katherine made their way to the engine car at the front to better see what was ahead. Engineer eggs were still stoking the egg-shaped boiler of the idling engine with egg-shaped clumps of coal.

"They occur naturally," explained Bunnymund before Katherine could even ask the question. "Egg-shaped coal is where diamonds come from."

Katherine liked knowing that, but North found the information distracting.

"Eggs!" he groused. "You talk too much about eggs!"

Bunnymund was offended.

"I do *not*."

"You do too."

"I DO NOT!"

"Yes. You. Do."

"Do not!"

"Do too!"

Katherine sighed. Here they were, the oldest and wisest creature on Earth and the greatest warrior-wizard of the age, yet they were behaving like a pair of brats. She'd been waiting for something like this to happen between them. They'd been aching for a fight since they'd met! Truth be told, she'd expected something more mature from them both. *Grown-ups, wizards, and Pookas! Are they all this muddled?* she wondered.

As the "do not"s and "do too"s continued unabated, Katherine made a decision: She would ignore them both. She turned to Kailash and told her to go to the back of the train and stay quiet. The gosling honked sadly, but Katherine insisted. As Kailash waddled back to the passenger cars, Katherine climbed down from the engine and walked down the tunnel. It was very dim. The walls of the tunnel grew less smooth and crafted. The egg-shaped lanterns that had been affixed to the ceiling for the whole length of the passageway thus far now appeared less and less frequently.

As she continued forward, she could barely make out where the tracks ended. The light of the lantern ahead of her—the last one she could see—was mistier than the others had been. Its shine hit in odd directions. Katherine paused, trying to sort out why that was so.

The ominous clanking they'd heard earlier grew louder and louder; she could feel the reverberations. But she continued forward until she stood under the lantern and its strange glow. The light looked as if it were being blown in the wind.

She followed its fading glow as it twisted farther away, but toward what? She took a few more steps forward, following the light. And with each step, the tunnel grew wider and taller—immense, in fact. And then, to her complete surprise, it stopped. Just stopped. A gray vastness loomed in front of her, a giant wall that blocked her from going any farther. But it didn't stop the light; Katherine could see that the misty stream of lantern light was actually flowing into this wall of dense, dark, metallic-looking rock.

And then she knew. She was at the Earth's core.

She approached the wall cautiously, her dagger at the ready. It occurred to her that her weapon couldn't possibly be of use against *a wall*, but perhaps it could defend against what was on the other side of the wall. So she kept her dagger raised, and she listened intently.

The sounds from within were deep and menacing, like growling thunder from an approaching storm. She heard what she thought was . . . laughing. Laughing? Could that be possible? Then she realized that it was Pitch's laugh. A cold shiver ran through her soul.

Katherine reached into her coat pocket and pulled out the locket that she had gotten from Ombric. She looked at the picture of Pitch's daughter. Again she felt a strange sort of sadness. She had lost her father before she'd ever really known him, and yet she missed him every day. Their time together had been so brief, but the bond lived on. She knew it would never fade or die. She studied the picture of that long-ago little girl and wondered: *Might this locket be a much more powerful weapon against Pitch than any dagger?*

Then a shift in the lantern's light caught her attention. The light was changing—twisting down and splitting into different threads, fanning out like a web that arched behind her. She spun around. Surrounding her stood a dozen or so Fearlings. The tendrils of the lantern light fed directly into their leaded armor.

"NORTH!" Katherine managed to scream before they whisked her away to the awful place behind the wall.

CHAPTER TWENTY-SEVEN

The Power of the Inner Pooka

REMEMBER," NORTH WAS SAYING, glowering at Bunnymund. "Pitch is *mine*." The Pooka's nose twitched.

Then they heard Katherine's scream.

North didn't wait for Bunnymund to respond. He turned on his heels and ran, his sword leading the way as if it couldn't wait to do battle. A knot of Fearlings plunged down at him. He could tell at a glance that they were more formidable than any Fearlings he'd seen before. They looked denser somehow, and though his sword was glowing far more brightly than usual, its light seemed to be sucked into the Fearlings themselves. North was startled. But the hilt of the sword wrapped itself tightly around his hand, and this gave him courage—he literally felt himself becoming stronger, faster. He slashed at the marauders as they descended upon him.

He had expected them to vanish with one quick touch, but they did not. Instead, he heard the clank of metal against metal as he struck at the Fearlings and realized that they were armored, like knights of old, but deformed, tangled, and terrible.

And armed.

How could that be? North managed to think as he lashed out again and again, barely able to stop the Fearlings' heavy swords from carving him up as they swooped down at him like giant murderous bats. They swerved in midair to attack again. North willed himself to be stronger and faster still, and as he did, the sword responded.

When the Fearlings dove at him again, he sliced them down with swift and brutal precision. Their armor hacked open, the Fearlings vanished into nothingness. The empty armor fell to the tunnel floor like hunks from a broken coffin.

North gripped his sword and stood ready for the next onslaught, but none came. In the tense quiet he had time to think one terrible thought: *What has happened to Katherine?*

The sword seemed to respond for, from its hilt, a small oval mirror emerged. At first North saw only his own face and Bunnymund and his army racing from the train behind him. Then the mirror showed another image—blurry at first, then sharper. It was Katherine, surrounded by Fearlings. Then it shifted to the face of Pitch as he looked down at her. The image faded and the mirror grew dark, reflecting nothing.

North gripped his sword so intensely that he began to shake. *This is my fault,* he thought. He'd dropped his guard. Let himself become distracted by—what? By a candy-making rabbit!

Bunnymund came up just behind North. Pookas have an uncanny ability to sense what others think and feel. He knew that North thought he was a silly creature. Ridiculous, even. But that didn't bother him.

He could also sense North's anger and determination, his need to help his young friend. The rabbit had kept his distance from the tumultuous feelings of living things for centuries, but now he knew he must respond as he would have in days of old.

He put his paw on North's shoulder in as friendly a way as a Pooka can. Then he sighed deeply. "Dear fellow," he said to North, "this will be more difficult than I had imagined. Drastic measures are required." He reached into his robe and pulled out three chocolate eggs.

"This is no time for sweets," North snapped in frustration.

"For you, perhaps," said the rabbit, then he popped the three chocolates in his mouth. The Egg Army gasped in almost-perfect unison. None of them had ever seen Bunnymund eat a chocolate. They had only heard rumors of what happened when Pookas ate the substance.

There was a curious rumbling. North turned around to face Bunnymund. The rabbit appeared to be growing before his eyes, becoming huge, then hulking, like a warrior from a mythology not yet written.

Bunnymund raised his egg-tipped staff above his head and let out a yell that shook the tunnel like an earthquake. The army of eggs did likewise. The sound was unlike anything North had ever heard.

It was the first time in a thousand years the world had heard the Pookan war cry.

And even Nicholas St. North was impressed.

CHAPTER TWENTY-EIGHT

The Battle Begins

PITCH HAD ALMOST NO time to relish the capture of Katherine. He knew that if the girl was here, North and Ombric must be near—and the magic library close at hand! But moments after the Fearlings had brought the girl to him, he heard that extraordinary, otherworldly sound.

He alone among all the creatures living had heard that war cry before. It was a sound he'd hoped to never hear again. He remembered it from the time he'd destroyed the Pookan Brotherhood. It was the one battle of the Golden Age he had nearly lost. "They've got a Pooka with them!" he hissed with alarm.

He knew he must act quickly.

"Make ready!" he bellowed to his Fearling Army. "The battle begins!"

The Fearlings gathered with enviable swiftness. Armor ready, weapons raised, they were a force no one would wish to face.

Pitch grabbed Katherine by the collar and dragged her with him. "Come, sprite," he muttered. "I've no time to dally with you just now."

He rushed from chamber to chamber, shouting commands, making sure his dark army was in place and ready, and all the while Katherine dangled at his side like a sack. She watched every movement of the Fearling troops, which was no easy feat, as she was being buffeted about with Pitch's grim grip tight at her neck. But she could see the trap that Pitch was planning. The Fearlings would let North and Bunnymund make their way deep into the hollow of the Earth's core, then surround and overwhelm them.

Her mind raced. As Pitch planned to destroy her friends, she plotted how best to stop him.

The Pookan war cry grew louder and closer. The Egg Army had obviously made it through the wall of lead that surrounded Pitch's lair.

Time was short. Katherine had so few choices, and none played to her favor. But then, as Pitch was hurrying into another chamber, she saw the metal cages holding the children. Her friends!

They'd crawled back up into the cages to avoid detection by Pitch, but Tall William and the others could see her as well. They yelled and stuck their hands through the airholes to wave. She tried to shout back, but Pitch swung her suddenly to his other hand. As he did so, she noticed, for only an instant, that this hand seemed different . . . changed . . . almost human-looking. Then she heard the opening of a metal door, and she was shoved into a small room. The door slammed behind her. She was immersed in a darkness that was total and complete.

And though he did not know it, Pitch had put her in the one place where she most needed to be.

CHAPTER TWENTY-NINE

The Voice

OMBRIC HAD BEEN FURIOUSLY preparing for his trip to the Earth's core. From the moment he'd figured out what had happened to his library and Mr. Qwerty's role in its disappearance, he'd worked nonstop to make a perfect reproduction of it. Every single book, every single history, calculation, chart, map, mixture, blueprint, plan, and spell had been duplicated and set down. The entire village had been busy, binding the texts that Ombric had dictated to the owls (who were brilliantly adept at writing and drawing with both talons at the same time).

It was fortunate that Ombric could call upon his unmatched memory to recite the entire trove of his knowledge.

When the last volume was stitched and bound, Ombric stood back to take in the whole of it. It looked as if his library had never been touched; it looked perfect. But it was all bogus. There were flaws carefully crafted into each bit of information. Because of Ombric's perfect memory, he knew exactly where to make a change here, a switch there. If followed to the letter, not one spell in this entire fabrication would work.

Ombric had no idea what form the real library was in since Mr. Qwerty had bravely devoured it. The wizard was impressed by this brilliant bit of strategy on Mr. Qwerty's and Nightlight's part, but he had to make certain that Pitch did not get the real library—

the phony one would have to be used to trick the villain.

This had been an extremely exhausting task, and he still had to muster the energy to astrally project himself and the immense library all the way to the center of Earth.

He sat in his favorite chair thinking about his store of knowledge. Remembering it had been both satisfying and bittersweet. He felt as though he had relived the entire arc of his life. He remembered learning each and every bit of magic: where he'd been, who he'd been with at the time. He realized that he'd achieved a rich, wild, vivid life. He had lived as he had believed. He had seen and known more wonder than almost any mortal ever had. So he felt a weary satisfaction. He would just need to rest his mind for a while.

Ombric leaned back and tugged at his beard, the

owls watching him worriedly. They had never seen their master so tired, so frail.

Ombric's breathing became quiet and rhythmic, and he drifted into a deep sleep.

He dreamed of when he was just a child in the city of Atlantis. There had been a day in his childhood that had always baffled him—the day of his first magic. And now he seemed to be reliving it. He hadn't been much younger than the youngest William, and had been secretly listening to the lessons of the older children; he had heard knowledge he was not yet supposed to know. He learned the secret of how to make a daydream come true.

The young Ombric stood in an open field and started to recite the spell. It was a difficult enchantment and required great concentration, but he was a boy with a talent for concentration. He focused hard, till his mind was clear of all distraction. He chanted the words slowly and thoughtfully. Ombric had always daydreamed of flying. And after a time he started drifting upward, at first just grazing the top of the tall, green field grass, then higher, and finally up into the sky. He flew in and around clouds, soaring and spiraling like a fantastic sort of bird.

But he had gone too fast and flown too high. His young mind grew tired. He could no longer maintain the spell, and he began to fall. Fear took over his thinking as he plummeted to the ground. He knew he must stop being afraid and focus on the spell, but his pulse was pounding and panic set in.

He began to tumble uncontrollably, spiraling end over end with sickening speed. Everything was a terrifying blur. He fell so fast that he began to black out.

And he was glad. He couldn't stand to feel a terror

this total, and he didn't want to face the instant that was coming—the moment when he would smash to the ground and be no more. As he began to lose consciousness, he felt a strange sort of calm. An acceptance of what would happen. Then he heard a voice whisper to him: "I believe. I believe. I believe." It was a pleasant voice. One he did not recognize, but at the same time, it sounded familiar. And he no longer felt afraid. Then, as all went black, he knew—*knew*—everything would be all right.

And it was. He opened his young eyes some time later. He was in the same green field. He was not hurt. Not a scratch or a bruise was on him. Only his red hair was tousled. Ombric never knew how he had survived or who had spoken the magic words to him. But on that day he had learned the power of fear, that fear was an enemy that must always be conquered.

Then the memory ended, but the dream went on. . . .

Ombric now saw himself in that same field from childhood. He was not a boy anymore but very old. He lay in the soft green grass. It was so cool and comfortable. There was a soothing breeze, and the sky above was alive with white clouds that drifted by like great galleons. *I am so tired. Maybe I will just stay here forever*, he thought. *It is peaceful.*

But now he heard the words again, echoing from far away. But this time the voice was different.

It was a young girl's voice. He struggled to sit up, and as he did, he saw Katherine standing near him. Then North appeared next to her. They beckoned him to join them.

They spoke, but he could not hear them. He

could only hear the mysterious voice from long ago: "I believe. I believe. I believe."

Then suddenly, he woke up. He looked around his library, startled. He could still hear the voice, but only the owls were there.

And for the second time he felt the minds of Katherine and North reaching out to him. Their thoughts and his had become connected. He felt— no, he knew—that they were in grave danger and that he must act instantly.

He grabbed the box that held Nightlight's moonbeam and the broken bits of the diamond dagger. Then he waved his staff over the new stacks of books. He felt strong again. Young again. Like Ombric in days of yore. Could he project himself to the Earth's core? In an instant! And the books? Absolutely! His friends needed him! The peace he felt in his dream could come later.

But that voice from the past . . . the voice that had saved him on that fateful day when he first learned the glory and terror of magic. It sounded so familiar now.

Who—or *what*—was it?

CHAPTER THIRTY

In Which All Is Linked by an Ancient Mind Trick That Has a Most Surprising Origin

NORTH WAS DAZZLED. BUNNYMUND was a madman, or rabbit, or whatever . . . a dervish! A devil! A juggernaut! There simply wasn't a way to describe the Pooka's electrifying deeds. He had taken his relic and fixed it to the end of his staff, then aimed it at the lead wall that blocked their way. If this ancient lead had never seen sunlight, starlight, or any light other than lava light before, it was seeing it now. The light that the relic contained blistered forth from a thousand tiny holes that opened up from its shell. This light would *not* be blocked or consumed; it could peel back the dense lead as smoothly as sealing wax from parchment.

But still, North felt wary—it was almost *too* easy. The Fearlings kept retreating without putting up much of a fight. They were going deeper and deeper into the Earth's core, and the wavy, peculiar lead-and-lava landscape was hard to mark or remember. North prided himself on his stellar sense of direction, but he now felt uncertain about how to find his way back out, and his warrior's instincts were telling him he was being pulled into an ambush.

It was at just that moment that there came a sort of ringing in his ears, the sensation blocking out the clatter of battle around him. He looked to Bunnymund, and he knew that the Pooka was experiencing the same sensation.

The magic sword could feel it too. The mirror

emerged again from its hilt, and North could see Katherine's face in it. Her lips did not move, but he could hear her voice. "There is no time to tell you everything. We must call Ombric here now!" she said. "He needs us, and we need him. Pitch has made a trap for you."

But how can we call Ombric? North wondered. Then he remembered when they were back in Santoff Claussen, when he had felt their minds unite as one. He knew that he must concentrate to make their minds combine again. Despite the skirmish going on around him, he closed his eyes, and all became quiet except for his and Katherine's voices: *I believe . . . I believe . . . I believe.* Then he heard Bunnymund's voice join theirs! And this surprised North. They had a new ally, a new friend.

But then North saw Ombric in the sword's

mirror. He was lying in a field of grass. He looked sad, old, as if he were dying. It scared North, and he could tell it did the same to Katherine and Bunnymund. So they shouted out to him, their minds as one, "Believe, believe, believe. You are needed!"

The mirror went bright, then Ombric was no longer visible. North heard Katherine say, "Be cautious. Wait for Ombric. Wait for me." Then the mirror went dark again.

North turned to Bunnymund, who was smiling.

"I haven't done the Pookan mind meld in centuries. I didn't know you and the girl knew how."

"Neither did we," North confessed.

"Even better," replied the Pooka. And off he hopped, like some warrior-rabbit-buffalo.

North had no choice but to follow.

CHAPTER THIRTY-ONE
The Mad Scramble

Ｎorth, Bunnymund, and the Warrior Eggs continued their push into the depths of Pitch's lair. Now mindful of the trap they were entering, Bunnymund left small groups of men (or, rather, eggs) to help mark their way out and to sound the alarm if an ambush was coming.

But the Fearlings continued to pull back, now without fighting at all.

"Something is definitely up, Bunnymund," said North.

"I'd say Pitch is making a tactical change

in his plans," the Pooka agreed.

"Do we split our forces?" wondered North.

"One of us goes forward to investigate while the other watches his back?" suggested Bunnymund.

"You read my mind," North said jokingly.

"Yes," replied the Pooka, "but only when I think it necessary."

North wasn't sure if Bunnymund was kidding or not, but before he could ask, the hulking rabbit gave him a good-natured shove. "Now, get going, my friend; you wanted Pitch to yourself."

North shot the rabbit a glance as he led half the eggs toward the heart of Pitch's hideout. "Come hopping if you hear anything," he called over his shoulder.

The Pooka decided to let North have the last word. He didn't mind the human's rabbit jokes at his expense. It had been at least seven hundred years since anybody had made any sort of jest to him. He'd almost forgotten the peculiar pleasures of kidding and being kidded, and how humans used humor to help them not be afraid.

And there was much to fear in this place.

With spears, swords, and clubs at the ready, North led a tight formation of eggs cautiously forward. The Fearling troops were continuing to back away, their clattering armor sending waves of uneasy echoes through the tunnel. It was dim—only the blue glint of the lead lava flows provided any light.

Then North heard the Nightmare King bellow, "Come forward!"

North's sword automatically tightened around his hand, but its glow stayed pale—North could tell it was doing all it could to avoid making him an easy target in this twilight.

Then they came to a huge open chamber. Great swirling lead columns formed a sort of circular shape to the room. The columns widened at the top as they merged into what could be called the ceiling.

Behind the lead columns, North could see only heavily armored Fearlings, a vast army of gray menace that completely surrounded the chamber and seemed eager to attack.

In the room's center, Pitch was standing triumphantly among every book from Ombric's library. They were stacked haphazardly in tall piles on the uneven floor of the chamber. North could see *The History of Levitation While Eating, Mysteries of Vanishing Keys,* and Ombric's beloved books on Atlantis. *What is the old man up to?* North wondered. Pitch gazed greedily from book to book, then grabbed one and began to scan its contents. He smiled to himself, then looked up at North, staring at him with gleeful hate.

North matched Pitch's stare, while, from the corner of his eye, he saw the children of Santoff Claussen huddled in cages that hung from lead beams.

Ombric was nowhere in sight, so North knew to bide his time and wait till the wizard made his play. North realized Pitch was expecting him to say something—explain the arrival of the books or demand that the children be released.

But North kept steady and quiet, as only the smartest warriors did. Let *the villain* make the first move.

"Why send a thief to do a Pooka's job?" Pitch asked mockingly.

North said not a word; he just moved in closer, the eggs at his side. He raised his sword as if to strike.

"Where'd you steal *that?*" Pitch questioned, suddenly curious. "It's a sword for a king, not a Cossack criminal."

North stayed silent. The magic sword glowed. Pitch, however, did not reach for his own weapon, but instead held out one of Ombric's books.

"At ease, brigand. I've got what I asked for. The books are here." Pitch turned to a Fearling. "Release the children," he ordered.

The Fearling unlocked the swaying cages, and the children jumped out. They tried to run to North, but the Fearling unsheathed his sword and brought it down in front of them, blocking their way.

Pointing to the sealed solid lead cage, Tall William shouted, "Katherine and Nightlight are in there!"

North inched closer, but still he said nothing. His sword glowed even brighter.

"No need to attack, Cossack," Pitch said soothingly. "The books are here. A deal is a deal. We can part and fight another day. Yes?"

North eyed him suspiciously. *Could this work without a fight?*

"But . . . ," Pitch continued, "I must be sure these books are what they seem." And he began to read a spell.

North knew that the incantation was directed at him. What would Pitch do? Turn him into a fungus, a slave, a Fearling general? He prepared to charge, but the sword held him back! He pushed against it, but it would not budge.

Then he remembered what Yaloo the Yeti had told him: "Perhaps the weapon is fighting *for* you."

The sword must know something, North decided.

Pitch, on the other hand, was growing angry.

Something was evidently not going as he wished.

Pitch repeated the spell from the book slowly, carefully, as if testing each syllable. Then North understood: The spell was useless; the books were sabotaged!

Pitch tried another spell. Then another. He snatched up the book of enslavement spells and read the words he knew by heart. "They're all fake!" he bellowed. "FAKE!"

North readied to strike. From behind him, he

could hear the charge
of Bunnymund and his
troops. Pitch threw the book
down and unsheathed his sword.

The room exploded into chaos.

The Fearlings rushed North. The earsplitting
clash of two armies bent on destroying each other
filled the chamber. Then the Pookan war cry sounded
out above the din—Bunnymund had arrived, his relic
staff sending beams of light crisscrossing the room,
engulfing the Fearlings.

The room was furious with spears, swords, clubs,
arrows, and armor. North was amazed. The Warrior
Eggs were incredibly agile fighters. They could roll,
leap, and charge with lightning speed, and their
armor was most difficult to penetrate. Their weapons
were injected with the ancient light of the egg relic

and more than held their own against the Fearlings.

North kept own his sights on Pitch, who was moving toward the children. North's sword glowed red; it was time to strike. He charged through the dense clusters of Fearlings and Warrior Eggs, easily felling every enemy that blocked his way.

Pitch was opening his cape. It rippled out and began to surround the children. North ran up the huge stack of books in front of him like it was a staircase, then leaped from the top, his sword at the ready, sailing over Pitch. Pitch's cape was curling around the children like a pair of massive claws, but before he could close it, North landed between them: Villain and thief were face-to-face, swords drawn.

North said to his sword, "Do what needs doing." With two deft swings, he sliced away the cape on either side of Pitch. The children were free! But in that one moment of victory, North's guard was down, and Pitch did his worst.

North staggered backward, gasping. The handle of Pitch's saber protruded from his side; the tip jutted out from the back of his coat. He'd been run through.

The children screamed. Pitch grinned. He pulled his sword back out. But North would not go down yet. He gripped his magic sword and it responded. It glowed with such brightness.

It was then that miracles occurred.

Nightlight's cage exploded open and light poured from it. The entire chamber was awash with light. The armor-covered Fearlings were almost blinded. Pitch pulled the cowl of his hood forward to block his face from the glare.

North charged again. Despite his wounds, despite the wrenching pain, he could feel an amazing power surge from the magic sword into him. It was almost as if the sword could remember Pitch and was eager to finish him. With indescribable fury, North hacked and lunged at the Nightmare King.

But Pitch had grown stronger since last they'd met, and even with the power of the magic sword, North was unable to best him. His wound was hampering him; he felt himself weakening. Then he saw the djinni, discarded in the corner. Without Pitch inside it, perhaps it would still heed his command.

"Djinni!" North shouted. "Attack him!" The djinni immediately stiffened and then ran toward North. It picked up two swords that were dropped in the battle. Was it coming to help or hinder?

The djinni attacked Pitch! *Now we've a chance,* North thought with relief.

When he next looked up, he was stunned to see

Ombric there as well, swinging at Pitch with his staff and landing more blows than North would have ever expected from the old wizard. Then Bunnymund literally came flying into the room, his ears twirling with such speed that they held him aloft like a helicopter. With the relic at the end of his lance, he charged Pitch like a jousting knight.

But Pitch was their match. He shouted out to the Fearlings and they began to merge into him. He grew bigger and stronger, their armor adding layer after layer atop his. Now Pitch was truly a monster in size as well as spirit.

The children huddled into a corner. They could see what was happening—even without Ombric's books of spells, Pitch seemed unbeatable. Fear crept into their hearts.

Then from the lead cage there shot another bolt

of light, and a shimmering, perfect laugh pierced the noise of the battle like an arrow.

Nightlight's laugh!

Nightlight flew straight toward Pitch, with Katherine riding on his back. His staff was outstretched, the diamond dagger repaired and aimed at Pitch's heart.

North caught a glimpse of them as they streaked toward Pitch. *Outstanding*, he thought. *The boy will do him in.*

But Nightlight pulled up short, hovering just within reach of Pitch's sword.

What is he doing?! North thought, pausing in mid-swing. "His heart, boy!" he shouted. "Strike him in the heart!"

Still Nightlight held back. Pitch, however, did not. He sliced savagely at Nightlight, but the spectral boy parried his blow, and his diamond dagger shattered

Pitch's sword. Now North and the others could move in for the kill.

But before they could strike, Katherine raised up her hand and held something out toward Pitch. Not a weapon—no, it was something she wanted him to see. *What is she holding?* North strained to look. The locket! With the picture of Pitch's daughter!

For a moment time seemed to stand still.

Pitch stared at the locket, his face twisted and monstrous. His gaze did not waver from the picture. Then his face began to change, the anger and fury fading, replaced by a look that was mournful, anguished, and unbearably sad. North and the others held steady, hardly believing what they were seeing. The King of the Nightmares was no longer horrifying but horrified. He reached out with his damaged hand—the one he had used to try to change

Nightlight into a Fearling, the hand that now looked human. He tugged the locket away from Katherine, and for an instant she felt his hand against hers. His touch was not of a creature of fear. It was the touch of a father who had lost his child. Pitch let out a long and haunted scream that came from the depths of whatever sort of a soul he still had.

He looked at the picture for one more moment, then faded, vanishing completely away. The Fearling Army disappeared with him.

And the battle was over.

CHAPTER THIRTY-TWO

North Is Fallen

THERE WAS A SUDDEN and strange calm in the chamber. There they were, together at last, the heroes of the battle at the Earth's core. Such an amazing and unlikely group: a spectral boy, a girl, a Cossack, an ancient wizard, a metal djinni, a huge Rabbit Man, and an army of Warrior Eggs. The children ran to the comfort of their friends and protectors. But North winced as the littlest William rushed into his arms. He grabbed at his wound, then dropped his sword and fell to one knee.

Ombric and Katherine hurried to his side. "How

bad is it, lad?" asked Ombric, bending close. North could not answer. As they laid him down, his face grew paler and even more drained of color. His sword lay next to him. It seemed to dim and darken. Katherine took his hand. It felt cold. North looked up at her as she began to cry.

CHAPTER THIRTY-THREE

The Bookworm Turns

IT WAS A BEAUTIFUL afternoon in the enchanted woods that surrounded Santoff Claussen. The children of the village were playing their favorite new game, called "Battle at the Earth's Core." The massive trees that edged the small open grove had bent their branches down in ways that looked like the lead columns of Pitch's lair. William the Almost Youngest was pretending to be Ombric, Tall William was Bunnymund, Fog was the djinni, and Petter was Nightlight. The bear was Pitch, which worked very well, as he was so large and very good at tussling with the children with just enough wildness that it was really fun. Plus, he was very difficult to hurt by accident.

A group of squirrels pretended to be the children, dressed up in tiny clothes that matched what they had been wearing during the battle. The birds of the forest were the Fearlings, and a number of actual Warrior Eggs (a gift from Bunnymund) played themselves.

William the Absolute Youngest always wanted to be North; he loved North so much, and it was he who had last hugged North before he fell.

Petter yelled for Katherine to join them, to play her own character, but she did not answer. She rarely joined in this game—she'd lived it, after all, so she didn't need to play it. Petter's sister Sascha gladly took her place.

Katherine was up in the topmost branches of Big

Root. She had made a small, ramshackle tree house in the crook at the highest point. She went to it often now. She could be alone there to think and to remember.

She spent her time making stories out of what she had seen. Sometimes she even wrote short little rhymes of their adventures. There was an egg that had fallen from a wall of Pitch's chamber during the battle. She was sure he would break, but his armor had protected him. If only the same could have been said for North. He had fallen. And no one had thought he could be made whole again.

Today she was combining those two stories into a rhyme, drawing pictures of a great egg that had shattered and couldn't be put back together again. She would sometimes make stories that were different from what had happened but were about how she felt or what she wished had been. This was a new way of thinking for her, and she loved it—needed to do it. These stories had become a mysterious new force in her, a way of healing and understanding the wonders and sorrows of her wild new life.

She was never actually alone in the tree house. Kailash would fly her up there and nap quietly as Katherine wrote, her long neck wrapped around the girl as she leaned against the soft, feathered body.

And there was one more companion with her: Mr. Qwerty. Or at least what he had become.

When Nightlight had told Mr. Qwerty to eat the library to save it from Pitch—yes, it had been Nightlight's idea—something remarkable had happened. The spells and magic contained in the thousands of pages had transformed the glowworm. In his cocoon he had changed, but it was not into a butterfly. He became instead something that the world had never seen before. He had wings, many of them, but they were made of paper—he had become a sort of living book! His pages were all blank. It was on these pages that Katherine wrote her stories.

Katherine could hear her friends playing in the woods. They were making a story too, of that great and terrible battle. It always changed as they acted it out. Sometimes whoever played Bunnymund would come too later, or the bear would run off too soon, or the squirrels would decide that they wanted to join in the battle and escape from the "cages" too early. But one part always stayed the same: when North fell. Somehow, it seemed important to do that part exactly as it had happened.

As Katherine sat in her tree house, she heard

her friends readying for their game's final battle. She stopped her writing to listen.

Down in the forest William the Absolute Youngest had fallen to the ground, the stick that was his pretend sword lying at his side. Sascha, Fog, Petter, and the others stood over him as he seemed to die. Then he reached for his magic sword.

Suddenly, a voice came booming from the trees at the edge of the clearing.

"No! No! No!" yelled Nicholas St. North. He came striding toward them. "That's not how it happened! Bunnymund gave me that magic chocolate first."

North came up to them looking very hale and hearty. He carried with him a large sack thrown over his shoulder.

"The magic chocolate saved me, I grabbed the

sword, and it began to glow again," he reminded them.

"But our stick sword can't glow for real," explained the youngest William.

"Well, this one can," replied North cheerfully as he dumped the sack upside down. Toy swords and staffs and relics and costumes spilled out on the ground before them. "I made them this morning. Well, the djinni helped a bit."

The children were delighted with their gifts. They grabbed their different costumes and weaponry and prepared to continue their game.

Katherine flew down on Kailash. She wanted to watch how her friends would act out the rest of the events now that they had props.

Bunnymund came popping out of the ground nearby, Ombric with him. The two had become close collaborators since the battle, once Ombric had discovered that it was Bunnymund who had saved him that long-ago day when he had tried his first magic. They traded spells and histories of this and that. He felt a strong kinship with the Rabbit Man—the only creature alive who was older and wiser than himself. Being with this marvelous creature made Ombric feel younger, almost like a student again.

The two of them stopped a moment and watched the children's game unfold. "So how exactly does the chocolate transform you, Bunnymund?" Ombric asked his new friend.

"My dear fellow," the rabbit replied, "I'm not entirely sure. Some mysteries need no solution. Does it help to understand why rainbows happen?"

"I think it does," replied Ombric.

The rabbit almost laughed. "You humans."

And from the trees above, a brave and gentle

spirit watched them all. Nightlight, the one who said the least but perhaps knew the most, thought only of the comfort he felt. He was among true friends. The moonbeam, back inside the diamond dagger, was happy as well. The dagger was bigger now. It contained the tears that Nightlight had taken from the children when they'd been kidnapped; he'd used them to bind the broken dagger back together again. Nightlight had always known that taking the sorrows of those you love makes you stronger in the end.

Remembering this now made him glow a bit brighter. Katherine could sense his gaze. She turned and looked up. She could not see him—he was hiding—but she knew he was there. The power of friendship was magical indeed. The happiness Nightlight felt spread to all of them. They had done what good friends should do: They had all saved one another. Whatever trials or troubles might come, from now on, their bond would be unbreakable. They were of one mind and heart.

And that heart would beat forever. Past time and tide and stories yet told.

THE NEXT CHAPTER
IN OUR ONGOING SAGA WILL FEATURE
THE DISCOVERY OF

TOOTHIANA

QUEEN OF THE TOOTH FAIRY ARMIES

Also by William Joyce

THE GUARDIANS: BOOK ONE
Nicholas St. North and the Battle of the Nightmare King

THE GUARDIANS OF CHILDHOOD: BOOK ONE
The Man in the Moon

Acknowledgments

Huzzahs all around to
Elizabeth Blake-Linn, Caitlyn Dlouhy,
Trish Farnsworth-Smith, Jeannie Ng, and Lauren Rille,
and with special appreciation to Laurie Calkhoven—
Guardians of the Book, all.

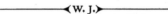